Recipe for Love

A Polwenna Bay novel

By

Ruth Saberton

Createspace

1st Edition

Copyright

Also by Ruth Saberton

The Island Legacy

Chances

Runaway Summer: Polwenna Bay 1

A Time for Living: Polwenna Bay 2

Winter Wishes: Polwenna Bay 3

Treasure of the Heart: Polwenna Bay 4

Magic in the Mist: Polwenna Bay novella
Cornwall for Christmas: Polwenna Bay novella

Escape for the Summer

Escape for Christmas
Hobb's Cottage

Weight Till Christmas

The Wedding Countdown

Dead Romantic

Katy Carter Wants a Hero

Katy Carter Keeps a Secret

Ellie Andrews Has Second Thoughts

Amber Scott is Starting Over

Pen Name Books

Writing as Jessica Fox

The One That Got Away

Eastern Promise

Hard to Get

Unlucky in Love

Always the Bride

Writing as Holly Cavendish

Looking for Fireworks

Writing as Georgie Carter

The Perfect Christmas

CHAPTER 1

It felt to Alice Tremaine as though Polwenna Bay had been fast asleep all winter and, now that February half-term had arrived, the village was stretching its arms and yawning as it slowly woke up. A watery sun was peeping out from behind the grey clouds, a few hopeful seagulls had decided to venture in from the cliffs in search of food, and shop shutters that had been tightly closed since New Year's Day were now being flung open. Whirly stands of postcards had been dusted off, the bakery window was filled with golden loaves and Cornish pasties, and the Harbourside Boutique had optimistically created a display of shorts and swimwear to catch the tourists' attention. Just looking at it gave Alice goose pimples. The sun might be shining and there might be snowdrops peeking through in her garden, but it was still chilly. The wind blowing across the village was northerly and carried snow in its breath.

It was just as well the newly refurbished beach café had good heating and a supply of hot coffee, Alice decided as she gazed out across the bay while her granddaughter Mo bought the drinks. This morning the sea was pewter and the sand was a pale gold sickle frilled with lace where the waves broke. Alice could see the Pollards, Polwenna Bay's father-and-son builder team, attempting to repair the beach steps while the tide was out, in a race against time that was somewhat hindered by their regular visits to The Ship for medicinal whiskeys and the odd burger – not to mention their general aversion to hard work. Maybe the steps would be ready for the coming season and maybe they wouldn't. *Dreckly* was the word Big Rog liked to use when anyone asked him for a completion time frame; it could mean anything from ten minutes to ten weeks.

It didn't help either that lately all the builder's energy was channelled into rigging a top-secret boat hidden away in the depths of his garage. Nobody was allowed inside and this as yet unseen vessel was fast becoming a Cornish mystery on a par with the Bodmin Beast. The other villagers were all dying to know what was going on. Sheila Keverne and Ivy Lawrence were eaten up with curiosity, and rumour had it that Keyhole Kathy Polmartin had asked Silver Starr in the mystic shop if her tarot cards could shed some light on the matter. Alas, Silver Starr's psychic skills had failed to reveal anything. Even Mrs Pollard pleaded ignorance, while Little Rog just looked blank (although in fairness this could be said to be his general expression).

"I have no idea what he's doing. He hasn't come to me for help and when I asked him what he was up to he just tapped his nose, winked and said it was his retirement project," Alice's marine engineer grandson, Jake, had said when she'd asked his opinion. Alice had found this rather alarming. In the run-up to the boating season Jake was always flat out; he had such a good reputation that customers came to Tremaine Marine from all over the county. She would have hoped that Big Rog would have asked for some expert help. If his boat building was anything like his handiwork around the village he'd soon be in big trouble once he set sail.

"You look serious, Granny." Mo Carstairs, balancing her baby daughter on her hip as she carried a tray laden with cakes and drinks, joined Alice at her window table. "Penny for them?"

"Goodness, they're not worth even that much," laughed Alice.

"Are you thinking about your wedding?" Mo asked, setting down the tray and inadvertently sloshing coffee into saucers. "Don't tell me you've finally set a date at long last? I need to be sitting down first for that kind of news."

"Cheeky monkey," said Alice mildly, although Mo did have a point. Her engagement to Jonny St Milton was starting to look rather lengthy – daft really when they were both in their eighties now and ought to be grabbing every second with both pairs of liver-spotted hands! The trouble was there was just so much else to think about before she could focus on their big day. The St Milton family, with their hotel, businesses and perpetual squabbling, were Polwenna's version of the Sopranos and kept Jonny busy. Alice, meanwhile, certainly had her hands full with her own brood. Her grandchildren might be in their twenties and thirties but that didn't stop her fretting about them and neither did it stop them getting into scrapes.

And then there was her son, Jimmy, who – despite being in his sixties – was the biggest child of the lot and caused Alice more worry than all his children put together. He was certainly behaving oddly at the moment with all those furtive phone calls and mysterious emails. Alice only hoped a woman was the cause rather than yet another of his get-rich-quick disasters. These schemes always turned into financial black holes and Alice really couldn't face, or afford, another one.

"I was thinking about Roger Pollard's secret boat," she told Mo, who grinned.

"You actually believe there's a boat, do you? Ashley and I reckon he's got a cannabis farm in there!"

"I hope not. I think we've had quite enough of that kind of thing to last a lifetime," her grandmother shuddered. Not so long ago the beach café had been at the centre of a drugs haul and the village had hit the headlines for all the wrong reasons. It had changed hands now and was run by a new arrival called Sam, a gentle divorcee who'd come to Cornwall for a quiet life. Alice thought there was little hope of that happening in Polwenna Bay but she hadn't disillusioned him. The poor man seemed stressed enough just navigating the coffee machine and it seemed kinder to let him believe he was in for the peaceful existence he craved.

"Fair point," said Mo, plonking herself down opposite Alice. "I still can't believe we were drinking our lattes all that time with tonnes of cannabis underneath the floorboards! I think it's more likely Big Rog has just made a man cave and is having some time out from the missus. I bet there isn't even a boat at all. Hey, Granny, can you take Isla for a second while I sort this lot out?"

She passed the baby across the table and Alice sat Isla in her lap, loving the chubby weight of the little girl and her delicious baby smell. She pressed a kiss into Isla's soft red curls. There were some good things about growing older: having a great-granddaughter definitely compensated for Alice's wrinkles and aching hip. It was wonderful to see Mo settled and happy too. Her fiery eldest granddaughter had certainly been the source of many of Alice's grey hairs and most of her worry lines.

"What have you done with Ashley this morning?" she asked as her granddaughter mopped up puddles of latte. Mo's husband wasn't usually far away from his wife and daughter. They were a tight unit, made even closer after his illness eighteen months ago.

"He's sulking at Mariners. I told him to stay there and not inflict his sour face on us. We don't want to see Daddy until he's in a better mood, do we, poppet?"

Immediately, Alice was concerned. "Ashley's upset? About what?"

Mo didn't reply. She was suddenly very intent on crumbling a savoury muffin for Isla. "There we are, sweetie! Muffin! Yummy, yummy!"

Having raised seven grandchildren Alice knew avoidance tactics when she saw them.

"Ashley's all right, isn't he?"

"God! Yes, yes of course! Sorry, Granny, I didn't mean to frighten you. Ashley's fine – well, except for being bloody annoying, which is nothing new."

Alice didn't say anything. Mo was clearly bursting to vent and all Alice needed to do was be patient. Three, two, one…

"I told him I want to get back into eventing this year. I missed the whole of last season and I need to be out competing this season before it's too late." Mo's freckled face took on the determined expression Alice recognised of old. Oh dear. This looked like trouble.

"And Ashley doesn't want you to."

"He wants me to concentrate on schooling and teaching. He thinks I should let Paula carry on breaking the horses in and he says competing's dangerous," said Mo scornfully.

Since her granddaughter's choice of career tended to involve her galloping horses across country and jumping huge fixed fences, Ashley had a point. Of course, Alice didn't dare say so. Instead she just jiggled Isla on her lap and fixed Mo with a searching look.

"Well, it is a bit dangerous," Mo conceded eventually, "but it's what I do, Granny Alice. It's my career and it's the only one I've ever wanted. I know I don't have to work and that Ash has more than enough money for us both but I'm not about to sit around and do nothing. I'll go mad!"

Alice was just on the brink of pointing out that being a mother was about as far from *sitting around doing nothing* as it was humanly possible to get, when they were joined by Summer Penhalligan, Jake's girlfriend. Summer was brandishing one of the national newspapers and her green eyes were shining with excitement.

"Have you seen this?" Summer placed the newspaper's magazine supplement on the table with such force that the cups rattled and coffee sloshed onto its pages. She snatched it up again hastily and smoothed the pages out before placing the magazine more gently on the table.

"Oh!" gasped Mo, leaning forward. "It's that piece about Symon! He said a journalist had been to The Plump Seagull for a meal."

"It must be the week for press. There was a double-page spread in *Cornish Coast* magazine about the Polwenna Bay Hotel," Alice recalled. Jonny had been beside himself with pride.

Mo's nose wrinkled. "The one about Evil Ella's wedding-planning business?"

There was little love lost between Mo Carstairs and the granddaughter of Alice's fiancé. They'd been rivals since school and things showed little sign of changing just because they were meant to be grown-ups now. Jonny felt that he and Alice should ignore Mo and Ella's feuding and leave the girls to sort it out, whereas Alice longed to orchestrate a truce. It was one of the few things Alice and Jonny disagreed on. Well, that and his quite frankly old-fashioned refusal to admit that Ella was far better suited to running the hotel than her feckless brother, Teddy. In Alice's opinion this was just ridiculous. Left to his own devices, Teddy would end up spending the hotel's every last penny within a matter of days.

"I know you don't like Ella, love, but be fair. She's put her heart and soul into that business," Alice said gently.

But Mo snorted. "Evil Ella hasn't a heart or a soul, Granny."

"I think she's not nearly as hard as we think," Summer remarked thoughtfully. "Maybe we should give her a chance?"

"Just because you feel guilty for stealing Jake doesn't mean I have to like her," retorted Mo. From the expression on her face, it was reasonable to assume that Satan would be making snowballs before Mo gave Ella St Milton the benefit of the doubt.

Alice sighed again. Bringing the two families together was going to be even harder than she'd thought. Maybe it was just as well she and Jonny hadn't set a date? At this rate the

Tremaines and the St Miltons would make the Capulets and the Montagues look like best friends.

Summer flushed. "I didn't *steal* Jake. He was never with Ella. Not properly."

"Tell that to *her*," said Mo. "She thinks she owns every good-looking guy in the village. Ashley was lucky I came along before she got her claws into him too."

"That's enough, Morwenna," said Alice in a warning tone that had never yet failed. It had worked when Mo was a teenager and it still worked even now she was a mother and, supposedly, an adult.

"Sorry, Sums. I didn't mean it. Just ignore me. I'm in a really foul mood," Mo sighed.

Summer smiled. "I'd never have guessed. What's up? Ashley and the horses again?"

While Mo told Summer all about today's disagreement with Ashley, Alice fished her reading glasses from her bag and turned her attention to the article. Sure enough, a small part of the broadsheet's weekend section was dedicated to her middle grandchild. There was a picture of Symon, looking deadly serious while he focused on searing scallops over leaping flames. She scanned through the write-up with her heart in her mouth – pieces like this could make or break careers – and was relieved to discover the journalist was singing Symon's praises. Of course he was. Symon was a wonderful chef and far too good, in Alice's opinion, to bury his talent in a tiny fishing village when at one point he'd been making a name for himself in Paris. This critic was comparing him to Rick Stein and Heston Blumenthal, so why on earth had her gifted grandson turned his back on the bright lights for this backwater?

Alice frowned. Something had happened to bring him back here, but what? Symon never spoke about his time abroad but the young man who'd returned was quiet and guarded; there was a sadness in his eyes that Alice hadn't seen before. His old sparkle had gone and its absence broke her heart. Oh dear. Yet another worry…

"What are you looking so down about, Granny? It's a fab piece. I bet Sy will be inundated with bookings after this," said Mo. "Maybe he'll actually get that second Michelin star people keep speculating about?"

"That would be amazing," Summer agreed.

"I'd rather he had a day off," said Alice. She folded up her spectacles and tucked them back inside her bag. "He's working far too hard. I wish he'd have a little more fun."

"Never fear, Granny Alice, I've got that in hand," Mo declared with a breezy confidence that made Alice feel the exact opposite.

"What's that supposed to mean?" she asked, but Mo just tapped her nose.

"You'll see."

"Have you been meddling?"

"Maybe just a little," Mo admitted. "It's all in a good cause though. You'll thank me in the end and so will Sy. Just wait. It's going to be perfect!"

This sounded ominously as though Mo had been matchmaking. Alice dreaded to think who she'd lined up for her brother. Somebody whose idea of fun was hurtling over five-bar gates? A female farrier? Paula the stable girl?

"Maybe it's best not to get involved, love?" she suggested.

But Mo just laughed. "It's a bit late for that now." Draining her coffee and jumping to her feet, she added, "There's no time like the present either. Would you look after Isla for me? I won't be long."

Alice's arms tightened around the baby. "Of course I will – but where are you off to in such a hurry?"

"To find Symon," Mo said, her blue eyes shining with excitement. "I had the most brilliant idea and I know Sy will thank me later, even if he goes crackers now. You'll never guess what, Granny! I've set him up on a blind date and he's going to be thrilled! Just you wait and see!"

CHAPTER 2

Symon Tremaine was in his kitchen, reading his review for the third time and allowing himself a moment of satisfaction. These didn't come very often in the restaurant trade. Mostly days flew by in a blur of hissing pans, shouting and sheer hard work, with his focus trained entirely on the dishes he was preparing. A chef was only ever as good as his last dish and Symon was determined that every single cover served in The Plump Seagull would always be perfect. It didn't matter whether it was an esteemed restaurant critic at the table or Little Rog Pollard; each customer would have a meal that delighted the taste buds.

This was the idea anyway – and although Symon was well aware that you couldn't please everyone, he certainly tried his best. He hadn't done anything for the reviewer that he wouldn't also do for any other customer. Although he'd realised who the reviewer was, Symon certainly hadn't made a song and dance about it. With hindsight, it had occurred to him that this could have been a mistake: perhaps he was supposed to feed the critic's ego as well as his appetite. When today's papers had been delivered, a flutter of butterflies had taken flight in Symon's stomach. A bad review could mean the

difference between a successful season and one that would
send him grovelling to the bank manager. Again.

"Happy with it?" Tara Tremaine asked, joining him and
pouring herself a coffee. She'd been working in the restaurant
for well over a year now and was a key member of the team.
Tara was resourceful and determined, and her marketing and
promotional skills had resulted in lots of coverage in the
Cornish press that was now catching the attention of the
nationals as well.

Symon nodded, pushing a lock of his deep red hair out of his
eyes and treating her to a rare smile. "Very, apart from the
photo. The way I'm searing those scallops makes me look like a
serial killer!"

"Rubbish," said Tara. "Anyway, those scallops had it coming!"

He laughed. "I still think it would have been a better image
without me in the shot. The focus should be on the food, not
the chef."

"Err, hello? You do know it's the twenty-first century? We're
in the celebrity age now. Everyone wants a face linked to a
brand and it's all about your Instagram and Twitter streams.
Just ask your nephew if you don't believe me."

Tara had tasked her young son Morgan, a budding
photographer, with the job of collecting images for The Plump
Seagull's online presence. Armed with his camera and a
determined attitude, Morgan had soon taken hundreds of

pictures. He'd also helped his mum build a simple website and patiently explained to her what Pinterest was. Tara now fed the restaurant's social media as frequently as Symon fed its diners. Symon scooted around this virtual world from time to time but it made him feel ancient and rather confused. When Morgan started telling him he should vlog and become a YouTuber in order to grow his reputation around the world, Symon had taken fright and bolted back to the safety of his kitchen. All he wanted to do was cook and live a quiet life. The last thing he wanted was to be visible or, God forbid, famous.

If that happened, Claudette might find him and Symon didn't want that. No way.

"I don't like my picture being taken," was all he said, knowing he couldn't possibly tell Tara the real reason for his reluctance to be an online presence. It was much better that his former sister-in-law thought he was a shy technophobe.

"You look great," Tara assured him. "With your fit body, those Tremaine cheekbones and that intense and moody expression you're *exactly* what a serious Michelin-starred chef should look like. Honestly, Sy, trust me. People are going to love this! I bet we'll be inundated with requests for interviews. That will be brilliant, won't it?"

"Hmm," said Symon, unconvinced. The less attention on him and the more on his food the better as far as he was concerned. Unlike his brother Zak, an up-and-coming musician and an expert show-off since childhood, Symon far preferred the shadows to the limelight. With any luck this fuss would soon die down and they could just enjoy some extra business. Still, Tara had a point: it was a great write-up. Scanning it again, Symon's heart filled with pride. He'd come a long way in the years since he'd returned home with only recipes, a rucksack and broken dreams to show for his time in Paris. Starting up his restaurant in a dilapidated cottage had been Symon's only reason to keep going in those bleak early days, so to have a Michelin star and a glowing review in the national press was quite an achievement. It almost made up for what he had lost.

Almost.

Not wanting to think about this for a second longer than he needed to, Symon returned his attention to the article. *Breathe in and breathe out*, he told himself. *In and out.* Long, deep breaths would steady the pulse and slow the blood currently galloping around his veins like one of Mo's horses. He needed to think about the restaurant, not Claudette Marsaud.

He never, ever wanted to think about her. The days when she'd filled his every waking thought and all his dreams were long gone.

Aware that Tara was looking at him askance, Symon pointed to a section of text highlighted by an eye-catching box. "He says he's still dreaming of how delightful the food was, even now. I think we can safely say he enjoyed the meal!"

"The phone's been ringing off the hook," said Tara. "We'll be booked solid until September at this rate."

"We need to be." Symon put the newspaper supplement down on the counter and picked up a brown envelope he'd opened earlier. The sight of it alone was enough to make a headache beat at his temples.

Tara paled. "Is that what I think it is?"

"If you think it's a letter from my landlord telling me that he's doubling the rent because that's what he'd get for a holiday let, and informing me that I can either pay up or terminate my lease, then it's exactly what you think it is."

They stared at one another and Symon saw his own dread reflected in Tara's horrified expression. This latest letter from his up-country landlord, Peter Marten, hadn't come as much of a surprise. All the same, Symon had been hoping it would have arrived a little later in the year. Property prices in Cornwall had rocketed in the last eighteen months and all over the village cottages were being painted up; invariably their window frames were given a slick of sage gloss and they received new names like *Crab Pot* or *Fisherman's Rest*. A holiday let could bring in up to four times the income of an ordinary rental, and as more and more houses in Polwenna Bay became second homes it was becoming harder to find premises to rent or an affordable property to buy.

When Symon had taken on the building that was now The Plump Seagull, it had been rather run down, having been occupied by the same tenant for over three decades. The elderly man who'd lived there had been making do with broken electrical sockets, lights that flickered and wiring that sizzled alarmingly. The walls were speckled with black mould, there were rotten floorboards and most of the surfaces were yellowed from nicotine. Nobody else had wanted to touch the place and Symon had been able to rent it at a reasonable cost and persuade the landlord to apply for change of use. Symon had carried out all the renovations himself and the project had been a true labour of love. The long days and even longer nights he'd spent there painting or sawing had been his salvation during those raw early days and he'd poured his heart, soul and savings into the place. Now the bright and cheery restaurant was barely recognisable as the dingy and neglected cottage he'd started with. With its low beams, its quirky uneven flooring upstairs and that glimpse of harbour view from Symon's attic bedroom, it was the archetypal dream Cornish cottage. Symon supposed it was hardly a surprise the owner had decided it could make far more money as a holiday let.

"What will you do?" Tara was asking.

"What *can* I do? I'll have to pay it or move out – and I can't do that until the season is over." Symon had spent several sleepless nights trying to think of a solution and, so far, winning the lottery was all he could come up with. That or selling a kidney.

"What about asking Ashley?" Tara suggested, adding swiftly when she saw his look of horror: "I know asking for help goes against everything you Tremaines stand for but he is part of the family now and he's got the cash too. Maybe he could be a partner and buy into the business?"

"Absolutely not. This is my business and I run it alone and my way." Symon was adamant on this score. There would be no partners for him, in business or in love. He'd seen first-hand how easily people could betray one another, family or not. Besides, he was far too proud to go cap in hand to his sister's wealthy husband. Claudette might have done her utmost to break Symon but at least he'd kept his dignity. He'd rather fry fish for Chris the Cod than lose that.

Tara sighed. She'd known the Tremaines long enough to realise exactly how determined and stubborn they could be.

"So if the worst comes to the worst and the rent is too high, will you look for another premises in the village?"

Symon grimaced. "I can't imagine where I'd find somewhere that works as well as this or that I can afford. I'll have to think outside the box if or when it comes to that."

"Well, it's not going to. Not with this fantastic review and the amount of extra bookings already," Tara said staunchly. "I'm going to update everything online and then see if I can drum up some more publicity. And no moaning!" she added sternly as Symon opened his mouth to protest. "If you want to make this work you'll have to give up being Polwenna's answer to Greta Garbo and work the brooding, sexy chef angle."

Symon laughed. "Should an ex sister-in-law make that kind of comment?"

"I'm speaking as your marketing manager. As your ex sister-in-law and slave-driven employee I know you're just a miserable git with all the worst Tremaine family traits. Thank God I'm with Richard now," Tara shot back with a grin as she set the newspaper supplement aside. "You never know, I might even have to put some adverts out for extra staff as well soon. We might be needing another pot washer and a waitress, if we get as busy as I think we will."

Symon was still smiling when she'd gone. Tara was much nicer since she'd divorced his brother, Danny. It just went to show that sometimes people could be totally wrong for one another. Claudette had sworn that was the case for her and Jean-Luc, but then she'd—

What was the matter with him today? He hadn't thought about Claudette Marsaud for ages and now it was impossible to get her out of his thoughts. He glanced at the clock. Almost noon. Maybe he should have a cognac to steady his nerves?

Or maybe not. Alcohol was a slippery slope and one he'd teetered on for a while. It was too easy to make an excuse for having a drink in this village. Meeting a friend in The Ship. Having a sunset cider in the beach café. A bottle of wine in the restaurant. Take your pick of venues to visit and then throw the holiday atmosphere into the mix, and there it was: the perfect recipe for a swift and booze-soaked decline.

He tucked the letter deep into the pocket of his checked chef's trousers. It was one to worry about another time and right now he'd be better off preparing some fillets of hake for the evening's menu. Besides, Perry would arrive any minute with the pink oyster mushrooms and the rest of the organic veg delivery. The last thing Symon needed was to be hitting the bottle when his old friend arrived.

Perry Tregarrick could drink for England (plus Scotland, Wales and Ireland for good measure), and if he saw Symon with a brandy they'd be on a pub crawl around the village before you could say *wasted*. They'd been leading each other astray since childhood, when Perry – full name Lord Peregrine Aldous Melville Tregarrick – had always returned home to Cornwall for the school holidays and had become an honorary member of the Tremaine clan. Perry claimed that downing vast amounts of alcohol was a family talent. It was one that could scarcely be argued with, since Perry's father had drunk away the family fortune with amazing efficiency. All that remained now of the Tregarrick family's once vast estate was Polwenna Manor, a mouldering medieval pile collapsing under the combined weight of a rotting roof and a tonne of debts.

Like Symon, Perry was also struggling to pay the bills. Death duties had walloped him hard. A gentle and rather eccentric dreamer, he'd been happy growing organic vegetables, pottering around the house with his pack of dogs and painting big splashy pictures that he truly believed would become masterpieces, until his father had died and the entire burden of the family name and estate had landed on his slight shoulders. Nice as the splashy paintings were, the galleries of St Ives had yet to call – and so it was the vegetables that paid the bills, or rather the interest on the bills. These days poor Perry looked as though he was in the same ready-to-crumble condition as his stately home.

Yep, Symon reflected as he pulled the hake out of the fridge, things could always be worse. At least he wasn't Perry.

"Hey, Sy!"

Here was Perry now, letting himself in through the back door and, bent almost double under the weight of his delivery, staggering across the kitchen. Replacing the fish quickly, Symon went to rescue him.

"Cheers," panted Perry, leaning against the counter while Symon rummaged through the vegetables. "I thought I was going to drop the lot or get a hernia."

"You could have made two trips," Symon suggested.

Perry looked stunned at the thought. "Gosh, I never thought of that. You're right. Maybe next time I will?"

Symon knew he wouldn't. Perry would have forgotten this conversation by the time he was back inside his battered Mercedes estate car. His head was too full of the latest splashy painting to find room for anything else. He had that familiar faraway look in his pale blue eyes and his sweater, on inside out, was daubed with streaks of crimson and blue. His fingers were smeared with jade and his burgundy cords were dotted with ochre. Even his scuffed brogues and frayed cuffs were speckled with paint. He'd either forgotten to put his smock on or couldn't afford a new canvas.

"Help yourself to a cold drink while I unpack," Symon said, running his hands over the produce and marvelling at just how wonderful it was. Perry had green fingers, that was for sure – both literally and metaphorically today. The oyster mushrooms were huge, with delicate pink gills the same hue as horses' noses, and the strawberries were plump and red. Symon hoped the manor's orangery would continue to hold out; Perry's produce was one of the key ingredients to the restaurant's success.

While Perry gulped back a Diet Coke, Symon unpacked the boxes. The systematic ritual of putting things in their allotted places was almost meditative and by the time the last mushroom was in the fridge he felt much calmer. The rent issue would be sorted and his thoughts of Claudette were just a blip and meant nothing at all because he was completely over her. All would be well.

Unfortunately for Symon, his sister Morwenna arrived just as he was starting to relax. Judging by her determined and slightly manic expression, any hopes he might have had for equilibrium were about to be dashed. Mo existed on a dizzying cocktail of enthusiasm and adrenaline, which made her a force to be reckoned with (especially when she was on horseback at one of her events) but left Symon feeling exhausted.

"There you are!" she said, bowling into the kitchen and hugging him.

"I'm normally here," Symon pointed out as he hugged her back.

"But you're not normally plastered all over the press! My little brother is famous!"

Mo loved hyperbole and Symon rolled his eyes.

"Hardly, Mo. It was a tiny column," he said, but his sister flapped his protests away with a dismissive hand.

"You're a celebrity now, Symon Tremaine. Watch out Padstow! Polwenna Bay's coming for you. And I bet Jamie's quaking over at Fifteen Cornwall in Watergate!"

"What's all this?" Perry asked.

"Oh hi, Perry. I didn't see you there," said Mo. Quite how she'd missed six feet of lanky paint-splattered aristocrat was a mystery, although Symon suspected her mind was on something else. His Morwenna madness antennae were on full alert. His sister was up to something.

"What's this about the press?" Perry repeated.

"Symon was in the national papers!" said Mo.

"Only one of them, in the food section," Symon explained.

"Didn't you see it?" demanded Mo, rounding on him.

Perry, trapped between Morwenna and the sink, looked quite scared. "Err, no. Sorry, Mo. Was it a good piece?"

"It was a great write-up about the restaurant and my brilliant, wonderful, kind brother," Mo replied proudly.

"OK, you can stop laying it on with a trowel," said Symon, very suspicious now. "Whatever you want, the answer's 'no'."

"Charming," huffed his sister. "What a thing to say. Can't I just be nice?"

Symon folded his arms and gave her a hard stare. "Don't give me that. I know you, remember? Spill. Or do I have to sit on you and—"

Mo shrieked in horror. "Anything but that! God, brothers are so gross! OK, then, this is it and you can't say no because I've already told her you'll go and it's all arranged and everything. Promise you won't go mad, Sy, but I've arranged for you to have dinner with a friend of mine."

Symon gaped at her. "What do you mean? Dinner?"

"It's a meal usually eaten in the evening," deadpanned Mo, but Symon wasn't in the mood for humour.

"You've set me up on a blind date? Seriously?"

"It's not *blind* exactly, because you know her. It's Tess."

"Tess Hamilton? The teacher?" Symon couldn't believe what he was hearing.

"Lucky you. She's gorgeous," said Perry wistfully.

Symon wasn't denying this. Tess certainly was gorgeous, but nevertheless he wasn't interested in her. It wasn't anything personal. He wasn't interested in anyone.

"No way," he told his sister. "You can tell Tess I'm busy."

Mo folded her arms and jutted out her chin. "I can't. I told her you were really keen. Besides, it'll do you good to get out. Tony will cover. I've already asked him."

Tony was Symon's second in command.

"You've been talking to my staff about this?"

"Just helping," Mo said. "They all think you need a night off too."

"Well you can help me even more by telling Tess it's not happening."

"I'll go if you don't want to," offered Perry. "You may have to lend me some funds though."

"It's Symon's date, Perry, and he isn't going to let Tess down," Mo said. "That would be unkind and cruel. She's really looking forward to this, Sy, and you'll absolutely devastate her if you don't show up."

"Why are you crossing your fingers behind your back?" Perry asked, and Mo flicked him a V.

"Ignore him. Come on, Sy. Please? Just one date? So she isn't stood up? So she doesn't feel like a total loser? So she doesn't cry herself to sleep?"

Great. Mo always did know what buttons to press. Symon was hopeless at coping with guilt. If only he hadn't been, he could have stayed in France.

"But Tess dated Nick," he said. It was the only excuse he could think of, but Mo wasn't having this.

"Who can just about read the back of a cereal packet and had nothing in common with her! They went out about twice and you're not Henry the Eighth so what does it matter if she dated your brother? This is Polwenna; everyone dates everyone."

"It's true," agreed Perry. "I've dated three sisters from the de Verney family. Terribly nice girls and big on shooting."

Mo ignored him. "Honestly, Sy, you'll have a blast. She's clever and funny and what have you got to lose? You can't let Tess down. She'll feel terrible. How would you like it?"

"Fine, fine, anything for a quiet life," said Symon. He'd have dinner with Tess because she was a nice girl and didn't deserve to be messed about just because his sister wanted to matchmake. He'd tell her gently that Mo had set them up and explain he wasn't looking for a relationship. That way honour would be satisfied and nobody would be hurt. There was nothing worse than hurt feelings. After having his own feelings well and truly shredded, Symon couldn't bear to make anyone else unhappy.

Mo punched the air. "Brilliant. You won't regret it."

"What about me? Do I get a date?" Perry wanted to know. "Preferably a rich one who'd like to fix up the manor – or, even better, buy it."

"You're selling?" Symon was shocked. Perry loved his home and felt a huge responsibility to keep it in the family.

"I may have to. The bills are crippling and it's falling down. I don't suppose you'd like to run your restaurant from it?" he asked hopefully. "The kitchen's huge. I think it's Tudor."

The manor's kitchen was indeed massive – and it also boasted a spit, an enormous chimney and a whole load of Tudor grime. Most likely it was still harbouring sixteenth-century pathogens as well. It certainly looked as though it hadn't been cleaned since Shakespeare was in nappies.

"I'm good thanks, mate," said Symon and Perry sighed.

"An heiress it is then. I'll have to ask Ella St Milton if she fancies marrying me for the title."

Mo's nose wrinkled. "God, things must be bad. Ella's a nightmare – isn't she, Sy? She drove you mad when you did the catering for the summer ball."

"She was quite demanding," Symon said tactfully. He wasn't going to badmouth Ella because firstly it wasn't gentlemanly and secondly he wouldn't mind more catering work at the hotel to help pay his increased rent. Ella had indeed been demanding – every detail had had to be a certain way – but then, like Symon, she was a perfectionist and cared about her business. He got that entirely. Still, in terms of romantic relationships, high-maintenance women like Ella St Milton were best avoided and the less Symon Tremaine had to do with them the better.

All of a sudden the date with Tess didn't seem quite so bad after all.

CHAPTER 3

The write-up about Symon Tremaine was good. Very good.

Ella St Milton, sitting on the terrace of the Polwenna Bay Hotel and enjoying a few moments away from her desk, took a sip of black coffee and leaned back in her chair. The critic was clearly impressed with his experience at The Plump Seagull and having eaten there several times she understood why: Symon was a truly gifted chef. Granted, in real life he was monosyllabic and gauche, but put him in the kitchen and a magical transformation took place. He was passionate and driven, a perfectionist who demanded only the very best from his team. There was certainly another side to Symon, one that thrilled and intrigued her.

Ella smoothed the page with a red-tipped index finger. Beneath her touch Symon smouldered up from the newsprint. She'd known him in a vague way for years and never seen him look at a woman with as much intensity as he looked at food, although to be fair Symon Tremaine never showed any interest in women – unlike his brothers, who'd worked their way through the female population of the village since their early teens. From what Ella could see Symon wasn't interested in anyone or anything apart from cooking.

He was straight, of that Ella was certain. Her gaydar was finely tuned – and even if it hadn't been, Tom Elliot, her assistant manager at the hotel, was good at keeping her up to speed on such matters. The fact was, all Symon lived for was his restaurant. It was hardly surprising that he was building such a name for himself, given that work was all he seemed to do.

She pushed the newspaper supplement aside and stared thoughtfully over the terrace and out to sea. The sun had popped its head above the clouds and the water was sparkling, no longer the grey sheet of minutes earlier but now blue and deceptively summery. There were a few guests on the terrace, seated beneath patio heaters and enjoying a leisurely lunch in the sunshine. She watched as they tucked into plates piled high with mussels, bowls of golden fries served with shavings of truffle, and crusty baguettes that shed crumbs on snowy linen. Delicious smells made her mouth water – and her stomach, which had been fed only its habitual low-carb breakfast of egg whites, grumbled. The hotel's chef was a genius and it seemed one of life's cruellest jokes that Ella spent all day thinking about menus and treats for her guests but never tasted more than a morsel herself. She didn't dare. Maintaining her size-eight figure was a full-time job in itself. Ella stuck to her strict diet and gruelling fitness routine with the same dogged determination that had seen her transform a rather dated country house hotel into one of Cornwall's most desirable locations.

It was this kind of single-mindedness, the absolute commitment to a vision, that she recognised in Symon. The write-up about him in the newspaper might only be a short piece with a small accompanying image, but Ella instinctively understood that Symon had fought hard to make it this far. Maybe he was still battling, who knew? She certainly was.

Few people in Polwenna Bay could imagine that there was anything about Ella St Milton's life that might be described as a struggle. To others it must look as though she'd been born with an entire set of solid silver spoons in her mouth. She had a wealthy family, an adoring grandfather, cars, designer clothes and bags, a hotel, trips to beauty salons, a perfect figure, a string of gorgeous boyfriends... On and on the list went. If she thought about it for too long, Ella actually felt quite jealous of herself. She had it all, didn't she?

At least, she did on the surface...

Ella bit her lip with frustration. Anyone walking across the terrace now and spotting her sitting at her table with the weekend papers spread out in front of her, next to the silver cafetière and bone-china cup, would see a glossy blonde oozing privilege. And she *was* privileged, Ella was the first to admit this. She'd never wanted for any material thing. Whatever she'd asked for had become hers, with an ease that had turned girls like Mo Tremaine (as she was then) and Summer Penhalligan pea-green with envy. She'd played on this too, taking pleasure in showing off all the wonderful things she had – and not just as a child either.

She sighed. Ella wasn't proud of it but not so long ago she'd sold a horse that she knew Mo had been desperate to keep at her yard. Ella had done this for no better reason than wanting to hit Mo where it would hurt most. For about three minutes Ella had gloated over her victory, before the annoying little voice of conscience that dwelt deep down inside had told her she was being a bitch. She'd tried to ignore it, but the inconvenient little voice had grown louder and louder until it had become impossible to ignore; in the end she'd cracked and tried to buy the horse back. This was when karma had really served her a double whammy, because it turned out that Ashley Carstairs, the sexy and rich Ross Poldark lookalike Ella had secretly had her eye on (if only to take her mind off Jake), had already bought the horse and placed it on livery with Mo again. The rest was history and now Mo and Ashley were blissfully married and parents to the most delicious plump bundle that was baby Isla – while Ella was in the wrong kind of relationship and, although she would rather die than admit it to a soul, starting to feel a little broody.

Serves you right. That's what you get for being a bitch, the little voice told her smugly. Ella couldn't help agreeing with it.

She had been a bitch. Come to that, she probably still was if you asked the hotel staff. If they thought she didn't know they called her Evil Ella then they were sorely mistaken. Some days it was almost like playing a pantomime version of herself. Not wanting to ruin her image, Ella did her best not to let them down.

"Table three needs clearing," she snapped at a waiter passing by with a laden tray. He jumped, crockery rattling, and looked stricken.

"I'm really sorry, Miss St Milton, I'll do it straight away."

"And there are empty glasses on the balustrade. Who's supposed to be bussing tables?" Ella's neat brows drew together in a scowl. Oh, that wasn't good. The Botox must be wearing off. She'd have to go to Truro for a top-up before anyone noticed. Ella spent all day dealing with problems and irate guests and was convinced that without her faithful doses of botulinum toxin she'd look like she needed ironing.

The waiter, on his toes now, delivered the drinks with great speed and was soon clearing up. When Ella said "jump" the staff always asked "how high?" and would probably have requested a springboard too if it were possible, just to impress her.

Unfortunately for Ella, there was one exception to this rule – a tricky and impossible-to-ignore exception who went by the name of Charlie Barton and happened to be the hotel's resident celebrity chef. Hiring him had been a major coup at the time because Charlie was both brilliant and broke, a potent combination which meant that he was only too happy to work for Ella. She'd agreed to pay his debts off (although she'd had to sell her Audi TT to do that, and think of a plausible explanation for its absence if her grandfather asked); in exchange, he'd lent his growing culinary reputation to the hotel. Ella had known that her chef's name would be the key to their success. After all, celebrity was what put well-clad bums on expensive dining-room seats. It seemed to her that Rick Stein had figured this out years ago.

When she'd taken the hotel over, Ella had set out to do her research and she'd done it with a thoroughness that was now paying dividends. She'd subscribed to all the Cornish and seaside-themed magazines, temporarily forgone her strict diet to eat her way around the area's top restaurants, and kept a close eye on the local and national press. With an influx of second-home owners from London and a plethora of celebrity chefs choosing to holiday and set up restaurants in the county, Cornwall was rapidly becoming a Mecca for foodies. Its fine dining appeared regularly in all the major glossy magazines, and Ella had been keen to tap into this trend. Charlie had been heavily featured in the local press and enjoyed a regular slot on regional television too. With his mop of bronzed curls, wicked dark eyes and rugby player's build he soon had the female viewers drooling as much over his raw masculinity as his delicious food. There was no doubt whatsoever that basing his restaurant in her hotel had brought in trade. This was great and Ella was thrilled. What was slightly *less great* was her subsequent discovery that Charlie made even the most famously difficult divas look low maintenance. In fact, if picking out green M&Ms or only bathing in champagne were all he demanded then life would have been simple.

It would be simpler too if Ella wasn't sleeping with him...

She grimaced. Having a fun romance with Charlie was proving to be a big mistake. She supposed she'd have to sort it out sooner rather than later, preferably when he wasn't halfway down a bottle of Scotch or putting the final touches to a wedding breakfast. For now, she was just enjoying a few rare minutes to herself before today's wedding party arrived and she ended up rushed off her feet making sure that everything was perfect. Thanks to the efforts of Jules Mathieson, their local vicar, Polwenna Bay was becoming a popular spot to get married and Ella's wedding-planning business was doing very nicely. Maybe there was a God?

If there was, then Ella hoped He'd heard her prayers asking for Charlie to calm down. All too often the chef was being led astray by her annoying brother; it seemed they were on a bender in the village pubs almost every other night.

Ella checked her watch and, seeing that she still had another five minutes left, poured a second cup of coffee. It was bitter on her tongue, rather like her frequent claims that things were "fine" and that life was "great". The truth was, Ella's own heart had been badly bruised when Jake Tremaine had chosen his childhood sweetheart over her. She'd never admit it to a soul, but Ella had fallen for Jake. She'd felt that way about him since they were teenagers, if she was honest with herself – and not so very long ago she'd allowed herself to hope that maybe there was a chance for them.

With his thick blond hair, laughing blue eyes and strong muscular body, Jake was the full package looks-wise. He was great company too and they'd enjoyed some incredible nights together. Then Summer had returned to Polwenna Bay. Immediately, Ella had been transported back in time to their schooldays: once again she was watching the Tremaines from afar, a noisy squabbling happy rabble of a family, and wondering how she could be included. The answer was that she couldn't. Now Jake was happy with Summer and Ella was on the outside looking in, just as she always had been.

What must it be like to have a family like that? As a child, Ella had observed the Tremaines with a mixture of bewilderment and wonder. Henry and Alice had been hands-on grandparents, if strict at times, but they'd clearly loved the children. And Jimmy, if far from an ideal father, had spent a lot of time when they were younger playing with them and thinking up new adventures. Treasure hunts, picnics, ghost walks... His imagination knew no bounds. Even when Jimmy hadn't been around, the family had always been up to something exciting, or at least it had looked that way from where Ella had stood. Her parents had split up and, busy with new partners and second families, had been more than happy to shunt Ella and her little brother Teddy from pillar to post. Living full time at the hotel with their grandfather had been something of a relief in the end – and if Ella had cried herself to sleep missing her parents then nobody except her teddy bear had ever known about it.

Lord! How pitiful did she sound? Annoyed with herself for still feeling eleven years old deep down inside, Ella drained her coffee and gathered up the papers. The hotel didn't run itself and she'd better get back to work. Her grandfather, Jonny, was old-fashioned and remained unconvinced that Ella should run the hotel when she had a brother who could do the job. It didn't seem to bother him that Teddy was younger, spent money like it was going out of fashion and treated the hotel like a personal bank account: he had a willy and that seemed to make up for all these defects. It was grossly unfair but Ella knew she had to work twice as hard to prove herself.

She'd do it too. The hotel and her growing wedding-planning business meant everything to her. In that respect, Ella entirely understood why Symon Tremaine was so antisocial. People only let you down in the end, whereas a successful business was there twenty-four hours of the day; it was a constant companion and proof that everything you did actually mattered. What was it her grandfather always said? *There are no prizes for coming second.* Well, Ella was determined to make the Polwenna Bay Hotel number one for everything.

With this goal in mind, Ella was particularly pleased with her appointment of Tom Elliot as the assistant manager. He'd worked for her before on a temporary basis and impressed her then; when the permanent position had become available, Tom had seemed like the obvious choice. He was experienced and sharp-witted, and the hotel guests adored him because he always went the extra mile to make them feel valued and important. Ella couldn't begin to imagine how many repeat bookings were down to Tom alone; there had to be hundreds. Conscientious and enthusiastic, Tom put in nearly as many hours as she did and was always full of good ideas. Sometimes these ideas weren't *quite* as brilliant as Tom thought they were, admittedly. Take Christmas, for example, when he'd almost caused a disaster attempting to play cupid with some guests. Still, his heart was in the right place and he ran the hotel so beautifully that without him Ella would never have managed to get the wedding-planning business up and running.

Not that she'd ever tell Tom any of this. In Ella's opinion it didn't do to let staff become too comfortable. It was far better to keep them on their toes and a little uncertain of her. That way they always worked as hard as possible, did what she asked and were keen to impress – which in turn made the hotel a first-class establishment.

It was a win-win situation and she only wished it worked with Charlie bloody Barton.

A man's never going to respect you once he's seen you naked, hissed the smug little voice gleefully. *He knows too much and he's got too close now. You should have stayed away.*

The voice was right. She should have stayed away. It was much safer to be single and Ella vowed that she'd remember this in future. Once Charlie was dealt with she'd make such an effort to avoid love that she might as well become a nun.

Her break was over. Holding her papers under one arm, Ella smoothed the creases from her trouser suit with her other hand and headed back through the lobby to her office. The smell of lilies and beeswax polish soothed her and she was pleased to see that the local florist had worked her magic: the various arrangements of cream blooms spilled from the windowsills, stood sentry either side of the big entrance and wound their way up the curling banisters. A quick peek in the ballroom confirmed that all was perfect there too. Meanwhile, fingers crossed, Charlie was working wonders in the kitchen and behaving himself while his film crew was shooting. Tom, who was currently checking in a guest, gave Ella a nod to indicate that all was well. Since the wedding party wasn't due for a while, she decided she had time to go through her emails.

Ella's office was a small room at the back of the hotel, overlooking the very glamorous recycling area. As she worked her way through the emails she watched a couple of seagulls attempting to rip open a refuse sack. It reminded her that spring was fast approaching and the usual seagull bin war was about to begin. There was so much to do before then that it made her feel quite dizzy. For one thing, she had her grandfather's wedding to plan – if he ever set a date, that was. To be honest Ella hoped he didn't because she couldn't think of anything worse than being related to Mo Carstairs. In addition, Georgie Angel's big day was looming on the horizon, as these six very urgent emails could testify.

She minimised the screen and rubbed her eyes with her knuckles until stars leapt and danced in her vision. The list of requirements was getting ever more ridiculous, but when an A-lister chose your hotel as their wedding venue you didn't quibble with anything they asked for, even if you did privately think that a hot-pink carpet was tacky or that matching thrones were very 1990s Beckham. Georgie Angel was the most talked-about celebrity of the moment and was currently starring in *Wreckers,* ITV's answer to *Poldark.* His handsome, glowering face was everywhere, from mugs to tablecloths. His now famous white shirt, slashed to the waist to reveal rippling pecs and tantalising whorls of dark hair just above his belt, drove women of a certain age mad. His wedding was certainly driving Ella mad because not a day went by without yet another demand.

Sorry. Did she say *demand*? What she meant was *request.*

She clicked the mouse and instantly another email pinged into her box. This time it was a message from Tabitha, the bride-to-be, suggesting the paparazzi be secretly allowed into the building to take pictures – even though last week Ella had been read the riot act regarding the need for privacy to protect magazine deals. All this was making Ella's head hurt. If any other customer had behaved in such a manner, she would have considered telling them to find another venue. The only thing stopping Ella from firing back a curt reply was the fact that Georgie was such a big star, whose wedding here was bound to generate invaluable publicity. If everything went well, it would cement the hotel's position as *the* place to get married.

She took a deep breath, flexed her fingers and started to type a reply. Ella was so deep in trying to explain why it would be unwise to invite the paparazzi – half the guests were celebrities, after all, and one Premier League footballer on the list was notoriously volatile – when the pressure of warm lips against the bare skin of her neck made her cry out.

Her heart hammering, Ella spun around in her wheelie chair to find Charlie Barton grinning at her. Her eyes widened. He was stark naked apart from a chef's hat placed in a strategic position.

"Jesus! Charlie! What the hell are you playing at?" Ella shot up from her chair and locked the office door. If anyone walked in on them she could kiss goodbye to having any authority with her staff.

"Giving my sexy boss a classic dish. I call it Charlie's Sausage Surprise," Charlie said, raising his eyebrows in a suggestive fashion. "Come on, Ella, don't be coy. You know you want me."

Ella knew for certain that, actually, she really didn't. As Charlie reached for her she caught a blast of his breath and recoiled.

"You've been drinking!"

It was only just past noon. Instantly Ella was on red alert. She had one hundred and sixty guests due at two o'clock, all of whom were expecting to sit down to a hugely expensive wedding breakfast prepared by Cornwall's very own Charlie Barton. Oh Lord. He hadn't been cooking naked, had he? Or, even worse, not prepared the food?

"A little," Charlie admitted. "I was making the champagne jellies and a red-wine *jus*, so I had a little tester. Chef's perks. A bit like this!"

He whipped the hat off his privates and attempted to pull her against him and bend her over the desk. It would have been sexy in a rather basic way, had he not been so plastered. Instead, he staggered and ended up in a heap on the floor.

"Oops!" he grinned, holding out his hand to her. "Never mind. The carpet's quite soft. Come and join me here, babe."

"Have you lost your mind?" Ella hissed. "There's a function on today! You should be in the kitchen!"

"Relax. It's all under control. I've worked the Charlie magic so it's all ready, the TV people have their footage and Klaus is in charge now. My work is done... in the kitchen anyway! Now come here!"

Klaus was an excellent sous-chef but it wasn't *his* food that her guests were paying for. Ella was furious. "Get up and cover yourself, for heaven's sake. You're being ridiculous. No, worse than that, unprofessional! I pay you to be a chef not an idiot!"

The humour faded and petulance flickered across his features. "Not nearly enough. I could get double if I went to Rock. Triple even."

Ella's heart clenched. She didn't doubt this for a moment and they both knew it was true. Charlie had been nagging her for a pay rise for months. She'd already given him one and thrown in her Range Rover too in order to keep him sweet, but she'd always known it wouldn't be enough. Nothing would ever be enough for Charlie Barton. He was avaricious to the last cell in his (naked) body.

But, as with vicious dogs, to show fear was to show weakness, so Ella just gave him a scornful look. "Not if you behave like this. What kind of a reference do you think I'd give you? You'd be lucky to get a job in the pasty shop."

Charlie hauled himself up, leaning heavily against the desk, and curled his lip. "You think I'd need a reference? Dream on. You'll need one from me, more like. Anyway, you know I'm good. You should give me a pay rise or I might just decide to go and see what's elsewhere. And then where would you be?"

An icy finger traced a path down Ella's spine. Up a well-known creek without a paddle was where she'd be. Georgie Angel was a fan of Charlie's and had booked the Polwenna Bay Hotel especially. She knew it and so did her chef.

"Ten grand a month should cover it – and that's on top of my basic." He reached out and grabbed his checked trousers from where he'd tossed them onto the filing cabinet, stepping into them as though he didn't have a care in the world while Ella's brain did some rapid mental arithmetic. Ten grand. Where on earth was she going to find ten grand?

She'd have to sell something. Lots of things. Already she was making an inventory of all her handbags and shoes. How much did second-hand Louis Vuittons go for these days?

Charlie, now dressed in his trousers, was unlocking the door. As it opened he swayed a little before clutching the doorframe for support. Then he laughed.

"You know something, Ella? It might have been easier just to have had some fun with me. You like it and I like it. Would it really have been so difficult? But I'm starting to feel very glad you didn't. I think our relationship just moved to a whole new level."

And with that he swaggered out, albeit a little unsteadily. She heard him laugh all the way down the corridor. Ella slammed her office door with such fury that the filing cabinet shook.

Even so, it wasn't trembling nearly as much as she was. Things with Charlie were about to get a great deal uglier – and right at the beginning of the wedding season, this couldn't have come at a worse time. What on earth was she going to do?

CHAPTER 4

Jules Mathieson closed the vestry door and leaned against it. Phew. Another successful wedding service at St Wenn's concluded and, outside, the wedding party happily posing for photos against the beautiful backdrop of Polwenna Bay. Even with the sun playing hide-and-seek and the sea alternating between blue and grey, Jules knew the happy couple would look back on their wedding album and agree they couldn't have chosen a better spot to take their vows.

As she shrugged off her cassock, showering the vestry floor with pink confetti (which she knew would give her verger, Sheila Keverne, a great excuse to moan), Jules couldn't help feeling smug. Goodness, she hoped this wasn't the Sin of Pride. But she did feel proud of what she and her team here had achieved in such a short time. Not so long ago the future of St Wenn's had hung in the balance: with a falling congregation and circling property developers, the villagers had been worried they might lose their church. After lots of ingenious ideas for fundraising (some of them *slightly* less ingenious than others, admittedly), the future was looking far less bleak. Jules knew they still had a long way to go and that the bishop would review the parish registers at some point, but they'd turned a corner and this was in no small part down to the church proving to be a very popular wedding venue. With Ella St Milton plugging Polwenna Bay in expensive magazines, the word was slowly spreading. Jules couldn't afford to buy these publications herself, but she'd sneaked a few peeks in Betty Jago's shop and been thrilled to see her church nestled between the property pages and features about driftwood art. She hadn't been *quite* so chuffed with the shot of her looking plump and tufty-haired; on the other hand, at least now Jules could say she'd been a model in a glossy magazine.

"It's not technically a lie, Lord," she said out loud. "And it's all for a good cause."

With any luck today's happy couple would show their pictures to all their friends, flood social media and upload so much video footage to YouTube that she'd be inundated with even more couples wanting to get married at St Wenn's. The register would overflow with names, there would be lots of christenings to follow and Bishop Bill would be thrilled that the future of her lovely church was safe for centuries more to come. Getting told off for the confetti was a small price to pay.

Still, Sheila could be quite scary and Jules made a mental note to hunt out the dustpan and brush from under the vicarage sink. She'd have a quick clean-up before tomorrow's early-morning communion service. Until then she'd just swish it under the rug. The flurries outside would have drifted all over the churchyard by now; dealing with them would be a job for Big Rog Pollard and his shiny new leaf blower. Assuming that Jules could ever prise him out of his shed, that was. Big Rog had missed the last Parochial Church Council meeting because, according to Little Rog, he was at a crucial point with his boat build. Jules wasn't quite sure what was going on but had decided she'd only worry when she spotted animals trotting two by two up the hill to the Pollards' cottage.

She hung her robes up, pulled her dog collar out from her shirt and donned a hoody. It was a lovely day but still chilly out of the sun – and since she was meeting her boyfriend Danny for a walk, Jules wasn't about to do the classic British thing of mistaking a ray of sunshine for tropical weather. Knowing Danny, he'd find somewhere interesting for their lunch spot and she didn't want to be cold. An ex-soldier, Danny might still bear the injuries that had forced him out of active service but he didn't hang about or hold back when he was hiking. Since they'd first started spending time together, enjoying a friendship that had slowly blossomed into love, Jules had lost over three stone keeping up with him.

Hmm. She still had a couple more to go, Jules thought critically. The trouble was that she lived in a village overflowing with pasties and scones. She also spent a lot of time visiting ageing parishioners and probably consumed her own body weight in cake every week. *The Vicar of Dibley* episode where Dawn French had had to scoff several Christmas dinners was closer to a documentary than a sitcom; many a time Jules had forced herself to eat another piece of sponge when her stomach was already fit to burst. Still, spring was on its way and with it the lighter evenings. She'd make a point of walking over the cliffs a couple of times a week. Maybe she could even ask her friend Summer if she could go running with her? Kind Summer wouldn't laugh at Jules's red-faced and wheezy attempts to get fit – and if anyone was a great advert for this form of exercise it was Jake Tremaine's girlfriend. Jules would be a size zero before she knew it.

Or maybe not. Jules shook her head at this unrealistic thought. She could run to Truro and back every day for the rest of her life but she'd never be as skinny as Summer. On reflection, Jules decided that she ought to stick to the walking and try to avoid the ice cream or sausage roll reward at the end.

The vicar locked up the vestry and made her way through St Wenn's, as always savouring the tranquillity of the place. The church was filled with a peace born of centuries of prayer and reflection. It wasn't unusual to find villagers in here at random times of the day, searching for answers or perhaps just looking for a few minutes out from the whirl of twenty-first-century life. St Wenn's belonged to the village and to anyone who needed it, and for this reason Jules tended to leave the main door unlocked. It was often surprising who came through it in search of the church's solitude and comfort.

Outside, the wedding party was busy taking part in the photo shoot. The bride and groom were posing in the arched gateway, with the village tumbling away behind them and the sun silvering the sea. The couple had their arms wrapped around one another and seemed unable to tear their mutual gaze apart. Jules felt a lump rise to her throat. They were clearly in love, and so happy. Knowing that she'd played a part in their special day meant a great deal to her, and as she paused to let the photographer perfect the shot, Jules offered up a quick prayer for their future. She was well aware that life threw all kinds of curveballs at couples and that marriage wasn't easy – her divorced and still warring parents were living proof of this – but moments like this filled Jules with hope. These newlyweds stood together now with the rest of their lives ahead of them like untrodden snow. How could Jules be cynical about love when she spent nearly every weekend marrying couples?

While the vicar reflected on these things, she watched the photographer attempting to arrange the bride's train. In the strong breeze, it was billowing like the sails of the boats in the bay. Despite this, the bride looked absolutely radiant. Her dress was a gorgeous froth of lace and silk, delicately embroidered with daisies and bees, and modest rather than exposing too much cleavage or unsightly goosebumps. As she'd conducted the service, Jules – who was somewhat of an expert in these things by now – had admired the gown and thought privately that if she ever got married (and lost enough weight, of course) it was exactly the kind of dress she would choose.

Not that Jules was expecting to get married or even engaged. Although she'd been with Danny Tremaine for over a year now and they were very happy, marriage wasn't something they discussed. It had become a big dancing elephant in the room, trumpeting loudly and waltzing around, but they both ignored it pointedly. Jules, regularly fielding comments from her mother about ticking clocks and dusty shelves, didn't want to make Danny feel cornered. Besides, Danny was only recently divorced and, she assumed anyway, in no hurry to repeat the experience. He didn't appear cynical about his marriage and he'd certainly made his peace with Tara, his ex-wife, but not once had he raised the subject of a second marriage with Jules.

"We're really happy," Jules told her mother over and over again. It was true: they were. Danny completed Jules. He brought out the best in her, was her best friend and truly her other half, and the time that she'd spent with him so far had been the happiest of her life.

"If you're so blissfully happy then why aren't you engaged?" her mother would snap, and then Jules would have to think hard for a plausible reason. This wasn't easy because for her part she really couldn't come up with one. The only answer she had was that Danny didn't seem in a hurry to ask.

"So ask *him*!" her mother would retort. "You're equals, aren't you?"

"We're okay as we are, Mum," was all Jules would say, uttering a swift plea to her Boss for patience. "Honestly, we're fine."

The trouble was, these conversations always left Jules feeling unsettled. She wasn't a bridezilla by any means and she'd certainly never been the kind of girl who'd spent her childhood dreaming of being swept off her feet by a handsome prince. Jules had always quipped that with her Dairy Milk addiction the prince would need a crane anyway. Unlike her friends, who'd fantasised over dream wedding dresses and chosen their stationery and flowers practically after the first date, Jules had been too busy studying. The only white flowing garments she'd hoped for were ecclesiastical robes. Marriage was about far more than a pretty dress and a guest list, she always told the couples who came to her asking to have their banns read. There was the symbolic union of Christ and the Church to think about, as well as the fact that it was a bond sealed in the eyes of God.

The problem was that, when it really came down to it, these considerations didn't seem to matter half as much to Jules as simply wanting to be with her soulmate and being able to utter the magic words "my husband" or sign her name *Jules Tremaine*. (Of course, if Jules had ever practised this on the blotting paper in the vicarage office, she was determined that it would stay a very closely guarded secret.)

The bride and groom were getting into line for the group pictures now, so Jules was able to make it through the gate without photobombing any shots. As she wandered down Church Lane and towards the village, she continued to mull everything over. By the time she was passing Magic Moon's shop window, Jules had come to the conclusion that she would have to talk to Danny fairly soon – even if the thought alone made her insides curdle.

It's not that I'm desperate, she thought. Nor, she told herself, had her mother's tick-tocking noises made her start to think about the fact that she was already into her thirties. Jules was far too busy with St Wenn's and the demands of her flock to be thinking about babies. No. Jules's issue was more of a practical one and would probably sound utterly ridiculous to most young women living in the twenty-first century. Some people might even think she was crazy. Not that this bothered Jules in the least. Or Danny.

Jules was a vicar and as a vicar certain things came with the territory. It wasn't just the dog collar and a draughty church Jules had taken on when she'd been ordained. Those were merely the outside trappings. What was more important to

Jules was that she'd promised to live her life in a particular way – however unfashionable this might seem nowadays – and to uphold the beliefs she held dear, even if at times she found this hard. She couldn't move in with Danny unless they were married and she certainly wouldn't be taking their relationship to the next level outside of wedlock.

"It's not that I don't want to," she said to the beady-eyed seagull watching her from the hippy shop's gaudy sign. The truth was that she wanted to very much indeed; even Danny's slightest touch was enough to make her unravel. But Jules had made promises she believed in, and she would keep them. She had always made this very clear.

Danny respected and understood Jules's faith and was careful never to make things difficult for her. Polwenna was a small village and certain people thrived on gossip. He and Jules were rarely alone at the vicarage and spent most of their time together at Seaspray, where they were inevitably in the vicinity of one of the Tremaines. Even their walks were often accompanied by Danny's son, Morgan. This was all very respectable but Jules was starting to feel like a character in a Jane Austen novel, constantly chaperoned and confined to small talk. All she needed was a bonnet and no one would be able to tell the difference.

Fifty Shades her life was not.

The seagull wasn't impressed. Instead it regarded her with a mixture of pity and triumph. *Spring's coming*, its gloating look seemed to say, *and with it lots of lovely avian rooftop frolics*. Oh Lord, thought Jules with a wry smile, it would have been easier to be a seagull than a vicar!

The sun had broken through the clouds properly and there was a hint of duck-egg blue sky. The cottages' window boxes were bristling with daffodils and the shrubs were coming back to life too, their buds tightly packed with blossom ready to burst forth. Everything in nature was waking up and tingling with energy, and Jules felt exactly the same. She was ready to move on to the next stage of her life too. More than ready!

There was nothing for it. She was going to have to be brave and talk to Danny. It shouldn't be so hard. He was her best friend and they told each other everything. He loved her too; Jules knew this with all her heart, and she certainly loved him. So what was holding her back?

Jules knew the answer. It was fear that tied a knot in her vocal cords every time she thought about raising the subject. Not the fear of saying how she felt – Jules was honest to the core and never shirked from telling the truth – but rather a stomach-lurching cold dread that if she told Danny how much she wanted them to get married he would panic and run. He'd been married before and hurt in the worst possible way, so she couldn't imagine he had a great affection for the institution.

Wasn't it better to just enjoy what they had instead of hankering after something that could destroy them?

No, because you're not being honest, said Jules's heart. She gave a sigh. Danny's brother Nick Tremaine always said that honesty was overrated (usually when he was dating three girls at once or keeping the true state of his bank balance from Alice), but Jules knew that without it there was nothing except the illusion of happiness. Relationships were built on trust and trust came from honesty.

She had to speak to Danny and soon. She needed to find out for certain whether they had a future as a couple. It was best to know the truth.

"Jules! There you are. I was starting to think you were buried under a pile of confetti and that I'd have to come and dig you out!"

Here was Danny now, smiling at her in that way of his that always made Jules shiver from the inside out.

"I've made a picnic," he added proudly. "We need to collect it from the marina office and then Ashley says we can borrow his boat. I thought we'd head out to Adriatic Bay and look for the dolphins. Nick says he saw a pod when they headed out to sea this morning."

Dolphins, picnics and sunshiny boat rides across the sparkling sea with Danny. What did she ever do to get this lucky?

"It sounds absolutely wonderful," Jules said.

"No, *you're* wonderful," Danny replied quietly, pulling her close with his good arm and brushing her mouth with his.

Jules kissed him back and felt all her resolutions take flight with the whirling seagulls. The sun was shining, the dolphins were waiting and the love of her life was beside her. She wouldn't spoil things today.

There was plenty of time to talk to Danny. Her worries could wait a little longer.

CHAPTER 5

Mo's choice of venue for a blind date wasn't particularly adventurous and it certainly wasn't anonymous. She might as well have taken out a full-page advert in *The Cornish Times* announcing that Symon Tremaine and Tess Hamilton were ON A DATE as book a table in The Ship. Polwenna's pub, a pretty, low-beamed affair so close to the harbour that it was almost paddling, was the centre of village life. It was also a hub of gossip, courtesy of landlady Rose Harper. There wasn't much going on in Polwenna Bay that Rose didn't know about, and as he stepped into the pub Symon resigned himself to being the subject of great curiosity.

"Evening, Sy. Pint of Pol Brew?" Adam Harper, the landlord, reached for a glass and was heading for the beer pump when Rose blocked his path.

"Symon's not here for a drinking session. He's here for a meal. Mo booked the table, remember?" she said, shooing her husband away.

"Ah yes. Hot-date night." Adam winked at Sy. "Maybe a bottle of wine would be better? If I was related to Morwenna I'd be on the booze, for sure. No doubt about that."

Symon laughed. "Yeah. Ashley deserves a medal."

"Tess is already here," Rose told him. "I've given you the table in the window and she's got the menus. There's a couple of specials on and the baked monkfish is nice – although not up to your standard, of course!"

The landlady was looking flustered as she said this and Symon groaned inwardly. He recognised Rose's expression: it was the horrified one he always saw on the rare occasions he chose to eat out locally. Rose ran The Ship's kitchen, where hearty plates of steak and chips or sticky toffee puddings were the order of the day. It wasn't haute cuisine but her food had fuelled many a stomp over the cliffs and she always had glowing write-ups in the local press. Symon, who lived and breathed fine dining, was actually looking forward to tucking into something that came with a mound of chips.

"Nobody does a better steak pie than you, Rose," he said warmly.

He was rewarded with a beaming smile. "Get on with you! I'm not the one in the national newspapers, am I?"

"Not yet," said Adam loyally. He patted his rotund belly. "You'll not have any complaints from me though."

"Or me," chipped in Big Rog Pollard, for once not in his shed but enjoying a pint at the bar.

"Dad likes a big dinner – don't you, Dad?" piped up Little Rog Pollard, perched next to his father and trying to pretend he wasn't being ignored by a gaggle of hair-flicking, giggling teenage girls.

"That's right, my boy, that's right," his father agreed. "I like to leave a place feeling full up with proper grub, not hungry after a few fancy bits – no offence, Symon."

The one and only time the village builder and Mrs Rog had visited The Plump Seagull, they'd pushed Symon's delicate dishes around their plates nervously, been bamboozled by the finger bowls and been spotted buying chips in The Codfather only minutes after leaving. Symon had offered them a refund or another meal but they'd only looked even more worried by this suggestion.

"None taken," Symon answered, passing a twenty-pound note to Adam in exchange for a bottle of Pinot.

"Foreign food's not really my thing," Big Rog continued. Then, glancing at his watch and draining his pint, he added, "Anyway, I can't stay here chatting all night. The missus is making lasagne for dinner. Bloody 'ansome!"

"Lasagne's foreign." This comment was from Caspar Owen, Polwenna Bay's resident author and general know-it-all, who was sitting at the far end of the bar and making a big show of scribbling in a Moleskine notebook.

"Don't be daft," Big Rog scoffed. "My Karenza makes it and she's proper Cornish."

"Doesn't mean lasagne is. Lasagne's Italian," Caspar informed him.

"Italian?" Big Rog echoed. "Since when?"

"Since it was invented in Italy," the writer said. "And that, I would suggest, makes it foreign."

While Big Rog struggled to come to terms with the fact that he'd inadvertently been enjoying foreign food for his entire married life, Symon escaped the discussion and wove his way through the pub towards the window table his sister had booked.

It was Saturday evening and the pub was filling up. A live band was booked and the musicians were busy with sound checks and plugging in amps. It didn't seem that long ago to Symon since he'd been helping his brother, Zak, set up in here with his band. Those had been carefree times spent meeting friends, having some drinks and listening to the music, and the memory of it all made Symon feel nostalgic for the lad he'd once been; so much had happened since then that he couldn't imagine ever feeling that light-hearted again. In any case, Zak's days of playing in local pubs were way behind Zak too. When they'd last hung out at Christmas, Symon's brother had been looking forward to recording his next few tracks in LA and poised for great things. Symon, who'd also once believed that the world was at his fingertips, could only hope that everything worked out for Zak better than it had for him.

A blast of static from the speaker, followed by several chords on an electric guitar, jolted Symon out of his thoughts. His eardrums throbbed and he guessed a lively evening was on the cards. As he negotiated all the cables on his way, Symon supposed that if conversation became too laboured he could always use the excuse that the music was too loud to talk. It would certainly be a reason to cut the date short.

Spotting Tess Hamilton seated at the window table with her cute nose buried in a book, Symon had to admit that most men would think he was crazy to want to cut short a date with her. Recently Tess had taken to wearing red-framed spectacles and coaxing her mane of dark curls into a bun; with her thoughtful brown eyes and serious expression it was the perfect sexy school mam look, and Symon imagined it drove a lot of guys wild. This evening, though, Tess's glasses were absent and she was wearing her hair loose. In her trendy printed dress, black leggings and chunky silver jewellery, she looked like a girl dressed up for a date. Symon almost turned tail and hotfooted it back to the safety of the restaurant, before reminding himself sharply that it was just one date and God only knew what Mo had told Tess. It was his job tonight to be a gentleman and find a way to tell Tess as kindly as he could that he wasn't interested in dating.

He'd never be interested in *that* again. Symon was tired of the games women played. From now on his heart belonged to his career.

Tess was so engrossed in her book that she didn't notice him approach. She seemed startled when Symon placed the bottle of wine and glasses down with a clatter.

"Sorry," Symon said, sliding into the seat opposite. "I didn't mean to make you jump."

"Don't apologise. I was miles away." Tess closed the book and smiled. It was a rather tense smile, Symon thought, and it didn't reach her eyes. She wasn't looking exactly thrilled to see him or like a woman who was keen to be here. He suspected Mo had been a little economical with the truth.

"Anything good?" Symon asked, nodding at it.

"It depends on your taste in books," Tess answered. She held it up and he saw that this was Caspar's latest offering, all six-pack heroes and heaving-bosomed swooning heroines.

He raised an eyebrow. "I must admit I had you down as a Penguin Classics kind of a girl. I'd have expected a Brontë or a Dickens."

Tess laughed. "Usually you'd be spot on, but Caspar insisted I read this proof copy and give him my opinion."

Symon sloshed some wine into a glass and passed it to her. "And?"

"And it's very compulsive reading! No wonder he sells so many. I'm desperate to know if Merribella can resist the dashing Regency rake who has his sights on her." She slipped the book into her bag and took the glass. "Thanks for the drink. I certainly need it after that last chapter."

"Developing a trashy bodice-ripper habit?"

"Somebody has to keep Caspar in cider and cravats," shrugged Tess. "Oh dear, I think he's about to get barred again."

They glanced across the pub. Sure enough, Adam Harper was frogmarching the author out of the door while Little Rog was pleading with his father, red-faced and shouting, to calm down.

"A row about the origins of lasagne. I nearly jumped in but I thought I'd let them sort it out in the time-honoured fashion," Symon explained.

Tess, who'd lived in the village long enough now to be used to this kind of behaviour from The Ship's regulars, raised her eyes to the beams. "Pasties at dawn it is. Still, you're the right man to set them straight on anything culinary. Didn't you train in France?"

Symon never talked about his time in France. Whenever he thought about Paris, it felt as though one of his chef's knives was slicing through his heart. An unbidden vision of dark eyes and red lips quirking upwards in a knowing half-smile flickered through his memory, and his fingers tightened on the stem of the glass. Jesus. He'd told himself he was over this.

Would it ever stop hurting? In despair, he knocked back his drink.

Luckily for Symon, Tess was now chatting away about how much she loved Paris and he had a few moments to collect himself. Nodding in what he hoped were appropriate places, Symon pushed the memories of Claudette back into the hidden place in his heart where he kept them locked away. By the time Tess paused to ask him about the city, Symon's heartbeat was steadier – and, unless she was extremely sharp-eyed, she wouldn't have spotted that his hand was still trembling slightly as he refilled his glass.

"Oh dear, I've not given you a chance to get a word in," Tess was saying. "I think having an uninterrupted adult conversation has gone to my head. You did live in Paris? Morgan said you trained at a top restaurant and with a really famous chef too. Fact!"

Tess taught Symon's nephew and she smiled as she repeated Morgan's favourite expression.

"Morgan's very proud of you," she added. "Who was it you worked for?"

Symon's mouth was dry. The noise of the pub faded and he was right back there in Restaurant Papillon Rouge watching Jean-Luc fillet fish with the precision of a brain surgeon, and hardly able to breathe for Claudette's proximity. He had never in his life been so intensely aware of another person's presence. It was as though even their blood was magnetised.

"I worked for Jean-Luc Marsaud," he said quietly.

"Wow."

Tess looked impressed, which wasn't surprising. Jean-Luc was one of the top chefs in Paris. Forty-six, driven and indefatigable, he was famous for his genius in the kitchen and his two Michelin stars. To train under him, let alone rise to become his second in command, had been a dream come true. Symon had hardly been able to believe his luck when he'd been taken on.

"No wonder you're getting such amazing write-ups in the papers," Tess said warmly. "I live on toast and Pot Noodles but even I've heard of Jean-Luc Marsaud. I think I saw a feature about his wife a while back too, in one of the Sunday supplements. They're a real power couple, aren't they?"

Claudette and Jean-Luc were certainly that. Her husband was the creative genius with the volatile temperament to match, but Claudette did all the networking, wooed the press, made sure the right celebrities dined in the restaurant and was generally agreed to be Jean-Luc's biggest asset. Together they had built the Papillon Rouge name up from its roots as a small backstreet bistro in Montmartre to one of the most celebrated epicurean establishments on the left bank. Claudette had been the driving force behind this; as Symon had soon discovered, when she set her heart on something she made sure that it was soon hers.

"So what brought you home?"

It was a reasonable question and Tess was only making conversation, but Symon, who'd been interrogated endlessly about this by his grandmother and sisters, was instantly on his guard.

"A combination of things," he replied shortly. "Excuse me for a minute, Tess. I must just check in with my sous-chef. Why don't you have a look at the menu? I'll have the steak pie if Rose comes to take the order."

He plucked his iPhone from his pocket and threaded his way through the growing press of evening drinkers. His younger brother Nick and several other fishermen were at the bar, still a little grimy from a long day trawling and celebrating a good catch with pints of Pol Brew, and his older brother Jake was chatting to Adam. It was all very normal and safe but to Symon it felt as though the pub walls were closing in on him. He saw mouths opening and shutting but no sound seemed to come from them; all he could hear was the rushing of his own blood in his ears. Panic silted his throat and it was only once he was outside and gulping great lungfuls of cold salty air that he felt his pulse slow.

Shit. He hadn't had a panic attack for months. Symon had thought he was through all that now. In the long, dark time after leaving Papillon Rouge he'd often woken up at night choking for air and with his breath coming in shallow gasps as his dreams ribboned away. Symon had thought this was in the past. He didn't think of France that often and he did his very best to never think of Claudette.

But it was hard to forget the first woman to take his heart, especially when he feared that it still belonged to her.

Symon killed a few minutes by calling the restaurant, was told very firmly by Tara that all was well and to stop checking up on them, and had no choice but to return to his date. When he rejoined Tess, the menu was still folded on the table and her wine glass was empty.

"I don't know what I said to upset you but, whatever it is, I'm sorry," she said.

"You didn't upset me. I just had to speak to Tony and—" Symon began, but Tess held up her hand and gave him a look that stopped him in his tracks. She must be formidable in the classroom.

"Don't insult me, please. I'm not an idiot. Besides, you look just like Morgan when you're fibbing. The tips of his ears go red too."

"My ears went red?"

"Not really. I made that up but it proves you weren't being honest," said Tess.

Symon stared at her for a moment, then started to laugh. "Well, I'm truly caught out, Miss Hamilton. No wonder the kids in this village don't get away with anything and my brother only lasted five minutes!"

Tess rolled her eyes. "The less we say about Nick the better. He's fun and cute but I think that's where we'd better leave it. I'm sorry though for upsetting you. I was just trying to make conversation." She paused and her brown eyes grew serious. "Look, Symon, don't take this the wrong way or anything, and I'm sure you're a really nice guy, but this isn't going to work between us. I don't want to hurt your feelings, and I know you were hoping otherwise, but I don't think we're ever going to be a couple. I just don't feel the same way as you."

"What?"

"It's OK, Symon, I know how you feel about me." Tess lowered her voice at this point and, unable to quite believe what he was hearing, Symon had to lean forwards to catch her words. "Mo's told me everything."

"Oh, has she?" Symon was starting to guess what was going on here. "And what exactly did my sister tell you?"

Poor Tess was suddenly fascinated by the beer mats. "That you'd wanted to ask me out for a while but were too shy? I only came tonight just because she keeps on telling me all this and I thought it would be best to speak to you myself. Blind dates aren't really my thing. You're a nice man, Symon, but there has to be a spark and I just…"

Her voice petered away and Symon wasn't sure whether he should laugh, feel insulted or go and strangle Morwenna. Probably all three.

"You just don't fancy me? Is it because I'm ginger?" he deadpanned.

"Oh God! No! Your hair is lovely and it's red not ginger and I…" Tess began and then groaned. "You're winding me up, aren't you?"

"Sorry, I couldn't resist." Symon reached for the Pinot and topped up their glasses. "You probably won't be surprised to hear that Mo said something very similar about you."

"And you came along tonight because you felt bad? You were trying to think how to let me down gently?" She shook her head. "I am going to kill your sister."

"Get in the queue," Symon answered.

Tess sighed. "She means well. I think she's worried about you working so hard."

"I'm aiming for my second Michelin star! I have to work hard. Besides, that's the nature of restaurant work. I love what I do and I haven't got time for a relationship even if I wanted one, which I don't."

"That's just how I feel about teaching," Tess said. She raised her glass at him. "To our careers and to being single!"

They clinked glasses.

"Now that's dealt with, I think my appetite's coming back." Symon passed Tess a menu. "Shall we order?"

"You still want to eat?"

"Sure. Why ruin a night off? Besides, it makes a good change to let somebody else cook for me," Symon said. "If you want to, of course. I'll totally understand if you'd rather go home and get on with your marking."

"Tempting thought, but I'll have some steak pie first," Tess grinned.

Their pub meals were every bit as hearty as Symon had hoped, and he and Tess tucked in with gusto. They'd just finished and were discussing whether they had room for pudding when the pub door flew open and a man stumbled into the bar. Tall, wide-shouldered and with a thick bronzed mane tossed back from a flushed face, he was hard enough to ignore anyway, even without the ripples of interest that spread through the place when people realised who he was.

"I'll have a bottle of champagne," he was hollering. "No! Bugger it! I'll have two. Teddy will be here in a minute and he'll drink mine if I let him, the bugger!"

"Hey! Isn't that Charlie Barton?" Tess asked, craning her neck.

Symon groaned. It certainly was and Charlie Barton wasn't a character he had a great deal of time for. He was a gifted chef, no doubt about it, but he was also volatile and erratic – and Teddy St Milton, who was joining him now, wasn't any better.

Charlie's restaurant based at the Polwenna Bay Hotel was probably the closest thing The Plump Seagull had to local competition, and Symon was all for some healthy rivalry. What he hadn't expected were the nasty rumours concerning his own establishment, as well as several thinly veiled insults that had been made by Charlie on his local television show. Symon couldn't prove where the rumours originated, or disprove this either, but he had his suspicions.

"I was going to ask him if he'd open the school's Spring Fair," Tess was saying, all thoughts of sticky toffee pudding vanishing as she watched Charlie clap Teddy on the shoulder and almost knock the smaller man over. "Do you think he would?"

It was on the tip of Symon's tongue to say that if there was a camera present Charlie would turn up to see a packet of crisps being opened, but the sparkle in Tess's eyes suggested that she wouldn't listen anyway. Celebrity chefs obviously appealed to her more than the nonentity kind.

"I guess you could ask him," was all he said and Tess nodded, already out of her seat.

"It's for the kids so I'm sure he'll say yes," she said.

What must it be like to have so much faith in people, thought Symon wistfully.

Leaving Tess to it, he picked up his jacket and headed outside into the night, where snatches of chatter and music lived and died on the wind and the full moon rose high above the sea. Pale and aloof, its out-of-reach beauty reminded him of Claudette. A scarf of grief wrapped itself around his heart. As he stared up at the moon, his head swam and for a horrible moment he felt so alone and so insubstantial that he thought he might float away.

Thank goodness for his restaurant, thought Symon as he walked away from The Ship and back to The Plump Seagull. It really was all that kept him anchored and he couldn't imagine what he'd do if he lost it.

He could only hope he'd never have to find out.

CHAPTER 6

Hitch-hiking in the UK was hard work, decided Emerald
Meyers as yet another car swished past while she stood at the
side of the road with her thumb held out in a hopeful fashion.
Either she now had amazing powers of invisibility (unlikely) or
folks in merry old England were just plain mean-spirited and
rude. Having spent most of her life hitching her way around
California, Emerald was drawing some conclusions that were
starting to make her wonder whether coming here was such a
good idea after all.

Take the weather, for example. As she shouldered her heavy
rucksack and resigned herself to trudging along the garbage-
strewn grass verge, Emerald realised that she hadn't seen
proper sunshine or even felt warm since her plane had taken
off from LAX. Having grown up taking bright blue skies, endless
sunshine and splashes of citrus colours for granted, the leaden
skies of Heathrow had come as something of a shock.
Everything was just so goddamn grey here! The people, the
sidewalks, the cafés – all were stained around the edges with
the same murkiness. It was as though somebody had turned
the colours down, the same mean entity that had also chosen to
sprinkle the world with icy drizzle and whip up a spiteful wind.
Just walking along the road was a battle as she bowed her head

against the rain and tried to ignore the cold water trickling down her neck. Used to warmth, Emerald was ill-prepared for the English weather and her thin Californian clothes were as much use at keeping out the cold as they were at repelling the rain.

This wasn't quite what she'd expected. It wasn't supposed to be like this.

Where were the thatched cottages? The castles? (Emerald couldn't wait to see a real live castle.) The morris dancers? At least she'd seen red buses and call boxes and been on a tube train. That tube ride was cool and so was the detour she'd made to see Oxford Street and Buckingham Palace. Emerald had grabbed a Starbucks (some things were the same the world over!) and then she'd posted several pictures to her Instagram account, which all her friends back in Sausalito had been way excited about. Within minutes, comments like *OMG! You're there! Sooo jealous! Say hi to Prince Harry!* had been pinging up on her Instagram feed, and Emerald had felt excitement rise in her like a hot-air balloon.

Emerald was half English, something her girlfriends found very exotic, and she had dreamed for years about actually seeing the country for herself. She wasn't daft enough to imagine that she'd bump into Prince Harry (although he did like American girls, or so she'd heard, and with her long blonde hair and blue eyes Emerald had secretly wondered whether she did stand a chance), but she was excited about seeing her dad again and meeting the rest of her family. She had brothers and sisters that she'd never met! Older than her, of course – because her dad had only met Mom when he was travelling later on in life – but nonetheless she had an entire new family waiting for her! That was way, way cool and Emerald could hardly wait to meet them all at last. Ever since Mom had told her the truth (and to be fair Emerald had long suspected that the stork hadn't delivered her and that Jim Morrison couldn't possibly be her dad), she'd been dreaming about this moment and planning it too. She'd had to wait until she was eighteen in order to get her own passport, but the minute her birthday had arrived Emerald had completed the forms and been on the phone to arrange her trip – and now here she was! In England and, according to Google Maps, only twenty-five miles away from Polwenna Bay.

Her mom wasn't convinced this trip was a good idea, but Leaf would no more have dreamed of stopping her daughter than she would of cutting her own long blonde hair or settling down in one place for more than five minutes. A perpetual flower child, Leaf Meyers was more concerned with campaigning against oil pipelines or being a birthing partner for the various women she met at the Outreach Centre than she was about what Emerald was up to.

"You have to be free to follow your own path," she'd always said, which Emerald's friends all thought was fantastic. They were wildly jealous of Emerald's freedom and of her pretty Mom with her flowing skirts, all jangling bells and shedding sequins. They loved the fact that Emerald was allowed to stay up as late as she wanted. If Emerald had envied them their mommies dressed in jeans and sneakers, their neat backyards and their cars that weren't held together with love beads and hope, then she'd kept this to herself. Now that she was older she could see that Mom had done her best. Besides, Leaf had only been young herself – not much older than Emerald was now, really – when she'd had her daughter.

Emerald's dad had been a mystery. All Emerald had known was that Mom had met him in San Francisco at a party and that he was English and quite a bit older than her. They'd had a great time and travelled together for a while, and then he'd gone home again before Emerald was born. Apart from him being fun and kind and very handsome, Emerald hadn't been told much more. Over the years he'd become a distant fantasy figure, a sort of mixture of Hugh Grant, Dick Van Dyke and Mr Darcy. Life was full and busy, Leaf was a fun mommy and since lots of the other kids Emerald grew up with didn't have fathers on the scene either, she never felt his lack.

A bit like having a father in her life, school too was optional in Leaf's view; because they moved about so much, Emerald had wound up being taught at home. Not that she and Leaf had actually gotten much done in terms of traditional academia, but there had been lots of nature walks, poetry and listening to Hendrix. Later, when Mom had hooked up with an ex English teacher (a gentle bearded soul with faded blue eyes and a huge collection of books), Emerald, a voracious reader, had been in heaven.

Mike. That was his name. As she trudged along the side of the A38, lorries rumbling past like monsters and with her glittery sandals rubbing her heels, Emerald recalled him with fondness. There'd been quite a few father figures drifting in and out of her young life – some better than others, it had to be said. Chuck with the motor bike had been fun and cowboy Mac, who'd taught her to ride on a barrel-racing pony, had been a big favourite too. Emerald had broken her heart when Mom had moved on from him, although admittedly this had been more about leaving Pepper the pony behind than worrying about Mac, who chewed tobacco and smelled funny.

Mike had definitely been one of the good guys. He'd walked away after a year or so, which always tended to happen, but while he had been around he'd chatted about books and writing and taught her so much about literature that the Brontës and Jane Austen and Lord Byron now felt like best friends.

Emerald was rarely without her nose in a book and she loved writing too. Her most cherished dream was to be a writer. Now that she was in England, the place that had inspired her literary heroes, Emerald was determined to make this dream come true. She'd already started a blog and filled several pages of her new diary as well, although with these failed hitch-hiking attempts and being thrown off the coach in Saltash because her ticket was only supposed to take her to Plymouth, she was feeling more Jack Kerouac than Brontë. Her feet were sore, she was cold and (although she hated to admit it) she was also feeling a little homesick. Still, writers had to suffer, right? And experience new stuff too. And take risks.

Coming to England to see her father and meet her family was all of these things…

It was only when she was in her teens that Emerald had started to ask questions. Leaf had done her best to avoid them for a long while; she hated confrontation and tended to skim over the surface of life's trickier issues like a pond skater. Nevertheless, Emerald's determination had eventually worn her mom down, until Emerald had a name and some sketchy details to be working on. It hadn't taken much more than a few clicks on Google and a scoot around Facebook to trace her father and a whole bunch of siblings she'd never known about. Suddenly Emerald's identity had been transformed. She was no longer an only child with a rootless mother who'd floated the two of them all around California. Instead, she was a member of a huge family who'd lived in Cornwall like *forever*, and in a clifftop house that looked as though it belonged in a du Maurier novel.

Rebecca had to be Emerald's all-time favourite book and now she knew why! Her family came from the very place the novel had been written! Cornwall was in her blood and she'd never had any idea. All the time she'd read about Maxim de Winter, imagined the overgrown garden at Manderley and pictured the beach with wild waves tearing up the silvery sand, that place had really existed and her family lived there. It was just like something out of a story and Emerald had been so excited. This was awesome!

Her father had been shocked when she'd contacted him via Facebook – which was fair enough, Emerald had thought. It couldn't have been easy for him to have found out that he had a teenage daughter when he was innocently flicking through his social media messages. He'd come out to visit a couple of times now and she liked him a lot and could see why he and Leaf had hooked up. They were two peas in an easy-going, carefree and (back then, she imagined) stoned pod. Having spent time with her newly discovered father, Emerald was keen to come to the UK and meet the brothers and sisters he'd told her all about. Her father had promised her that they were equally keen to meet her and that soon, very soon, he'd arrange a trip. He called her regularly and they Skyped a lot, but whenever she asked him again about her visit or raised the possibility of speaking to the rest of the family, the subject was swiftly changed. It was one of her mom's classic avoidance tricks too and Emerald was instantly on her guard.

Another lorry trundled by, the driver pointedly ignoring her outstretched thumb. Jeez, these British truckers were miserable! Emerald hoisted her rucksack onto her other shoulder and plodded on. She was always hitching in California and never failed to get a ride. Granted, out there the sun was usually out and she looked pretty good – all tanned body, white vest and swishy ponytail – whereas here she resembled a drowned rat. That probably had a lot to do with it. No wonder England had so many amazing authors. If it rained this much everyone was inside writing!

If she was honest, Emerald was starting to feel a little underprepared for her big adventure. During her bus journey to Saltash all she'd seen of England were acres of freeway, and raindrops trickling down the steamed-up bus window. It couldn't be that far to walk to Polwenna Bay, surely? England was tiny, right? She gritted her teeth and trudged on. Emerald wasn't a quitter. She clearly didn't get this side of her personality from her dad or her mom, both of whom struck her as lovely but total dreamers, so it must be a throwback gene to someone else. Maybe someone she was only hours away from meeting? A sister? A brother or maybe even a granny? Emerald knew she had a grandmother in Cornwall and she could hardly wait to meet her. She'd always wanted a grandmother.

It had been worth spending all her savings on a plane ticket, Emerald told herself firmly. Even if she was cold and wet and feeling a bit lost, this was still the right thing to do. She could hardly wait to see her father's face when he saw her. He was going to be so surprised. Her fingers were itching to message him, but so far she'd been able to resist. It was tempting to call his cell and ask him to come and pick her up, but she'd been dreaming about this moment for so long – the knock on the front door and the cries of delight when her family saw her there at last – that she wasn't going to let a bit of silly old rain spoil things now. No way, siree!

The sun was coming out now anyhow, edging the pewter clouds with gold and drying up the drizzle. As though in direct response to the brightening day, Emerald felt her spirits rise too. Everything was going to be perfect. She just knew it! Just moments later a car pulled up alongside and the window hissed down.

"You look drenched, love!" A middle-aged woman with a couple of children squashed in the back seat and plugged into earbuds was peering out at her, looking concerned. "Can I give you a lift somewhere?"

Talk about the Law of Attraction! Her mom would say this was the Universe delivering up what she wanted in response to her positive thinking. Leaf loved stuff like this and right at this moment so did Emerald. Go the Universe!

"Polwenna Bay?"

The driver's eyebrows rose. "You don't sound as though you're local."

"California, ma'am," Emerald told her. "Sausalito? Do you know it?"

"Bless you, I'm lucky to get to Bristol," laughed the driver. She leaned across the car and opened the passenger door. "You're miles away from home, you poor thing, and you're miles away from Polwenna too, but hop in. I'll give you a lift."

Emerald didn't need asking twice. The car was warm and it was a relief to sit down and give her blistered feet a break. It still felt odd to be seated on the wrong side of the vehicle but she'd get used to that, just like she'd get used to the greyness and the rain.

"Thanks," she said. "I sure appreciate this."

"It's a pleasure." The driver turned up the heating. A blast of dusty air had never felt so good and Emerald made a vow to never again complain about the heat in California.

"I'm Amy Jones," the driver said, pulling back onto the road and slotting into the traffic with ease. "Mum to these monsters and I live in Fowey. And you are?"

Emerald took a deep breath. This was it. The minute she said it, it would be real and there would be no going back. Was she ready?

Of course she was. She'd been waiting for this day for a very long time. If she wasn't ready now she never would be.

"My name's Emerald," she said slowly. "Emerald Tremaine and I'm going to meet my family!"

CHAPTER 7

Alice Tremaine loved Sundays at Seaspray House. Traditionally this was when her family gathered for a big roast dinner, caught up on news and generally carried on with their everyday teasing and squabbling. It was something she'd started doing when Jimmy had been newly widowed, firstly because her grief-stricken son had seemed incapable of feeding himself, let alone seven children, and secondly because she'd wanted to find a way of gathering all her loved ones close and taking care of them. Some members of the family were now long departed but fondly remembered – like Great Auntie Hannah, for instance, whose marvellously crispy roast potatoes were still talked about. Others were living far away from home. New members had arrived too, as her grandchildren had married and met partners. Some, like Jake and Symon, had been gone for a while but had then returned to the fold; nothing gave Alice more pleasure than seeing them home and happy.

Actually, this wasn't wholly accurate. Jake was happy, at least; as he laughed at something Summer had just said, it was obvious to Alice how in love the young couple were. Jake had been so lonely without Summer, and Alice was thrilled to see her eldest grandson smiling again now that they were back together. But Symon… Well, Alice couldn't put her hand on her heart and say he was happy. In truth she couldn't have said what was going on with her middle grandson. Symon was so self-contained these days and no matter how many times Alice tried to speak to him about what had happened in France, her efforts were about as productive as trying to prise barnacles from the rocks on the beach. Something had happened to change him from the open, sunny-natured boy she'd raised, into this quiet and career-driven young man – and Alice had her suspicions what it was. She'd also had an uneasy sensation all morning. Maybe it was because she was so worried about Symon. Or perhaps it was because Jonny was pressing her to set a date for their wedding, and still Alice wasn't convinced that the St Miltons and the Tremaines were ready to combine forces.

"Are you OK, Granny?"

Dragged from her thoughts, Alice realised she'd frozen over the dishwasher midway through loading plates. No wonder Mo was looking concerned. She probably thought her grandmother was going gaga.

"Sorry, love, I was miles away."

"No you weren't," said Morgan, looking confused. "You're right here."

"It's an expression, love. It means I was deep in thought," Alice explained. Morgan often took things literally – which had been interesting when old Miss Powell at Polwenna Primary had told him to "pull his socks up", for instance. Tess Hamilton, a far more enlightened teacher, was now helping Morgan to negotiate the choppy waters between what was literal and what was metaphorical. He was much happier these days, enjoying school and making friends too. Alice couldn't thank Tess enough for this. It just showed what a difference a good teacher made to a child.

"You shouldn't be clearing up anyway," Summer scolded. "Not after you've cooked for everyone and done all the hard work. Sit down and let us take care of it all."

Alice waved her hand. "I'm more than capable of stacking the dishwasher, you know!"

"No one's doubting your dishwasher-stacking ability, Gran. We just want you to be looked after for once. Now sit down!" This order was issued by Danny, and Alice laughed.

"You're not in the army now, young man! Shall I remind you who's the General in this house?"

"Me?" her son Jimmy offered hopefully. In his sixties and constantly giving Alice more headaches than all the grandchildren combined, Jimmy Tremaine could hardly organise himself, let alone lead an army. A kind-hearted and entertaining dreamer, he drifted from one hopeless scheme to the next and constantly needed keeping an eye on. Only last year he'd accidentally been caught up in a drug-smuggling operation – and he'd made several expensive trips to the USA, which had convinced Alice that he was gambling everything away in Vegas. Once upon a time his wife, Penny, had grounded Jimmy and he'd been truly happy with her and his young family. However, Penny's cruel death had left him unanchored and adrift, and Alice feared he'd never find a safe harbour again.

Oh dear. It seemed it was a mother's lot in life to always worry about her children no matter how old they were.

"Duh, Jim-pa. It's not you. It's Grand Gran. Fact," said Morgan.

"Fair enough, old sport." Jimmy said, passing by and ruffling Morgan's hair. Placing a hand on Alice's shoulder he gently manoeuvred his mother away. "No protests, Ma. As a lowly member of the cannon-fodder ranks I can probably cope with stacking a dishwasher."

"Make sure you put the knives in upside down and rinse the plates," Alice said quickly, knowing her son would shove everything in, shut the door and hope for the best. In fact, he probably wouldn't even get that far; he'd wander off leaving it half stacked as soon as something more interesting flashed up on his mobile or he had to take a Skype call from his mystery American woman.

"Chill, Granny. I'll supervise him," said Mo, positioning herself at her father's shoulder. Jimmy rolled his eyes at this but set to work cheerfully.

"I'll make some coffee if you like," offered Ashley. "Alice, would you hold Isla?"

"I can't think of anything I'd rather do," Alice said, holding out her arms to her great-granddaughter. "Come here, love."

Alice settled herself on the sofa by the Aga with the baby on her lap and glanced around Seaspray's kitchen with pleasure. It was a large room, filled with light streaming through the windows. The sea could be glimpsed from here and the waves were dancing and wild today, the water alternately lit with flashes of gold and darkened with smudges of indigo as squalls galloped across the bay. There was something wonderfully cosy about being inside the kitchen, wrapped in the warmth of the Aga and with the air heavy with the smell of Sunday lunch while the elements squabbled outside.

As Jimmy stacked the dishwasher and the family cleared away, Alice sang to Isla and jiggled her on her knee. Ashley brewed coffee, Jules and Danny bickered good-naturedly about where to walk that afternoon and Mo, always one to face danger head-on, turned to Symon, who was quietly scrolling through messages on his phone.

"Sy, I'm dying to know. How was the big date?"

Symon placed his phone on the table. "I was meaning to have a word with you about that, actually."

"Oh?"

"Don't give me that look. You totally stitched me up – and Tess too. Seriously, Mo! Didn't you think we'd talk to each other? You fed us both a line about the other being desperate for a date."

"What have you been up to now?" Ashley asked his wife.

"Matchmaking," grinned Summer.

"It could have worked and then you'd be thanking me," Mo huffed.

"I don't need you to set me up, thanks!" Symon said. His voice was quiet but a flush of annoyance stained his cheeks.

"You bloody well do. You're a hermit," his sister shot back.

"And that's my choice! I don't need you interfering! And I don't want to date Tess!"

"You're seriously missing out, fam. Tess is brilliant. Wish she hadn't dumped me," sighed Nick. "Mo, if she's that desperate tell her I'm free. I won't hold a grudge."

"Don't be stupid. Tess needs a man who can read words of more than two syllables," snapped Mo, and Nick gave her the finger.

"Tess isn't interested in me and I'm not interested in her," Symon said firmly. "We have nothing in common."

"Ashley and I have nothing in common either and we're happy," Mo said, hands on hips and red curls bouncing in temper. "Aren't we, Ashley?"

"Of course, dear," Ashley said, grinning at Symon. "Blissfully happy."

"Ignore him. We are happy," Mo told her brother. "And everyone said it wouldn't work. All you lot, for a start."

"Did they?" Ashley said. "Gee. Thanks, you guys."

"I didn't," said Jules, blushing scarlet. "For the record, I always thought you'd be good together."

"Even though she thinks you're way too fond of Mammon," Danny added. "Ouch!"

Jules had elbowed him in the ribs. Hard. "Dan! That was a joke!"

"You are very rich though, Ashley. Fact," said Morgan.

"Thanks, mate," said Ashley. "I'm not as rich as I was though. Mo's doing her best to spend it all on horses."

But his wife was far too busy glowering at Symon to take this bait. "Stop being so stubborn, Sy. Get over whoever it is that's turned you into such a misery guts and have some fun. She can't be that great if you're not with her, anyway. Did she dump you?"

Symon stared at Mo. His blue eyes glittered with anger. He had a slow temper and when it erupted everyone ran for cover. Any minute now…

It was time to step in, Alice decided. She'd refereed enough family squabbles in her time to know the signs but there was something about the tight set of Symon's mouth, and the way his fists were clenched as he fought to keep calm, that made her very uneasy.

Had Mo inadvertently hit on the truth?

"Stop it, all of you!" Alice said as Isla, picking up on the atmosphere, began to wail. "Now look what you've done. Honestly, this is worse than when you were kids."

"Here. Pass her to me." Ashley reached for his daughter, just as the doorbell shrilled and Isla howled even harder at the sudden noise. "Come on, Isla. Shall we go and see who this is and leave all these mean people to argue?"

With Isla in his arms, he headed out of the kitchen.

Alice exhaled wearily. "Morwenna, please stop interfering in Symon's business. It's absolutely nothing to do with you."

"I was only trying to help," Mo said sulkily, looking about fifteen. "Fine. I won't bother again."

"Thank God for that. What do you do when you don't want to help?" Jake asked. "Pop people up on Tinder and then run and hide?"

"Oh! I never thought of Tinder! Over a billion people have found love on Tinder, Sy!"

"Don't even go there," Symon warned. "You got away with it this time and luckily Tess wasn't too upset, but do me a favour in the future? Don't meddle in my affairs."

"Fine. Be a miserable git and die all lonely and unloved. See if I care," Mo scowled.

Her brother grinned. "Thanks. I probably will, but do you know what? It'll be my decision and it'll be peaceful."

World War Three averted, Alice heaved a sigh of relief and returned to enjoying her coffee. It would be impossible to stop worrying about her family but at least she was still here to keep an eye on them. Who would prevent Symon from strangling Mo or make sure Nick was up in time for work if she wasn't living here? It was another reason she was reluctant to set a date for her wedding and move into Jonny's apartment at the hotel.

"Jimmy? There's a visitor for you," said Ashley, returning from answering the door.

As he stepped aside, still holding Isla in his arms, Alice saw the young woman standing behind him. She was slim-built with long blonde hair and delicate features, and was glancing about the kitchen with wide eyes. When she spotted Jimmy a huge grin of delight spread across her face.

"Hey, there you are! Awesome!"

There was a crash of porcelain on flagstones. Jimmy, still loading the dishwasher, had turned as white as the shards of plate now scattered on the kitchen floor.

"Emerald? What are you doing here?"

"I know you weren't expecting me, right?" the girl continued, stepping forwards and still smiling, although the smile was slightly less certain now as everyone in the room stared at her.

"Mom said I should have called but I wanted it to be a surprise.
"

Judging from the expression on her son's face, Alice reckoned the visitor had surprised Jimmy all right. Shocked was probably a better word. Knowing him as well as she did, Alice was certain that if there had been a way out of the kitchen that didn't involve leaping out a of window, Jimmy would have been long gone.

The girl glanced around and the smile melted away as her perfect white teeth worried at her bottom lip.

"You are pleased to see me, right?" she asked, sounding very young. She looked young too, Alice thought. She couldn't be more than eighteen. Surely this wasn't Jimmy's girlfriend? She looked young enough to be his daughter!

"I... I..." Jimmy seemed unable to form a coherent sentence. "Emerald, I..."

The girl's blue eyes were bright with tears. "You said I could come anytime! You promised!"

Jimmy cleared his throat. "I know I did. I was just going to speak to everyone here first. I was going to tell them all about you first."

The girl was open-mouthed with disbelief. "You haven't told them about me? But you said you were going to!"

"I meant to," said Jimmy. He had that look on his face that Alice recognised of old. It was his classic *being caught out* expression. As his mother, she'd seen it on numerous occasions, from pies going missing out of the larder, to skiving off school, to taking off travelling and leaving her and Henry with seven heartbroken children, to driving a truck for crooks like Mickey Davey.

"Jimmy, what have you done now?" she said.

"Aren't you going to introduce us, Dad?" asked Jake.

The visitor fixed Jimmy with confused and wounded blue eyes. "Why didn't you tell them? Like you said? Like you promised? Why did you lie to me? Are you ashamed of me?"

"I had no idea you were coming here, love," Jimmy said faintly. "You never told me."

"I wanted to surprise you, that's why! I'm eighteen, I've finally gotten a passport and here I am! I thought you'd be pleased!"

As she flung these defiant words at Jimmy, the girl raised her chin and tossed her hair back from her face. If Alice hadn't known better she would have sworn it was her youngest granddaughter Issie standing there, although that tilted chin was pure Mo. The kitchen suddenly felt very hot and very crowded and there was an odd rushing in Alice's ears. Those same bright blue eyes were replicated in her grandchildren, just as the delicate nose, high cheekbones and determined jut of the chin were stitched through every member of the Tremaine family.

She'd never seen this girl before but Alice realised she knew exactly who the visitor was. The missing money, the flights to LA, the odd phone calls… At once these all made perfect sense and the pennies were dropping so fast she was in danger of being concussed.

Her hands on her hips, the girl stared Jimmy down. Fury crackled from her.

"So, come on then," she said. "Isn't it time you introduced me to the rest of the family? *Dad*?"

CHAPTER 8

Emerald couldn't believe it.

Her father hadn't told the others about her.

As she stood in the kitchen, surrounded by faces familiar after months of gazing at their photographs and fantasising about the day they'd finally meet, it was painfully apparent that until several minutes ago none of Jimmy's family had even had a clue she existed. Instead of the cries of delight and hugs Emerald had dreamed about, there were gasps of shock swiftly followed by silence.

"Jimmy? What is this? What's going on?"

An elderly woman sitting by a monster of an oven was the first person to speak and Emerald knew that this had to be her grandmother. Alice, that was her name, wasn't it? She looked exactly how a granny should look, with her soft grey hair held back in a bun and a kind face crisscrossed with lines that had probably been etched by a lifetime of smiling. She wasn't smiling now, though, and the last drops of excitement Emerald had been cherishing ever since her plane had landed at Heathrow trickled away.

"You're our sister?" This was the red-headed girl, her big sister Morwenna, and she was staring at Emerald without a great deal of enthusiasm. Turning to Jimmy, she added, "Is this a joke? Or do we seriously have a sister *you conveniently forgot to mention*?"

"Mo," began the dark-haired man who'd shown Emerald in.

But Morwenna ignored him and spun round to confront Emerald instead. "You're his *daughter*? Really? You're the reason Dad's been flying to the States?"

Emerald nodded. Her voice had vanished and she didn't blame it one bit. She wished she could vanish too.

"Jeez, Dad!" Mo sounded exasperated. "We thought you had another woman but not another family!"

"I don't have another family," Jimmy said quietly. "I have one daughter and I've only recently met her."

"Well, that's OK then," said Mo. She folded her arms across her chest and gave Emerald a hard stare.

Suddenly Emerald wanted nothing more than to be back home in California, thousands of miles away, and chatting to Leaf as they strolled along the sidewalk in town or planted herbs in the community centre's garden. Her mom might be a flake but she was a flake who loved Emerald and was proud of her, and it was abundantly clear that Jimmy's feelings were the total opposite. Emerald was his shameful, guilty secret. No wonder he'd closed his Facebook account, been increasingly hard to contact by telephone and been so cagey about setting a date for her visit.

As for asking her not to contact her siblings but to wait for them to get in touch? Well, then she should really have smelt a rat. Emerald felt horribly lost. It was all very well reading English literature, being a dab hand at balancing chakras and learning to barrel-race a pony, but it might have been more helpful if her mom and the procession of father figures had taught her a little more about human nature instead.

"I'm so sorry. I shouldn't have come here," she said, her voice sounding all funny and tight – nothing like her real self at all.

"Of course you should have come. I only wish we'd been able to give you a proper welcome. But that isn't your fault. Is it, Dad?"

This comment was from a tall blond man with gentle blue eyes, who smiled shyly at Emerald. He had his arm around a beautiful woman with glossy dark hair and the kind of figure that would make a prom queen jealous.

"No," said Jimmy sheepishly. "I'm sorry, sweetheart. I've been an idiot."

"You didn't tell them about me," she said again, and the words were like razor slashes on her tongue. When she thought how excited she'd been only minutes before, how she'd willed the car journey here to pass as quickly as possible, how eagerly she'd sprinted up this huge hill with her lungs burning and her breath coming in sharp gasps, she wanted to weep for the person she'd been back then. It was only moments ago, but it felt like another Emerald altogether. One who was trusting and hopeful and so, so dumb.

"I'm so sorry. I just didn't know how to begin," her father said hopelessly.

"You've got another sister in America? That might have been a start?" suggested the blond man wearily. "Dad, honestly. You are the utter limit."

Emerald sifted through the names and faces that she'd been studying ever since she'd found out she had a family and *Jake* seemed to fit this brother. The other man beside him, with shorter blond hair and livid scars bisecting his face, had to be Danny, the brave veteran. And presumably that younger guy was Nick? So the other man with the deep red hair must be the chef, Symon. Then there was a little boy with a serious expression, a plump woman with a gentle smile and the tall handsome man who'd answered the door with a gorgeous baby in his arms. All of them were members of a big happy family, who until a few moments ago had been having a lovely Sunday lunch, totally oblivious that their world was about to be blown apart.

"You're my aunt? Fact?" said the little boy, walking over and giving Emerald the once-over. He was the only person present who wasn't looking concerned.

She nodded and tried to explain but the words seemed to wither on her vocal cords.

"You look just like Issie," he observed and, unperturbed, returned to the table and his laptop.

"Don't be mean, Morgan. She's nowhere near as ugly as Issie," said Nick kindly. "You do look a bit like Mo, though. Without the nasty temper, I hope?"

"Oh sod off, Nick," answered Mo.

At least Nick didn't seem put out to see her, Emerald thought, and as though reading her mind, her brother added happily, "God, Dad! You're in *so* much trouble with Granny now. Nothing I ever do will seem bad again!"

"You're not wrong there," agreed the elderly lady faintly. "I think you have some explaining to do – not just to us, Jimmy, but to…" Her words faded and she flushed. "Oh, my dear. I don't even know your name." Possibly someone had said it, but Alice was too shocked to have taken it in.

"Emerald," said Emerald and Jimmy together.

"That's a lovely name," said the dark-haired man with a smile. Emerald decided that she liked him. He wasn't a member of the family as such (he was Mo's partner, by the look of it), but there was something about his quiet confidence and the gentle way he held the baby that suggested strength and reliability. Maybe he would be an ally?

"Yes, it's a lovely name," Alice Tremaine managed to say.

"Yeah, well, my mom chose it, not me," Emerald replied, shrugging one shoulder. "Dad wasn't exactly on the scene. Y'know?"

"We do, and welcome to the club," snapped Mo, shooting her father a look that should have laid him out on the stone floor. "It seems to be a bit of a theme with our dear Papa. Have some sprogs and bugger off."

"That's not fair, Mo. I only found out about Emerald recently," said Jimmy quietly.

"Not quite as recently as us," Mo shot back.

"I was going to tell you all; I was just waiting for the right time!"

In fairness to her father he did look upset, Emerald thought, although whether this was because he was in trouble or because he was genuinely sorry she couldn't tell. Out of everyone present he certainly seemed the least pleased to see her. This was hardly surprising, since the entire Tremaine family were mad at Jimmy. Emerald hadn't known her father very long but she'd already worked out that he was the kind of man who needed approval and admiration like the rest of the world's population needed oxygen. He was fun and she'd enjoyed getting to know him but Emerald had spent the past eighteen years with men just like Jimmy drifting in and out of her mother's life and she was under no illusions. You didn't rely on men like them.

"You said you'd tell them all about me," she said, hating the reproachful note in her voice. "You said they'd be thrilled to meet me!"

It was too much to take in and her head began to spin. How naïve she'd been! How quick to take this exciting new English father at his word. If she looked back with her newly acquired twenty-twenty vision it was painfully apparent how Jimmy had dodged any tricky questions about her siblings and persuaded her not to approach them through social media because it would spoil the wonderful surprise when they finally met.

Surprise? Jeez. What a joke that had turned out to be!

"I was going to, sweetheart. I was just waiting for the right moment," Jimmy insisted again. "I wasn't sure how to tell everyone. To be honest I was still coming to terms with it myself. I didn't even know you existed until you got in touch."

Alice's eyes widened. "You had no idea you had another daughter?"

Her son rounded on her. "Of course I didn't! I'm not a monster, Ma! I was a wreck after Pen died, you know that, and I did a lot of travelling and met a lot of people."

"Nice euphemism," said Mo sarcastically.

Her father ignored this pointed remark. "Leaf was one of a few girls I dated back then. She was lovely and sweet but we parted and I eventually came home. To tell you the truth I hadn't thought of her in years until Emerald traced me. It was a huge shock."

"Oh, Jimmy! Why didn't you just say?" Alice Tremaine smiled sadly at Emerald. "We'd have been so excited to meet a new member of the family. And we *are* excited, my love. It's just a little unexpected!"

"Aren't things always with this family?" said Symon wryly, looking across at Mo.

"Only because some people keep way too many secrets," she hissed back.

All her life Emerald had yearned to belong to a big, noisy, happy family. She'd grown up watching reruns of *The Waltons* and dreamed about what it would be like to have brothers and sisters to play with and talk to. With only her lovely but often distant mom around, she'd imagined there could be nothing better than being surrounded by a group of people who knew her inside out and loved her unconditionally. Now, as the kitchen erupted into a cacophony of chatter while Jimmy tried to explain events to his mother – with Jake and Danny butting in, Mo and Symon squabbling, Nick making smart remarks and the baby crying – Emerald wondered whether it was time for a big rethink. Rather than being all apple pie and smiles, her new family was loud and chaotic and everyone seemed to be involved in everyone else's business.

Suddenly Emerald could see *exactly* why this hadn't appealed to her mom.

This was way, way too much. She should never have come here.

She turned on her heel and was out of the house and running through the garden before anyone inside had even noticed. They were all far too busy arguing to care about her anyway. Tears prickled her eyes and she blinked them away furiously. She wasn't going to cry now. No way.

Was it really only ten minutes ago that she'd walked through this garden with a heart full of hope and a head full of dreams? It felt like another lifetime. She'd been rendered speechless by the beauty of the wild coastline and the racing waves galloping across the bay. There was nothing like this in the USA. Sure, Sausalito was pretty, with its brightly hued houseboats and glimpses of Richardson Bay, and places like Carmel had a seaside charm – but they felt smart and new and too much like film sets compared with this place. As she'd brushed past rosemary bushes and followed the twisty path through unruly rhododendrons, Emerald had felt as though she was the heroine of *Rebecca* dreaming of Manderley. The gulls wheeling above and filling the air with haunting cries had only added to the illusion. She'd felt poised on the edge of a huge adventure, her stomach freefalling as though she was peering into the

Grand Canyon again and just a stumble away from soaring with the condors, ready for adventure and flight.

How dumb was that?

The garden blurred and, furious with herself, Emerald dashed tears away impatiently with the ragged sleeve of her hoody. This was not how her adventure was supposed to be.

"Emerald! Wait up!"

A figure was stumbling down the path towards her, slightly out of balance and most definitely out of puff. Blinking away her tears, Emerald saw that it was the plump woman who'd been standing next to Danny. Her sweet face was red with exertion and when she drew alongside Emerald she bent double and gasped. Moments later Danny joined her.

"Beat you," wheezed the woman.

"You cheated. I'm physically impaired, remember?" Danny said. To Emerald, he added, "Don't be fooled just because she's a vicar. She's a dreadful cheat and she even hides Monopoly money under the board."

"Once, just once," the woman puffed, straightening up and smiling at Emerald. "He exaggerates."

"Once is enough," Danny told her sternly. "Besides, you shouldn't have been playing to win. What is it Jesus said about camels and eyes of needles again?"

Oh! This must be Jules. Jimmy had mentioned that his son Danny was dating a pastor. Leaf wasn't big on organised religion, unless you counted fads on yoga from time to time, but Emerald was impressed. Mind you, this fairly young woman in her jeans, sneakers and sweatshirt didn't look much like a priest.

"He wasn't talking about Monopoly! They didn't have a Nazareth version!" Jules said. "Ignore Danny. You'll soon learn he's your most annoying brother, which is saying something as Nick's stiff competition and Zak's a force of nature. Dan'll have you playing Monopoly or walking for miles if you don't watch out."

Emerald had heard that Brits walked everywhere and usually in the rain, whereas in the USA they drove across the parking lot just to get to another shop in the same mall. She'd already been stunned to discover that you couldn't get a car anywhere near the family house. What the heck was that all about? Nobody at home would put up with it! She eyed Danny nervously.

"That's a joke. I hate Monopoly," said Danny quickly. "Anyway, we didn't break our necks following you to talk about board games."

"I'm going if that's what you're worried about," Emerald replied, raising her chin and looking Danny in the …eye. OMG. He really had been hurt. Jimmy had told the truth there at least.

"Wow! You look just like Mo!" Jules gasped.

"This could be big trouble. As if one wasn't bad enough!" Danny grinned. "And yes, of course we're worried you're leaving. I know we must seem like absolute lunatics but we don't generally hurtle down through the garden. You slipped away so fast we thought you'd gone and we had to find you."

Emerald stared at him. "You came to stop me leaving?"

"Of course we did," said Danny. "You'll soon get used to that bunch bickering; they don't mean anything by it. They all want you to come back up to the house. Granny Alice is in pieces and Dad's really upset."

"Although it's his fault," frowned Jules. "He should have told us about you ages ago."

"No shit," said Emerald and then clapped her hand over her mouth. Swearing in front of a priest was so not good. "Sorry. I mean, no kidding."

But Jules wasn't looking at all concerned by this profanity.

"Jimmy's a lovely guy but he's hopeless when it comes to dealing with real life," she sighed. "I'm sure he'll explain lots of things and I know that when he met your mum he was very lonely and unhappy. She must have really helped him through a tough time."

That was one way of putting it, Emerald guessed.

"Please come back to the house," added Danny. "I'm sorry about the crap welcome. We'll do our best to make up for that."

"Are you sure it'll be all right?" Emerald asked, feeling nervous all over again. "I haven't upset things too much?"

"It's going to take a bit of getting our heads around for a day or two, but of course not. We'd love you to come back and give us another chance," Danny promised.

"Even Jimmy?"

"Especially Jimmy. He's really sorry and he's only still inside because Alice was terrified he'd scare you away if he followed."

Emerald thought of Jimmy with his silver ponytail, tall tales and air of general confusion. It was hard to imagine him scaring anyone. Besides, running away was his thing, wasn't it? And Emerald never ran from anything.

"He hasn't scared me away," she said.

"Good," answered Danny. Then a smile spread across the uninjured part of his face, lighting him up from inside. "After all, it's not every day we get a new sister – and Gran's desperate to cluck over someone new. Please come back and meet her properly. You'll be doing us all a favour! And you'll probably distract Sy from killing Mo too. We need you, Emerald!"

Emerald wasn't convinced they did. Everyone seemed fine before she'd arrived, but the word *sister* undid her and she found herself following Danny and Jules back up to the house. Her heart was racing, although whether from the climb or from nervousness it was impossible to say.

She was their *sister*. They were her family. That had to be worth a second chance, right?

After all, it was why she was here.

CHAPTER 9

"If it had been any other child I wouldn't have believed it but you know Morgan, he doesn't make things up," Tara said to Symon the next morning as he let her in to The Plump Seagull. "He came home, announced he had a new aunt from America and then asked if he could have some crisps. I've been gagging to find out more but he was more excited by Monster Munch than he was about his granddad's secret daughter."

"To be fair to Dad, she was a secret to him too until pretty recently," Symon replied, stooping to pick up the mail and feeling his stomach curdle when he recognised his landlord's scrawl. What now?

"So, tell me more. I've been desperate to know what happened."

Following Symon into the kitchen, Tara headed straight for the coffee machine and began to twiddle with dials and settings.

"Latte? Mocha? Espresso?" she called over her shoulder.

Symon, who generally preferred a mug of bog-standard Nescafé, glanced down at the letter clutched in his hand and thought privately that he'd need a brandy if the envelope contained what he feared it did. As if the family trauma of discovering a new sister wasn't enough to be getting on with, he now suspected that Peter Marten was about to play hard ball.

He placed the envelope on the counter. It was one to deal with once he'd answered the questions Tara was evidently bursting to ask. It was hard to tell what was bubbling the most, her curiosity or the coffee machine. To be honest, Symon was still trying to get his head around the appearance of Emerald. Unlike Mo, who'd stormed out in a fury with Jimmy, or Alice, who was devastated at missing eighteen years of her granddaughter's life, Symon felt relatively calm about it all. One more sibling wouldn't affect his life either way and Emerald seemed like a sweet kid. He was also worldly enough to understand that these things happened. After all, who knew better than him how easy it was to lose your head when a beautiful woman was involved and you were far away from home? Jimmy had been grieving and lost and Symon couldn't find it in himself to blame his father for seeking comfort.

Symon could just vaguely remember his mother. Sometimes he'd be taken aback by brief flashes of a warm smile, soft auburn hair, and the scent of flowers. All these images were layered in his mind like faded snapshots in a half-forgotten album, the pages of which were only occasionally flicked through. He remembered the ache of losing her and the choked sobs that had come from Jimmy's room when he'd thought the children couldn't hear. He also recollected hearing extracts of

Alice and Henry's snatched conversations when they'd believed they were alone. It was Jake who'd looked after Symon and the others while their father had withdrawn into himself. Then Jimmy had gone away for a while, something Symon recalled as being a shock but had dealt with at the time. Life had found a new rhythm and, as an adult, and knowing his father as well as he did, Symon had come to appreciate how losing the woman he'd loved had sent Jimmy spiralling into a vortex of despair that had changed him forever.

Maybe Symon had more in common with his father than he'd thought?

"Sy?" Tara was waving at him and with a jolt he plucked himself from the past and back into the kitchen. "Wow. You were miles away there."

Years rather than miles, Symon reflected. More than eighteen years ago, in fact.

"Thinking about it all?" she asked, handing him a mug.

"I guess," Symon said. "Although to be honest there's not a lot to tell really, Tara. You'd be better off going up to Seaspray and finding out for yourself. From what I could gather yesterday, Dad met Emerald's mum when he was in California and they had a relationship. She sounds like a bit of a free spirit and she never told him she was pregnant. Emerald traced him when she grew up and now here she is on our doorstep. I don't think we can actually blame Dad too much for all this. He only screwed up by not telling us as soon as he found out about her."

"It's like something from a soap opera," said Tara. "Seriously, you Tremaines are way more exciting than my family. Their idea of drama is choosing Sainsbury's rather than Waitrose."

"I'd be happy with that. Right now Mo's in a strop with Dad, Issie's apparently distraught and threatening to come back from Florida, and Granny Alice is frantically trying to make everything all right." Symon was worried because there was no way Alice could possibly fix this. Mo always blew up and then simmered down, while Issie was used to being the baby of the family and was probably feeling put out – but a new sister, unlike a cut knee, wasn't going to go away with a kiss and a plaster.

"So Emerald's staying at Seaspray?"

"I think so. She was keen to pitch a tent somewhere but Granny wouldn't hear of it." From what Symon had seen of Emerald she seemed a self-reliant type. He certainly admired her courage. Coming to England all alone and facing a strange family must have been hard enough in itself, so discovering that nobody knew she existed must have been doubly difficult. Emerald had eventually faced the situation head-on, telling them all about her upbringing in California, and by the time he'd left Seaspray Symon had decided that he liked her a lot. She had Mo's fire, Jake's honesty, a dash of Zak's creativity, resembled Issie and was a million times braver than Jimmy. Was there any of him in her? Symon had wondered. Maybe. There was certainly an air of independence and a determination to do things on her terms.

He hoped she was more sensible than he had been at her age.

"I'll look forward to meeting her," Tara said. "As will the entire village. I thought Betty Jago was going to pop with the news, and Sheila Keverne's telling everyone she meets that Jimmy's *love child* has arrived at Seaspray."

Symon raised his eyes to the beamed ceiling. Superfast fibre-optic broadband had nothing on the speed of village gossip. No wonder he played his own cards close to his chest. "What century is this?"

"You know how it is. Even Big Rog is agog. I heard that he was going to give the shed a miss and paint the window frames at Seaspray."

"The same ones he was supposed to do last summer?"

"The very same. Isn't it lucky he's got a gap in his schedule today of all days?"

Leaving Tara laughing, Symon picked up the mail and wandered outside into the small courtyard garden. It was mild today and spring was in the air. The slice of sky above the closely packed cottages was baby blue; beneath it, seagulls squabbled on the chimney stacks, fighting for prime real estate on which to build their nests. It was a time of hope and new life and optimism – all of which were very much at odds with the sensation of dread that washed over Symon when he opened the letter and scanned the contents.

This time it was worse than just a rent hike. The landlord was writing to inform Symon that he'd been reflecting on the situation and come to a new decision. When their current tenancy agreement expired, the lease on the restaurant wouldn't be renewed. That was it. The Plump Seagull was over. The years of gently building up its name, the hours spent restoring the crumbling building one scoop of filler and one lick of paint at a time, and the effort of slowly putting Polwenna Bay on the map as *the* place to dine were all for nothing.

He crumpled the letter and let it drop onto the cobbles. At once a gull swooped upon it and then shrieked its rage when it discovered there was nothing to eat.

"You'd better get used to it," Symon told this would-be glutton as it flew back to its chimney pot and glared down at him. "And so had I."

He leaned against the wall and closed his eyes. The warmth of the sun and the day-to-day noise of the village soothed him for a moment. The constant burble of the River Wenn was the background to his life here; it lulled him to sleep at night and sang him awake in the morning, just as the scrabbling of gulls' feet on the slates above his head and the hoots of owls told him the time. He rose early and went to bed late, living and breathing this place and giving it all the love and devotion that Claudette had rejected. Without the restaurant who was he? And what the hell was his purpose?

He knew that thoughts like these could send him spinning into that dark place where the lid slammed shut and where, no matter how loud he yelled, nobody came. Symon had been there once and he was determined never to find himself there again. He opened his eyes and took a long breath to slow the racing of his heart. The Plump Seagull was a brand name and it would travel with him. Wherever he, Symon Tremaine, decided to base himself next would by some mysterious alchemy become The Plump Seagull. All would be well. Hadn't Jean-Luc and Claudette taken Papillon Rouge with them from the narrow backstreet in Montmartre to the beautiful boulevard not far from the Eiffel Tower? They were Papillon Rouge and the restaurant bound them more closely than love or marriage. Who knew that better than him?

There was no need to tell his staff about this, Symon decided as he retrieved the screwed-up letter and smoothed it flat before tucking it into his trouser pocket. Tara and the others were already hard at work in preparation for the lunchtime service and worrying them wouldn't achieve anything. Anything could happen between now and the end of the lease. He might find an even better venue, or the landlord might have a change of heart, or Symon might win the lottery...

He laughed out loud. He'd *need* to win the lottery to buy a place in Polwenna Bay these days – or even to rent one. He supposed he could ask Ashley for help, but to go cap in hand to his brother-in-law went against everything Symon believed in. No, he would do this on his own merits or not at all. There had to be a way to make some cash that didn't involve selling souls to the devil, flogging vital organs or developing a scratch-card addiction. All he had to do was think of it.

"I'm just popping out for a moment," he called to Tony and Tara. "If Perry comes while I'm gone, can you ask him for some more wild garlic? And extra rocket for the tortellini?"

Tara called something back, which Symon took as assent. God, he hated to think that she might be out of a job if he had to move further west to find somewhere more affordable. The same went for Kelly, who wouldn't want to be far from the fisherman she'd started dating recently – and Tony was a local man with an elderly mother to think about. Jobs were as rare as gulls' teeth in these parts and his employees depended on him. There had to be a way to solve this problem.

Leaving his team prepping, Symon slipped out of the side gate and headed towards the harbour. The sea was calm today and he longed to hop into a sailing boat and zip across the bay. The whipping of sails and the slap of waves against the hull would be a wonderful antidote to the churning dread in his stomach. There was nothing like racing over the water and leaving everything else far behind.

As if his feet longed for the water too, Symon found himself entering the marina and meandering along the pontoon. Boats rose and fell with the water, their hulls creaking against the safe dock and their rigging clinking against the mast and chiming in perfect time with the motion. Gull scarers whirled and at the furthest end of the jetty an engine coughed and belted out puffs of blue smoke as the owner attempted to start it after months of inactivity.

"One for me, I think." Jake joined Symon on the pontoon, shading his eyes against the glare of sunlight on water. "Alternator maybe? Or perhaps the fuel injection's got some dirt in it?"

Symon never failed to be impressed by how his brother could tell these things. To him one engine sounded just the same as another, yet Jake heard every nuance and every vibration.

"How are things at home?" Symon asked.

"Pretty much as you'd expect," said Jake. "Dad's gone AWOL, Mo's in a sulk and Gran's trying to make amends for being Jimmy's mother."

"No change there then. And Emerald?"

"Asleep when I left. I think she must be jet-lagged and worn out by it all, poor kid," replied Jake. "Imagine arriving and meeting us lot en masse. No wonder she almost did a runner."

"I can't believe Dad knew about her for months and never said anything," Symon remarked.

Jake gave him an arch look. "This is Dad we're talking about. Of course you can believe it. He thought if he hid for long enough the problem would go away. It's what he always does."

This was true. In a past life Jimmy must have been an ostrich.

"So what next?" Symon asked. "Is she staying?"

"I think so, for a bit anyway. Summer says she'll show her around this morning and I think Danny and Jules will be about later. Best not to overwhelm her with the whole tribe. She's an only child and not used to siblings."

"Lucky her," grinned Symon. "But a new sister. Can you believe it?"

"Like the other two aren't bad enough," said Jake. "I don't know. Maybe she'll be fun? She seems like a switched-on girl and she's got guts, that's for sure. Nick couldn't wait to take her to the pub but apparently she doesn't drink. He's horrified."

"I bet. That's his new partner in partying crime ruled out," Symon observed.

"He needs to get his head down and work before Eddie Penhalligan decides to sack him again," Jake commented. Given that Eddie was Summer's father, Jake knew what he was talking about. Symon was alarmed; the last time Nick was sacked he'd come to work in the restaurant instead, where he'd lasted about twenty minutes before growing tired of scrubbing pans and being given the brush-off by the waitresses. Never again.

"Is everything all right with you?" Jake asked.

Symon's fingers, buried in his pocket, brushed against the letter. He was about to answer when Jake added, "Gran's really worried about you."

Symon paused. The last thing he wanted was Alice fretting. She had more than enough on her plate. "I'm great, thanks. Just busy."

"Yeah. That's what I told her," said Jake. Then he glanced at his watch. "Do you think Ella will be in her office?"

Symon was used to his brother changing tack (metaphorically and literally, when they went sailing), but this nearly had him overboard.

"Ella St Milton? What on earth do you want with her?"

Jake looked around to see whether anyone was listening in. Even though their only audience was a snoozing gull, Jake's lowered voice was so soft that Symon had to lean closer to hear it.

"Justin Anderson's on the guest list for that big celebrity wedding at the hotel."

Premier League footballer Justin Anderson was Summer's ex-fiancé and they were currently embroiled in an ugly court case. Summer and Jake were both highly stressed about the whole deal.

"How on earth do you know that?" Symon asked, taken aback. The hotel's wedding plans had better security than GCHQ. "Ella must sleep with the guest list under her pillow."

"Tom Elliot *accidentally* let it slip. He thought we should know. Can you imagine what it will be like for Summer to think that bastard's anywhere nearby? And if the press gets a whiff of it they'll be crawling all over us looking for a story."

Jake's jaw was clenched with anger and Symon understood why. He'd known Summer for years, having grown up with the Penhalligans, and when she'd returned to the village he'd been shocked by how thin and frightened she'd been. Life with a violent bully had driven Summer to despair, and Symon knew that Jake wanted to kill Justin with his bare hands for this.

"What are you going to do?" he asked.

"Nothing stupid, so don't panic. Much as I'd like to take Anderson out to sea and throw him overboard, I'm going to start by visiting Ella and asking politely for him to be removed from the guest list."

Symon wasn't convinced this would work. Ella St Milton wasn't a huge fan of Jake's. In fact, she wasn't keen on any of the Tremaines. Poor Granny Alice and Jonny St Milton were like a superannuated Romeo and Juliet.

"What makes you think she'll agree?"

"Not old time's sake, that's for certain," Jake answered wryly. "I don't know. Decency? Empathy? Female solidarity? The fact that Granny Alice is about to marry her grandfather?"

"Maybe," Symon said doubtfully, although from what he knew of Ella these were not qualities she possessed in abundance. Determination, arrogance and single-mindedness sprang to mind far more readily.

"I have to try," his brother said.

"And if she says no?"

A dark expression shadowed Jake's face. "Then I'll do whatever it takes to protect Summer," he promised grimly, "and, Granny's wedding or not, the St Miltons had better not stand in my way."

And with this he was gone, striding along the pontoon and leaping the steps up to the quay two at a time. Symon stared after him until Jake was just a matchstick figure crossing the fish market and then vanishing into the warren of narrow streets.

Symon exhaled slowly. The folded letter pressed into his leg, the words burning against his skin in much the same way that the threat of losing the restaurant was seared into all his waking and dreaming moments. It seemed to Symon that everything he knew and loved was hanging by a thread – and he hadn't a clue how to keep it all safe.

CHAPTER 10

"You want to postpone our wedding? You can't be serious?"

Jonny St Milton stared at Alice in disbelief. All of a sudden his dapper suit looked slightly too big for him, his mouth seemed to droop and even the jaunty feather in his tweed hat appeared dispirited. It was as if her hesitant suggestion that they put their wedding back a few months had been a sharp pin popping the balloon of his usual confidence. At this moment, the man she loved looked every one of his eighty-odd years.

Alice sighed and passed a hand over her eyes. She was certainly feeling her age. Since Emerald's unexpected arrival the previous afternoon she'd felt weary to her bones. Hauling herself out of bed this morning had been a huge effort; all she'd wanted to do was pull the covers back over her head, close her eyes and shut the world out. But this was Jimmy's way of carrying on, not hers, and Alice knew that however difficult today might be, she couldn't hide from the fact that her granddaughter was bound to have questions she needed answering.

Thank goodness Danny and dear Jules had managed to persuade Emerald to come back. Alice had been horrified when her squabbling family had driven the poor child away, and hugely relieved when she'd reappeared. They'd spent some time together but mostly Emerald had been monopolised by the other grandchildren, who were fascinated by her – with the notable exception of Mo, who'd had a massive row with Jimmy and stormed home to Mariners with an apologetic Ashley in hot pursuit. Mo would come round, of course; she always did. In any case, this wasn't about the appearance of a new sister as much as it was about reaching the end of her patience with Jimmy. Alice had explained this as best she could to the new arrival, but by this stage poor Emerald had been almost passing out with jet lag. Eventually Jake had carried her up to the spare room – where, the last time Alice had checked on her, she was sleeping soundly.

Alice was quite envious. She wished she could do the same, but this dragging, grinding heaviness wasn't just normal tiredness. It was bone deep and nothing like the physical weariness she'd reluctantly become accustomed to these days when walking home from the shop or after a few hours of minding Isla. If the mere thought of trying to organise her wedding, referee the feuding between the two families and move all her belongings into Jonny's apartment at the hotel was enough to make Alice long to close her eyes and give up, then the reality was impossible. Besides, how could she move out now? Her new granddaughter was going to need her and so were all the others.

"It's not forever," she said gently. "Just until everything's sorted here. Emerald arriving out of the blue has turned everything upside down. You can understand that, surely?"

Jonny nodded. "Of course I can. It must have been a huge shock."

Alice considered this for a moment. "In some ways, yes, definitely – but in others I wonder if deep down I always knew Jimmy was hiding something? It's a mother's instinct I suppose. You always know when your child's keeping a secret and Jimmy's always been a hopeless fibber."

"Not for want of practising," Jonny commented sharply.

Alice tutted. "He never means any harm and I'm sure if he'd known about Emerald from the very start he'd have been a part of her life. That's one thing I can promise you with my hand on my heart. I can say many things about my son, Jonny, but he loves his children."

Jonny took her hand and raised it to his lips. "I was just teasing, my love. The kids adore Jimmy and we all know he never means any harm."

"Things just seem to happen to him," Alice sighed, hearing the excusatory note in her voice and not liking it much. Oh dear. More than sixty years on and she was still having to sort out her son's problems and justify his actions. Jimmy had always got himself into scrapes and made things ten times worse by not knowing how to put them right. She supposed he would never change.

"In fairness it could happen to any man," said Jonny kindly. "It's you I feel for, Ally, because as usual you'll be the one who'll end up having to deal with it all."

"Exactly!" Now he was finally understanding and Alice was relieved. "So the last thing I have time to do at the moment is organise a wedding or move out of Seaspray."

"Ella can plan the wedding for us, love. It's what she does," Jonny told her.

Alice nodded absently. She was wondering whether Emerald was awake yet. What would she want for breakfast? Didn't Americans eat pancakes? Luke, Issie's boyfriend, always ate those with bacon and maple syrup, and grits too, whatever those were. Did Betty Jago sell them?

"Maybe," she said. "We'll see."

"She's in the middle of planning Georgie Angel's wedding right now, so I think two pensioners who want a quiet do with just friends and family will be a breeze," Jonny said shortly.

His tone was so unusually sharp that Alice was jolted.

"Unless you're just looking for an excuse not to get married?" he added.

"Don't be ridiculous," she said.

"I'm not being ridiculous." Jonny dropped her hand and rubbed his temples. "I'm offering solutions for how we can make this happen – and everything I come up with, you manage to find a problem with."

"I just don't think we need to rush it!" Alice was exasperated. "What's the big hurry? It's not as though we're teenagers anymore. There's plenty of time to get married once Emerald's settled and the family's taken care of."

"I hate to break it to you, Ally, but I don't think we've got forever," Jonny replied bluntly. "We're in our eighties and we'll be lucky if we even have five good years. We can't put off getting married because there *isn't* plenty of time. If we don't do it soon it might never happen."

His voice wobbled, his body swayed and his hands clutched the kitchen table for support.

"Calm down, Jonny! Think of your heart," Alice said, pulling out a chair – which he pointedly ignored.

"Why should I think of my heart when you don't care about breaking it?"

"Oh, for goodness' sake, you daft old man! Don't be so dramatic!"

Alice was starting to lose patience with the men in her life. Why was it that everything always had to be about them? She'd been up until the small hours listening to Jimmy complaining about how none of the day's events had really been his fault and how upset he was, and now all Jonny seemed bothered about was getting his own way with the wedding dates. What about how *she* was feeling? And, even more importantly, what about that poor young girl? It really did break Alice's heart to imagine how Emerald must have felt arriving here so full of excitement, only to discover that Jimmy had been keeping her a secret and that the rest of the family had no idea who she was. She'd looked utterly crushed. The least the child deserved was some time to get to know her family – and Alice was determined to give this to her.

"I'm not being dramatic," insisted Jonny. "We've waited years to get married!"

"Exactly. So a few more months will hardly matter," Alice countered. "Now sit down before you fall down and let's talk about this properly."

"Fine, have it your way," muttered Jonny, lowering himself onto the chair and glowering at Alice over the toast crumbs and plates left over from breakfast. Summer had been in the middle of clearing these away but had retreated tactfully when Jonny had arrived. Usually Alice would have busied herself finishing up while she chatted to him, but this conversation deserved her full attention. She took the chair beside his and reached out for his knotted old hands, marvelling that she'd first held them almost a lifetime ago. How was this even possible when it felt like yesterday?

"I still want to marry you," she told him.

Jonny made a noise that was halfway between a sob and a laugh. "Strange way of showing it. You've been putting off setting a date for what feels like forever."

"I know," she said quietly. "It isn't because I don't want us to get married though, love. I just don't think it's the right time to leave my family. They need me here."

"They're adults!" Jonny couldn't hide his irritation. "You've given them years of your life, Alice. Years! It's time for you now."

"And I will have my time but not at Emerald's expense," Alice said quietly. "She's only just arrived and she's going to need her family. She's going to need me."

"She's Jimmy's daughter," Jonny pointed out. "That makes her his responsibility, not yours."

But Alice shook her head. "You know as well as I do that it doesn't work like that with Jimmy. Maybe I went wrong somewhere as a mother? Was I too indulgent? Too soft? Or perhaps Henry was too hard on him? I don't know anymore but I do know that I have to see this through. I need to be here for Emerald and the others."

"So that's it? No wedding?"

"No wedding *at the moment*," she answered. "Maybe later on, in the summer? Or perhaps even Christmas? A Christmas wedding's always beautiful. Imagine the church all decorated for us."

"And then it will be a spring wedding and then a summer one," Jonny said bitterly. He felt for the engagement ring on her fourth finger and stroked it tenderly. "Oh Alice, time's not going to stand still for us and we've wasted so much already, can't you see that? It's time we stepped aside and let the young people take charge. They've got to make their own mistakes and live their own way because we won't always be there to hold their hands. We're not going to be around forever."

There was a lump in Alice's throat. Nobody ever wanted to face their own mortality, and when she thought about leaving her family behind – whether it was moving in with Jonny or going somewhere a little more abstract and much further away – it made her heart shiver. They needed her. How would they manage without her?

A tear slipped down her cheek and splashed onto the table.

"I know it's difficult, my darling," Jonny said softly when she didn't reply. He squeezed her fingers as though holding onto her would anchor him too. "I've clung on to my business far longer than I should have done because I've been afraid of what I'll become without it. It's hard to know what's worse: that they need us dreadfully or that they don't need us at all. That's why I've come to a decision about the hotel."

"Have you?" This did surprise Alice. The Polwenna Bay Hotel was Jonny's pride and joy, and although he'd talked for months about handing it over fully, nothing had happened. She'd secretly thought that it never would.

He nodded. "I want to spend all my time with you, Ally. I don't know how long we'll have but I want to make every minute count. Lord knows we've both worked hard enough and this is our time now. I want us to see Paris, visit Rome, take cruises to the Med and spend our winters in the sunshine. I can't do that if I'm tied to the hotel, can I?"

Alice supposed not. He'd painted a wonderful picture of their new life together and she could just imagine them both sitting on a balcony in Italy and watching the red sun sinking low on the hills as they sipped Prosecco. She'd always wanted to travel and never had the chance…

"So I'm handing the hotel over," Jonny concluded.

"You're going to let Ella run it?" Alice was pleased. Ella wasn't everyone's cup of tea but she lived and breathed the hotel. Even Mo would admit that.

"Ella?" Jonny looked taken aback. "Whatever gave you that idea? No, of course not. I'm putting Teddy in charge. He's the heir to it all, not Ella."

"But it's Ella who does all the work," Alice pointed out. Heaven only knew she was no great fan of Ella St Milton, but credit where credit was due! The girl had poured her heart and soul into the business. You didn't need to be her number one fan to see that. The hotel's assistant manager Tom Elliot, who was friends with Nick and Issie, was a regular at Seaspray and always sang her praises.

Jonny shrugged. "I guess I'm old-fashioned but I still think a business needs a man to run it. A steadier hand at the helm."

That wasn't Teddy St Milton. He was more likely to drive the entire thing onto the rocks.

"Old-fashioned doesn't come close," said Alice. "You do know women have the vote now? Some of us even have jobs."

"Very funny," said Jonny. "Look, I know times have changed and that I'm an old fossil, but that's my point! I'm out of touch and that's why it's time we stepped aside and let the youngsters run the show. Look, just for you I'll wait and see how Ella gets on with this big wedding and then I'll make my decision regarding who I place in charge. Either way though, I'm going to make the most of the time I have left and see a bit of the world while I still can." He turned to face her now and his expression was serious. "I want to do that with you beside me, Alice, but I can't wait forever because time's running out. I need to know where I stand."

"Is that a threat? If I don't set a date soon then you're off anyway?"

"It's not a threat but it is an intention," Jonny said quietly. "I love you, Alice Tremaine, and I want to spend the rest of my life with you. That's a given, seeing as I've loved you since I was a teenager, but I suppose what I'm saying is that I have to have an answer soon. If Emerald's your latest excuse to put the wedding off then that's all I need to know. Just be honest with me. I'm a big boy. I can handle the truth."

"For heaven's sake, Jonny! Emerald's not an excuse! She's a perfectly good reason to stay here at Seaspray for a little bit longer!" Alice cried, snatching her hand away in temper.

"Fine! Stay for Emerald. Or Jimmy. Or Mo. Or whoever you feel needs you next." He rose creakily to his feet. "Look, I think we should give it a break for a while."

"A break?" Alice echoed, not quite able to believe what she was hearing. "You want to call our engagement off?"

"No! Never that."

"Then what?"

"Then let's really think hard about whether or not we're actually going to get married," Jonny replied.

Alice saw his love for her etched in every line of his dear face, and her chest constricted. "I still want to get married," she insisted. "I really do. I just need a little more time."

"But that's the one thing we don't have. I think we both need to take some time out to consider what we really want. Perhaps it isn't the same thing after all?" he said quietly. "I want to be with you, Alice. That's it. There's no secret and there's nothing more complicated going on. I love you and I want to marry you. Whatever time I have left, be it a day, a year or even a decade, I want to spend every second with you. The question I need you to answer is whether you feel the same way?"

Her breath was caught in her lungs and Alice couldn't speak.

"*This* is our time right now, Alice, and we have to seize it while it lasts."

Jonny dropped a kiss onto her cheek, squeezed her shoulder and then walked out of the kitchen with his head held high and his stick tapping on the floor. Alice watched him go with her feelings in ribbons, but she didn't call him back. How could she when she couldn't tell Jonny what he wanted to hear? Her heart might long to cry out that she was ready to throw caution to the winds, get married and see what they could of the world while they still had the chance, but she knew this was impossible while her family still needed her. Her family came first; it had to. That being the case, she'd surely made the right choice.

But whether she was making the right decision or not, the kitchen suddenly felt very big and very, very empty.

CHAPTER 11

As Monday mornings went, this one was from hell. Already two of the cleaners had phoned in sick and the computer system had crashed – just as Ella had discovered that Teddy had helped himself to several thousand pounds from the hotel's bank account. It was only half past ten but she felt shattered.

It was always a fight to keep her head above water here, but now that Charlie's demands had been added to all her other problems, Ella's nerves were beginning to fray. Not that anyone else would have realised this was how she felt. Like a gliding swan, Ella made running the hotel look effortless, even if beneath the surface her feet were paddling like mad. And they had never paddled harder than today. Her hair was perfectly straight and swishy, her make-up and nails were immaculate (courtesy of the girls in the hotel spa) and her designer suit and crisp white shirt were the epitome of businesslike chic, but inside she was the emotional equivalent of bed hair and baggy jogging bottoms.

"Hold your nerve," Ella said out loud to herself as she sat at her desk. "It's all going to be fine. There's nothing here that you can't deal with."

Feeling slightly better for this pep talk, she turned to her in-tray and psyched herself up for a morning's firefighting. So far there were four apparently urgent calls from Georgie Angel's people, a complaint from a guest, a parking fine for her Range Rover (bloody Charlie, why couldn't he just buy a ticket like everyone else?) and the IOU from her brother. A headache started to beat near her temples. This couldn't continue; the hotel wasn't Teddy's personal bank account. Her hand hovered over the telephone as she toyed with the idea of calling her grandfather and asking him to have a sharp word, since Teddy wasn't listening to her. Then she sighed because what would be the point? Jonny was certain to take her brother's side and bound to see any request for help as yet another example of why a woman couldn't run a business. Ella would rather pull her newly applied acrylics off with her teeth than ask her grandfather for his assistance. She'd just have to think hard and find a way of dealing with her brother – preferably one that didn't involve murder or incur the cost of a hitman.

The computer system was still down, so her emails and booking updates would have to wait. Instead, Ella busied herself with reading the latest magazine article about the hotel, feeling irritated to discover that most of the copy was devoted to Charlie. The main picture didn't even feature the hotel, but was a shot of him clad in chef's whites and posing on the quayside. Infuriating! The whole point of spending vast amounts of money on a celebrity sodding chef was that he was meant to bring publicity to the hotel. He wasn't supposed to detract from it. She scanned the article and with every line felt more annoyed. Charlie had barely mentioned the place. The piece was in a national lifestyle glossy and Ella had spent weeks and a small fortune schmoozing the journalist who was putting it together. A champagne lunch in Truro paid for by her, a free night in the hotel and far too many brushes of his clammy paw on her leg later, and they'd had a deal – or so she'd thought.

In frustration she shoved the magazine away, howling in pain when she knocked hot coffee all over her desk and her trousers.

"For Christ's sake!" Ella shrieked, leaping up in agony. Her trousers were ruined, her paperwork was sodden and now she probably had third-degree burns to boot. What a crappy start to the day.

She was still attempting to mop up the mess with Kleenex when there was a sharp rap on the office door. For heaven's sake, what now? Tom knew better than to disturb her. Before she'd even had a moment to bark that whoever it was could go away, the door swung open and Jake Tremaine strode into the office.

Great. Just great. Of all the moments she might have picked for her ex to see her, this wasn't one of them. Wearing coffee-stained cream trousers and hopping about in pain wasn't exactly her best look. Ella had entertained many fantasies about her ex-boyfriend turning up unannounced and pleading for her to take him back, but in these daydreams she was usually dressed to kill and he was down on his luck. Right now he was anything but the heartbroken mess she'd so often pictured. Jake's tall, broad-shouldered and muscular body was every bit as good as she remembered, and so were those sexy denim-blue eyes and that full beautiful mouth. In spite of all the ill feeling that had passed between them and the fact that he was blissfully loved up with Summer Penhalligan, Ella felt her heartbeat quicken.

He was still the most handsome man she'd ever seen.

She closed her eyes briefly, held her breath for a few seconds and prayed that this was all a horrible dream.

Sadly, when she opened her eyes Jake was still in the office and his expression was grim. It didn't look as though he'd come over to tell her he'd made a huge mistake and to beg her forgiveness. Not that she would want this anyway, of course, but hypothetically it would have been nice to have had the chance to turn him down and get her own back. Ella didn't let many people get close to her heart, but Jake Tremaine had come dangerously near and she hated herself for being weak enough to have allowed this.

Ella forced herself to meet his angry gaze. God, what had set him off now? The Tremaines were such a touchy bunch. They were always flying off the handle about something. She could only hope her grandfather came to his senses before he married into the clan.

"Isn't it usually polite to wait to be invited in?" Ella snapped while her body quivered, clearly deciding it still responded to Jake's proximity.

"This isn't a social call," Jake said shortly.

"So you always charge into people's offices uninvited?" She pointed to her stained trousers. "I could have been changing out of these. It might have been a little embarrassing, although I guess there's nothing here you haven't seen before."

He had the good grace to look a little awkward. "Sorry. That was bad-mannered and I apologise."

"Apology accepted. So, why did you need to see me so urgently?" A thought occurred to her and her stomach lurched. "Nothing's happened to my grandfather, has it?"

Jake looked horrified. "God, no. Nothing like that. I never meant to worry you. Actually, I passed him when I was on my way to the marina and he looked as fit as a fiddle."

This was a relief. Jonny was difficult at times and old-fashioned, and she'd lost count of the occasions when she'd wanted to throttle him, but he was the closest thing Ella had to a father since her own had pushed off. She loved him dearly. Lobbing the tissues into the bin, she returned to her desk. She felt much more in control there, once her coffee-drenched legs were tucked away out of view. The last time she'd been alone with Jake Tremaine she'd been stark naked and hurling insults at him, while he'd been hastily gathering his clothes.

It wasn't a happy memory.

"So what's the problem?" she asked, pushing aside the swift recollection of how his body had looked, naked and close to hers. Thank God Jake wasn't a mind reader.

"Justin Anderson's the problem." Jake answered, and Ella saw that his fists were clenched as he fought to keep calm.

She frowned. Justin Anderson was a Premier League footballer well-known for his volatile temper and ongoing feud with the paparazzi. He was also one of Georgie Angel's wedding guests, something that was top secret and causing her no end of headaches as the bride-to-be tried to drum up maximum publicity.

"What about him?"

"Don't play dumb, Ella. It doesn't suit you," said Jake. "I know he's on the guest list for the big wedding."

Ella stared at him while her brain raced around at a million miles an hour trying to think of a reply. How the hell did Jake know this? The guest list was crammed with A-listers and it was highly confidential; all the hotel staff had been warned about mentioning it on pain of losing their jobs. Who'd spoken to Jake? Was it Tom? Had Nick overheard when delivering fish? Or maybe Charlie had been shooting his mouth off in the pub?

"I don't know where you got your information—" she began, but Jake just laughed.

"It doesn't matter how I found out. You know he's Summer's ex and they're not on good terms."

Ella did know. You'd have to live on the moon not to, because the tabloids had truly gone to town with the story. Summer hadn't breathed a word about all this, but the rumour mill had it that Justin Anderson had been violent throughout their relationship. He had a reputation for getting into fights and certainly had a troubled past. Then again, so did lots of people.

Ella shrugged. "And your point is?"

"My point is that I don't want him coming to Polwenna Bay or anywhere near Summer!" Jake flared. His blue eyes blazed with anger and Ella felt a twist of jealousy that it was Summer and not her who'd fired this fierce protective instinct.

"If he is on the list, and I'm not at liberty to divulge that information, then that's the business of the bride and groom and nobody else," she said.

Jake gave her a scornful look. "Don't give me that crap, Ella. You run this hotel and you call the shots."

"I don't decide who people invite to their weddings!" She pinched the bridge of her nose between her thumb and forefinger, fighting to quell her rising temper. "That isn't my call to make."

"Fine. Whose call is it? Jonny's? Teddy's?"

"It's Georgie Angel's decision!" Ella shot back, riled by his comment – which was way closer to the knuckle than Jake knew. "It's his wedding and his guest list. I can't interfere with it just because your girlfriend's oversensitive!"

Jake stared at her with such contempt that Ella felt as though she'd been punched in the stomach. Even as she'd said the words, she'd known that they were bitterly unfair. When Summer had returned to Polwenna Bay her bruised face had told its own story. Who could blame Jake for wanting Justin Anderson kept miles away?

"You really are hard as nails, aren't you?" Jake remarked, shaking his head. "And to think I felt bad about you."

"Don't feel bad on my account," Ella said crisply. "We had a meaningless fling. That was all."

In reality she was trying her hardest to hold back the sobs that were tightening the back of her throat. She shouldn't be upset, not when she'd worked this hard to cultivate her ice-maiden image. She wanted Jake to think she didn't care. The less he knew of the nights she'd soaked her pillow with tears on his account, the better.

Jake's beautiful mouth was pressed into a tight line.

"So there's no point appealing to our past friendship or even asking you to see this from Summer's point of view?" he said. "Maybe Summer should go to the press? That would be interesting. Not quite the publicity you probably had in mind for the hotel or the flagship wedding, but needs must."

Oh Lord. Georgie Angel would flip. Ella felt quite faint at the thought. There was way too much depending on this wedding being a success, and she couldn't risk Georgie and Tabitha pulling the hotel as a venue.

"Look," she said finally, "I really can't say anything because there are confidentiality clauses in our agreement, but the security for this wedding is going to be super tight. There's a magazine deal in place with exclusive picture rights – and several big A-listers are attending too. I promise that any guests won't be leaving the hotel. We've even got a special marquee and tunnel being set up, to hide their arrivals. If the person you mention is coming, and I can't tell you either way, then they certainly won't be wandering down into the village. They'll be here for twenty-four hours at the most."

Jake's blue eyes were narrowed and dark with suspicion as he looked at her. *He trusts me as far as he can throw me*, Ella thought and this idea made her feel very sad.

"Do I have your word on that?" he asked.

Ella nodded. This was something she could promise. She'd spent days sorting out the security for this wedding, taking every eventuality into account. Justin Anderson wouldn't be going far.

"Absolutely," she said. "If he was here he wouldn't leave the wedding. I promise."

Jake exhaled a ragged breath. "OK, Ella. That's good to know. Thank you."

"Did I just hear you thanking me? Wow. That must have been hard."

His lips curled upwards. "It wasn't easy but I'd do anything for Summer, even ask a St Milton for a favour."

Ella felt a sharp pang in her chest. What must it be like to have a man love you so much that he'd do anything for you? Most guys she met took what they wanted – money or sex; it didn't seem to matter which – and then pushed off. And yes, she counted Jake Tremaine in their number, even though in fairness to him he'd told her it was over almost as soon as Summer had returned to Polwenna Bay.

"You must really love her," she said, and he nodded.

"Yes, I really do." Then he smiled at her and she saw sympathy in his eyes. "I'm sorry if I ever hurt you, Ella. I never meant to."

She waved her hand at him dismissively. "I'd almost forgotten about it. Now, I don't know how the marine trade is right now but I'm flat out. Apart from interfering with my wedding-planning business, was there anything else you wanted?"

"No," said Jake. "I think that was just about it."

Once Jake had gone, Ella remained at her desk staring into space. His visit had shaken her more than she cared to admit. The problem wasn't his anger or even the business with Justin Anderson – these she could deal with. Rather, the feelings that had been stirred up in her own heart made settling down to work impossible. Witnessing the protective intensity of Jake's love for Summer had been like holding a mirror up to her own life: the reflection had revealed just how empty it was. The stupid flings, the mess she'd made with Charlie, the lonely nights spent working… All these images played through her mind like a bleak movie. What would it be like to have a man who truly loved her? The way the Tremaine men loved once they gave their hearts, with passion and loyalty and utter selflessness, made Ella want that love for herself with a longing that took her breath away.

She sighed and reached for her paperwork. What was the point of yearning for what she'd never have? She might as well long for the moon and the stars, because true love was just as far out of her reach.

Ella St Milton was on her own and she suspected that was the way it always would be.

CHAPTER 12

OMG. The old couple had just split up because of her? Seriously?

Emerald hadn't meant to eavesdrop on her grandmother but it had been pretty hard not to when she'd heard her own name batted backwards and forwards like a soccer ball. Venturing downstairs after waking up in a huge bed straight out of *Bedknobs and Broomsticks*, she'd begun following the smell of toast and coffee to the kitchen. The sound of raised voices had stopped her in her tracks.

"Emerald arriving out of the blue has turned everything upside down. You can understand that, surely?"

This was her grandmother speaking. Emerald's heart leapt into her throat. In her excitement about heading to England, she'd never dreamed her family would be upset by her arrival. Before falling asleep she'd heard her father and Jake arguing. Mo had stormed out hours before – and although Nick and Symon had been kind, Emerald could see that they too were thrown by her unexpected appearance. It had been a relief when exhaustion had claimed her and she'd fallen fast asleep. Things always looked better in the morning.

Except that this time they didn't. They were actually looking worse because now people were arguing about *her*.

Emerald peered through the crack in the door. Granny Alice was standing beside the monster oven and had her back to Emerald, facing an elderly man who was wearing a hat and the kind of tweedy clothes the royal family favoured. He had thick white hair and a crinkled face that looked as though it smiled a lot, even though at this moment it was folded into a frown.

"Of course I can. It must have been a huge shock."

His words hit Emerald like hammer blows.

She was a *huge shock*.

While Alice did her best to pretend otherwise and the conversation ebbed and flowed, Emerald's heart raced. Her legs suddenly felt so wobbly that she slid down the wall and crumpled into a heap. This wasn't what she'd expected. All her dreams about meeting her brothers and sisters and getting to know her father seemed childish now. She'd watched way too many syrupy Hallmark movies, that was her trouble, but these weren't real life.

Real life sucked.

"She's Jimmy's daughter. That makes her his responsibility, not yours," said the old man crossly.

She was a responsibility? Emerald was stung. Being someone who was generally quite self-reliant and independent, the idea that she was now an old lady's problem didn't sit easily. She hadn't come here to be a burden.

The conversation continued. Most of it didn't make any sense because she didn't know the people they were discussing, but with every word spoken her spirits sank lower.

"Fine! Stay for Emerald. Or Jimmy. Or Mo. Or whoever you feel needs you next." There was the sound of a chair scraping across flagstones. "Look, I think we should give it a break for a while."

The old man was heading towards the door now and there was no way Emerald wanted to bump into him. Jeez. She'd only gone and ruined everything for him and Alice. If it wasn't for her they'd have been happily planning their wedding (another thing that Jimmy had forgotten to tell her about) and life would have continued in its usual pattern with everyone remaining oblivious to her existence.

If she wasn't here everything would go back to normal.

The solution was obvious. She had to leave.

Emerald turned away and sprinted back up to the bedroom. Her rucksack was propped up against the bed and, since she'd not had time to unpack it, all she had to do was pick it up. Then it was only a matter of seconds before she was down the stairs again, slipping out of the front door and heading through the garden towards the footpath. There was no point sticking around. She was out of here.

Life with her mom hadn't always been a picnic but one thing Emerald had learned was to be pragmatic and cut her losses.

So far this trip had wound up being unbelievably complicated. Emerald was more upset than she cared to admit, but what was it Mom always said? *When life gives you lemons, make lemonade.* It had been written on a wooden sign they'd once had in the kitchen of the house in San Luis, back when Leaf was seeing Mike. Emerald had liked living in San Luis, and Polwenna Bay reminded her of the nearby Californian coastline. Here in Polwenna there were pastel-hued ice-cream shops, holiday houses, beach cafés and souvenir shops jostling for pole position along the seafront – providing a perfect contrast to the roughness of the quay, where nets and lobster pots were heaped in seaweed-strewn piles and fishing boats tugged at thick ropes. There probably weren't any seals, though. This thought was accompanied by a dart of homesickness because Emerald loved the fat noisy creatures who lounged beneath the piers and basked on the pontoons.

C'mon! They'll still be there when you get back, she told herself sharply. This was England and there was so much to see and do. She shouldn't be fretting over what she had left behind. It was the trip of a lifetime and since she'd spent all the money she'd saved from her part-time job in a café, she was going to make the most of it. She'd hitch a ride, check out some youth hostels and see the place by herself. Jimmy could always find her on Facebook if he really wanted to. Who needed him anyway? She never had before. He'd not been in evidence this morning; his bedroom door was still firmly closed, and Emerald guessed he was in hiding. Well, let him hide.

It was all very disappointing but, now that she thought it all through, not in the least bit surprising. He'd never actually invited her here anyway, had he? There'd been all kinds of vague comments about what they'd do together when she visited, but there'd never been anything concrete. If she hadn't been so swept away by the romance of having a family in merry England, she might have noticed his lack of commitment. Emerald sighed because it was too late now. She was here and she needed to make a plan. Her flight back was weeks away and, besides, she wasn't a quitter.

It was a windy day and the light was an odd sickly yellow shade, seeping from between purple clouds and turning the sea to dark navy. It was stormy, squally weather that would send sudden salvos of rain hammering down for a few intense minutes before bright sunshine flooded the place again. Puddles glinted in the streets, the harbour gates were closed against the swell, and people sploshed by in colourful spotted wellies and huddled beneath umbrellas. Emerald wished she had something a little sturdier on her feet than sparkly sandals. California was a neat place to grow up but it didn't prepare a girl for colder climates. Maybe Mom could transfer a few bucks to her bank account so she could sort herself out? She glanced down at her soggy toes. They were as blue as the Californian ocean. Jeez. That couldn't be good.

Shivering now that the sun had tucked itself behind a cloud, Emerald shifted the rucksack higher onto her shoulders and headed out of the village. She wasn't sure where she was going but her mom always said that was the most exciting part of the journey. With luck she'd find somewhere fairly nearby where she could camp out – or maybe she'd even discover a super-cheap guest house. That way she wouldn't be imposing on the Tremaines, but she could still be close to where they lived and (maybe) spend some time getting to know them. It was a vague hope but Emerald wasn't the kind who gave up easily.

The path rose steeply and clung to the hillside. A narrow lane forked off towards a pretty church, where Emerald guessed Jules must spend a great deal of time. It looked way older than anything she'd ever seen back at home – but then again this whole country was way, way ancient. She climbed higher up the hill, with the straps of the rucksack digging into her shoulders and her breath coming in sharp pants, until the lane veered sharply to the left and the village was hidden from view. There was a small forest on her right and a little further along were fields where horses grazed, swaddled in muddy rugs and looking far better suited to surviving here than she was in her shorts and sandals.

Emerald loved horses. Riding Pepper, the ancient barrel-racing pony, had been one of the highlights of her childhood. She'd been a good rider too, and Mac had told Mom that with a bit of practice she could be a big star on the rodeo circuit. He'd taken Emerald and Leaf to a rodeo and it had been the most exciting thing she'd ever seen. Country music had blasted over the speakers, while in the arena dashing cowboys had sat astride bucks that looked as though they could launch them into space. Women had sashayed across the stands, their skin-tight jeans glittering with rhinestones and their white Stetsons blocking the view so that Emerald had had to crane her neck to see. And what sights there were! Her eyes wide, she'd watched as bulls and bucking horses shot out of pens while the crowds cheered and swooping spotlights followed every heart-stopping move. When the bull-riding had begun, Emerald had thought her heart really might stop. It hadn't seemed to matter to the cowboys how mean the creatures they sat on were, though; they rode it, lassoed it and roped it whatever! Now and then a rider hit the floor in a puff of dust – to the gasps of the crowd – but the contender would always stagger to his feet and walk back to the corral, hat in hand and spurs jingling, to ride again.

The stands had been crowded, the soupy Californian air had been thick with the stench of hot horses and cheap perfume, and she'd been jostled and shoved as cowboy-booted folk squeezed by – but Emerald hadn't cared. Even though Mac had bought burgers, dripping with onions and ketchup, Emerald hadn't been able to manage a single mouthful because by this point the barrel-racing had started. Girls in sequinned jeans and hats that sparkled in the floodlights had torn around the arena on gallant ponies, approaching each barrel in a flat-out gallop before sinking low and spinning on their hocks in the race to reach the next. It was fast and exciting and Emerald had wanted to be one of those girls more than she'd ever wanted anything in her life.

Poor Pepper, retired and rather grumpy, hadn't been best impressed at being dragged into the corral so that Emerald could practise; before long, Emerald had been begging for rides on other horses. Fearless and determined, she'd ridden pretty much anything. She'd landed face first in the dirt on more than one occasion but she'd soon learned to stick on. In time, she'd built a reputation at the barn for being good.

Then Mom and Mac had split up. Emerald and her mother had left the area and headed back to San Francisco, and that had been the end of Emerald's dreams of rodeo stardom. All that remained was a little fizz of excitement when she glimpsed a Stetson – and of course her love of horses. Whenever she saw one, she longed to jump onto its warm back, wind her fingers in the flowing locks of mane and race towards the next barrel, her hair flying as her legs drove the animal forward.

At eighteen now rather than eight, Emerald knew she'd never be a rodeo queen. All the same, fragments of that cherished dream still clung to her. Spotting these English horses now, she shrugged off her rucksack, rolled her shoulders to ease the ache and hopped over the fence for a better look. Immediately the horses abandoned their grazing and ambled over, their soft noses nudging her in the hope of treats.

"I've not got anything for you guys," Emerald told them, scratching their necks and blowing into their noses. Wow. These were big animals: well-muscled warmbloods built for jumping and galloping across country, rather than the nippy little quarter horses she was used to. They were beautiful and a lot muddier than Pepper. She wondered what had happened to him. Was he still alive? Was Mac? This was one of the hardest things about living with her mom: there were so many unfinished stories. Sometimes it felt like reading a book only to discover that the last page was missing, leaving you wondering what the ending might have been.

That was why it had been so exciting to think that she had roots here. It had never occurred to Emerald that her newly discovered family might not want to read her story. She rested her head against the warm neck of a friendly bay horse, closed her eyes and for just a brief second allowed her disappointment to smother her.

"Hey! You there!"

Emerald's head snapped up. A woman, snugly wrapped against the British weather in a padded coat and wearing jeans tucked into green wellies, was striding across the paddock. Red curls sprang from beneath her black bobble hat and her chin was set at the same determined angle as Emerald's own when she realised who this was.

It was her sister Mo and she was looking as grumpy now as she had yesterday. Just great.

"Oh, it's you," said Mo, the horses stepping aside like little lambs when she reached the fence. "I thought it was some emmet feeding them again. Last week some utter moron tried to feed Mr Dandy a pasty. Can you imagine?"

Emerald couldn't. What was a pasty?

"It's such a menace in the summer. I never know what's going on and the last thing I need is colic," Mo continued. "Shoo, Mr Dandy! Splash! Nothing for you here!"

The horses, who clearly knew better than to push their luck with her, wandered back to their grazing.

"I can't stand horses being titbitted," Mo said crossly. Even her red curls looked angry. "Can you?"

Emerald had spent hours picking grass for Pepper. Did grass count as a titbit? She was pretty sure the cubed sugar she'd collected from the diner where Leaf had worked did. Maybe best not mention that?

"So you like horses then?" Mo asked, and Emerald nodded.

"Yeah, horses are cool. These ones are really nice."

Her sister looked pleased with this comment. "They are, aren't they? These two are my top horses and should be getting fit for the season, if bloody Ashley ever lets me near them again." Her eyes narrowed. "Do you ride?"

"A bit, I guess," Emerald said. She wasn't sure that much barrel-racing went on here, but it couldn't be that different, right?

"That means you can. Real riders are always modest and novices always brag," Mo told her. She glanced at Emerald's rucksack slung down on the grass and frowned. "What are you doing up here in the drizzle? You're not leaving, are you?"

Emerald shrugged one shoulder. "Doesn't seem much point staying at the house. Nobody wants me there and I've upset everyone by turning up. Don't deny it," she added when Mo opened her mouth to protest. "I'm not an idiot. You were really pissed."

"I wasn't pissed! Oh, you mean angry! Well, yes, maybe I was a bit but not with you," said Mo, looking flustered. "It was everything. Ashley's been necking Nurofen and thinks I haven't noticed, Isla's teething, I'm trying to get the horses fit and then you arrived. As usual it's all Dad's fault. As if I wasn't stressed enough! Don't take it personally."

Emerald didn't say a word. To be honest she wasn't really sure what Mo was talking about.

"And if there's one thing I know about Dad it's that if he thinks there's a problem he'll vanish, usually to the pub or out on a boat. I bet you've not seen him today, have you?" Mo added.

Emerald shook her head and her sister sighed.

"What a surprise. Look, I'm sorry if I was a bitch yesterday. None of this is your fault and, genuinely, I'm pleased you've found us – but this is so typical of Dad. He's always getting himself into situations because he isn't upfront to begin with, and it drives me mad. Jake and Danny have been picking up his chaos for years. Honestly, Emerald, if he'd told us about you we'd have been dead excited, I promise."

"Really?" A small arrow of hope took flight from her heart.

"Really," said Mo firmly. "Symon's thrilled to meet you, even if he's very quiet. He's probably thinking you're a vast improvement on me, at any rate. Jake and Danny are pleased too, and Morgan couldn't care less but that's just his way, so don't take it personally. Granny Alice is delighted to have somebody new to fuss over and Nick will be desperate to take you down to the pub and party. In fact, the entire village is dying to find out about you. Betty Jago and Sheila will be gutted they missed seeing you walking past in your backpacker disguise."

"It's not a disguise," Emerald said, glancing down at her clothes.

"*We* know that," said Mo, "but they'd have been expecting you to walk past dressed in cowboy boots or something, saying 'howdy'! Anyway, the point is that everyone wants you here, honestly, and I'm sorry if I made you think otherwise. Please stay."

For a split second everything seemed possible. Maybe she could get to know her family? Spend time with her new siblings? Even Jimmy might come good once he knew that nobody was angry? Emerald was just about to nod when she remembered the argument between her grandmother and the old man.

"I can't. It's causing too much trouble," she said sadly. Then she explained to Mo what had taken place. She'd only been here a short while but had already broken up an engagement. This surely had to be some kind of a record?

But Mo didn't seem at all concerned.

"I shouldn't worry about any of that," she said. "Jonny and Granny Alice have been on and off since the nineteen-forties! Between you and me, I think Granny's looking for an excuse not to move out of Seaspray and you've just given it to her. I can't say I blame her either. Who'd want to be related to Evil Ella? Not me! So, now you know it's not your fault and that we're quite frankly all bonkers, how about you come up to the yard with me, have a coffee and warm up? You look terrible."

"Gee, thanks," Emerald said, and Mo laughed.

"Yeah, I'm the tactful member of the family! Come on, I'll take your bag. I think I've got some biscuits, or should I call them cookies? I can probably find you a coat too."

Emerald's head was starting to throb with a combination of jet lag, no breakfast and the barrage of information she didn't understand. She felt absolutely exhausted and she was chilled to the core. This watery English sunshine wasn't anything like California's oven-hot blast, that was for sure. Coffee and cookies sounded very good.

"Are you sure?" she asked.

Mo nodded. "Of course I am. What are sisters for? And besides," she paused and gave Emerald a conspiratorial smile, "if you like horses half as much as I think you do, I've just had a brilliant idea..."

CHAPTER 13

Jules didn't tend to socialise in the week. Since early-morning services were best conducted by a vicar who wasn't yawning through the liturgy, Sundays sermons didn't write themselves and her parish council seemed incapable of holding a meeting without needing her to act as a referee, most of her evenings were taken up with work and going to bed early. Sometimes she might have dinner at Seaspray or an early drink in The Ship, but as a general rule Jules was normally home by nine – or even earlier if she had a meeting. It was hardly a rock 'n' roll existence, and if she did venture out on a weeknight Jules always felt a prickly sensation of guilt, as though she ought to be in her bedroom doing her homework.

Thirty-something years old and she still felt like she was at school. What on earth was that about?

"It's no life for a young woman," her mother often lamented. "You should be out enjoying yourself and spending time with Danny, not cooped up inside reading all those daft romance novels of yours! Why bother with fiction when you've got the real thing? You're not getting any younger either, love! Tick-tock!"

It was a reasonable question if you were a) not a vicar and b) unsubtly hinting about wanting grandchildren, Jules thought.

Besides, apart from being flat out with work it was often hard to see Danny. Usually he was either collecting Morgan from school and looking after him while Tara worked, or busy helping Jake run Tremaine Marine. With all this plus the extra issues that came with her faith and vocation, it was no wonder that lately she spent more time with the product of Caspar's pen than with her very own romantic hero.

It came back down to the same issue: if she and Danny wanted to spend more time together and move their relationship to the next level, there was only one solution, wasn't there?

They would have to get married.

Jules had been mulling this over all week and by Sunday she'd been ready to pluck up the courage to talk to Danny. She loved him and he loved her and they always told one another everything, so keeping back her thoughts about their future didn't feel honest. Jules had prayed a lot about it, hoping a bolt of heavenly lightning might zap Danny into proposing beforehand. Alas, by the time they'd been to church and enjoyed Alice's spectacular roast dinner there was still no sign of a celestial intervention; apparently, God wanted Jules to speak to Danny and sort the matter out herself. That was fine because Jules had a backup idea. She'd planned a walk over the cliffs to the next cove (past plenty of gorse bushes that could easily burst into flames should He so wish) and had picked out a suitable resting point, on a bench that overlooked the ocean and the sweep of the bay. This bench was tucked just a little way back from the main path and so was generally unnoticed by walkers, who tended to press on to the village in search of pasties and cider. It was, Jules had decided, the perfect spot for A Very Serious Conversation. She'd been determined that once they reached this spot, she'd take Danny's hand and tell him exactly how she felt.

But, like the famous saying regarding the plans of mice and men, just as she and Danny were pulling on their walking boots Emerald Tremaine had arrived out of the blue. Of course, this had turned everything upside down and any hopes Jules might have had for a quiet talk were swiftly dashed in the following chaos. They'd ended up fetching Emerald back when she'd tried to leave, and then stayed at Seaspray for most of the afternoon and evening. With the family dynamics in so much chaos it didn't feel like the right moment to bring up the subject of marriage; in any case, it was impossible to have a conversation without being interrupted. Jules had resigned herself to waiting until life returned to an even keel, or at least what passed for this in Polwenna Bay. She and Danny were happy and, to keep the nautical metaphors going, why rock the boat? She could wait. Family issues had to take priority.

At this point Jules had prayed very hard for patience – or at least an opportunity to speak to Danny. Jules had been a vicar for a few years now and her faith in her Boss was strong, but even she was taken aback when Danny phoned the next day to invite her out to dinner so that they could talk.

"It's all gone crazy up at the house since Sunday," he'd sighed. "And before you point out that it's only Monday now, let me explain that in the Tremaine household hours work a bit like dog years!"

"What's happened now?" Jules, who had Mondays off and was lolling on her sofa with Caspar's latest bare-chested hero, had sat bolt upright. "Tell me Emerald hasn't got a football team of brothers Jimmy also forgot about?"

Danny had laughed at this. "Not yet, but give it time. It's not even noon and already Jonny and Gran have had a big fallout, Dad's gone AWOL and Emerald's decided to move in with Mo."

"Emerald's moving in with Mo?" The last time Jules had seen Danny's eldest sister, she'd been storming out of Seaspray with Ashley hard on her heels.

"Apparently they met up earlier, bonded over a shared love of all things equine and now Emerald's moving into the caravan at Mo's yard to help out with the horses. Mo's thrilled, Ashley's relieved and Granny Alice is distraught that she can't fuss over the new arrival. Even Dad thinks he's off the hook now the girls are friends."

Jules rubbed her eyes in case this was all a weird dream – but apparently not.

"How long have I been asleep?"

"See what I mean about Tremaine time?" Danny said. "Look, I'll explain it all when I see you later. We've got a lot to talk about, Jules, so dig your glad rags out. I've booked us a table at The Plump Seagull. Sy's giving us the table at the back so we won't be disturbed."

"*The Seagull?*" Jules squawked. "That's a bit decadent for a Monday, isn't it? I'm more than happy to go to the pub."

"With everyone listening in in case we're talking about our latest family drama? No thanks," said Danny firmly. Then a softer note crept into his voice. "Besides, there's something really important that I need to talk to you about, something that could affect our future if we choose to let it. It could be life-changing."

Jules could hardly breathe. "What is it?"

"I'm not telling you over the phone and I'm certainly not telling you in the pub," Danny replied. "I don't want anyone to overhear what I need to ask you."

Her heart thumped. Was Danny saying what she *thought* he was saying? Jules thought she'd explode with anticipation. Danny was going to propose! That had to be it! What else could it be? He was going to propose properly with a ring and everything.

It was just as well she was on the sofa, otherwise Jules thought she might have fallen over with the shock.

The rest of Monday passed in a blur of excitement, hair-washing and frantically pulling out of her wardrobe every garment she possessed in the hope that there was something amazing in there that she'd forgotten about.

What did a girl wear for a proposal? In the movies it would be something flowing and white, Jules guessed, but the only clothes she had like this were her vicar's robes. Tee shirts, jeans and hoodies just wouldn't cut it; a clerical shirt wasn't in the least bit romantic; and even her faithful little black dress, hanging unloved at the back of the wardrobe, was way too tight. She tugged hard at the zip, hoping that the laws of physics might bend a little just this once, but there was a loud ripping sound as the fabric admitted defeat. Oh, if only she'd paid less attention to the biscuit tin and more to her diet!

Having ruled out dresses, Jules settled for a swingy red tunic with bell sleeves, teamed with black leggings and funky knee-high boots. With some light make-up and her hair playing nicely for once by curling into spirals, which she pinned out of her eyes with glittery clips, Jules thought she didn't look too bad. Maybe even pretty? The pink flush across her cheeks was certainly all her own, as was the sparkle in her eyes. As she twirled in front of the hall mirror, Jules wondered whether Danny's ring would shine as much.

"You look lovely," Danny said, kissing Jules gently when they met outside the restaurant. He took a step back and appraised her. "Have you done something to your hair?"

Danny was partially sighted, but Jules knew this wasn't the reason for him not noticing her new hairstyle or make-up. No, that was just down to Danny being a man.

"I washed it," she said.

"Is it that time of year again?" he teased and, taking her hand, led Jules into the restaurant before she could think of a witty retort.

She was too busy drinking in the sight of him to find words anyway. Sometimes Jules couldn't quite believe her luck that Danny was really and truly with her. He was just so absolutely gorgeous, with his short blond hair, wide-open face and high cheekbones. The scars and injuries didn't detract at all from his beauty; in fact they only made him more attractive because they spoke volumes about his honour and bravery and the journey he'd been on. Jules was immensely proud to have played a part in that journey – and when he smiled at her she thought she would melt.

Jules loved eating at Symon's. The restaurant, with its candles and subtle lighting, had an intimate and welcoming atmosphere. You could sit and talk quietly to somebody or celebrate a special occasion, feeling that you were being spoilt by Symon and his team. Whenever she'd eaten there, even if it was just a lunchtime bowl of soup, Jules had been made to feel valued and looked after. Usually Kelly or Tara greeted diners and seated them, but this evening the chef himself took their coats and saw them to their table.

"As promised, the quietest seats in the house," Symon told them, while Jules and Danny settled themselves at the back of the restaurant. He gave them both his sweet, shy smile and Jules was struck by just how like Danny and Jake he really was, despite the different hair colour. Symon's deep-red curls – the same sleek hue as autumn leaves, and at the moment tied up with a bandana – made his eyes seem even bluer. As always, his soft way of speaking made her want to draw closer, keen to hear more. Nevertheless, she thought that lately Symon had had a more pensive air about him than usual. His smile appeared less often, and Jules sensed something was worrying him deeply. You didn't work as a vicar without developing an instinct for these things.

"Thanks, fam, we need some time out," Danny said.

Symon nodded sympathetically. "Not a lot of peace at home right now, I can imagine? I did pop up earlier and it was all a bit chaotic. I think the only people who weren't in a state were our sisters, old and new. They seem to have palled up."

"More in common than they might have thought?" Danny wondered. "Gran's devastated that Emerald's staying in a caravan. She's longing to cluck over her."

"Maybe she should cluck over Dad a bit instead?" Symon suggested.

"Dad?" echoed Danny. "This is all his mess."

"Maybe, but perhaps we ought to think about why?"

"Err, because he's hopeless?" said Danny.

Symon handed them both a menu. His expression was thoughtful. "Is he really though? Why does he behave the way he does? Why did he run away when Mum died? Why's he never found anyone else? When you lose someone you care about – someone you love truly and deeply – you never get over it. It's like part of you has been… amputated."

"Tell me about it," said Danny, and Symon coloured when he realised what he'd said.

"Oh God, that was bloody tactless of me. Sorry, Dan."

"No, no, it's actually a pretty good analogy," said Danny slowly. "I'd never thought of it quite like that before."

Jules had; Jimmy's past behaviour seemed to her like evidence of a breakdown. Now, though, she was wondering who'd hurt Symon so badly. His words had come from the heart, that much was clear.

Poor Symon, puce with embarrassment, was talking about the menu instead.

"Tonight I recommend the monkfish," he was saying, "with the fresh dill and organic garden *pommes de terre* with butter and parsnip puree. Maybe some mackerel pâté for your starter? And blood-orange sorbet as a palate cleanser?"

Jules's mouth was watering already.

"Sounds good to me," Danny nodded. "I'm loving the way you describe Perry's potatoes! Garden *pommes de terre*? Maybe I could have a side of fries with ketchup instead?"

His brother winced. "Philistine. Jules? For you?"

"I'll have the same, please," Jules told him.

"And to drink? Sparkling water for you, Dan? Jules?"

Danny no longer drank alcohol but Jules decided she could always order herself a glass of champagne later on to celebrate.

"Sparkling water sounds perfect," she said.

Symon collected their menus and once he'd departed for the kitchen, Danny reached across the table and took Jules's hand.

"There's something I need to ask you and I'm so excited I don't think I can wait for our starters to arrive. Is that OK?"

Jules nodded her assent. Her heart was bouncing like a spacehopper. Oh goodness! This was it! He'd picked the perfect setting: the snowy table linen and the soft light from the candle couldn't have been more romantic.

"Jules, I've been trying to find the right time to tell you this," Danny began as his thumb caressed the back of her hand and longing licked through her like a flame, "but we're always interrupted or one of my family does something crazy and the moment goes." He laughed nervously. "I'm not very good at this telling people what I'm thinking stuff. Maybe I'm more like Dad than I thought?"

Usually Jules would have started babbling at this to put him at ease, but she held her tongue: these were words Danny had to speak.

"I've been thinking a lot about the future," Danny continued. "I love my life here in Polwenna with Morgan and my family and you. I love you, Jules. I hope you know that."

Jules nodded encouragingly and felt a flicker of excitement. This was it. Danny was getting ready to tell her something big. She could tell by the way his face had taken on a serious expression and the grip on her hand had tightened.

"Go on," she said gently.

He took a deep breath.

"I love you, Jules, but I love the army too. It was my life and I miss it every day. Working with Jake is great and being hands-on with Morgan is fantastic but I sometimes feel that there's something missing. Maybe it was being part of something bigger? I like feeling that I made a difference and I know I was good at my job. I have a duty to the army and I feel that I haven't finished with it yet." Warming to the topic, he carried on excitedly, "I've been talking to my old Lieutenant Colonel – he's the guy who commanded me for both my front-line tours – and he's suggested I apply for a desk-bound Staff Officer role in

London. I'll keep my rank too." He beamed at her. "I'd be back in the game. What do you think?"

What did she think? Jules couldn't think at all for a few seconds. She was utterly floored.

She'd always known that Danny's passion for the army had never waned and that he missed his career dreadfully. It hadn't just been his arm and some of his sight that had been lost when he was injured. But he was thinking about returning? And had been actively discussing going back? This was a huge shock.

And what did she think? That she couldn't have got things more wrong if she'd tried. Danny hadn't brought her here to propose. That had never been his intention. Her own pathetic hopes and dreams had stopped her from seeing what was really going on. It was all obvious now.

Danny had brought Jules here tonight to tell her he was leaving.

CHAPTER 14

Symon didn't often take time off but the past couple of weeks had been exceptionally stressful. His landlord wasn't prepared to renegotiate the lease, so the restaurant's future hung in the balance. On top of that, Emerald's arrival had thrown the family into uproar and the approaching tourist season meant that he was up until the small hours experimenting with new dishes to wow his customers. When Mo invited him over for a barbecue lunch, Symon found himself accepting and, what was more, actually looking forward to a break from work. He'd spent all morning preparing fish chowder, a firm favourite at the Seagull and famous for being served in sourdough bread bowls with a side portion of truffle fries. He'd also been making goujons from the delicate lemon sole Nick had delivered the day before. When Symon had left the restaurant, Perry had been in the kitchen unloading the latest produce, while Kelly, Tara and Tony had been readying the place for the lunch service. They were fully booked, his staff were doing their usual fantastic job and all was under control.

So why did he have an unpleasant churning sensation deep in the pit of his stomach?

Symon mulled this over as he walked up to Mo and Ashley's place – a large house known locally as Mariners, which stood on the headland keeping watch over the bay. The fact was, unless he found a new venue soon (which was bound to involve finding extra money as well), he was going to have to break some pretty bad news to his team. They worked so hard for him and Symon felt dreadful that he would be letting them down.

"Who died?" was Mo's opening gambit when she answered the door. Her wild red curls were pinned up on the top of her head with a bulldog clip and Isla was sitting on her hip, beaming her gappy smile at him.

"Nearly me! Your path is bloody steep," Symon grumbled, ruffling Isla's hair and giving his sister a hug. The Tess incident was forgiven, if not quite forgotten, and Mo leaned forward and hugged him back.

"Tell me about it. Nobody wants to deliver the shopping and I have to park miles away at Fernside. I'm starting to wish I'd never made all that fuss about Ashley bulldozing a road through the woods!"

"I thought you guys were getting a helipad? That's what Sheila Keverne told Kelly," Symon teased, and Mo rolled her eyes.

"If he's got money for a helicopter then he can get a new horse lorry first," she said. "I'll need it to get out and about this season."

"You're going to compete?" Symon was surprised.

"Of course I am," said Mo. "I've got Emerald helping with the horses now and that's given me lots more time. She rides like something out of the Wild West but I don't hold that against her. Paula's taking over the schooling, which means I can go out again."

"And Ashley's cool with that?"

A cloud flittered over Mo's face. "It's my decision, not his. Anyway, never mind all that right now; the others are on the terrace. I thought we'd eat outside as it's so mild."

That was a "no" then, thought Symon as he followed his sister through the vaulted open-plan expanse of Mariners' ground floor. The modern conversion had been designed by an award-winning architect and until recently had been an immaculate vision of blond wood, white sofas and painfully trendy (and Symon suspected even more painfully expensive) pieces of artwork. Now though, the place was littered with baby paraphernalia and Mo's tack. A baby gate guarded the bottom of the floating glass stairway, a bouncy swing had been set up in the huge archway between the kitchen and the living areas, and two saddles were slung over the sofa. Toys were everywhere too and for a surreal moment Symon wondered if he'd died and gone to Hamleys. For somebody who could barely walk, his niece certainly had a lot of kit. Symon wasn't convinced she needed a giant rocking horse when Mo had the real thing – and as for a Scalextric? That had to be Ashley's indulgence!

Mo shoved open a pair of enormous bifold doors and they stepped onto the terrace, where a big table was set up, complete with patio heaters and a barbecue being tended to by a fraught-looking Ashley. Smoke was rising, flames were leaping and oh no! That wasn't how it was done at all. What Ashley needed to do was—

"Don't you dare," warned Mo, seeing Symon glance over. "You are not to so much as flip a burger. Grab a beer and relax for once. *We're* cooking."

It was on the tip of Symon's tongue to say that things might be bad but that dying from food poisoning wasn't top of his list; however, the determined expression on Mo's face kept him quiet. Besides, he could always claim he was full. To be fair, it was true that he didn't have much of an appetite lately.

The fear of losing your business was certainly a good way to lose weight. Perhaps he could market that and make enough to save the restaurant?

It was a mild March day: the sky was blue, the sun was warm and the hedges and banks were exploding with flowers. On an afternoon like this in Cornwall, it was hard to believe it wasn't summertime. Mariners' terrace had the most spectacular view across the sea and a few determined day trippers had even braved the beach. A flotilla of yachts was peeping around the headland, their sails pregnant with the wind and the wake spreading behind them like lace as they zipped across the bay. Helping himself to a beer, Symon decided there were worse places to feel sick with worry.

Mo went to make sure Ashley was doing a good job of incinerating the burgers and Symon joined the others at the table. Tom Elliot from the hotel was in the middle of a story about his latest hotel nightmare and doing a wonderful impression of Ella giving him a telling-off, which had everyone in stitches. Nick was explaining the context of this to Emerald, who was understandably bemused, while Alice tutted and shook her head. Jake and Summer were deep in conversation with Tess, who caught Symon's eye and looked away hastily, and Morgan was busy taking photos. Even Jimmy was present, still looking sheepish, but making an effort to spend time with his newly discovered daughter.

"All right?" Danny asked, clinking his Coke bottle against Symon's Bud.

"Yeah, I'm good, mate." There was no point worrying his brother, Symon thought.

"No Jules today?"

Danny shrugged. "She said she was busy."

"Too busy for a burger? That doesn't sound like her," this was from Mo who, having passed Isla to Summer, was reaching into the cooler for a beer. "Are you guys OK?"

"I think so," Danny said. Then he frowned. "I can't think why we wouldn't be. She's been a bit off the past couple of weeks though. If it was anyone else I'd have thought I'd upset them, but you know Jules; she's always upfront. That's one of the things I love most about her."

"She seemed very quiet when you left the restaurant that Monday," Symon said. Jules had hardly touched her food and he'd fretted that there might be something wrong with it. She'd been very pale too and barely said goodbye. "Was she ill?"

"No. She was fine. Insisted on walking home by herself, which we had a bit of a squabble about, but there was nothing else going on." Danny took a big gulp of Coke and coughed as it fizzed up. "Shit! Beer never did that!"

Mo's blue eyes were narrowed. "What exactly were you guys doing in the Seagull on a Monday anyway?"

"Eating," said Danny. "It's this weird thing people do in restaurants."

"Ha ha. Very funny, smart arse," said Mo. "But on a Monday? It wasn't a special occasion or anything?"

"That's what I wondered when you asked for a quiet table, Dan," Symon agreed. It was probably best not to mention that Kelly and Tony had been taking bets on a proposal taking place. Big Rog had been certain he was going to win and, in the end, sick of endless texts from nosey villagers, Symon had confiscated Kelly's phone.

"Why wouldn't I ask for a quiet table? I had something really important to say about our future." Danny was looking perplexed.

Mo's hand flew to her mouth. "Oh my God! You've asked her to marry you! Congratulations! Can Isla be a bridesmaid?"

"Of course I haven't proposed!" Danny said. "What on earth gave you that impression?"

"Err, a secluded table in a romantic restaurant and on a Monday? Talking privately about the future?" Mo nudged Symon, slopping Budweiser onto the table in the process. "Go on, Sy. I bet you thought the same."

"Maybe," said Symon carefully. Not speculating about your customers was one of the golden rules of running a restaurant. No diner wanted to think they were being spied on by the chef and the waiters – as he'd tried to remind Kelly and Tony that night.

"And if we thought that, you can bet Jules did too!" Mo shook her head despairingly. "Men! You are all absolutely clueless and, yes, I count my own husband in that too before you ask. Lord, no wonder she's been off with you, Danny! I bet she thought you'd hidden a ring in the fish pie or something!"

Danny stared at her in horror. "No way!"

"Yes way," said Mo. "Out of interest, what did you want to talk to her about?"

"Mo, I don't think that's really our business—" Symon began, but Danny had drained of colour.

"I took Jules to dinner to tell her I've been thinking of applying for a desk job in London," he explained. "The army might want me back and I was hoping to sound her out and know what she thought. *That* was the news I had to tell her. I wasn't proposing."

"You utter muppet, Daniel Tremaine," said Mo. "You took Jules out for a romantic dinner to tell her you want to move away? Are you for real?"

"It wasn't like that at all," protested Danny. "I was excited about the job and the possibilities. It could be amazing for us both."

"But did you tell Jules that?" Mo asked, and Danny's groan was all the answer she needed.

Time to intervene, Symon decided. He'd been making peace between his siblings for years and he knew that once Mo got her teeth into something there wasn't a lot that would make her let go. The stricken expression on Danny's face told Symon that the last thing his brother needed was a Mo lecture.

"Are you going to let Ashley cremate the food or do I need to step in?" he asked as a cloud of black smoke billowed from the barbecue. This was enough to distract Mo and with a howl she fled across the terrace, leaving Danny and Symon alone.

"I've really messed up," groaned Danny.

"Nothing you can't fix." Symon thought of Claudette and his heart shivered. That was unfixable.

Danny stared at the horizon. The light played on the water, making it sparkle, and for a while he seemed totally absorbed. Symon sat quietly, not wanting to interrupt.

"The thing is, I do love Jules," Danny said finally, still looking out over the water. "She's everything to me but I love the army too and I'm excited about the prospect of a new role, even if it won't be active service. I still feel that I need to do my bit for the country and make a difference. I could come home at weekends, maybe even do four days a week? I think Tara and Morgan would be cool with it and I could see Jules too. Maybe she'd even move to London? Have a parish there?"

"Maybe," said Symon cautiously. "You'd be asking a lot of her though. She loves it here."

"So do I." Danny shook his head. "I feel so torn. Not about Jules – I love her and I want us to be together. That's settled in my mind and I thought it was in hers. But the army…" He sighed. "What can I say? This isn't about not loving Jules or my life here. It's about the army, Sy. I miss it. I *really* miss it."

"I understand," Symon said. "I miss Paris."

The two brothers didn't say any more. They didn't need to. An entire subtext flowed between them. Neither had ever questioned the other about the events and circumstances that had led them back to Polwenna Bay. There was a language of regret and despair in which they were both fluent; it was based on the tug of mutual sympathy. Symon sipped his drink and reflected that, unlike his brother, he didn't have a way back to the past. For him it literally was a foreign country.

"Maybe you should explain all this to Jules?" he said eventually. "Tell her how you feel about everything?"

"I intend to," Danny said. "In fact, I know exactly how I can show Jules how much she means to me and that my wanting to go to London doesn't mean the end for us. I've had a brilliant idea and it's actually down to Mo!"

Symon was about to ask what this might be, when they were joined by Tom.

"You two look very serious," he said, perching his designer-jean-clad backside on the bench beside Symon. "How can I cheer you up?"

"Lend me a few hundred grand?" Symon answered without thinking. Great. He'd just let Tom know he was worried about money. The whole village would find out within twenty minutes.

Tom whistled. "I couldn't lend you a tenner right now. In fact, I was thinking about asking Ella to sub me until payday. Not that there's much chance of that. She's tighter than a bodycon dress these days."

"What do you need a few hundred grand for?" Danny asked Symon quietly.

"Just a figure of speech," Symon said.

"He wants a sports car so he can keep up with Charlie," Tom grinned. "Rumour has it he's just had another pay rise too. You should be a celebrity chef, Sy. It's where the money is."

Symon shuddered. The money would be nice but all the press and exposure and people prying into your private life? *Especially* people prying into your private life. No thanks. It had been wonderful to have the glowing review in the national newspaper, of course, but that was as far as his interest in being famous went. There were some things that were better left hidden in the past. Time to leave this conversation and see what was going on with lunch. Maybe Ashley would like a hand? Symon knew from experience that there was nothing like cooking to take his mind off everything else.

Money worries, a broken heart, family matters; all these things melted away when he was focused on preparing food. Symon was determined to keep it that way.

CHAPTER 15

"You want three hundred orange gerberas? And three hundred purple dahlias? For next Saturday?"

Ella could hardly believe what she was hearing. With the big wedding under a week away the bride-to-be was calling now to tell her that she wanted to change the entire colour scheme and flower arrangement? Was Tabitha insane?

"I think the white lilies you chose are classic and beautiful," she said through gritted teeth, hoping that her irritation wasn't crackling down the lines. If it was, Tabitha Morr, ditzy star of *Born in Mayfair*, was too busy explaining her sudden change of heart to notice.

"I thought so too, Ella, but then I saw a psychic last week, that one off the telly. What's her name? Sally somebody or other? She's the real deal, everyone says so! Apparently she told Katie Price she was going to get married again, and she did! How awesome is that?"

Ella's new acrylic nails beat a tattoo on her desk as she fought to keep her cool. The customer was always right, she reminded herself sharply, even when they were a lunatic.

"Very awesome," she said, but Tabitha wasn't listening.

"And so Sparkly – you know Sparkly, right? She's on the show and she's dating that fit guy from *TOWIE*? Anyway, she said I should see that psychic too before I got married and OMG! She only told me orange is my wealth and prosperity colour and purple is my lucky colour. So I have to have those colours instead, because white is really unlucky for me. I was really freaked out for a bit but then Georgie said to call you and get you to sort it. He says that's your job. So thanks!"

It was at times like this that Ella wondered why she even bothered. Not only was she fighting Teddy, her grandfather and her head chef, but now even her clients were determined to make life as difficult as possible. She could walk away from all this, catch the first flight out to see her mother in Palm Beach and spend the next five years getting her nails done, going for lunch and dating billionaires. Why was she killing herself trying to prove to Jonny that she was the right person to run the hotel?

But Ella already knew the answer: this was who she was. Her mother was a trophy wife and Ella knew that twenty minutes of that existence would be enough to drive her insane. People around here might think she was a spoilt bitch who'd just walked into the family business, but they didn't see the whole story. They had no idea how long her days were or how much she'd given up to do this – and they would never find out either.

If she could take on her grandfather and survive knowing that most people in Polwenna Bay couldn't stand her, she could certainly sort out some flowers. *Woman up*, Ella told herself as she ended the call and promised Tabitha she'd deal with it. After all, girl power hadn't ended with the Spice Girls.

Ella replaced the phone in its cradle and massaged her temples. Right. Deep breath and then she'd break the news to the florist. The hotel would probably have to cover the costs of replacing the original order, which would eat into any profit, but she guessed she'd just have to suck it up. Ella was viewing this wedding as something of a loss-leader anyway. With luck, it would generate so much publicity that she'd be booked solid for months, if not years, ahead. She'd have to chalk up several thousand pounds spent on lilies as an advertising cost. It was fortunate that lilies were classic and classy; Ella would use them around the hotel anyway.

Ella was just writing *call florist* on her list of things to do when the office door flew open and Charlie Barton swaggered in – fully clothed today, thank goodness, but still wearing the same arrogant smirk. *How did I ever find Charlie attractive?* Ella wondered. Just the sight of him now was enough to make her teeth itch.

"What can I do for you, Charlie?" she asked evenly. Her face might have retained an impassive expression but inside she was frantically trying to pre-empt his next demand. It couldn't be a car, because she'd done that, and he'd already had a shockingly big pay rise. When it came to worldly goods Ella was almost cleared out, so she wasn't sure quite what else she could offer. Her first-born son perhaps, when (or if) the time came?

"Absolutely nothing," Charlie said. He stepped forward and placed an envelope on her desk. "Here. This is for you."

Ella's brows drew together. What was he writing to her for? And, more importantly, why was he dressed in jeans, a shirt and a leather jacket rather than his chef's uniform? It was lunchtime and all systems go in the hotel kitchen.

"What's this?" she asked, suddenly fearful.

"It's a letter," said Charlie. His eyes were bright with malice and he gave the envelope a shove in her direction with a stubby forefinger.

"I can see that," said Ella. She didn't pick it up. She had the sensation that it would burn her fingers, as acid might.

He looked at her expectantly. "Open it then."

"Why write to me? I'm right here," said Ella. "Whatever it is you need to say, just say it. I know things between us have become a little *complicated* lately but that shouldn't affect our working relationship. We're professionals." She paused. "This is about work?"

"It's not a love letter if that's what's worrying you," Charlie retorted, his voice dripping with sarcasm. "Quite the opposite, actually. It's my resignation."

Panic bloomed in Ella like black mould.

"Your resignation?" she echoed. "What are you talking about?"

"I'm leaving." He folded his arms across his chest, the leather jacket creaking as he did so. "I'm quitting. I'm out of here like last week."

"You can't resign. You're under contract."

Charlie laughed mirthlessly. "So sue me. It won't make any difference. I'm leaving. I've had enough of your airs and graces and superior attitude."

He was angry because she wouldn't sleep with him and Ella could have kicked herself for getting involved in the first place. He'd seemed fun and she was lonely, but in reality Charlie was a prima donna; men like that had fragile egos. She should have been gentler with him, carried on their relationship even, at least until the big wedding was over. She couldn't lose her celebrity chef right now. Georgie Angel would flip. He might even cancel the wedding.

Orange and purple flowers no longer seemed such a big deal...

"I'm sorry you see it like that or if I've given you that impression," she said slowly, trying her best to placate him and buy some time. "You're a wonderful chef."

Her voice didn't tremble and Ella hoped her expression remained neutral. She'd been cultivating her ice-maiden persona for occasions such as this, when to show one tiny flicker of fear would be admitting weakness. Characters like Charlie loved nothing more than feeling powerful and Ella would rather face an angry Georgie Angel than give Charlie the satisfaction of knowing he had the upper hand.

"You're not sorry at all. You just don't want to lose me from your precious hotel," said Charlie. "Well, hard cheese. I'm going. I've been offered a head chef job in Rock for twice the money you pay and half the crap."

Ella stared at him.

"But what about Georgie Angel's wedding? He and Tabitha are so excited about you doing the food," she said, attempting to appeal to his better nature. This was pointless, of course, since Charlie didn't have one.

"They'll get over it," answered Charlie. "See you, Ella. And good luck. You'll need it."

And with this parting shot he was gone, sauntering out of her office without so much as a backwards look.

Now the panic really did set in. Ella didn't think Georgie and Tabitha would *get over it*. Charlie Barton was one of the main reasons they'd booked the Polwenna Bay Hotel in the first place. For the first time in her life Ella had no idea what to do or how to sort this problem out. Her head was spinning.

A drink. She needed a drink. Once she had a whiskey in her hand and her heartbeat had slowed she could try to make a plan and get ahead of the game once more – but right now she just needed some time out.

Five minutes later she was sitting on a stool at the hotel bar with one empty glass being swiftly replaced by another. Alcohol burned a trail of fire into her belly and as she sipped her next drink Ella was seriously tempted to throw caution to the wind and just get blindingly drunk. How blissful would it be to slide into oblivion and let somebody else deal with this mess? If only there was somebody she could turn to, someone who would put his arm around her and tell her everything would be just fine. But women like her didn't have that luxury, did they? Summer Penhalligan and Mo Carstairs did. Even the vicar had Danny on side. Tears prickled Ella's eyelids. She was so, so tired of always carrying the load.

Was this what defeat felt like?

"Are you OK?"

It was Tom Elliot. Clad in his suit and with his spiky red hair gelled and styled to within an inch of its life, her assistant manager was looking alarmed. Ella didn't blame him. In all their months of working together, Tom had never seen her hit the booze.

"Ella?" He leaned closer and his eyes widened when he sniffed her drink. "Is that whiskey? Drinking on shift is frowned on at the Polwenna Bay Hotel, you know. What if our boss finds out?"

"Go away, Tom," said Ella. Was it really too much to have just a few moments out?

"Is this because of Charlie walking out?" Tom was asking, hopping up onto the stool next to her and gently unpeeling her fingers from the glass and placing it out of reach. "Don't let that tosser drive you to drink."

Ella groaned. If Tom knew then so did the rest of the staff. There went any vague hopes she might have had of keeping Charlie's absence a secret until the wedding was over. "You all know about that?"

He nodded. "Afraid so. Charlie couldn't wait to gloat about it. He always was an utter, utter dick."

"An utter dick who's a genius chef and who's supposed to be catering for Georgie Angel's wedding." Ella reached for her drink. "Give that back, Tom. As your boss I'm ordering you."

"And as your very responsible assistant manager I am not letting my senior manager get plastered when we have a crisis on our hands. Anyway, this isn't the disaster you think it is."

It wasn't?

"Have *you* been drinking? Tom, this is as bad as it gets. Our celebrity chef has just walked out days before the biggest wedding we've ever had."

"He's overrated anyway," Tom said airily. "We all know Klaus does the work while Charlie poses for the cameras and flirts with the waitresses. We'll cope without him. You'll see."

"But Klaus isn't a top chef," Ella pointed out. "He's good and he does work hard but Charlie has that dash of genius. Yes, we all know it borders on megalomania, but when he's on it, he's fantastic. That's what Georgie Angel is expecting and Klaus just won't cut it. We need a top chef."

Tom nodded. He got it. "So what's the plan now?" he asked. "Apart from getting drunk, obviously."

Ella stared thoughtfully into the mirror opposite. Her fragmented reflection danced among the bottles and optics. "I need a top chef and I need one by the weekend," she said. "So unless you can find me one I think getting drunk may well be our best option."

They sat in silence for a few moments before Tom whooped and clapped his hands so loudly Ella nearly toppled off her stool.

"Not for the first time do I amaze myself. I really am your fairy godmother!" cried Tom. "I know *exactly* where you can find a brilliant chef by the weekend. Even better, he's only minutes away and I know he needs the cash! You can hire him this afternoon!"

Ella fixed Tom with one of her killer stares. "What on earth are you talking about now?"

"Not what, who! Symon Tremaine, of course! He's an incredible chef, a zillion times better than *Charlie by name Charlie up his nose Barton*! Ella, it's a perfect solution! I'm a bloody genius. You should have given me the Range Rover and the pay rise."

"Symon Tremaine? You have to be kidding."

"I'm deadly serious. He's a brilliant chef, he's local, he's catered here before, he's practically family, he trained in Paris," Tom was checking all these attributes off on his fingers and looking more excited by the second. Ella wished she shared his enthusiasm.

"Why on earth would Symon want to help me? The Tremaines loathe the St Miltons."

Tom rolled his eyes. "This isn't the time for petty squabbles. Besides, Symon doesn't hate you. He's not like that. He doesn't hate anyone. He's a really nice guy."

This was probably true. Ella had never heard anyone say a bad word about Symon (except perhaps Big Rog Pollard, who'd moaned that there hadn't been enough food on his plate at The Plump Seagull). Unlike Mo and Issie, Symon had always been polite to Ella – and he hadn't broken her heart like Jake had, either.

Maybe he would help? Since top chefs weren't exactly queuing at the door it had to be worth a try.

Reaching across for her drink, Ella downed it, slammed the glass onto the bar and hopped off her stool.

"Where are you going?" Tom asked, startled.

"To see Symon," Ella replied.

After all, what did she have to lose? Except the hotel's good name of course. Besides, it couldn't hurt to ask him; Symon Tremaine might just surprise her.

CHAPTER 16

March was a quiet, in-between kind of month in Polwenna Bay and on a weekday trade at The Plump Seagull tended to be fairly slow. Symon, standing in the kitchen doorway, could count his customers on one hand. The initial buzz following the write-up in the newspaper seemed to have died down somewhat.

The window seat was taken by a forty-something couple sharing a bucket of moules and some crusty bread. A bottle of sparkling water, a bowl of fries and some complimentary onion tartlets were laid out before them, but Symon knew from experience that this would be the full extent of their order. There would be no ice buckets of champagne; nor would there be any caviar or expensive cheese courses making their way to this table. Judging by their sturdy footwear and the anoraks that Tara had placed in the cloakroom, these two were walkers stopping off to refuel before continuing on their way to the next bay. They wouldn't want anything too heavy.

The only other diner today was Richard Penwarren, the local GP and Tara's partner, who'd popped in to see his girlfriend and grab a bite to eat. He was sitting in a corner tucking into a bread bowl of chowder. Symon knew that Richard would order a coffee after this before dashing back to the surgery – again, no wine or desserts for him.

Better not order the Ferrari yet.

It was a sparkling and crisp day, the kind that showed Cornwall in its best light. The window boxes were exploding with primroses and crocuses and the beach was basking in honey-hued sunshine. Much as Symon loved the spring weather, he'd been quietly hoping for a drizzly grey week – not wet enough to keep the day trippers and early visitors inside museums or holiday cottages, but just damp enough to make them long for hot soup and comfort food inside a cosy restaurant. On sunny days like this they were far more likely to grab something from Patsy's Pasties and eat on the quay, or even brave The Ship's beer garden.

Usually Symon popped into the dining area and chatted with his customers, asking them about their food or telling them a little bit about the village, but today he didn't have the energy. Or maybe even more than that, he didn't have the heart. The couple were enjoying being together and Richard was engrossed in a book propped up against his bread bowl. It was almost quarter to two and since there was no sign of anyone else arriving Symon was better off prepping for tonight. That would keep him busy and stop him worrying about the day's low takings and the increasingly pressing question of what to do when the lease on the premises expired. Past experience had taught Symon that chopping, slicing, filleting and marinating emptied the mind and kept all other problems at bay. It had saved him before when he'd thought he was broken beyond repair, and it would save him now from spiralling into a rapidly deepening chasm of debt and despair.

He turned his attention back to the kitchen. The longer he could put off facing reality the better.

"Shall I make a start on the monkfish, Chef?" Tony was asking, his round face bright with enthusiasm. He was a talented local chef and the thought of letting him down made Symon feel ill. The same for Kelly who, although she drove him mad, was gradually becoming something of a sommelier. If he could only afford to train her properly or send her to Paris to spend a week with Claudette... Unbidden, the image of dark eyes smiling at him over a glass of blood-red wine flickered through his memory and Symon's heart turned over.

"Chef? Shall I start?"

Shaken by the memory, Symon nodded hastily. "Yes, good idea. I'm going to think about what can go with it."

"I can help with that!" This was Perry, staggering through the back door and laden with a huge crate. All but collapsing onto the floor with it, he announced proudly, "The celeriac's looking amazing, if I say so myself."

"Perfect. Celeriac and sweet potato mash," said Symon. Food. Think of food. He had a million recipes crammed inside his head, surely enough to ensure there was no room for thoughts of the past?

While Tony set to work, Symon helped Perry unload, marvelling at the beautiful field mushrooms with their delicate gills, the frilly winter greens that were the same jewel-bright hue as his new sister's name, and the mass of sweet potatoes still clad in peat. Already his mind was imagining what wonderful dishes he could create to do justice to all this, and the old excitement was igniting.

"You've certainly got a flair for growing excellent produce, Perry," he said, and his friend flushed at the praise.

"Just as well I'm good at something. Maybe I should try paying off the overdraft with veg? What do you think the exchange rate is for carrots?"

Symon laughed bleakly. "I was wondering the same for chowder. At this rate you and I will be bankrupt together."

"That bad?"

"Between us, yes, I think so," Symon told him. Once they were out of earshot and unstacking Perry's produce in the cold store, he added, "My takings are a bit low at the moment, even after that review. Worse, the landlord doesn't want to renew the lease when it comes to an end. He probably wants to convert the premises into a holiday cottage, I imagine. I don't know how I'll afford another place with the way things are; all the prices are sky-high."

"He's seen a potential goldmine in this building," Perry observed.

Symon nodded. "It's going to happen right across the county, especially if people stop buying second homes abroad and head to Cornwall."

"Maybe an oligarch will want to buy the manor," Perry said hopefully. Then his face fell. "Bugger, forgot the bloody place is entailed. I'll probably have to live in a caravan and rent it out for glamping. Hey! That's a brilliant idea, don't you think? Glamping's huge. That could work!"

Over the past two years Perry had been the enthusiastic genius behind many brilliant ideas, none of which had turned out to be quite as brilliant as he'd originally believed. Polwenna Manor's tithe barn contained the relics of these grand schemes: they included a rusting cider press, crates of mildewed leaflets for Polwenna Ghost Tours, ten beehives purchased for the Manor Honey venture (Perry was allergic to bees as it turned out) and a punctured bouncy castle. It didn't require a huge leap of imagination to picture a pile of cobweb-draped yurts joining this collection.

They set to unpacking, both men deep in thought, and by the time they'd finished Symon was ready to throw himself in the River Wenn. Judging from the expression on his friend's face, Perry wouldn't be far behind him. With everything now stored away, Symon made them both a coffee, which they carried into the empty restaurant.

"Something will turn up. You're very talented," Perry said, but he didn't look too hopeful. If even Perry's optimism was on the wane, then things were looking grim.

Symon was about to reply that no mattered how talented he might be, nothing short of winning that evening's lottery would help. It was at this moment that the restaurant door opened and a tall slim blonde glided inside.

His heart sank. Ella St Milton. What now?

"Lunch is finished, I'm afraid," he said politely.

Ella tucked a strand of hair behind a shell of an ear. Her face was flushed and she looked decidedly hot and bothered.

"I'm not here to eat," she replied.

Of course she wasn't. Women like Ella didn't eat. They lunched *à deux* in trendy restaurants where they pushed a few Parmesan-sprinkled rocket leaves about their plates before declaring themselves *stuffed*. Similarly, Claudette would rather have died than eaten more than a morsel of the beautiful food served in Papillon Rouge.

"I'm here to see you, actually."

"Right," he said, feeling cautious. What was it? Were Granny Alice and Jonny back on again? Had Nick delivered the wrong fish? Or maybe this was industrial espionage and she was on a mission for Charlie Barton?

Ella looked nervous. A triangle of pink tongue darted over her lips and she was clasping her hands tightly in front of her.

"I've got a proposition for you. Hear me out before you say anything, because I think it could work really well for us both."

Ella was rarely seen in the village; something must be up, for her to make the effort to visit the restaurant. Judging from her rosy cheeks and the slightly untidy hair she was smoothing back into place, she'd actually walked down over the cliff path rather than hopping into one of her fleet of luxury cars. Despite not liking the woman, Symon was curious.

"In that case you'd better have a seat," he said, rising and pulling one out for her. "Can I get you a drink? Perry and I are on coffee but the bar's fully stocked."

Was it his imagination or did she colour even more at this?

"I don't drink when I'm working," she snapped.

So this was a work proposition then. She probably wanted some catering done for one of Charlie's day's off. Mentally, he was already totting up his costs and adding another couple of noughts for good measure. Yes, that might help.

"Let me fetch you a coffee and we can talk," he said.

"In private would be good," Ella told him, looking pointedly at Perry. "And I don't need a coffee. Thanks."

Symon's hackles rose. Who did she think she was, swanning into his restaurant, demanding to speak to him and deciding who could and couldn't be present? Typical St Milton behaviour. Only they would lord it over an actual Lord!

"I'll go and finish up in the kitchen," Perry said tactfully.

"So what's all this about?" Symon asked Ella once his friend was gone.

That pink tongue flicked over her lips again. They were full and plump and Symon looked away. He felt oddly disconcerted.

"Look, this isn't easy to say so I'll come straight out with it." Ella's hands were still clenched tightly. She was on edge, almost trembling with nerves, and her grey eyes seemed troubled.

Symon, who had a kind heart, smiled encouragingly at her. "Go on."

"I need your help. Charlie Barton's walked out on me and we've got Georgie Angel's wedding on Saturday. I'm without a head chef."

Symon whistled. This was low even for Charlie Barton, who in his opinion was a first-class tosser. No wonder Ella looked stressed.

"It's a mess and I have no idea how we can carry on without him unless another chef's able to step in. I know it's at short notice but would you possibly do it?"

Short notice? The wedding was three days away. Everyone in the village was talking about it. Little Rog was convinced that if he staked the hotel out one of Little Mix would be bound to take pity on him. Meanwhile, Jake was so wound up about Justin Anderson's imminent arrival that he was all but chiming.

"I don't think so, Ella." Symon couldn't think of anything worse than having to pick up Charlie's mess. He knew lots of the staff at the hotel and they'd all told him horror stories. In fact, Klaus had visited The Plump Seagull several times to sound out the possibility of a job. Symon could imagine that the bulk of the preparation was still to be done and that Charlie, the kind of chef who flew by the seat of his pants, hadn't even thought about finalising the menu. At Charlie's behest, someone had probably persuaded the bride and groom that it was best to wait for their celebrity chef to come up with something bespoke nearer the time, rather than planning too far ahead in advance and spoiling the surprise. In other words, the menu would be made up on the spur of the moment when Charlie could be arsed to think about it.

It would be utter chaos and Symon's head ached just at the thought.

"I'm flat out here too," he added, crossing his fingers under the table. Bookings were bound to pick up soon, weren't they?

An expression that looked like panic flickered across Ella's perfectly made-up face.

"I know it's a big ask but I'll pay you really well. I'll match what Charlie would have made and I'll even throw in a bonus. It will win you a lot more bookings for here too. You know it will, Symon. The hotel will be crammed with celebrities all eating your food, hearing your name and talking about you. It'll be fantastic advertising."

She was good.

"It sounds like I should be paying you," Symon remarked drily.

Ella smiled. "You've said it! But seriously, I'd really like you to do this. You're an exemplary chef and we both know you're ten times better than Charlie anyway. Just think of the opportunity this could be to showcase your talent, get media attention for The Plump Seagull and stick two fingers up at Charlie, who'll be expecting it all to fall flat on its face. You can really show him."

Charlie was a huge show-off and Symon had been the recipient of many sneering comments from him, as well as having his suspicions about the origins of some nasty rumours. He had to admit that it would be very satisfying to better his rival. The extra money and publicity were enticing too. All the same, Symon knew that this job could be a poisoned chalice. Part of him wanted to tell Ella to stick her offer anyway, because she'd treated his family appallingly in the past. And yet, he sensed that beneath Ella's apparent confidence and her smooth sales pitch she was utterly terrified. Taking everything into consideration, Symon was sorely tempted to rise to the challenge.

"How much are we talking about?" he asked, and Ella named a figure that made him glad he was sitting down. He couldn't turn this down. No way.

"OK," he said. "I'll do it."

"You will? Oh, that's brilliant!"

Symon hadn't seen Ella St Milton smile properly before. He'd seen her lips curve upwards in a polite expression, but he'd never witnessed her real smile. It was one that filled her eyes with sparkles, softened the sharp edges of her face and popped two cute dimples in her cheeks.

Symon stared at her transfixed. She was utterly beautiful.

"Thank you!" Ella cried. "That's wonderful!"

"It's a pleasure," Symon replied, feeling a little as though he'd looked too long at the sun and couldn't quite focus anymore. Her smile was imprinted on his vision even though it had swiftly been replaced by her habitual measured expression. Feeling thrown, he added, "Just make sure Justin Anderson keeps out of my way."

"Totally," Ella promised. "You won't even know he's there. I promise."

She held out her hand and they shook on the deal. Ella was now busy discussing the details, but Symon was unable to put aside the unexpected glimpse of that excited girl behind the icy façade. This aspect of Ella had vanished as quickly as it had appeared; by the time Ella departed, promising to email some further information and a contract once she was back at her desk, Symon was wondering if he'd imagined it.

Of course he had. This was Ella St Milton, wasn't it? Everyone knew she didn't have a nice side – and Symon told himself sharply that he ought to keep this in mind.

After all, nobody knew better than him exactly what could happen when two people were thrown together in a hot and busy kitchen.

CHAPTER 17

"You are going to love Symon's grub! Trust me on this one! Our brother might be socially inept but he's a great chef."

Emerald hadn't known her brother Nick for very long, but there were two things she thought she'd figured out. The first was that Nick liked to party hard and the second was that when he said to trust him it was really best not to. So far, he'd told her to trust him when he said that Cornish pasties were the world's greatest culinary experience ever (two days on, Emerald's stomach still hurt from the carb-filled assault) and to trust him that all his mates were "mint". Bobby and Joe Penhalligan were nice enough, even if their conversation about fishing and constant questions about cheerleaders soon became wearisome, but the one called Little Rog hardly said a word. Instead he just stared at her. In the end, convinced that she must have something in her teeth or a massive spot thanks to her new English diet of pasties, fries and cream teas, Emerald had fled to the bathroom to check.

"Don't mind Little Rog. He doesn't get out much, that's all. I heard he went to Plymouth once but that might be an exaggeration," Nick had explained when Emerald asked what the problem was. "You're from America, that's why he's gobsmacked. You may as well have come from the moon!"

Emerald was learning that the Brits had a very odd sense of humour. Nick was exaggerating. Right? Or maybe not? It was very hard to tell.

And anyway, what on earth did *gobsmacked* mean?

"And while we're talking about our friends, do you have any who are cheerleaders? Or, even better, who work at Hooters? Would they like to visit?"

Nick had yelped when Emerald had walloped him and called him a sexist, which had been the end of that conversation.

Today Emerald was meeting Jimmy in The Plump Seagull and she'd bumped into Nick on the way. Together they'd wandered through the village, with Nick pointing out characters and landmarks and filling her in on gossip and history. Emerald tried to take it all in but there was so much to remember that her brain felt as though it was overflowing. She'd wanted roots and history though!

"And that's Silver Starr. She runs the psychic shop and she's a total fraud. Don't ever get your hair cut in Kursa's salon: she'd be better off topping verges for the council. And unless you want to be his latest muse, avoid that guy over there. He's our resident writer."

"Gotcha," Emerald said. The man in question looked like he'd stepped out of a Jane Austen novel. Did guys really still wear cravats and frock coats here?

"OK. That's the end of today's tour. I'm off to the pub. Sy's place is just up that road," said Nick, pointing to a narrow cobbled side street. "And well done on pinning Dad down, by the way. None of us can ever manage it!"

A lunch date with Jimmy was indeed something of a coup. In the short time since she'd arrived, Emerald had soon learned that her father was as elusive as the Cornish mist and equally capable of vanishing in an instant. It had come as a surprise when Jimmy had pulled up at the stables and asked her if she wanted to have lunch. She'd hardly seen him since she'd arrived in Polwenna Bay, but then she'd been so busy getting to know the rest of her family and helping Mo out. This arrangement was generally going well, with the exception of her sister freaking out when Emerald rode one of the horses like a barrel-racing pony.

"What the hell are you trying to do? Break your neck?" Mo had screeched, flying across the arena and practically dragging Emerald off the horse. "This isn't the Wild bloody West!"

"He was going real fast!" Emerald had protested. She was totally confused. Wasn't this the whole point?

"He's not supposed to go fast in here! It's a dressage arena!" Mo had sprung into the saddle and then spent the next ten minutes trotting around in circles, which looked neat but made Emerald yawn. She couldn't imagine a stadium filled with cheering crowds wanting to watch *that*. Not for the first time since she'd arrived in England, Emerald felt lost and rather homesick. Not that she'd admit this to a soul. No way. When her mom called, Emerald just told her what an awesome vacation she was having – and Leaf, being Leaf, didn't question this. If Emerald went to sleep each night in the rather damp caravan wondering why she was here and longing for warmth, she'd rather die than let on.

Besides, it all made great material for her vlog. Maybe she'd be the next big YouTube sensation. An American teenager in England? It could work. As soon as she got some decent broadband she'd upload some of the entries. You never knew and, anyway, her friends back home would just love to see what she was up to. The English guys were kind of hot too, if you ignored their wonky teeth and love of beer…

"Hey, you two!"

It was her brother Danny, waving and hurrying towards them. His face was split with a smile and he looked excited. Morgan, camera in hand, was with him and on seeing Emerald started taking photos.

"It's to add you to my family pictures," he explained and Emerald, thrilled to be included, posed happily.

"Glad to have caught you, Nick," said Danny. "I need a favour."

"I'm not babysitting for the squirt," Nick said, ruffling Morgan's hair and neatly sidestepping as his nephew lunged at him.

"I'm not a baby!"

"It's just a turn of phrase, mate," said Danny quickly. "Anyway, it'd be you looking after your uncle and you'd need danger money."

"I'd just take him to the pub," Morgan told his father matter-of-factly. "Grand Granny says he lives there anyway."

From what Emerald had seen of her new brother this was a fair assessment. What was it with Brits and pubs anyway? No wonder the legal drinking age in the UK was eighteen – as Nick had delightedly told her. When Emerald had informed him that she didn't drink, he'd been floored.

"So what do you do for fun back at home?" he'd asked and she'd shrugged.

"Read books? Write? Yoga? Go hiking?"

"Blimey," Nick had said. "Are you sure we're related?"

"What I need from you guys is some practical help," Danny continued now. "I'm organising the village Easter Egg Hunt and I could do with a hand – seeing as I only have one these days!"

"I thought that Easter egg stuff was Jules's job?" Nick asked. "It's all in the Bible, right?"

Danny gave him a withering look. "Oddly enough I don't think the Easter Bunny and chocolate eggs feature strongly in the New Testament. Anyway, Jules has got enough on. What I'll need is some help placing the eggs and organising the children. There's one egg that I'll need to make sure they don't find because it's going to be a big surprise for Jules."

"What is it? A monster Easter egg? Giant chocolate bunny?" guessed Nick, but Danny tapped his nose.

"None of your business. So, can I count you in?"

"Sure," nodded Emerald.

"Buy us a pint and I might consider it," Nick agreed grudgingly.

"See what a mercenary this brother of ours is?" Danny said to Emerald. "He won't even help the vicar without a bribe. Isn't that shocking?"

Nick was unabashed. "There needs to be something in it for me, fam! Those kids are savage when they're hunting for chocolate!"

Emerald laughed. She could imagine that kids looking for candy were a force to be reckoned with. And talking of kids hunting for things, now that Jimmy had resurfaced Emerald didn't want to miss him by running late. She was glad that they'd have some time to catch up at last. Their sun-drenched lunches in California and drives along Big Sur felt as though they belonged to another father and daughter. Emerald totally understood that she'd put Jimmy on the spot by turning up here unannounced, but she hadn't expected him to be constantly busy.

He was avoiding her – but not for much longer. Today she would finally pin him down and ask a few questions.

Once she'd said goodbye to her brothers, Emerald headed towards Symon's restaurant. The short walk gave her a few moments to gather her thoughts as well as to marvel at the cobbles and the whitewashed cottages, as picturesque as anything she'd seen at Disney. With the diamond-paned windows, crumpled rooftops and a merry little river chuckling under a tiny bridge, she thought it was a dead ringer for that street in Harry Potter where the magic wands were sold.

This was more like it! Emerald paused to snap a couple of pictures to upload to her Instagram feed.

#England #Cornwall #cute #cottages

Her friends at home would go crazy. They'd already gone crazy over her pictures of Nick – not that Emerald would tell him so. Nick was already full of his own blond good looks and didn't need encouraging. Several of these friends were also cheerleaders, something else that Emerald was keeping to herself. She wouldn't put it past Nick to borrow her phone and start texting them all. Besides, her friends would be way more excited about Zak Tremaine. They'd think having a rock-musician brother was so cool and although Emerald had only spoken to him on Skype, she had to agree. Zak had an easy-going vibe – unlike her sister Issie, who'd made it obvious during their FaceTime session that she wasn't happy to meet an interloper.

Emerald sighed. This was all way harder than she'd ever imagined. She hated to admit it but maybe her mom had been right? Leaf had thought it was better to let her new family seek her out, but Emerald had been so excited at the thought of her English roots and family, as well as charmed by Jimmy on his visits, that she'd ignored this gentle advice. Now she was beginning to wonder (secretly, because she'd never admit as much) whether this hadn't been a huge mistake. Everyone apart from Issie was being accommodating, but they had their own lives to deal with, didn't they?

At least having Mo's caravan as her base was working well. It afforded her a little break from the intensity of her new family and Emerald guessed they might well feel the same. After all, she was the new arrival and, now that she knew her existence had come as a shock to everyone, Emerald was keen to give them some space to take it all in. Mom was big on giving people space for their own soul journeys; in Mom's case this applied to boyfriends and landlords mostly, but even so Emerald figured that in terms of taking pressure off it worked. Living up at the caravan and helping Mo with stable chores was the perfect compromise. She was getting to know Mo and having fun learning to ride English style too. Granny Alice was kind but much too full on; she always wanted to cook for Emerald and look after her. Having fended for herself for much of the past eighteen years, Emerald found this suffocating. Nick's endless questions and insistence she came out drinking with him was exhausting as well. Danny and Jake were nice but they were older and had their own things going on, and Symon seemed to do nothing but work. Then there were the partners and children and complicated family histories to unravel… All in all, it was making Emerald's head hurt and she was starting to wonder whether her dream of a big family should have stayed just that.

But too late now. Here she was at The Plump Seagull and there was Jimmy, sitting in the window seat. With his grey hair pulled back in a ponytail, and wearing wrap-around mirrored shades perched on the top of his head and an open-neck shirt with a gold chain, he looked like most sixty-something guys in San Francisco and oddly out of place in Cornwall. His top teeth were worrying his bottom lip and his brow was crinkled. Emerald felt her stomach fold with tenderness. Maybe it was because she didn't know Jimmy as well as the others, or perhaps it was simply because she didn't have their expectations of what he should be as a father, but at that very moment Emerald felt she really saw *him* as a person. Jimmy was as scared and confused and lost as everyone else on the planet; being her father didn't make him any wiser.

As though sensing her thinking about him, Jimmy glanced up. Catching sight of her, he waved delightedly. Emerald waved back. He was a nice man, too nice to face reality, which maybe was his hamartia? His fatal flaw? (Mike, the English teacher, had been a fan of Aristotle.) Mulling this over, Emerald joined him inside, where they hugged hello, talked a little then browsed the menu, eventually plumping for the chowder. It was a San Francisco favourite she often enjoyed and Emerald was horrified to feel tearful as she thought of Pier 39, the vibrant sunny streets and the trolleys clanking up the steep hills. Luckily Jimmy was busy chatting to the waitress taking their order, which gave Emerald time to blink the tears away.

"Where's Symon today, Kelly?" Jimmy was asking, peering over the waitress's shoulder as the service door swung open. "He's not taken a Saturday off, surely?"

The girl laughed. "Yeah, right. Your son doesn't know what a day off is. I'm lucky I get one! No, he's up at the hotel doing the wedding."

Jimmy looked blank.

"The celebrity wedding at the Polwenna Bay Hotel? Georgie Angel and Tabitha Morr?" Kelly shook her head when Jimmy still didn't react. "The whole village has only been talking about it for months."

Jimmy gave Emerald a rueful smile. "I've had one or two other things on my mind lately. So how come Symon's involved? I thought they had a famous chef?"

"Who decided to quit at the eleventh hour," Kelly said, wide-eyed and loving the drama. "Sy's stepped in to save the day. We've hardly seen him since Ella came and begged for help. Tony's going spare."

"Sounds like Symon," said Jimmy, ignoring the last part of this. "He's got such a kind heart, that boy. I hope the St Miltons aren't taking advantage."

"We all reckon Evil Ella's paying him loads," Kelly said. "Nobody would work for her otherwise."

Emerald was trying to keep up with all of this but it was impossible. Figuring out who was who in this village was like watching all the episodes of a soap in one hit and not in the right order. Everyone seemed to be related to everyone else or had been married to them or was feuding with them.

"Welcome to Polwenna," was Jimmy's wry response when Emerald voiced this observation. "And talking of being related to everyone, how are you finding it? Are the kids being nice to you?"

Emerald, who'd been about to take a sip of her mineral water, spluttered into her drink at this casual remark.

"If you'd been about lately, you'd know," she shrugged. "Why have you been avoiding me?"

The blue eyes slipped away like ketchup slipping down a hot dog.

"I haven't, love. I've been busy working at the marina."

"That's bull." Emerald gave him a stern look. "You've hidden because you think I want something or that I'm going to upset your family. And you feel guilty about them and bad about me. You can't please us all, so you hide."

Jimmy stared down at the snowy white linen. "I do feel bad about it all. I feel awful that you grew up without me and I'm ashamed that I wasn't there."

"But I know that wasn't down to you! It was Mom's choice."

"Maybe, but I should have kept in touch with her at least. She was a sweet girl and she was there for me when… when…" He paused, visibly gathered himself and then continued. "Your mum was there for me during a rough time in my life. I wish I'd been there for her in return."

Emerald nodded. She and Jimmy had already had this conversation.

"Hey, it's OK. Mom never thought that. She wanted a baby," she said gently. "She wanted me."

"And so would I have done if I'd known about you." Jimmy reached across the table for her hand. His was trembling. "Emerald, I feel like I've let you both down and I guess I didn't want my family to know that. It's pathetic but that's how I felt. They already think I'm a useless father, yes they do!" Seeing

Emerald about to protest, his tone grew firmer. "I've heard Jake and Danny talking about me. They think I don't know it but they don't trust me near the business. I don't blame them; whenever I have an idea it goes wrong. Christ, I used to hear my mother and father too. Useless. Weak. Feckless. Those were the words your grandfather used to like to use when describing me."

"He sounds like a real fun guy," said Emerald drily.

Jimmy laughed. "I don't think Pa knew what fun was. It was all about duty and the army with him, and I was never going to be forces material. I grew up listening to him criticising me on a daily basis and maybe he was right? Maybe I am a useless waste of time."

Not having a dad was better than growing up with a bad one, Emerald realised.

"Of course he wasn't," she said. "Hey, you're a great dad, I can see that. The others love you to bits no matter what."

But Jimmy wasn't listening. "My old man had some good qualities too, don't get me wrong. He was determined, stubborn and brave – so you can see where you get those parts of your personality from! I suppose he was old school. He'd fought in the war and he had high standards. I just didn't reach them. When I met Penny, my wife, it was as though the world suddenly made sense. Penny liked me. She saw me. She believed in me. Together there was nothing we couldn't do. "

He was still holding her hand. Emerald squeezed his.

"You must have missed her so much."

"I still miss her every day," Jimmy said quietly. "Pen made me believe I could be the man I always wanted to be. I was able to be the person she deserved, the person she saw. When I lost her it felt as though I lost everything."

There was a silence, interrupted only by the chink of cutlery against china and the rise and fall of murmured conversations.

Emerald thought she understood.

"Your family are all you have left of that love. You were afraid that if you told them about me then that would destroy everything that was left."

Jimmy sighed, slipped his hand away and reached for his drink. Swirling it thoughtfully, he said, "I suppose so. Deep down I wanted to uphold that perfect love. Unsullied. Pure. You mum and I were friends…"

He flushed and Emerald, who'd grown up with Leaf and her string of *friends* took pity on him.

"It's OK, Jimmy. I'm not here thinking you and Mom were Romeo and Juliet. I know how these things go. It was fun and that was all. You travelled, tried to mend your broken heart in a faraway land and then came home. The way I see it, it's no big deal. It's how life is."

He shook his head wonderingly. "How did you get so level-headed so young?"

Emerald smiled. "You get to watch a lot of Oprah when you're home-schooled! And I read a heck of a lot. Heathcliff never got over Catherine, right? And you never got over your Penny. I think it's really romantic – and so will the others if you tell them what you've told me."

"There's been nobody since," he said softly. "Or at least nobody who matched up to Penny. There never could be. You see, Emerald, when a Tremaine gives their heart they give it one hundred percent, body and soul. We love for life."

And Emerald, in the warmth of the restaurant, shivered at these words. In reality, they didn't seem quite so romantic. Hearts once given could be broken, in some cases never to be mended again, and the idea of giving your love totally and utterly suddenly seemed very scary indeed.

If it was love that had made Jimmy Tremaine this sad and lonely then, thought Emerald, you could keep it.

CHAPTER 18

As long as she lived she was never going to be responsible for another celebrity wedding, Ella St Milton promised herself as she hid behind a giant arrangement of purple and orange flowers to enjoy a few seconds' peace. It had been manic from the moment she'd opened her eyes. One member of a re-formed boy band was distraught because orange fake tan was smeared on his white linen suit, another former pop star had twisted her ankle, and Justin Anderson had enjoyed a scuffle with the paps – all before the bride and groom had even exchanged vows. Now that the reception was in full swing, Ella was ready to collapse in a heap.

She wouldn't be surprised if all her hair went grey by tomorrow from the stress of it all; Georgie Angel's wedding had probably taken a few years off her life too. From the frantic scramble to find the purple and orange flowers to the military-style security required to guard the exclusive pictures, to the bride's meltdown when she'd snapped an acrylic nail, today had been nothing short of an ordeal – and it wasn't even over yet.

Thank God that in the frantic run-up to the big day nobody from the wedding party had been too distraught by Charlie Barton doing a runner. Ella had done her best to smooth over the shock of his departure by making sure that her clients were aware of Symon Tremaine's credentials. After some initial hysterics (Tabitha) and threats of suing the hotel's arse off (Georgie), they'd calmed down sufficiently to read reviews of The Plump Seagull and to let Symon devise a menu. They weren't happy but they'd been mollified by Symon's Michelin star and a massive discount on their bill, which might have cost Ella most of her profits but had ultimately ensured that Charlie's bid to sabotage her flagship wedding would be unsuccessful.

Ella made a mental note to never, ever get romantically involved with staff again. *Especially* temperamental chefs.

She knew she owed Symon Tremaine big time for agreeing to step in at the eleventh hour. As she'd suspected, and as Symon had predicted, Charlie hadn't done any preparation at all for the wedding breakfast. Worse, it transpired that he'd forbidden Klaus from getting on with anything without his say-so. The freezers were empty, nothing had been ordered and even the kitchen staff, used to Charlie's erratic manner of doing things, were terrified. When she and Symon had assembled them to explain what was happening now that Charlie had quit, everyone had looked delighted to have a plan. Poor Klaus had almost shed tears of relief.

"Have any orders been placed or menu plans agreed?" Symon had asked them. He might be quietly spoken and have none of Charlie's swagger, but he was certainly able to command respect. Ella had noticed that as soon as he'd entered the kitchen everyone, from the lad who scrubbed the pans to the sous-chef, had stood up a little straighter and given him their full attention.

"Not as far as I'm aware, Chef," Klaus had replied, wringing his hands. "In fact, I'm almost certain nothing's been ordered. He wouldn't let me do any of it."

"Nothing's been ordered? What the hell were you thinking?" Ella had bellowed, rounding on Klaus. Terror sharpened her voice and panic made her cruel. "Are you an idiot? What kind of kitchen orders nothing for a wedding breakfast?"

Symon had placed a hand on her arm, and something in his touch had calmed Ella. Without him needing to utter a word, his blue eyes had promised that all would be well. Admittedly her pulse had still been racing somewhat, but she'd had the oddest conviction that this quiet man with his fox-red hair and unassuming manner was the life raft that would keep her afloat.

"I'm so sorry, Miss St Milton," Klaus said. "This is how Charlie likes to work. He's creative. He says he has to be free to have ideas. I should have said something. Of course, I take full responsibility."

Poor Klaus must have suffered dreadfully having to work with such an erratic, disorganised and despotic chef, but he'd never once resorted to bitching and moaning about the situation. In fact, none of the kitchen staff had. Realising this, Ella had felt ashamed for taking her panic out on them. Deep down, in the brutally honest and self-aware part of her that Ella did her utmost to keep hidden, she knew she had to accept responsibility for this mess as well. After all, she'd been more than happy to leave Charlie to it, and once their relationship had soured beyond repair she'd actively avoided the kitchens.

"It's not your fault, Klaus. We understand how Charlie likes to work – don't we, Ella?" Symon had said gently.

Ella had found herself nodding. Oh yes, she understood that Charlie liked to fly by the seat of his pants, just as she also understood that Charlie would be laughing his head off right now. Where on earth was she supposed to source food for one hundred and sixty guests with only a few days' notice? The nearest supermarket?

It was impossible. As good as the local supermarkets were, their finest wouldn't cut it with Georgie's celebrity wedding guests, and neither would a quick bulk order from Patsy's Pasties.

All Ella's hard work had been for nothing. The hotel's reputation would never recover from this. She'd failed.

"What are we going to do?" she'd asked. Her mouth was dry.

Symon's lips had quirked upwards. "*We* are going to do nothing, Ella. You are going to press on with organising the final details for this wedding, while my team here and I put together a wedding breakfast that people will be talking about for months."

Ella had stared at him. "You think you can do that?"

"I know I can do that," Symon had replied. He'd turned to the assembled kitchen staff. "Can't we, everyone?"

"Yes, Chef!" they'd chorused, brimming with confidence now that Symon had arrived.

"Now, if you don't mind leaving us to it, we've got a wedding feast to plan," he'd said.

Ella was so taken aback by this new authoritative version of Symon Tremaine that she'd done exactly what he'd said. The next couple of days had been a blur of preparations and their paths had barely crossed, but on the several occasions when she had managed to poke her head into the kitchen, everything had been a hive of activity. Pots were boiling, chefs were chopping and at one point even Patsy Penhalligan was there, with her sleeves rolled up and wearing one of Symon's bandanas as she kneaded pastry with grim determination.

Oh God. What was he going to serve the guests? Ella had fretted as she'd tossed and turned in bed that night. Pasties? Saffron buns? Cheese and baked-bean slices? What on earth was he up to?

Ella's fears hadn't been allayed the next day either, when she'd spotted that gormless idiot Perry Tregarrick's ancient

Mercedes lumbering up the hotel drive. Perry grew organic vegetables, but as far as Ella knew this was a hit-and-miss affair. At one point he'd been delivering veg boxes; however, the enterprise had come to an abrupt end when he'd mentioned in the pub that he was thinking about installing a compost toilet at the manor, to help produce more fertiliser. Ella supposed this was yet another of Perry's hare-brained schemes that had never actually been implemented, but you never quite knew for sure.

Then Chris the Cod had pulled up in his clapped-out van and proceeded to unload what looked like a tonne of spuds onto the spotless front steps of the hotel.

Pasty and chips? Poopy vegetables? Ella had started to pick at her acrylic nails, which was always a bad sign. She'd persuaded herself to have a massage in the spa to relax, but on the way back to her office the sight of Nick Tremaine lugging fish boxes through the hotel lobby immediately raised her blood pressure again. Dirty footprints on the polished oak floor aside, Ella was now terrified that the wedding guests would be eating mackerel pasties served with chips and a garnish grown in aristocratic waste.

She couldn't stay away from the kitchen a moment longer: Ella had to know what was going on.

"Has anyone ever told you that you have trust issues?" was Symon's response when she cornered him and demanded to see the menu.

"Has anyone ever told you that you're way too secretive?" Ella countered.

A shadow flickered across his face. "I prefer to call it private."

Private was one way of putting it. On each occasion when Ella had tried to see what was going on in the kitchen, she'd been politely but firmly told to jog on. Well, not this time. Ella was the hotel manager and she was pulling rank. Symon Tremaine was working for her, not the other way around.

"Private's one thing but you're creating a menu – you haven't signed the Official Secrets Act."

He laughed at this, and Ella thought how much she liked the warm sound and the way the serious mask seemed to slip, revealing a mischievous twinkle in those blue eyes that reminded her of his siblings. Symon didn't laugh very often and she wondered why that was. There was something there that held him back from sharing his thoughts with other people; Ella recognised it, because she exercised the same restraint. Don't get close. Stay at the edges. Never let anyone see the real you. These were all mottos that had worked for her, and she suspected her new chef lived by them too.

"So you want me to tell you what I've come up with just in case I'm about to serve seaweed porridge or seagull goujons?" he teased.

"Very Heston Blumenthal," Ella said. "Actually, that sounds like the sort of thing these guests would rave about. But seriously, the last time I chose not to check in with my head chef it didn't end so well, so I'm feeling a bit nervous."

Symon nodded. "That's fair enough, although I wouldn't beat myself up too much about it if I were you. Charlie Barton doesn't strike me as the most organised character. He's got by on account of his flair and with a fair bit of good luck too."

And by charming his way into his boss's knickers, Ella thought bitterly. She didn't kid herself that she was the first woman he'd worked for who had fallen for Charlie's good looks – and she probably wouldn't be the last. She'd learned her lesson though; Ella was steering clear of chefs for the next few thousand years.

"I guess I have been keeping things under wraps a little," Symon admitted. "First of all I didn't want to panic anyone or alert the press by revealing just how much there was to do, and secondly I wanted to really impress you with a final reveal. I wanted you to be happy with what I'd come up with and I wasn't going to show you any half measures." He shook his russet head ruefully. "I guess what I'm trying to say is that it's been a hell of a job pulling this together at such short notice and I've had to call in some very big favours. I wanted to be sure I've delivered the goods before I showed you."

Ella was touched. She was used to people wanting to impress her only because they were scared, so it made a nice change that Symon genuinely hadn't wanted to let her down.

"And there was a lot to do?"

He grimaced. "Just a bit. You can imagine how much we needed to buy in, and it hasn't been easy at short notice. Luckily for me Perry has the best produce for miles around and it's organic too. Chris the Cod had potatoes going and Patsy's a genius with pastry. Nick and the Penhalligan boys have given me the pick of their catch as well. With all that, we've pulled it off. There was just about enough there to create a Cornish-themed wedding breakfast."

Ella's heart lurched. Pasties and chips it was. Oh God.

"Don't look so worried! I'm not feeding them pasties and scones," Symon said. Mind-reading skills as well as cooking were clearly in his repertoire. "Well, not in the traditional sense anyway. Come on. I'll show you. I've just finished doing some samples. You'll need to have the menus printed tonight in any case."

He held the door for her and Ella stepped into the hotel kitchen for the first time in almost three days. The change in the place took her breath away. Gone was the tense atmosphere that could have been sliced with one of the filleting knives. Instead there was a sense of industry and purpose. Each member of the kitchen staff was busy attending to a task, while the waiters bustled in and out. The whole operation was running like clockwork; every surface gleamed and the food being plated up onto chunky white ceramic platters looked divine. Even Ella, who as far as possible tried to avoid eating, felt her mouth start to water.

"Klaus has been brilliant at keeping the restaurant ticking over," Symon said warmly. "That freed me and some of the others to concentrate on putting together something really special with whatever I could get my hands on at short notice." He looked shy all of a sudden. "I think it's time you had a look at my Cornish-themed creations."

Ella followed him across the kitchen and leaned against the farthest counter while Symon and another chef fetched several domed dishes, which Symon arranged in front of Ella.

"*Et voilà!* The starters!"

He whipped the first lid off and beamed at Ella, who was speechless. Every single item on the platter looked stunning.

"Pollock cakes with beet-and-apple salsa, creamy wild mushrooms with crumbled Cornish blue cheese, smoked mackerel crostini with mixed baby-leaf salad, and mini leek and Yarg pasties," Symon said proudly. "Do you want to have a taste?"

Ella didn't need asking twice. She picked up one of the mackerel crostini and bit in. "Oh my goodness! That's amazing!" she groaned. It truly was to die for.

Next she reached for one of the fishcakes, which she devoured with almost indecent speed. "That pollock is fantastic," Ella gasped, needing every inch of self-control to hold back from grabbing another. The food was fresh and the flavours were incredible. The guests would go crazy for this.

"Fresh off the boat last night. See, Nick does have some uses," Symon said. "Try the pasties. Patsy's magic touch is in the pastry but the rest was down to me."

Again, Ella gladly obeyed. Her stomach, denied a good calorie fest for so long, was in utter heaven. She couldn't even remember when she'd last had a pasty but it had been worth the wait. The Cornish Yarg and leek were a winning combination, and the light and buttery pastry melted in her mouth.

"Main courses now. We've got roasted haddock, creamy sweetcorn chowder and spring-onion scones here. Then there's the roasted butternut squash and Cornish Blue wellington with sage drizzle and balsamic beets. We've also got bass fillet with lemon mash, basil oil and Mediterranean vegetables."

Each of these creations was more delicious than the last, and by the time she'd tasted a little bit of everything Ella felt ready to explode. Goodness only knew how many workouts it would take to burn this lot off, but it would be worth every aching, pain-filled rep!

"Puddings?" Symon asked once he'd cleared the main courses away. "Can I tempt you with apple pie and clotted Cornish cream? Or vanilla and saffron mascarpone with poached pears?"

Ella placed her hands on her stomach and shook her head. "I'd love to but I can't eat another mouthful. That was incredible!"

He flushed with pleasure. "Then it looks as though my work here is done."

It was more than done. Ella knew that the food Symon had produced was far superior to anything Charlie might have come up with. Her previous chef's dishes were designed to win him maximum attention and column inches, which they generally did, but Charlie's cooking didn't have the authentic Cornish twist that Symon had nailed so beautifully.

And neither did it have that sprinkling of magic. There was something special about Symon Tremaine. He seemed still and quiet on the surface but underneath she was sure that deeper passions swirled, as dangerous and as enticing as the eddies around the Shindeep rocks. The driven energy in him, the single-mindedness, was channelled into his cooking – but what would he be like as a lover? How would it feel to be the focus of that intensity? The sole target of his undivided passion?

"What is it?" Symon asked. "You're staring at me, Ella."

She was? Whipped back to the present and horrified by her thoughts, it was Ella's turn to blush.

"I was just thinking that you're very gifted," she said swiftly. "You really are, Symon. You should be out there with the television shows and the big restaurant, not tucked away in Polwenna Bay."

He shuddered. "I can't think of anything worse than being a celebrity. I'm more than happy to leave the showing off to Zak."

"But you're truly talented and you've worked miracles with this wedding, you really have."

Symon shrugged. "I'm glad you approve. I can't take all the credit though. It helps to have a great team and a few local contacts who can help."

They hadn't just helped, Ella thought. Perry, Nick, Patsy and her own kitchen staff had all gone the extra mile for Symon. There was something about him that inspired confidence and made you want to give your best. While Symon cleared away, she mused over what it was that could have brought him back from Paris to a backwater like Polwenna Bay. Hadn't he worked in a renowned restaurant? With his talent, he could have gone straight to the top – and unlike others she could mention, he didn't need to screw or bribe his way there either. What had happened?

"Didn't you train in Paris?" Ella ventured when Symon returned.

"I did." He shut the fridge with a thud, as though informing her that the topic was closed too, but Ella ignored the signal. She was intrigued by this enigmatic member of the Tremaine clan.

"So why come back here?"

"Life," said Symon shortly, "and I'd rather not discuss my private business with all and sundry."

Well, that told her. Yet again rebuffed by a Tremaine. This was nothing new and Ella, dismayed to find that her chin was wobbling from the sharpness of his tone, quickly arranged her face into her best haughty expression.

"Get over yourself," she said coldly. "I was only making conversation, not asking you to bare your soul."

An awkward silence fell. Then Symon gave a weary sigh, breaking the tension.

"We all have secrets and a past, Ella. I expect there are things in your life that you're not proud of? Things you'd rather never think about again?"

The image of Charlie, naked and swaggering through her office, darted across her mind's eye. Oh yes. There were lots of things she regretted. Jake Tremaine was another.

"So my life is no different. Paris was fun but it didn't work out the way I hoped it would, and I came home again," Symon continued. "End of story."

Ella very much doubted this. To her it sounded like the start of the story. Nevertheless, the shuttered look on Symon's face and the swiftness with which the easy atmosphere of their food tasting had vanished kept her silent.

"I've left that part of my life behind and I don't want to dredge it up just to *make conversation*," he said, untying his apron and tugging off the bandana before raking a hand through his thick mane of sunset hair. "It's been a long day and I'm exhausted. There's the wedding tomorrow, and I also need to make sure The Plump Seagull is surviving without me and prep there. So forgive me, but the last thing I'm in the mood for is an interrogation."

"Understood," Ella said tightly. "From now on I'll restrict our conversation to food and the weather."

Symon stared at her for a moment, as though battling internally, and then pulled a face.

"God, I can be a pompous arse," he said, relenting. "Look, the truth is I fell in love with the wrong person and I couldn't bear to stay. It hurt too much and I ran back here. There's not much more to it than that but I'd rather it wasn't common knowledge. My gran would want to know every detail and I'd never hear the end of it from Mo. Besides, I think they have enough to deal with now that Emerald's arrived, without my woes adding to the mix."

Of course. The new sister. This had been the talk of the town.

"I understand," Ella replied. If she could have left Polwenna Bay when Jake had told her that he was in love with Summer, Ella would have done so in a heartbeat. Running from pain made perfect sense. She held out her hand. "I swear I won't say a word."

Symon took it and they shook. They were so close that Ella could feel his breath fluting against her cheeks, and she was shocked to feel a ripple of longing as his fingers closed over hers. Surprised and confused, she pulled her hand away sharply.

"I'll catch you tomorrow," she said, and Symon nodded.

"Until then," he answered.

Ella had beaten a hasty retreat from the kitchen back to her office, and the rest of the evening had passed in a blur of phone calls and logistics. Keeping busy was the key to dismissing the weird pull of desire she'd felt for Symon; by the time she'd fallen into bed, Ella had put this down to either a strange allergic reaction to all the unaccustomed calories or sheer exhaustion. Once the wedding was over she'd treat herself to a couple of days off. Tom was more than capable of covering, and if she paid Symon a bit extra maybe he would run the kitchen until she managed to appoint a new head chef.

Oh Lord. Here he was in her head again, Symon flipping Tremaine. This was evidence, if ever she needed it, that it was time for a rest.

Anyway, Ella reflected now, the wedding had gone smoothly so far, the paps had been kept at bay and although she hadn't seen much of Symon the guests had been very appreciative of the results of his labours. The bride and groom were being showered with compliments about discovering a talented Cornish chef and disaster had been averted. It was enough to make Ella seek out Jules Mathieson and tell her she now believed in God.

It was that stage of the reception where the food had been eaten, the speeches were over and there was a lull in the proceedings while everyone took a breather before the evening celebrations. The guests had wandered outside, where they flitted across the terrace like designer butterflies, their cigarettes glowing like small red eyes in the darkness and their chatter rising and falling with the breeze. Lambswool clouds were stitched across the darkening sky and a small slice of moon was peeping through them. Inside the ballroom, all was still save the gentle chink of cutlery against bone china as the hotel staff cleared the tables, rudely interrupted every now and then by the screech of feedback from the amps as a famous re-formed band warmed up. Ella had solved a minor crisis or two and even helped unpin Tabitha's heavy train so that the bride could mingle more easily with her guests.

Maybe it was time to grab a quick coffee, while she had the chance.

"Excuse me, are you in charge here?"

A rail-thin woman with a sharp blonde bob was looking at Ella questioningly. She didn't look upset but you could never tell. That coffee would have to wait.

"I am," Ella said pleasantly. "How may I help you?"

"I'll get straight to the point because I'm sure you're busy, but I was wondering who did the catering today? The food was wonderful! I loved that Cornish artisan and city fusion theme you had going on."

Ella had no idea what she was on about but if this guest was happy she could call the food whatever she wished.

"I'm delighted you enjoyed it—"

"I more than enjoyed it!" The woman didn't seem in the mood to chat. She was much too busy rummaging in her designer clutch bag. "Look, here's my card. I'm a producer for the Food and Drink Channel. You've heard of us, I'm sure."

Of course Ella had heard of the Food and Drink Channel, or F&D as it was known. It was a showcase for some of Britain's most famous chefs and had become a launch pad for many household names. Charlie Barton had been gagging to find a way in; he'd even been prepared to lower himself for a stint on game shows like *Get! Set! Bake!* in his shameless quest for exposure.

Ella took the card and turned it over.

Sara Hopkiss, Producer, F&D

"I'm a friend of Tabitha's father," Sara Hopkiss explained. "Our families go back years. But look, never mind all that. The point is, I've been searching for a genuine Cornish chef to front a couple of features for us. This county's where everyone wants to be right now. Do you think your guy would be any good in front of a camera?"

Symon was a Tremaine and the camera adored them all. His blue eyes, fine bones and swathes of sunset hair would be captivating, there was no doubt about that. However, whether he'd want to be filmed was less certain.

"I can't think of anything worse than being a celebrity. I'm more than happy to leave the showing off to Zak."

Ella was just about to say that she didn't think her chef would be interested, when Sara added casually, "We'd film here and give your gorgeous hotel a massive plug. And we'd pay the chef too, of course. I don't suppose you need me to tell you where this could lead. For all of you."

Ella certainly didn't. It was an incredible opportunity and exactly what she'd been dreaming of. Her grip on the card tightened and her pulse raced. This was her chance to put the

Polwenna Bay Hotel well and truly on the map and show Jonny just what she was capable of.

Now all she needed to do was find a way to talk Symon Tremaine around. Ella knew she would do whatever it took to win him over, because there was no way she was turning this golden opportunity down. No way at all. Ella St Milton didn't like taking no for an answer.

CHAPTER 19

"The answer's no. Absolutely not," Symon told Ella firmly.

Standing in the hotel's plush bar with a glass of celebratory champagne in his hand, all he could think about was finishing up in the kitchen before going home and passing out from sheer exhaustion. The last thing he was in the mood for was a big discussion with Ella about potential television deals and doing even more work at the Polwenna Bay Hotel.

"Symon! Didn't you hear what I just said?" Ella asked, stepping forward and waving a business card under his nose. "This is F&D we're talking about! They want to feature the hotel and your cooking in a couple of their flagship shows! This card is from their producer, Sara. She gave it to me herself and she asked personally for you. Come on, Symon! You only live once!"

Symon had heard these words before, another country and a lifetime ago. Claudette had wound her arms around his neck and pressed her mouth against his, flickering her tongue over his lips until he gave in and kissed her back, breaking all the promises he'd made to himself and destroying forever his friendship with her husband.

"None of that matters, *chéri*," she'd murmured when Symon had attempted to protest. "Let us enjoy the moment, *non*? You only live once."

That may well be true, Symon thought, but he'd died a thousand times since from regret and heartache.

Fortunately these days he wasn't so easily swayed by a pretty face and a sexy body. And Ella St Milton was gorgeous, there was no denying it. Her mouth was beautiful, whether she was frowning or treating him to a rare smile, and her slender body had curves in just the right places. There was a sensual appetite too that was kept rigidly in check by the same iron will that imposed her strict diet, gruelling exercise regime and long working hours. When he'd watched her bite into those sample dishes, her eyes closing as she'd groaned with pleasure, Symon had glimpsed the passionate woman she truly was. As he'd watched Ella licking flakes of pastry from her lips, Symon's groin had tightened in a way that he'd almost forgotten. The urge to step forward and wipe the pastry crumbs away with his thumb had been horrifyingly strong. It had taken all his self-control to focus on the next dish.

"Well?" Ella was saying now, her head cocked and her voice softer. "Do you want to give it a go?"

"Didn't you hear what I said? I'm not interested."

Symon folded his arms and gave Ella what he hoped was his most determined *I have made my mind up* expression. What part of "no" didn't she get? He'd neglected The Plump Seagull for too long already and could hardly wait to return to his own kitchen and the banter of Kelly, Tara and Tony. He couldn't think of anything worse than having to stay at the hotel dreaming up fancy food for rich and picky guests.

Wait. Yes, he could. How about being *filmed* dreaming up fancy food for rich and picky guests?

"Look, I know what you've said before about not wanting to be a part of the whole celebrity thing, but this could be an incredible opportunity for you," Ella pointed out, her wide grey eyes holding his as though sheer willpower alone could persuade Symon to come around to her way of thinking. Beneath the flimsy bodice of her strapless party dress her swelling breasts rose and fell, and Symon forced himself to look away hastily. This was the oldest trick in the book, after all. Hadn't Claudette thought she could manipulate him in just the same way?

And hadn't she succeeded?

Focus, he told himself sharply. What was wrong with him? It must be the wedding atmosphere or maybe the sense of spring in the air. At this rate he'd have to take a trip to the chiller cabinet.

"And how does that opportunity work exactly? I neglect my own business to generate loads of publicity for yours?"

"Of course not," Ella replied, sounding exasperated. She took a sip of her drink and then set the glass down on the bar with a determined thump. "The way I see it is that any publicity we get from this benefits us both. It builds the hotel's reputation and ultimately yours too. You'll get even more bookings at the Seagull."

"I've already got loads of bookings," Symon fibbed, but Ella wasn't listening.

"They'll pay you too," she continued, ignoring his protests and pressing home this point. "Believe me, Charlie was earning good money from his appearances on local television but this collaboration with F&D will be in another league altogether. There could be cookbooks, vlogs, even your own show. Think about it, Symon! You'll make good money, enough to sort out any rent issues you might have, or maybe even enough to buy somewhere of your own?"

He stared at her. "Who have you been talking to?"

Ella tapped her nose with a manicured nail. "I have my sources."

"Tom, I suppose," said Symon. Typical. There were no secrets in Polwenna Bay, except perhaps what Big Rog was up to in his garden shed. That really was a mystery.

"I can't possibly divulge such classified information," Ella said, but Symon saw her expression shift momentarily to guilt. Tom, then. "Anyway, that's not the point. Are you up for it? You could make a lot of money, I can prove to my grandfather that I've really put our hotel on the map, and between us we can also flip Charlie Barton the bird. It's a win-win situation."

Symon wasn't all that concerned about Charlie Barton or impressing Jonny St Milton, who might or might not still be engaged to Alice, depending on which day of the week it was and which individual you spoke to. He did care about his restaurant though. If he could earn enough from this, it would broaden his options for moving to new premises and he could start making some plans. Having the extra money to tide him over when the current lease ran out might mean being able to keep his staff on during the inevitable upheaval. Usually Symon wouldn't dream of selling his soul to the media, but if a spot of TV moonlighting could be the answer to his problems then perhaps he ought to consider it?

"Get behind me, Satan," he sighed.

"Just give Sara a call and talk to them," Ella suggested, sensing him weakening. She pressed the card into his hand. "You might be pleasantly surprised. Who knows? You may even enjoy it!"

Symon raised his eyebrows. "Don't let's pretend this is all for my benefit."

"I'm not pretending for a minute that this wouldn't be good for the hotel too," she said. "You know my feelings on the matter. I'd say 'yes' in a heartbeat but the point is that it isn't just the hotel they're interested in. They want you too, Symon. In fact, without you there's no deal. You're what they really want. So, what do you say?"

She was determined, Symon would say that for Ella St Milton.

"I'll think about it, OK? I said *think*!" he added as she punched the air in a most uncharacteristic show of excitement. Symon couldn't help feeling touched; the gesture made her look about fifteen.

"Thank you for even thinking about it," she said, her dove-grey eyes full of warmth now. "I really appreciate it and I really appreciate what you've done already too. Without you, today would have been an utter disaster – but you've made it a huge success."

The glow her words caused took Symon aback. *Careful*, he told himself. *She knows the effect she has on men.*

"It was a pleasure," he said. "Stressful, yes, but I enjoyed it. Chefs are masochists that way."

"After spending time with Charlie I'd have said a sadistic streak was more of a requirement," Ella said bitterly. "He nearly ruined everything. I honestly thought it was all over for the business and for me. He'd have loved that."

Ella needed this break just as much as he did, Symon realised with a sudden jolt of understanding, if for different reasons. Money would never be an issue for her; however, Jonny St

Milton was old-fashioned and everyone in Polwenna Bay knew he favoured the utterly useless Teddy, which was ridiculous. Ella was smart and determined and worked harder than anyone else Symon knew. Just a few days at the hotel had shown him that much. He'd also seen how much respect the staff had for her. Sure, they called her Evil Ella, but they did so in a fond way and they were proud to be a part of her team. Tom sang her praises and now Symon could see why. Mo would never believe him but there was certainly more to Ella St Milton than the spoilt-brat image. Beneath the surface she was fighting for her business every bit as hard as Symon fought for his.

"I promise I'll think about it," he told her, pocketing the card. As he did so, it occurred to Symon that if he did agree to the filming it would be because it meant so much to Ella rather than because it offered him a way out of a tight corner. The oddest sensation gripped him – and if he hadn't known better, Symon would have said it was tenderness.

What on earth was that about?

If Symon had thought Ella was persistent when she'd wanted him to cater for the wedding, this was nothing in comparison to her subsequent campaign to persuade him to film for the Food and Drink Channel. After a few days of being bombarded by press cuttings about the wedding, finding copies of *Heat* and *OK!* mysteriously left on the restaurant's doorstep and receiving flurries of emailed links to glowing write-ups in the national press, Symon was starting to weaken. The final straw came on the Thursday, when yet another huge bill arrived. Paying it would wipe out everything he'd earned doing the wedding and a great deal more besides.

"It's only two episodes," Tara said when Symon gathered his team for a council of war. It was a gorgeous March morning and the restaurant's small courtyard was basking in warmth. Above them, the sun was shining through a halo of cotton-wool clouds; to Symon's mind it looked rather like a celestial fried egg on a bright blue plate.

"She's right," Tony agreed. "What have you got to lose?"

Symon grimaced. "My dignity? My integrity? My privacy?"

"You'll never make it big worrying about those," Kelly chipped in from her seat on an upturned milk crate. "My brother's been working at Rock for months on that new house of his. It wasn't built by fretting about his privacy and keeping himself to himself!"

Symon was about to open his mouth to make a noble point about some things being beyond a price, but then it occurred to him just how much it cost to buy a house in Rock, never mind demolishing one and starting again. Maybe he was being a little hasty here?

"Hasty and snobbish," Tara nodded when Symon said this aloud. "There's nothing wrong with making cooking more popular. It could be amazing. Morgan will be beside himself at all the web opportunities and Instagram updates – and think of the publicity for Polwenna Bay if we have our very own celebrity chef! Tourists will come for miles, just like in Padstow."

"It wouldn't matter if we had a wet summer then; the emmets would still come," Tony added slowly.

"We could open more in the winter!" Kelly gasped. "Or even all year round?"

Everyone looked thrilled at this thought. Seasonal work was hard and although he would have loved to have paid everyone a retainer when The Plump Seagull closed for the quieter months, as things stood Symon couldn't justify this financially.

He felt horribly guilty. This wasn't just about him. There were a lot of people depending on the success of the restaurant. Symon knew he had to think of the bigger picture.

"I'm not about to become a celebrity chef. That is *not* what I want," he warned, knowing it was important to make this clear – otherwise Kelly would tell her mum and by lunchtime the whole village would think he was the new Rick Stein. "It's just two slots on a digital channel. I don't suppose anyone will even see it."

"Then you may as well say yes and take the money," said Tara.

Symon knew when he was beaten. He drained his coffee and nodded.

"Fine, I'll meet Ella and tell her the good news. But just remember: you guys thought this was a good idea. Not me!"

Symon had suggested that Ella meet him in the revamped beach café. Pleased to have a break from working, she was enjoying the walk down the hill into the village. With the spring sunshine on her face and astounding views of the coast everywhere she looked, Ella felt that luck was on her side at long last. If Symon was going to say no, then surely he wouldn't have invited her out for a coffee? Excitement bubbled deep down inside her. He was going to agree! This was the big break she'd been waiting for.

For the past few nail-bitingly tense days – or rather, anxious days of picking off her acrylic nails – Ella truly hadn't been able to guess what Symon's decision might be. He needed the money, that was obvious, but the Tremaines were a funny bunch when it came to finances and fiercely proud too. Mo would rather die than ask for help, Alice was refusing to give up her home to move in with Jonny, and now Symon had made it clear that he thought television and publicity work were nothing more than a sell-out. Apparently, he didn't want to betray his principles. Several times Ella had been forced to bite her lip very hard, to refrain from pointing out that beggars couldn't be choosers. It was beyond infuriating that he seemed unable to grasp just what a golden opportunity this was for both of them!

Ella had spent a happy hour that morning sifting through the latest press coverage of the wedding. Predictably, all the celeb magazines had splashed Georgie and Tabitha across their front covers and crammed their inside pages with snaps of boy-band members, soap stars and assorted other guests dancing, eating and latterly falling over drunk. The security team had been briefed to confiscate mobile phones and cameras, so how these shots had been leaked was a mystery. Oddly enough there were none of the bride though, which gave Ella a clue.

She'd been busy taking a snapshot of the lovely write-up from *OK!*, to be emailed across to her website guy as well as added to the hotel's Instagram feed and Facebook page, when Symon had called to arrange their meeting. After this she'd been unable to settle back into work; even when Teddy had sauntered in and raided the petty cash, Ella had remained in a state of eager anticipation. She knew with every fibre of her being that Symon's talent was exactly what F&D were looking for and that, with the hotel's breathtaking Cornish setting too, they had a winner on their hands. Ella thought she would combust with excitement, and the walk into the village was just what she needed to let off steam. She'd toyed with putting on her running kit but in the end had plumped for indigo skinny jeans teamed with a long-sleeved white tee shirt and a basic pair of pumps. Her make-up was fresh and simple and she pulled her hair up into a high ponytail, reminding herself that it was only Symon Tremaine she was meeting. It wasn't as if she wanted to impress him.

The beach café was busy when Ella pushed open the door and scanned the room for Symon. Now that it was spring the tourists had started venturing down to the coast, and the simple shabby chic building had broken out in a rash of Joules and Seasalt attire. The sheer number of patterned wellies made Ella feel dizzy.

There was Symon, sitting by the window. He was gazing out across the beach to the horizon, where a flotilla of sailing boats was heading out to infinity. Ella could tell that he was deep in thought.

"Thinking about running away to sea?" she asked.

"Ella!" Symon rose to his feet and kissed her cheek. He smelt delicious, of newly baked bread and fresh air. "I've ordered us both black coffee."

"Great. I'm still trying to shake off the weight I put on after tasting your menu," Ella said, sitting down. She glanced at him, wondering if she would be able to guess what it was he wanted to tell her, but as always there was no clue. He played his cards as closely to his chest as she usually did, and Ella was impressed. He was looking great though. His fox-red hair, not tied back for once, fell in thick waves to his shoulders and his skin glowed with sea air and exercise. He was wearing jeans, a blue sweater and an olive gilet that looked perfect with his colouring.

Goodness, Ella thought with surprise, he really was a handsome man. How had she not noticed before? She supposed it was because he was so quiet in comparison with the others and that he kept himself busy with the restaurant. He'd be incredible on screen.

"It's weird meeting here," Symon remarked. "I'm used to having to sort out issues. I'm not used to sitting down and relaxing."

Ella nodded. "I know. Where are the menus? The staff? The countless cock-ups from Charlie that need sorting?"

He grimaced. "Never again."

The café's new owner, a sweet-faced man in his late forties, brought them their coffee. Ella sipped hers while wondering what Symon was about to tell her.

"So, you want to know what I've decided to do about F&D," he said eventually.

Didn't men just love to state the obvious?

"Yes," Ella replied. Under the table her fingers, legs and toes were crossed. Maybe she should try her eyes too – but they seemed to be locked on Symon's and, no matter what she did, they refused to leave his searching blue gaze.

Symon took a deep breath. "I might live to regret this but, OK, yes."

"Really?" Ella hardly dared hope she'd heard him correctly. "You're going to do it?"

"I must be mad, but yes, I'll do the filming and see where we go from there."

"That's brilliant!" Ella gasped. "Thank you!"

Excitement and relief broke over her like a giant wave and she reached across the table to kiss his cheek. Except that it didn't quite work like that, because Symon must have moved and suddenly Ella felt his lips on hers. His mouth felt so good, so warm and so utterly right, that before she could stop herself Ella was kissing him and it was a kiss that she never wanted to stop. Like his cooking, Symon Tremaine was totally addictive.

Symon's mouth moved against hers and his fingers cupped her face as he kissed her in return. For a beautiful, fleeting moment Ella floated on air before reality kicked in and she pulled away.

What was she thinking? Her heart was racing and she felt light-headed. Light-headed and terrified. She never lost control like that. Never.

"You needn't think that will happen every time you tell me you'll film a piece," she said, doing her very best to rearrange her face into a cool expression, even if her heart was pounding at an alarming rate.

"Pity," said Symon. "I was starting to think I could get to enjoy this television lark."

His lips, the same beautiful lips that she could still feel against her own, were twitching. Was he laughing at her? Ella couldn't bear to be laughed at.

"I have to go," she said abruptly. "I'll be in touch with the schedule."

Before Symon could reply, she grabbed her bag and was walking away from him. Even though she didn't turn around, Ella knew he was watching her all the way to the door, as still and as thoughtful as always – except that now she knew there was a latent power beneath the stillness. For some inexplicable, dreadful and compelling reason this thought thrilled Ella more than anything she'd ever known.

Oh God. What was happening to her?

From now on she would have to be very, very careful. She was in danger of letting Symon Tremaine get far too close to the real Ella St Milton.

CHAPTER 20

"And then garnish with a sprinkle of dill and serve on a bed of lemon rice." Symon Tremaine stared confidently out of the television and Emerald, watching the Food and Drink Channel on Ashley's monster flat screen up at Mariners, felt a surge of pride for her brother. Out of all her siblings residing in the village, Symon was the one she'd spent the least time with, but this was hardly surprising given that his television career had gone crazy over the past few weeks and he'd been flat out.

This was the first of the shows featuring Symon and the Polwenna Bay Hotel, so the Tremaine family had gathered at Ashley and Mo's house, where there were about a million satellite channels to watch. As she'd curled up on the sofa next to Alice, Emerald hadn't been sure quite what to expect. After all, Symon was always so quiet and so serious. Emerald was used to fast-paced American TV where everyone sported dazzling white teeth, were tanned to within an inch of their lives and did their utmost to hold the audience by speaking manically – so this gentle show, with its gorgeous shots of Polwenna Bay and Symon's genuine eye contact with the viewer, was something out of the ordinary. She'd been glued.

Of course, she was biased because Symon was her big brother, but to Emerald he seemed like a natural in front of the camera. If anything, he was more at ease on the small screen than he was in real life. He chatted away with confidence and had a certain kind of magnetism; no doubt women up and down England would be dreaming about his slow smile, sculpted cheekbones and sleepy blue eyes. That British accent was to die for and Emerald just knew that if the American viewers saw this it would turn to TV gold. She hoped she could find a link so that her friends could watch.

She had a TV star for a brother! How awesome was that?

As the credits rolled everyone clapped and Symon, who'd been watching the broadcast through splayed fingers, shook his head in embarrassment.

"You were absolutely wonderful, my love. All the girls in England are going to fall in love with you," Alice said proudly, beaming at him.

"I don't know about that, Granny," said Symon, blushing. "I don't think I've ever cringed so much in my life!"

"You actually didn't look that bad – for a ginger," Nick told Symon kindly.

"Take that back, squirt," said Symon, and the brothers tussled for a moment until Jake dragged Nick away and sat on him. Emerald watched in fascination. This was exactly what she'd imagined it would be like to be a member of a big family. Childhood insults, scuffles, old quarrels and a shared history were all things her siblings took for granted, but witnessing them made Emerald feel sad and a little bit jealous. She felt even less a part of things now that she was here and watching from the sidelines.

Go figure.

"Ouch! Get off me, fatso!" Nick squeaked as Jake pinned him down.

"Make me," grinned Jake as the two boys wrestled. "Danny? Sy? Want to bundle?"

"Not near the sculpture!" Ashley cried in alarm as flailing limbs narrowly missed what looked like a pile of twigs balanced on a tennis ball.

"Boys! Calm down!" Alice Tremaine shot her grandsons a look that had them sheepishly returning to the sofa in seconds. Emerald was impressed. Her grandma might look frail but Alice was tougher than she seemed. Just look at how she was still refusing to go and talk to Jonny St Milton even though he was sending flowers and letters most days.

"It's not about *you*, my love," Alice had promised when, worried that she'd caused a rift between the elderly couple, Emerald had spoken to her grandmother about it. "This situation's arisen because Jonny isn't listening to me and I'm far too long in the tooth to be ignored! If we're going to get married, he has to understand that I need to be listened to. He's a good man but he's also a stubborn old fool!"

Emerald hoped her grandmother was telling the truth because she hated to think that she'd caused any upsets. Jimmy was relaxed and happy with her being around and the others all seemed to have accepted it, but sometimes she still wondered. Maybe it was time she thought about heading home?

"Have you finished the TV work now?" Jules was asking Symon, who spread his hands in a gesture that implied he had no idea.

"I thought I had, but it seems that the producers have suggested three more segments for future shows. And of course, Ella's really keen to proceed."

"I bet she is," muttered Mo. "Tell her where to go, Sy. Don't let her push you around."

"No, that's your job, my angel," said Ashley mildly.

Mo glared at him. "You might have been taken in by her, *darling,* but I know a harpy when I see one!"

"And what's that supposed to mean?" Ashley demanded. "Is this because I once went on a date with Ella? You can't still be holding that against me! It was before we were even together!"

"Of course she can, mate: she's a woman," grinned Nick, and Ashley rolled his eyes.

"I don't hold it against you. I just think it shows a huge lack of judgement on your part," Mo said sulkily. "Evil Ella is foul."

"She's not so bad once you get to know her," Symon commented.

His sister rounded on him. "Just because you fancy her, don't make the mistake of thinking she's a decent human being!"

"Of course I don't fancy her."

"So you were just snogging her face off in the beach café to pass the time? Don't deny it! Saffy Jago saw you."

"Busted!" crowed Nick.

"I wasn't *snogging her face off*, as you so delicately put it. We'd just agreed to do the TV show and we were celebrating. Granted we got a little swept up in the moment but it didn't mean anything," Symon countered. "Christ, Mo. What are we? Six?"

His voice was soft but Emerald noticed that Symon's cheekbones were stained pink and his hands were clenched into fists. He was fighting to keep his temper. Jeez. Sisters sure knew how to wind brothers up and Mo had really touched a nerve.

"She was a cow when she was six too," spat Mo.

Symon shook his head. "That was more than twenty years ago! For heaven's sake! Ella's not had it easy, Mo, and she works bloody hard too. Why don't you give her a break? You might even find you've got more in common than you think."

"Drown me now if that's the case," said Mo. "Come on, Jake, tell this poor deluded man what Ella's really like! And you, Summer. You've been on the sharp end of her tongue."

But Jake shook his head. "Everyone deserves a chance, Mo – and, besides, Sy's right. Credit where credit's due: Ella works her socks off."

"She made sure that Justin was nowhere near me when the wedding took place," added Summer. "She even called to reassure me that there wouldn't be a problem."

"Did she?" Symon's attention was straight there when he heard this.

Summer nodded. "I thought it was you who'd asked her."

"No, I never mentioned it. That was all Ella's doing," Symon said slowly.

"And she's going to be part of the family when Alice and Jonny get married," added Jules.

"Looks like I'm outnumbered by the Ella St Milton fan club then," said Mo bitterly. "Well, Jules? Haven't you got a Bible verse for me? He who is without sin casting the first stone or something? Logs and splinters in eyes?"

Jules said gently, "Those aren't my first choices. I'd go for John, chapter thirteen, verse thirty-four myself: 'love one another. As I have loved you, so you must love one another.'"

"Make me feel really crap, why don't you?" said Mo. "Oh, have an Ella love-in then, if you all must. I'm going to check on Isla."

Once Mo had flounced out of the room things calmed down considerably. Alice and Summer made tea, as usual; they seemed obsessed with the stuff, for reasons that escaped Emerald. Meanwhile Symon, who didn't seem to be enjoying his new-found fame, sloped off to the restaurant, and Nick and Jimmy decided to have an early pint in the pub. Wondering what she could do to help, Emerald went to find Mo, only to catch her and Ashley in the middle of a heated debate on the upstairs mezzanine. She was about to slip away when the mention of her own name made her freeze.

"For God's sake, stop fussing! Now Emerald's here I can concentrate on riding. It's not a difficult course and I know I can win!"

It was Mo, sounding just as angry as she had earlier, only now her temper was aimed at Ashley.

"I don't want you out competing, Mo! It's bloody dangerous."

"You've always known that, Ashley! You bought me The Bandmaster, remember?"

"That was before we had Isla," Ashley's voice was low and tight with emotion. "If having your sister helping out at the yard is encouraging you to risk your neck then I'd rather she didn't help at all!"

Emerald felt as though she'd been walloped in the chest. She liked Ashley. He was dry-witted and they'd chatted a bit about California. To discover that he thought she was causing a problem came as a physical blow.

"*Encouraging me*? I'm not a child!"

"I can't lose you, Mo!" Ashley said quietly.

"Well, now you know how I feel!" Mo yelled back. "Would you like to tell me just how many Nurofen you've been taking lately and why?"

Although she didn't understand quite what they were quarrelling about, Emerald knew this wasn't a subject she was meant to overhear. Somehow she was responsible for causing Ashley and Mo to argue, and that had never been Emerald's intention.

Upset, she crept back down the stairs and out of the front door. She wasn't sure where she was going but Emerald needed some space.

Jules loved the view from Mariners. The house felt as though it was perched on the headland and poised to soar over the bay. Sky and sea met in a sweep of a thousand shades of blue and as the waves broke onto the dark sand, their crashing mingled with the cries of the gulls. This was the soundtrack of Polwenna. As she stood at the garden gate, Jules wrapped her arms around Danny's waist and rested her head on his shoulder. How very blessed she was.

Being with Danny was like spending time with her best friend, only a million times better. He knew her inside out and from the very start she'd felt connected to him, as though he had a direct line to her heart. She'd always been able to be open and honest with him, so not telling him about her worries about the future felt wrong. Usually there was nothing she kept from Danny – and if they were to stand any chance of taking their relationship to the next level, it needed to stay that way.

In the days that had followed their meal at The Plump Seagull, Jules had felt like the biggest idiot on the planet. On the surface she'd been her normal self, but whenever she'd been alone she'd replayed the evening over and over again, wincing when she recalled the excited Jules who'd dressed up for the occasion with such delicious anticipation. What a fool! Danny was a wonderful man and she loved him with all her heart but he'd been badly hurt in love. Getting married again was a step he'd have to think very carefully about, when or if he chose to take it. Had a man's quiet thoughtfulness ever been misinterpreted so badly?

He still seemed distracted but Jules knew now that Danny was pondering the job opportunity rather than gearing up to propose. She was broken-hearted at the thought of him rejoining the army and moving to London, even if it was only during the week. Nonetheless, for the past few weeks she'd been putting on a brave face. She was excited for him because

Jules knew just how much Danny loved the army, but on a selfish note she would miss him terribly if he went. She didn't want him to go. She wanted to be with Danny all the time and in every way. She wanted to marry him. As they stood wrapped in each other's arms, Jules knew she had to tell him the truth.

"Dan, we've been together for a while now," she began, "and it's been the most incredible time of my life."

"Same here," Danny said, dropping a kiss onto the top of her head. "I've never been happier. I mean that, Jules. I love you with all my heart. I know things have been a bit weird lately with the job to think about, but it doesn't change the way I feel about us. I want us to be together."

Jules flushed with pleasure. Danny loved her and she loved him. It was simple – so what was she worrying about? It was time to be brave.

Here goes, Jules thought.

"So if you love me and if I love you then maybe we should think about—"

"Emerald?" Danny called out, interrupting Jules. "Hey! Are you OK?"

His new sister was hurrying down the path, her ponytail bobbing and her feet almost tripping over in her haste to be away. Her face looked pinched and unhappy.

Although Jules was frustrated at not being able to finish her piece, her heart went out to the teenager. What a time of it the poor girl had had since she'd arrived.

"I'm fine," Emerald said, shoving open the gate and hurtling onto the path. "Just fine!"

"When a woman says she's fine I'm always terrified," Danny remarked. "Usually it means the exact opposite."

"You're learning fast," Jules said. "Obi-Wan has taught you well."

Danny laughed and Jules loved it that they had so much in common. This particular joke between them had resulted from Jules having to sit patiently through all the Star Wars films. Aside from this, their lengthy conversations on all kinds of topics had forged a special bond between them, so that they now shared their own language and secret codes (most of which would have been utter nonsense to anyone else, of course). They were a strong couple, Jules told herself, and they would make it through whatever life decided to fling at them – and if that was Danny leaving for London, then she'd pray hard for courage and patience.

"Shall we go after her?" Danny asked.

"I will. You'd better wait for Morgan though," Jules said. "I'll catch her up."

Danny kissed her and Jules set off after Emerald. It didn't take long before she spotted her heading towards Fernside woods to take the shortcut back to the stables.

"Emerald!" Jules called, waving. "Wait up!"

She jogged along the path, a stitch sewing up her left side until she drew level with the younger girl.

"You walk fast," Jules gasped, bending over to catch her breath.

Emerald shrugged one shoulder. "I guess."

"You wanted to get away? Something upset you?"

Another shrug. That was a yes then.

"Look," said Jules once she had her breath back, "you can tell me to push off if you like but I'm a pretty good listener and I also have a good selection of biscuits at my house. Or maybe I ought to say cookies? Biscuits are scones in America, aren't they? You eat them with gravy, don't you?"

Oh dear, she was babbling now. *Shut up, Jules! The poor girl will think you're the local nutcase.* Actually, maybe she was? Jules certainly felt like it some days and Sheila Keverne acted as though she thought Jules was barmy.

But Emerald was nodding.

"Sure, I'd like that. You know these guys too, whereas I just get it all wrong."

"I'm sure you don't," said Jules. "In fact, I think you've coped brilliantly. A new country and a new family would be enough for anyone to deal with, never mind having the Tremaines thrown into the mix. It's not you: they really are as mad as cheese."

Emerald laughed. "That's a neat way of putting it! I think maybe all you Brits are?"

Jules smiled. "How else could you explain a nation that's so fond of Marmite?"

Emerald made a gagging sound. "Nick puts that on his toast like chocolate spread. I nearly hurled when I tried it."

"So there you are. It really isn't you. It is definitely us," Jules said.

They strolled back to the vicarage, narrowly avoiding being flattened by Teddy St Milton in his latest sports car, and by the time Jules had brewed tea and dug out the chocolate biscuits, she knew all about Emerald's hippy-chick mother, love of literature and passion for castles. The thing about castles made Jules feel guilty because she and Danny had promised to take Emerald to St Michael's Mount and then forgotten all about it. The proposal-that-never-was, followed by the news of Danny's potential move to London, had totally driven it from her mind.

"We'll drive you to St Michael's Mount as soon as we have a sunny day," Jules assured her. "It's magical. The first time I saw it I could hardly believe it was real."

"You don't have to," answered Emerald. "I don't think I'll be here much longer anyways."

"Are you due back? I thought you were here for a while?" Jules said.

Emerald looked down at the table. "Yeah, me too, but I don't think it's working out. I'm just upsetting everyone by being here and I never wanted that to happen. I thought they'd all be pleased to meet me. Jules, I would never have just come here if I thought nobody knew about me. Jimmy said he'd told you all."

Some days Jules could swing for Jimmy Tremaine. She prayed hard for patience with him but it was a close thing at times.

"But you and Jimmy have sorted that now and everyone's pleased to be getting to know you. Alice thinks the more the merrier!"

"I broke her and the old guy up."

"You most certainly didn't. Jonny and Alice are old enough to make their own choices and this postponement is about them deciding what's right for their future. If your arrival's made them think even more carefully, then that's a good thing. Marriage isn't to be undertaken lightly," Jules said firmly. Nobody knew this better than her, both personally and professionally.

Emerald looked slightly more cheerful, and to seal the deal Jules passed her a chocolate digestive.

"Dunk it in your tea," she suggested, doing so with her own.

"Dunking. Cool. That's another British tradition, right?"

Jules chuckled. "It's right up there with afternoon tea and the Changing of the Guard."

They dunked and munched thoughtfully for a moment as Emerald considered what Jules had said. Jules noticed that the teenager was looking much happier now – proof that there was nothing tea and biscuits couldn't make a little better.

"As for the others," Jules continued, her voice thick with biscuit, "I know Danny and Jake think you're great and Nick does too. He's always boasting about you."

Emerald rolled her eyes. "Yeah, but only 'cos he thinks I might know some Playboy Bunnies!"

Jules couldn't help smiling. "That sounds like Nick. I'm sure Zak and Issie will be fine when you eventually meet them. And Symon's pretty relaxed about life in general."

Actually, Jules wasn't so sure about Symon lately. He certainly wasn't his usual even-keel self whenever Ella St Milton was mentioned – which was interesting, especially if Saffy Jago's story contained even half a grain of truth.

"So that just leaves Mo, and you get on brilliantly with her," Jules concluded.

Emerald groaned. "I've caused a fight between her and Ashley. Jules, I'm a bad-luck curse."

"Nonsense," Jules answered. She wasn't having this. "They fight a lot. They only met in the first place because Mo was fighting Ashley's plans for the house. It's how they are. Mo's pretty fiery and he's certainly no pushover. I think they enjoy it."

"But this really was my fault."

Jules glanced at the younger girl, unsure how she'd come to this conclusion. "I really don't think that could be the case."

"It is!" Emerald insisted. In her agitation, she'd reduced the remainder of her biscuit to crumbs. "Mo wants to go eventing because I'm looking after the horses, which gives her time. But Ashley said he'd rather I didn't help at all if she does that. He says competing's too dangerous." Her eyes, that deep Tremaine blue that Jules loved so dearly, were wide with distress. "If Mo hurts herself it'll be my fault."

"Oh, Emerald, of course it wouldn't be your fault. Mo's a fantastic rider and she knows the risks. So does Ashley. I think he even bought her a couple of horses. Eventing's what Mo's always done and I suspect what she'll always do. Whether you're helping out or not won't stop her. She's stubborn – but then all of you are."

There was a ghost of a smile. "Mom said I was stubborn coming here. She thought I should wait."

"Typical Tremaine," Jules sighed. "You guys are hard work but we all love you."

The younger girl bit her lip. "Ashley said he can't lose Mo and she said she felt the same about him. He said Isla needs her too much."

"There you go, you see. They're fine. Bonkers but fine. You haven't broken them up, if that's what you were worried about."

Emerald looked relieved and took a sip of her tea, her nose wrinkling. "What's Nurofen?"

Taken aback, Jules spluttered into her drink. "What?"

"Mo said Ashley was taking a lot of Nurofen. Is it a drug?"

Horror pulsed through Jules's heart. Oh Lord, not again. No wonder Ashley didn't want Mo risking her neck and leaving Isla all alone if... if...

Jules slammed her mental brakes on. Hard. *Don't go there.*

"It's a painkiller, like Advil," was all she said. Tonight she would pray very hard.

Unlike Jules, Emerald appeared reassured by this. After another cup of tea and several more biscuits, all talk of returning to the USA had stopped. By the time she left for the caravan, Emerald seemed much more upbeat and was looking forward to her day out at St Michael's Mount.

Jules shut the vicarage door and leaned on it, her eyes closed and her heart heavy. Sometimes this job was difficult to bear. Her thoughts whirled so fast she felt dizzy: Danny, London, marriage, Symon, Alice, Jonny, Emerald, Summer, Mo, Ashley...

So many people to think about. So many burdens to shoulder. Suddenly Jules needed to talk too and she needed comfort. There was only one place to go and one person she needed to hear her. She would spend a quiet hour talking things over with her Boss in the peace and holiness of St Wenn's Church.

CHAPTER 21

The next two weeks passed in a blur for Symon. His days were spent filming at the hotel, shopping for new clothes with the F&D stylist and having his hair cut and artfully arranged with gel before giving interviews to endless journalists and food bloggers. The hours were long and gruelling in the restaurant trade, but they were nothing compared to this. When he was cooking in The Plump Seagull, time always seemed to have wings; although he often felt stressed and might not stop for hours, Symon loved every challenging and creative minute.

It had been the same at Papillon Rouge. When they'd started out, the restaurant had been little more than a bistro, tucked away in a side street and frequented by artists and musicians. They'd spent as much time partying after hours as they had cooking, and Symon had lost count of how many nights and days had been cognac-fuelled. As word had spread, the restaurant had gained a reputation for being the place to eat late and party even later – and Symon and Claudette had been more than happy to oblige. Understanding that their flamboyance was equally important to developing the brand, Jean-Luc had encouraged this and they'd worked together as a team.

And they had continued to do so until Symon had screwed things up...

He shook his head as though trying to shake away the memories. That was another life and that version of himself felt like another man altogether. Symon hardly recognised who he used to be. Nobody in Polwenna would believe that there was once a time when his capacity for partying and drinking had made Nick and Zak look like choirboys.

The producer was the one shaking her head now, and frowning.

"Cut! Can we take that again? The lighting needs adjusting and can we have make-up over here? Now? And somebody take that pan off the gas, for God's sake!"

Before Symon had a chance to protest that the hollandaise sauce was at a crucial point, a runner had taken the saucepan away. Now it would curdle. Great. Just bloody great. This was the fifth time now and he was starting to lose the will to live. This television work might be well paid but Symon really wasn't enjoying it. Some chefs might be happy to act like performing seals whenever there was a camera trained on them, but he wasn't one of them.

Symon tried to arrange his features into a neutral expression as the make-up girl swathed him in a robe and the stylist adjusted the jade bandana they'd decided was just perfect for his colouring. Meanwhile, his thoughts were engaged in a fierce mental debate as to whether the pros of filming outweighed the cons. Financially it was a no-brainer, of course. But there were more important things in life – like integrity for one, and giving his full attention to his own business for another. Already there was talk of a series and a tour to drum up publicity, and Symon knew exactly where this could lead.

What was wrong with him? Most people would be thrilled with the opportunity for fame and fortune, so why was his stomach folding over with dread?

Because, said a small voice deep down, he didn't want to be famous. He just wanted to live peacefully here in Cornwall. He loved the village with its quirky characters and dramatic coastline; he loved running The Plump Seagull and seeing his family; and he loved going sailing across the bay. These things were true riches. What more did he need?

The money to buy the premises, said the small voice, and Symon exhaled, causing clouds of face powder to rise and the make-up girl to tut. He would have apologised, but she was applying a subtle lipstick and he didn't want to make more work for her or hold up filming. She'd probably have sighed if she'd been in his position though. That morning Symon's landlord had called to break the news that he was putting the restaurant on the market at the end of the summer.

"I need to realise some capital," he'd said. "You know how things are at the moment, son. These are tough times. You've got first refusal, of course."

He'd then gone on to name a figure so high that Symon had laughed in sheer disbelief. "This is Cornwall! Not Chelsea!"

There was no way he could afford the price Peter Marten was asking, and Symon didn't imagine that the banks would be in a rush to lend him such an enormous amount either. In any case, he was too proud to ask for help – and this was *his* business and Symon wanted to run it his way. He supposed he could sell his soul to the TV company, but this would come at a price too: it would cost him the time he could be putting into his own business instead. In the food industry reputations were slow to build and fast to ruin.

"OK," said the make-up girl, whipping off the robe and standing back to appraise him through narrowed eyes. "You're good for the next half an hour."

And that was when Symon knew he couldn't do this. He'd honour his commitment to Ella and F&D, but after that there would be no more filming. The likes of Charlie Barton could keep it. Symon just wanted to return to his own kitchen. He'd find another way to save the restaurant, or even a new place that would be even better and where he could expand, but he wouldn't be selling out or neglecting his business. He'd only been filming for a few weeks but already there was an impact on his usual routine. By the time the producers were satisfied, it was generally so late that the restaurant was closed and the village was fast asleep. When he returned home, the only light guiding him downhill was from the stars or from the orange glow of the streetlamps. Symon would let himself in to the deserted restaurant, where – without Tony or Kelly to chat to – he'd climb the stairs and fall into bed until his alarm dragged him out of sleep. Then it was up, shower and get into the car they sent for him to do it all over again.

Hamsters running on wheels probably had more fun. He was thankful for this opportunity but the more time he spent on filming and doing publicity, the more he knew that this wasn't for him. He missed the adrenaline rush of having to produce twenty or thirty covers at once and the challenge of ensuring that each meal, from the simple fishcakes to his signature lobster ravioli, was as perfect as it was possible to make it. Most of all though, he missed the camaraderie of working with his team. Drinking coffee with Tara first thing in the morning, bantering with Perry as they unpacked the fruit and veg, teaching Tony the skills that would take him from being a good chef to a superb one; Symon loved all these things just as much as he loved creating his new dishes.

It was the sense of being part of a team and working together towards a shared goal that drove him, Symon realised. The great reputation, the Michelin star and the write-ups in the food press were just the icing on the cake, but it was the teamwork that really mattered. After all, it had been one of the things he'd loved the most about working at Papillon Rouge. They'd been a tight unit, him, Jean-Luc and Claudette, and they'd worked hard together and played even harder. It had been the best time of his life.

Until he'd ruined everything by falling in love…

Whenever he thought about Claudette, Symon still felt a jolt of desire, which was always followed swiftly by shame. He hadn't seen her since he'd left the restaurant but this didn't stop him thinking about her and wanting her. She'd made the world vibrant and colourful and every second he'd spent with her had felt like being plugged in to the mains. He fizzed, he crackled, he was wired. It was crazy and stupid and he'd been an idiot because it had meant nothing to her.

Women like Claudette were not to be trusted. For ages Symon had hated her, but not nearly as much as he hated himself. He'd promised himself that he would stay away from women. They were nothing but trouble. It had been a successful policy – until recently, when Ella St Milton had somehow managed to slip under his guard.

Symon was at a loss to understand how this had happened. Was it through working together on the wedding? The intensity of filming? Seeing in Ella the same determination to succeed on her own merits that he saw in himself? Or was it because he couldn't put their kiss out of his mind? That kiss had been incredible, so delicious and so full of promise, but what had it actually meant? Nothing or everything? Was she, like Claudette, playing games?

As he looked into the camera now, smiling and chatting about hollandaise sauce, Symon's emotions were a mess. He simply couldn't concentrate.

"Cut! Cut!"

Jolted from his thoughts, Symon realised that the sauce was burning. Instantly several crew stepped forward to relieve him of the scorched attempt and a fresh pan had materialised.

"Let's take that from the top," suggested the director. "Symon, if you could go back to the bit where you say how easy it is to make your own hollandaise?"

"I think I've already proven that's a fib," said Symon. His head was aching and he knew from experience that any further attempts would be a disaster in this frame of mind. He also knew that he didn't have any real option but to press on. He'd signed a contract and the money was already in his bank account. He'd be extremely relieved when this was over. Thank God they were stopping at lunchtime.

Or they would be, if this bloody sauce was ever made…

He sighed and then forced himself to smile brightly into the camera.

"Shall we try again?" he said.

"Ah, there you are, my dear. May I have a quick word?" Jonny St Milton asked his granddaughter.

Ella looked up, her heart sinking. Since Jonny and Alice had put their engagement on hold her grandfather had been at a loose end, which meant he was distracting himself by interfering with running the hotel.

Err, she meant getting involved with running the hotel. She must be patient.

"Can it wait for a just a little bit? I've just got to go through these job applications."

Ella was working her way through the pile of impressive CVs from the applicants for Charlie's job. Her aim was to shortlist three and then persuade Symon Tremaine to help her interview them – if he ever spoke to her again, that was. Things between them had been awkward since their meeting in the coffee shop and he'd been so busy with filming that Ella hadn't found a moment when he was free. In some ways this was quite a relief. After all, what could she say? That she'd temporarily lost her senses and couldn't help kissing him? The memory of that kiss alone was enough to send a longing flickering through her like flames. For a moment she lost herself, imagining what it might be like to take that kiss further and feel his skin against hers...

"No, that's exactly what I wanted to talk about," said Jonny. He shuffled forward and sank onto a chair with a grunt. He looked his age today and Ella was reminded that however difficult he could be, her grandfather was an old man. She took a deep breath. *Patience*, she told herself. *Be kind.*

Be kind? Where did that come from? It sounded like something Symon Tremaine might say. It certainly wasn't the way her Evil Ella alter ego would think!

"These are the chefs I've longlisted," Ella said, pushing the CVs across the desk to him. She was pleased with the selection so far. "They're all extremely well qualified and I think they could bring a lot to the party. I'm just about to make the final cut."

Jonny peered at the documents for a second, before pushing them aside. "I'm sure they're all very impressive, my dear, but you needn't carry on. I've already found a head chef."

Ella did her best to remain calm at this bombshell. Jonny was given to these kinds of strange decisions and generally she was able to talk him out of them. *Count to ten*, she told herself. *Don't react or show your emotional side because he'll only see that as feminine weakness.*

"Right," Ella said slowly. "I'll add him to the shortlist, shall I?"

"No need. I've already told him the job's his."

"What?"

"Don't look at me like that. This is going to be great. You know him anyway, Ella. It's Ricky Mellington-Smyth, Jane and Edmund's boy? Teddy's friend from school? Apparently he's had a bit of fun running a pop-up restaurant in Somerset, at a festival, and he's very keen to be a chef. Ted's sure he's the guy for the job and I'm willing to give him a chance."

It wasn't often that Ella was speechless but this was one of those moments. Ricky Mellington-Smyth was a nice enough guy, if a bit of a chinless wonder, but since when was he a chef? The last time Ella had bumped into him in London he'd been an estate agent and before that he'd been something in the City – what that something was nobody quite knew, but she would bet her life that it wasn't a chef. She doubted he even knew how to flip burgers. No way would he be able to run a professional kitchen and produce the fine dining the hotel was becoming known for.

Ella felt sick.

"Is he qualified?"

Jonny waved a hand. "He's a nice boy. His grandfather and I go back a long way, so I'd like to give him a chance. Teddy says he's a fantastic chef. Apparently this pop-up thingamajig made a fortune."

In a field in Somerset during a festival? Ella wanted to scream. For heaven's sake!

"Grandpa, we need the best. Since we were featured in the press and on F&D I've had over fifteen wedding enquiries and the phone hasn't stopped ringing for restaurant reservations.

We can't risk that by appointing a head chef who isn't up to the job. That would be insane!"

"Give him a trial run," Jonny suggested. His face wore the determined expression Ella often saw in the mirror and her heart sank even further. At this rate, it would be in her shoes before very long. "A month to see how he goes. You might be surprised."

"I'd be amazed," Ella said. "Look, Grandpa, you can't take risks like this with the hotel's reputation. We've been building it up steadily for a while now and we're getting a name for wonderful service and food. That was why I hired Charlie Barton."

Jonny regarded her over his glasses. He might be old but his gaze was still razor-sharp and when he spoke his words sliced like blades.

"Yes. Charlie Barton who charged a fortune for his services and took you for a fool. The very same Charlie Barton who drove your cars and walked out just days before your biggest wedding? Forgive me, Ella, if I choose to question your ability to hire chefs."

Ella curled her hands into fists, the nails digging into her palms, and forced herself to keep calm. "Charlie was a gamble but he attracted a great deal of attention for us."

"A gamble that could have left us looking incredibly stupid," Jonny countered bluntly, and Ella winced. "You were damned lucky Symon Tremaine was there to bail you out."

Ella bristled. "Symon didn't *bail me out.* I employed him to do a job and in doing so I hired a qualified chef with a Michelin star. Not a public school boy who's decided he wants to play at being Jamie Oliver or because Teddy needs a chum to drive him about when he's too pissed to see straight!"

The gloves were off now but Ella was beyond caring; there was no way this was happening just because her grandfather once played golf with Ricky's granddad or something equally ridiculous.

Jonny's bushy white eyebrows shot upwards. "I'm not sure what you're insinuating but I don't like it."

"Don't you really, Grandpa? Are you sure about that?" Ella held his gaze and Jonny looked away first.

"So he's a little bit wild and needs to settle down. He's not the first young man to behave like that and he's harmless."

"He's not harmless if he drives too fast or drinks and gets behind the wheel," Ella replied. She was worried for her feckless, silly brother. She buried herself in work not to feel and Ted buried himself in booze. What a pair they made.

"I agree," Jonny said. "Teddy needs a focus and he needs to know we trust him. This is a family business after all. He's equally entitled to make decisions and be involved."

"Not this time!" Ella cried, unable to believe what she was hearing. "He hasn't got a clue! We'll be bankrupt in months. Come on, Grandpa! We're doing so well here. Don't ruin it now."

But Jonny shook his head. "I think allowing him to make some management decisions is exactly what he needs. You chose the last chef and now it's his turn. That's only fair."

"For God's sake! This isn't a game of snakes and ladders!" Ella exploded, standing up so abruptly that her wheelie office chair shot across the room. "I can't let you do this!"

"It isn't your place to tell me what I can do or to give me permission. Let me remind you, young lady, just who owns the Polwenna Bay Hotel!"

"And let me remind you who was appointed as the manager!"

"You may be the manager but I'm the owner and I'm telling you that this decision is going to be Teddy's. You need to step aside and let your brother take some of the load."

Ella was in anguish. If she *stepped aside* and allowed Teddy to pop his hopeless cronies into roles they were no way qualified for, the business would be ruined. It was so obvious to her and she was beyond frustrated that her grandfather was so blind to the reality. It seemed that her brother could do no wrong in Jonny's eyes just because he was a boy.

Her heart was hammering in her chest. "I can't do that, Grandpa."

Jonny leaned forward and his voice was lower but as firm as ever. "I'm not asking your permission, Ella. I'm telling you what's going to happen. This is Teddy's call, not yours."

Ella knew it was over before the sentence was even completed. All her work, all her achievements, all her pride in building a team and a superb reputation counted as nothing to her grandfather, just because she happened to be female. It didn't matter how hard she worked or how well the hotel did; in Jonny's eyes she would never be as good as Teddy. Her grandfather was never going to allow her to take over the business fully, was he? She'd been deluding herself by imagining otherwise.

What a fool.

Ella felt as if she'd been punched.

"Then I quit," she said quietly. "You can find yourself a new manager as well as a new chef."

Jonny grimaced. "Don't overreact, Ella, for heaven's sake."

"I'm not overreacting! I'm telling you calmly and politely that if you choose to do this I can't be a part of it and neither can I have my professional reputation ignored. If you give Jonny carte blanche to hire Ricky then I can't remain in a managerial role here."

Her grandfather glowered at her. He wasn't used to people saying no to him and Ella felt a growing admiration for Alice Tremaine. No wonder Jonny was having a hard time believing that she really was postponing the wedding.

"If you walk out of this office now, Ella, then that's it. No second chances."

She walked past him and paused in the doorway, fighting the tears stinging her eyes.

"That works both ways, Grandpa. Just remember that."

All Ella wanted to do was escape and find a quiet place to try and calm her racing thoughts, but as she hurried away from her office she bumped straight into Symon Tremaine on his way out after filming. Oh no. This was all she needed. The last time they'd been alone she'd embarrassed them both by kissing him, and now she was on the edge of breaking down. Why was it that he always caught her when she was least in control of her emotions?

And how was it that even though she was so upset she still felt a flash of longing?

"Hey, what's up?" he asked.

"Nothing," Ella fibbed. She gulped back her tears and bit the inside of her cheek hard because Ella St Milton never, ever showed weakness.

"I have two – no three – sisters and I think I can tell when a woman's upset," said Symon. "What is it?"

His gentle tone undid Ella and tears spilled down her cheeks. Symon reached out and brushed them away, which only made her cry harder. Nobody had wiped her tears away for as long as she could remember, but as Symon's thumb caressed her cheek she felt as though he'd been doing this all her life. She had the strangest conviction that it didn't matter at all if he saw her crumbling. He wouldn't judge or exploit her for being upset; rather, he understood.

"I've quit," she choked.

Symon stared down at her. "Sorry, Ella. I think I must have hollandaise sauce in my ears or something because I thought you just said you'd quit?"

Ella half laughed and half sobbed. "It's not the hollandaise sauce. I really have quit. I just told my grandfather. Oh God. I've just taken bookings for three summer weddings too. What a bloody mess!"

Oh great. More tears. What the hell was happening to her? Now Symon would want to know all the ins and outs and she was way too raw for an interrogation. Ella braced herself for an onslaught.

But Symon Tremaine didn't ask her anything. Instead he simply put his arms around her. Ella pressed her face against his chest. He smelt the same as before, of salt and fresh air and soap.

"Maybe it's not a mess at all."

She looked up at him in surprise.

"What do you mean?"

"Maybe it's a good thing?"

"Don't be ridiculous," Ella snapped. "And don't you dare come out with a load of hippy drivel either about coincidences and serendipity. I'm not Silver bloody Starr."

But Symon just smiled at this, which riled Ella. She took a step back and, placing her hands on his chest, pushed him away.

"I have no idea what you think is so funny but, go on, gloat if you must. I probably deserve it. Go on, have fun."

The smile slipped away but the blue eyes that met hers were so full of kindness that Ella's fury vanished. Oh God. Please come back. Being angry was something she could do automatically. Dealing with sympathy and kindness? That was more of a challenge.

"Oh, Ella. Whatever's happened to you that makes you think anyone would take pleasure in this? I'm laughing because you're far better than Silver Starr! Talk about serendipity and fate. You've actually beaten me to it. Who would have thought?"

"What's that supposed to mean?"

Symon breathed out slowly as though he'd been holding onto something.

"I made a decision today that lots of people won't understand. I'm not sure I understand it either but it feels right and that means I have to listen to it. The only problem was that I was worried that in making it I was going to let you down."

Ella was so intrigued that she forgot her misery for a moment.

"What decision?"

"This whole television thing? It really isn't for me."

"But you're brilliant!" Ella had watched Symon filming and he made it look easy. She'd also watched him smoulder out of the television screen and had been unable to drag her eyes away. Recalling this now, she felt hot all over.

He flushed and tucked a strand of fox-red hair behind each ear, a nervous gesture that she found touching.

"That's very kind of you but the truth is I absolutely hate it. I hate the filming and the styling and being the centre of attention. Maybe it's a middle-child thing, but I like being away from the spotlight – perhaps that's what I enjoy about being a chef? You might be the star of the kitchen but outside of that space the diners don't care who you are or what you look like."

It sounded a lot like being a hotel manager. She managed everything from behind the scenes but let Jonny take the credit and lovely, smiley, people-friendly Tom be the face of the operation.

"I miss being in the Seagull and I miss my real life," Symon continued. "I'm probably a freak in this world of *Big Brother* and *X Factor*, but I don't want to be famous. To be honest I've only stuck the filming this long for your sake."

"My sake? How do you work that out?" Was he alluding to their kiss? Ella's heart started to thud against her chest. Did she want him to mean this? Her head began to whirl as her carefully ordered world began crashing out of orbit.

"I can see how hard you work and how much this opportunity meant to you," Symon continued. "Don't get me wrong: I'm not a saint and the money could certainly help me, but most of all I didn't want to let you down when I could see how excited you were." He paused, then added softly, "I think far too many people have already let you down and I'm not going to be another."

Ella didn't know what to think. Nobody had ever said anything like this to her before, not even the therapists Jonny had spent a small fortune on when she'd been a teenager. Ella had been something of an expert at hiding the truth from them and in the end it had almost become a game before morphing into a habit. How the hell had Symon Tremaine managed to see beneath the armour she'd worn for so many years?

"So if neither of us are working here anymore, what are we wasting time for? Let's get out of here." Symon held out his hand and, without hesitation or quite knowing why she did so, Ella found herself taking it.

"Where are we going?"

"That's a secret but there's something I'd like to show you. I've been mulling it over for a while and now we're free agents I'd value your opinion on it."

Her fingers laced with Symon's, Ella followed him back through the hotel. As always, the place was a busy beehive of activity and, watching the staff and looking around at the gleaming oak panelling and sparkling windows, she felt the old familiar thrill of pride. This was swiftly replaced by a pang of grief.

Oh my God. Had she really just quit?

Her eyes filled, but she blinked the tears away. There was no way she would let any of her staff (or maybe she ought to say her ex-staff) see her upset. She might not have her job anymore but she still had her pride.

Symon walked fast and Ella, suddenly exhausted at the thought of all she'd lost, could hardly keep up. She'd never noticed before how tall Symon was. He was just as tall as Jake and Danny, and his strides were long and powerful. He was still holding her hand and she was half running to match his pace. By the time they reached the back entrance of the hotel, the less glamorous area where the staff left their coats and sometimes snuck to enjoy a crafty cigarette, Ella was gasping.

She needed to up her workout regime.

Symon was holding the door for Ella. He let go of her hand and she felt bereft because holding onto him for those few moments had been like clutching a life raft.

They stepped into the bright spring sunshine and he turned to her with a grin.

"Apologies for the speedy exit. I wanted to make a break for freedom before one of the TV crew spotted me and dragged me back for cutaways or, God help me, another take on the sodding hollandaise sauce."

Although his tone was light Ella could see that Symon was only half joking.

He pointed his keys at a car parked opposite, so muddy it was impossible to tell its make, and when the lights flashed Ella realised it was his.

"Hop in," said Symon. "I know it's not a Range Rover but it's not as bad as it looks, I promise."

"I don't have the Range Rover anymore," Ella told him once they were inside the vehicle. "I had to give it to Charlie to keep him on at the hotel."

"Bloody hell. He was blackmailing you? What a bastard!"

"I hadn't thought of it like that but I guess he was in a way," Ella said quietly. What an idiot she'd been. She should have stood up to Charlie a long time ago and her grandfather too. Thinking about the row she'd had with Jonny made her feel quite sick and as Symon drove out of the hotel grounds, she looked down at her hands rather than at the beautiful building and sweeping lawns. Walking away from all this was going to break her heart. Without the hotel and her job, who was she? What was she for?

Where would she live? What would she do? She supposed she would have to fly out to Palm Beach and ask her mother and stepfather for some help. It wasn't a happy thought.

"We're out," announced Symon as they rattled over the cattle grid and onto the lane. "You are now free to talk and I have escaped death by hollandaise."

In spite of everything Ella laughed.

"That's more like it," he said. "You had me worried for a moment there. It actually looked as though you were crying."

"Me? Never. I'm made of stone," replied Ella. "Haven't you heard what they say about me?"

He gave her a sideways look. "I have and I promise it's not as bad as you probably think. In fact, it isn't bad at all. The staff think you're great."

They did?

"Really?"

He nodded. "Yes, really. Now, before your head gets too big, put your seat belt on and let's go for a drive. I don't know about you but I could really do with a change of scene."

Ella felt the same: she didn't care where they were headed as long as it was as far away from the hotel as possible. As Symon accelerated she fastened her belt and she didn't look back. She couldn't.

Seeing the hotel slide into a phase of her life that was now over would have broken her heart.

CHAPTER 22

They had driven about two miles out of Polwenna, up the hill past Mo's stables and high onto the next windswept headland along the coast. The views were glorious from here and the hedges were splashed with primroses and early bluebells, as though nature had decided to flick blue and yellow paint everywhere. Even a few late daffodils had popped their heads out to feel the sunshine. Ella couldn't help thinking that it was hard to feel down when the world was on the brink of exploding with life. Although the narrow lanes were thick with mud and still relatively free of worried holidaymakers struggling to reverse or doggedly following satnavs rather than their own eyes, it felt as though spring had truly arrived in Cornwall. Today the sun was out and the wide sweep of blue sea was sparkling like something Ella's mother would wear to a gala.

The drive was quiet, neither of them speaking much, but the atmosphere was comfortable rather than strained. Ella had cried on Symon and she wasn't sure if this was less humiliating than kissing him, but thank goodness he hadn't referred to either extreme of her behaviour. The kiss he must have forgotten about and the tears she supposed he was used to with Mo and Issie and Summer around. Not that Mo cried about much at all. When Mo had cut Ella's ponytail off all those years ago at school and been punished for it, Mo had refused to say sorry or shed a tear – even when she was suspended from the school for a week.

Actually, years on Ella felt bad about that. She'd been so jealous of Mo and Summer and had wanted to goad them both. The odd thing was that when she'd achieved her aim, Ella hadn't felt good about it at all. Quite the opposite. She'd felt horrible. Mo might have snapped and Ella had ended up with a bad haircut, but the fact that Mo had got into trouble for the incident hadn't made Ella feel better. Summer and Mo still wouldn't be her friends and now Ella had had a guilty conscience as well as envy to contend with.

Was Jonny's preference for Teddy a punishment or just more evidence that she was unlikeable?

She was still mulling this over when Symon swung the car to the left and through a pair of massive stone gateposts topped with what might once have been majestic lions in full roar, but which were now sad mossy felines with crumbling ears and long-lost manes. Then the car dodged potholes for a good mile along a winding drive, edged with camellia bushes and guarded by thick rhododendrons. Ella wished she was wearing a sports bra and wished even more that she'd told Charlie Barton where to go, and kept her Range Rover. Whatever Symon's car was, it didn't come with state-of-the-art suspension or even the most basic kind.

"If this is where you bring women to cheer them up, then I hate to imagine what you do if you think they're happy," Ella remarked. "Is it meant to be some kind of sick and twisted metaphor for what's become of my career? Or do you genuinely think visiting Perry Tregarrick's vegetable plot will make everything better?"

"Have faith," said Symon. "Just sit back and enjoy the whole medieval manor experience."

The grounds must have been glorious once but were now overrun with weeds and creeping gorse. The views across the landscaped park to the coast were still astonishing though, and the ornamental lake would have been a perfect blue mirror if it hadn't been choked with the type of weeds Ophelia might have been found floating in. No wonder Perry looked suicidal; spending his time here must be like living in a Pre-Raphaelite painting.

"Why on earth are we here?" Ella wanted to know.

Symon didn't answer but drove slowly towards the front of the manor. At some stage there would have been beautiful flower beds either side of the building's sprawling wings, but these had been carved up into allotments or crammed full of slithering polytunnels and bright yellow hosepipes.

Ella winced. Looking at all this, she dreaded to think what Perry Tregarrick had done to the inside of the house.

Polwenna Manor was the real deal. Its thick stone walls, narrow mullioned windows and arched front door dated back centuries. Ivy smothered the façade and dog roses clung to the porch, peering into the windows as though curious and trailing languid stems over the sills. Woody lavenders had taken over what had once been neat herb gardens, the rosemary and thyme having eventually lost their battle for space. The gardens might be overgrown and the old house was falling down in places, but the building was timeless and romantic and everything that an ancient Cornish manor house should be. What potential it had and what a history!

In spite of everything that had happened today, Ella experienced a flicker of something deep inside that felt oddly like excitement.

"I've not been up here for years," she said. "Didn't Perry have a party when he was sixteen? I think the theme was *Austin Powers*? I seem to remember some hippies, anyway."

"That's right," said Symon. "Although the hippies were actually his parents. You wore a green dress, didn't you?"

"Wow! You have a good memory," Ella said, impressed. Symon was spot on. She'd borrowed one of her grandmother's old Biba outfits and teamed it with some knee-high boots. With a slick of heavy black eyeliner and her hair pulled back into a high ponytail, she'd thought she really rocked the sixties' sex-kitten look. At the time she'd been crazy about Jake Tremaine, who'd predictably spent the whole night with eyes only for Summer, and Ella had gone home feeling dejected. She couldn't remember seeing Symon there at all.

He laughed. "There were lots of pretty girls in knee boots and miniskirts! It was one of the highlights of my teenage life! In fact, maybe I should say of my entire life?"

They were passing back down the drive now, leaving the manor house slumbering in the sunshine. Perhaps it was dreaming of the past – maybe even of a teenager's birthday party over a decade before? There must have been so many parties here and so many memories. Ella turned in her seat and looked back. It really was a beautiful setting. Perfect for a wedding or a film.

And totally wasted on Perry Tregarrick, who seemed intent on destroying the place...

"So, apart from a trip down memory lane, we're here why exactly?" she asked again.

Symon slowed the car and parked it just off the rough driveway.

"I'll show you," he said, reaching over to the back seat and pulling out his rucksack. "Come on."

He was shrugging the bag onto his back and striding across the parkland before Ella even had a chance to reply. Great. So she was going to have to follow him across tufty grass dotted with crap on some kind of wild goose chase. She wished she'd been left alone to be miserable in peace. Still, there was nothing for it now but to follow him. Just as well she'd worn Skechers today and not her Jimmy Choos.

By the time Ella caught up with Symon, he was sitting at the top of a bluebell-covered bank and pulling out a bottle of water from his backpack. This was followed by a hunk of French stick, a wedge of Brie and some olives.

"You've brought me on a picnic?"

Symon laughed. "Actually, this is my lunch but you're more than welcome to share it."

He patted the grass beside him and, casting a careful eye around for sheep droppings, Ella joined him. She waved away the bread but took a big gulp of the Evian.

"So, you've quit," said Symon.

Ella sighed. "I didn't have much choice. Jonny's overruled me and appointed a total moron as head chef."

"Ah, well, the St Miltons do that from time to time. They pay their chefs in Range Rovers, or so I've heard."

"Very funny. Well, how about this for a real laugh? Grandpa's also given Teddy carte blanche to run the place."

"Christ. Teddy couldn't run a bath," muttered Symon, and Ella laughed bleakly.

"Tell that to my grandfather. He thinks Teddy's baby Jesus and Richard Branson all rolled into one. He really can't do any wrong."

"The hotel will be run into the ground if Teddy's in charge. It'll be free drinks for all his friends until the cellar's dry. What is Jonny thinking?"

"He's thinking that Teddy's a man and should be the heir to the family business." Ella knew she sounded bitter but she was beyond caring. Besides, she *was* bitter. "So that's why I've quit. I can't stay and watch everything I've built up be destroyed. Tom's good but he won't stick around to bail them out."

"Maybe I should poach him?" Symon said thoughtfully. "He'd be a wonderful host."

"You'll have to do a lot more filming to afford Tom," Ella said. "I haven't quite paid him in Range Rovers yet but it's only a matter of time. I'll have to catch him and make sure he picks up all my loose ends too. That won't be much fun. I've got three potential weddings booked in and they'll have to look elsewhere just when places are getting booked up. It's a disaster."

Symon didn't say anything to this. He tore a chunk off the French stick, sliced some Brie with his penknife and bit in, chewing thoughtfully for a while. Ella drew her knees under her chin and wrapped her arms around her legs, hugging them close. They sat like this for a while as the sun dipped in and out of the gathering clouds, sending golden light and silvery shadows dancing across the landscape. The manor sat in the middle of this, tranquil and unmoved by the passage of the elements and the years, and Ella thought it was one of the most beautiful spots she'd ever seen. If it was cleared, the lake would mirror the house perfectly; she could just picture the reflection trembling in the water. She looked again at the house, with heavy-headed roses nodding above the glittering windows and all around it those woody lavender bushes. She imagined them thick with beaded blooms, scenting the air as she brushed past and trailed her fingers through them. In the dip of the hill behind the manor was the faint azure line of the sea, and as she gazed on it Ella felt again that delicious tingle of knowing that something special was hovering just out of reach. She'd felt it once before when she'd first been allowed to take over the hotel and she knew it meant something now. This place could be magical.

"Of course, there is a flip side to all of this," Symon said, breaking into her thoughts. "Maybe quitting the hotel isn't a disaster at all?"

"What do you mean? How can it be anything else?"

"Because without that safety net of family money and a family business you have no choice but to find out what you're really capable of."

"You're saying I've only got this far because of who I am?" Ella's hackles were up at this. "I worked bloody hard to turn that hotel around *in spite* of my grandfather questioning every step I took and Ted using the place like his own personal bank!"

Symon held his hands up. "I'm not saying that at all. You're an intelligent and resourceful woman. I might not have worked with you for long but I can see just how driven you are. How enormously talented. I also know how hard you've worked. But for all that, the hotel's never really been yours. It's always come with conditions, hasn't it? No matter how kindly intentioned."

This was true. Jonny had been so generous in many ways but had held her back in others. Her role as manager might have looked impressive from the outside but deep down Ella had always known it was all smoke and mirrors. This morning was the ultimate proof of just how little autonomy she really did possess.

"I understand how it feels as though you're falling right now, Ella," Symon continued, "but sometimes the ground has to be ripped away if you're to really learn how to fly. God! That sounds like something Silver Starr would come out with – but it's true."

"You're right about falling. It feels like I've lost everything," she said quietly.

He nodded. "I can imagine it does, but what if this is just the start of something even better? You're a smart woman and you know that you'd gone as far as you could in that role. Maybe it's time to start over and find a blank canvas. It's hard but it's the best way to find out just what you can really achieve. The hurt is still there but it lessens and success is a great balm."

Ella looked at him with interest.

"It sounds to me as though you know what you're talking about."

"Maybe." He turned to meet her gaze and there was a sadness in his eyes that took her breath away.

"Is that what happened to you?" Ella blurted. She couldn't help herself; she had to know. There were all kinds of rumours in Polwenna Bay about Symon Tremaine, ranging from his business in Paris going bankrupt (which was possibly true) to him being gay (which, as Ella could vouch, was nonsense). "Why did you leave Paris?"

Symon stared at her long and hard. "That was a different life. I don't talk about it."

"Because you went bankrupt?"

"Ah! Is that what the rumour mill's come up with? I thought it was because I was gay and my French lover broke up with me?"

"I haven't heard that," fibbed Ella.

He laughed. "You're not a very good liar. You turn pink when you fib!"

"I do not!" Ella could feel her cheeks growing warmer. Then she laughed. "OK, maybe I do. But just for the record, I never believed that rumour."

He reached forward and tenderly stroked her face. "I should hope not."

She held her breath. His lips were just a kiss away. Was Symon Tremaine going to kiss her? And did she want him to?

"We've known each other a while now," he said softly. "Maybe you should hear the real story? I'm afraid it's not as exciting as anything the village gossips could come up with, though."

Then, and Ella was shocked at just how disappointed she was by this, he pulled away and the moment was lost. Reaching into his rucksack he delved for his phone and passed it to her.

"You want me to call someone? Ask the audience? Fifty-fifty?" she quipped, puzzled.

"I'd say phone a friend but I don't keep in touch with any of them," he answered. "Google *Papillon Rouge party chef* and then find the YouTube link. I haven't checked it's still there, and I live in hope it's been taken down, but probably not."

Ella frowned but she took the phone and Googled the words he'd suggested. Minutes later she was scrolling through links until she saw the one he'd meant and then clicked on it.

"Oh!"

"Sounds like you've found the one," Symon said.

The video footage was shot in a kitchen where an array of boiling pans was hissing and spitting away. Music was playing and the kitchen was filled with elegant people drinking wine, talking in French and gesticulating enthusiastically, while a beautiful woman with a chic black bob held court and laughed, throwing back her head and opening her bright red lips. It was some party. In the midst of all this a chef was hard at work flambéing over roaring burners and tossing handfuls of mushrooms and onions into a pan, as hellish leaping flames lit his face. Ella couldn't tear her eyes away from him. Her gaze took in his bare chest, pumped pecs and swelling biceps. He was a vision of pure sex and raw passion, and with his wild hair caught back with a bandana, he looked as though he'd stepped straight off the cover of a racy novel. Her jaw dropped.

It was Symon.

As the clip continued the party grew more rowdy. Symon was now taking regular swigs of cognac straight from the bottle, all the while managing the pans with expert dexterity. Around him, the music blasted and the conversation rose and fell. At one point there was a scuffle and then Symon tossed the food onto plates, downed more brandy and pulled the dark-haired woman into his arms, planting a kiss on her cheek. He held her for only the briefest of seconds, but it was enough for

Ella to notice the intensity of the look they exchanged. The electricity between the two of them made Ella's fingers tingle against the edge of the handset. This was a couple who were having wild and passionate sex, there was no doubt about it. Ella was horrified to feel jealousy coil itself around her heart like a poisonous snake.

She was relieved when the clip ended abruptly.

"Some bash," she said coolly, hoping her emotions didn't show on her face.

"Yeah. Life was pretty much one long party," Symon confessed, reaching across and reclaiming his phone. "Every night there was a crowd of us pushing on through to the small hours. I seem to remember that a fight broke out on the night you just saw. A food critic had written a snide piece and was arrogant enough to turn up for dinner and drinks. Jean-Luc, that was my boss, pulled a knife on him. I had to wrestle it away. They called the police."

Ella was seeing Symon Tremaine in a whole new light. She didn't know quite what to say. Five minutes ago she would have thought that his idea of a crazy night was having a half in The Ship. Then Ella recalled the way his mouth had felt against hers, the power and passion she'd sensed simmering beneath his quiet surface, and she shivered.

There was another side to Symon, just as there was another side to her.

"Polwenna Bay must seem a bit dull," was all she could manage.

"Are you kidding? With all the drama about who said what in the village shop and Big Rog's mystery boat?"

"I could probably live without it," said Ella drily, and Symon chuckled.

"Yeah, me too. But actually there's a lot to be said for coming back, especially when things don't work out as you hoped and you've lost everything."

He stared across the park and the expression on his face was bleak.

"It looks like you were having lots of fun in France," she said. Oh great. She sounded like Sheila Keverne.

Symon shot her an amused look.

"Oh, I was, believe me. I worked hard and I partied even harder and we built a bloody good reputation. Everyone wanted to be seen at Papillon Rouge. I was the sous-chef at the hottest restaurant in Paris and my dishes were getting great write-ups. Jean-Luc, my head chef, taught me everything from when I arrived fresh from my initial training in London to the day I left. He was brilliant. Everyone thought I was mad when I quit but I didn't have any choice – not when I was in love with his wife."

"The woman with the black bob." It wasn't a question.

"How did you know?" Symon asked, looking surprised.

Ella shrugged. The way the woman was watching Symon as though she could gobble him up? The fact that all women recognised when another was staking her claim on a man? The fact that she'd behaved that way herself in the past?

"Women's intuition."

"God, I must make certain I never underestimate that! But you're right. That's Claudette. She was older than me by at least ten years and she was also my mentor's wife – the last woman I should have become involved with," Symon said quietly. "I was flattered, stupid, wrong, young... Call it whatever you like, but I fell for her and I fell hard. Claudette was the front of house and we were constantly together. You know how it is in a kitchen."

Ella nodded. In that pressured environment temperatures and passions ran high. She imagined their affair had been heady and exciting and that Symon had found himself swept away on a tide of sensational sex and insatiable desire. Her stomach folded with an irrational jealousy.

"It was like I'd had a hit of the most addictive drug in the world and all I could think about was scoring more." Symon shook his head. "Christ. I hated myself for betraying Jean-Luc but I couldn't stop. I was in love with Claudette and I thought she felt the same way about me. Turns out I was wrong and I'd ruined everything. What a stupid idiot."

He took a big gulp of water, wiping his mouth on the back of his hand as though trying to remove the memory. Ella imagined he was wishing he could travel back in time and warn his younger self that no matter how sexy Claudette might be or how flattering it was to be the object of her attention, the price he would pay was far too high.

It must have been. He wouldn't be back in Cornwall otherwise.

"What happened?"

"Like a fool I told her how I felt and I asked Claudette to leave Jean-Luc to be with me. She always said he worked too hard – neglected her – and I thought we really had something special. I was wrong. She laughed at me and said that we were having fun and she'd never leave her husband for a sous-chef without a Michelin star to his name." He shook his head as though trying to shake away the memory. "So I left there and then. I had no reference and no job. Everything I'd loved was in Paris and I walked away from it all with little more than my passport and a few euros. I was in pieces."

"And came home to Cornwall," Ella finished. He'd been mending his heart here; of course he had. Now it all made perfect sense.

"And came home to Cornwall," agreed Symon. "It's OK, Ella. Don't look so worried. I'm not about to top myself in the lake or anything. It was quite a while ago now and I've made my peace with it as best I can. I'm not proud of some of the things I did but I'm doing my best to make up for them now."

"Why are you telling me all this?" Ella asked.

"Because I want you to know I'm not bullshitting you when I say that losing everything isn't always the end of the world. I'm not going to lie; at the time I really thought my world had ended. But without any of the crap happening, I wouldn't have come home to Cornwall or started The Plump Seagull or even have been awarded my own Michelin star. I was acting like an utter cock too, and if I'd carried on down that road then I wouldn't have been a person I'd have liked very much. Sometimes things work out for a higher purpose than we can see."

Wow. This had to be the longest speech Ella had ever heard Symon make. She was moved that he'd chosen to share his story with her.

"You're not that person," she said softly. "And Claudette was an idiot to let you go."

He smiled, but it didn't quite reach his eyes. Was the pain still there? Did he still love Claudette?

"Hey, she did me a favour, just like Jonny has for you. Now, forget about my tale of woe for a moment and look around. What do you see?"

Ella's heart was racing. "I see *you*, Symon Tremaine."

And she really did. Symon was absolutely beautiful. Her feelings for Jake, once all-consuming, were nothing in comparison to how Ella felt now. As she stared at Symon, with his intense blue eyes and flame-bright hair, she realised this was different from her teenage crush. There was more than just the strong tug of physical attraction. Ella found Symon's honesty, his considered thoughts, his clever mind and his deft hands and creativity just as sexy as that sculpted body of his, which she longed to feel pressed against hers.

It was everything. She couldn't believe it had taken her a lifetime to see it.

Symon raised her hand to his lips and kissed it. "And I see *you* too. I have for a while now. I see that the chippy attitude hides a woman who's super talented, and clever and brave, and who really cares about what she does. But apart from the emotional wreck that I am, what else do you see here? I mean, what do you notice about this location? What really strikes you about this place when you look at it?"

"The house. The views. The amazing parkland," said Ella, only just managing to stop herself adding that all this was totally wasted on Perry Tregarrick. After all, he was Symon's friend and harmless if hopeless.

"Exactly!" Symon cried, so delighted with her answer that Ella felt as though she'd just passed a difficult exam. "Now imagine all of this in perfect condition and running as a restaurant."

"Or as a luxury hotel with wonderful dining, top-class service and a real sense of history!" Ella interrupted. Oh! She could see it now! The place restored to its former glory, the gardens manicured and filled with beautiful blooms, the lawns as smooth as bowling greens, marquees for weddings...

She understood now why he'd brought her here and what he'd been thinking.

"Oh, Symon! This is your blank canvas! It's perfect!"

He turned to face her, his eyes bright with excitement. The passionate nature he'd kept so tightly in check was bubbling to the surface once more. "You get it, Ella, and I knew you would. You see it too. You feel it!"

Ella did. She felt it all: the high she always experienced when she successfully pulled off an event at the hotel; the thrill of the write-ups in the press; even the satisfaction of sourcing orange and purple bloody gerberas. She knew this must be exactly how it was for Symon too. But feeling things was risky and sometimes you got hurt. It was far safer not to feel anything.

"Perry needs a sound business to keep this place afloat and I need a new restaurant," Symon explained. "It came to me last night that this could be the perfect solution. It'll take time and money and it'll be slow and hard and probably almost bloody impossible, but I think Polwenna Manor could be it. When you said that you'd left the hotel, I knew I could share the idea with you. What do you say, Ella? You could put some weddings on here, small-scale ones at first maybe? Tents and picnic benches and the whole rustic rubbish thing that looks like tat to most guys?"

"Marquees! And rustic chic, not rubbish!" laughed Ella. "But yes, that could be amazing. We'd have that whole Port Eliot Festival vibe going on here, or something like it. I think people would love it!"

"We?" said Symon, and Ella could have kicked herself hard. What was she thinking, allowing herself to get swept away like this? She'd made herself look vulnerable; now that he'd seen her excitement he'd take advantage, make her prove herself ...

But Symon was nodding slowly.

"*We.* Do you know, I like the sound of *we* very much. I think we could make a great team. But do me one favour? Drop Evil Ella? She's a great defence mechanism but I like Excited Ella far more and I think she's a lot more fun to be around."

"If I drop Evil Ella who will I be?"

"The sexy, clever, brave Ella, the Ella I haven't been able to stop thinking about since she kissed me in the beach café," Symon replied softly. "That's the Ella who drives me crazy."

And then his hands were cupping her face and his mouth was on hers, and all Ella's fears melted away. As Symon Tremaine lay Ella down beside the bluebells, his arms holding her so close and his lips straying to her throat, nothing else mattered.

CHAPTER 23

"So, Jonny St Milton," said Alice Tremaine. "Are you going to tell me the truth about what's happening at the hotel or am I supposed to believe the gossip in the village shop?"

"And are you going to accept that you're not needed at Seaspray any longer and marry me?" Jonny countered, his mouth set in a stubborn line.

Alice sighed. It seemed that all they did was argue and she was so weary of it. After Jonny had told her that she had to make a choice, Alice had gone quietly to her bedroom and shed a few tears before drying her eyes and going back downstairs. She loved Jonny very dearly but he had to understand she wasn't the teenager he'd fallen in love with all those years ago – she was a woman in her eighties now, with a family and all kinds of responsibilities. She couldn't give him her undivided attention even if she wanted to. Of course Alice understood his frustration and his fear that their happiness was already based on borrowed time, but she couldn't just walk away. Since their big argument he'd sent her flowers and letters and told her a thousand times how much he loved her and that he just wanted them to have their time together, but they didn't seem to be able to reach a compromise. It was breaking her heart that she would have to choose.

"We've talked about all that," she sighed, reaching out for his hand and covering it with her own. "Jonny, I am needed. There's Danny with his job opportunity, Mo's worried about something too, and then there's Symon who really doesn't like filming but is keeping something from me, and Nick never manages to get out of bed on time—"

"They're adults, Ally." His voice shaking with frustration, Jonny slid his fingers away and made a big show of packing his pipe with tobacco so that she couldn't see how bright his eyes were. Alice hated being the cause of his unhappiness. "And before you mention Emerald, even she's moved out. I love you and you love me. Please let's not waste any more time."

Alice was torn. The life Jonny had imagined for them was like a beautiful dream and she longed with all her heart to say "yes" and step straight into it. On the other hand, how could she enjoy that life if it came at the expense of her family? Oh dear, they'd only come out to have a quiet lunch and already they were at loggerheads.

It was lunchtime on a sleepy Wednesday, that still interim between the bustle of half-term and the vibrant activity of Easter, when the village had a chance to catch its breath before the holiday season began in earnest. As Alice had walked down to the harbour café to meet Jonny, ostensibly for a coffee but in reality for another discussion about their relationship, the village had been quiet and the shops had been empty. A few wealthy-looking day trippers were about, but the explosion of cars stuffed with visitors, suitcases and beach gear was still a little way off.

Easter wasn't until April this year, which gave the Pollards even more of an excuse to slope off to the pub rather than repaint door frames and fix window boxes. The Pollards aside, there was the sense that Polwenna Bay was being spruced up for the main event. Now, as Alice sipped coffee at their sun-dappled table, she could see her grandson Nick doing his bit to tidy up by stacking yolk-yellow fish boxes and coiling ropes on the quay. A seagull snoozed on the wall beside her, watching Alice with a half-open beady eye, but even he was far too relaxed in the sunshine to bother harassing her for a bit of sandwich. He was probably saving his strength for the serious business of mugging tourists for ice creams and pasties.

Alice wished she could follow the seagull's sleepy example. She didn't feel relaxed in the slightest. The arrival of Emerald had knocked her sideways and she was still stressed about whether the poor child was happy here. Emerald was a sweet girl – very independent, in a determined way that reminded Alice of Mo and Symon – and she seemed delighted to be in Polwenna Bay, but it couldn't be easy for her. If only she would stay at Seaspray with them rather than camping out in Mo's damp caravan. Alice had worried enough when Mo had lived there but, unlike the new arrival, at least Mo was accustomed to the chilly weather and the driving Cornish rain, whereas poor Emerald looked half frozen. A warm bed in the house and a tummy full of stew or hot soup was what she needed, and Alice was longing to fuss over her new grandchild. Dear Lord! They'd lost eighteen whole years of Emerald's life. Now *that* was what Alice called wasting time. She could never make up for that, of course, but she could do everything in her power to show Emerald just how loved she was.

"Maybe we've been looking at this the wrong way round?" she said slowly as an idea took hold. It was glaringly obvious and she could hardly believe it hadn't occurred to her before. "Rather than me moving to the hotel after we're married, why don't you move into Seaspray with me?"

Oh, it would be so wonderful to share her family home with Jonny! Already Alice was picturing them taking afternoon tea on the sunny terrace or pottering in the garden together. The walk up was very steep for him but she was sure they could sort something out there – Nick was always nagging Jake to buy a quad bike and organise vehicle access. Alice could just imagine her and Jonny hooning around on one like a pair of teenagers. What fun!

But to her disappointment Jonny didn't jump at her suggestion.

"I can't leave the hotel, Ally. Especially now Ella's quit."

So it was true. Sheila Keverne and Ivy Lawrence had been full of the story when Alice had bumped into them at her WI meeting. She suspected that Symon knew more than he was letting on too, since he and Ella were thick as thieves lately. Even so, Alice was shocked. Ella St Milton was a difficult girl, always had been, but she loved her job and was a superb hotel manager. She'd also managed to persuade Symon to film for that food show – which had certainly impressed his grandmother, who knew just how hard it was to make Symon change his mind about anything. Alice had her quiet suspicions that this change of heart wasn't just down to Ella's skills in staff management, but she hadn't said anything aloud. Symon was intensely private and after Mo's near miss when she'd set him up with Tess, Alice was giving her grandson's love life a very wide berth.

"Why on earth did she quit?"

"She took offence to a decision I made and threw her toys out the pram. Typical Ella, having hysterics."

This didn't sound like Ella to Alice. That girl had great self-control, and one of her icy looks could probably give you frostbite.

"And what was that decision, exactly?"

Jonny looked shifty. "She didn't like my new chef."

Alice knew when she wasn't being told the whole story. Years of raising her grandchildren had given her lie-detecting superpowers.

"Why not?"

He spread his hands out in defeat. "Because I said that Teddy could pick him. Don't look at me like that, Ally! It's high time the boy stepped up to the plate and had some input. Ella's had the hotel to herself for long enough and if it's going to be Teddy's business at some point he needs to learn how to run the place."

"So you pulled rank and employed Teddy's choice over hers." Alice gave up. No wonder Ella had decided enough was enough.

"I wouldn't have put it like that," huffed Jonny. "She didn't have to walk out in a tantrum."

"She did if she felt you don't take her seriously because she's not a man." Alice shook her head in exasperation. She loved Jonny dearly but sometimes Alice wanted to grab him by the cravat and drag him into the twenty-first century.

Jonny gave her the kind of look Nick often did when he knew he was in the wrong but would rather swim around the Shindeep rocks than admit it.

"She's made her choice and that's fine by me," he said sullenly. "She's been bloody stubborn and she's told me her decision's final. She's even moving out of her flat."

"Goodness," Alice said. "Where's she going?"

He shrugged his tweedy shoulders. "Blowed if I know. Your Symon might. She's been talking to him non-stop ever since she gave her notice. If I didn't know better, I'd say she was sweet on him."

Alice also suspected this. They might seem an unlikely pair but they had far more in common than most people realised. Both were self-contained. Both were passionate about their work. And both, she was certain, had been unlucky in love.

"Can't you talk her around? Let her choose her own chef?" she asked gently.

Jonny crossed his arms and jutted his chin out. Talk about eighty-something going on eight.

"She's made her mind up and unless she apologises I'm not saying a word. Besides, Teddy deserves a chance and he needs to settle down. This will be the making of him. You'll see."

Privately, Alice thought it would take more than a hotel to do this. Maybe losing his sports car and having his endless funds curtailed would be a start? Teddy could be charming when he wanted to be, but he was reckless and arrogant and when her granddaughter Issie had briefly dated him Alice hadn't been happy. She'd been sure that no good would come to her family from that quarter. It had all been superstitious nonsense, of course, but she'd been very relieved when their liaison had ended.

"So I'm standing by my choice. Teddy's going to run the hotel from now on. He'll need a lot of guidance from Tom Elliot and from me."

He certainly would, thought Alice, otherwise the hotel would be in the red by teatime. So now Jonny couldn't move out of that place even if he wanted to. Oh dear, so much for her lovely dreams of them zooming up and down the cliff path on a quad. Why couldn't Jonny see that he was choosing the wrong grandchild? The silly old fool was making a huge mistake.

"Don't," he added.

"Don't what?"

"Look at me like you're thinking *Jonny St Milton, you're a silly old fool and making a big mistake.*"

Just as well she wasn't an actor or a spy, thought Alice.

"It's your choice, love, although for the record I think it's the wrong one." She placed her cup in the saucer and stood up, smiling gently down at him. "But maybe now you know how I feel? It isn't so easy to give up your home and family when you know they still need you, is it?"

Jonny looked stricken. "I never wanted to make you feel you had to choose. I love you, Alice. Don't you love me enough to at least try?"

"It's not about not loving me enough or me loving you enough. It's about having to make that love go around and being unselfish. And love, they tell me, isn't selfish." She tucked a five-pound note under the plate and retrieved her bag from the back of the chair. She was done with discussing this. "Let's stop going round in circles talking about all this and just enjoy the afternoon. How about a walk up to the church and a look at the view?"

"Sounds like a plan," agreed Jonny, taking the hint. "And maybe we could have a drink in The Ship afterwards."

He rose to his feet and Alice's heart ached to see how slowly he did this. It always took her aback to see an elderly man superimposed over the vibrant boy she'd fallen in love with all those years ago.

Suddenly Alice knew she didn't want to waste the time they'd been gifted; it was too precious to spend it bickering.

"We're so lucky to get this second chance, Jonny," she said gently, as she took his arm and they strolled away from the water's edge. "Let's not ruin it."

He dropped a kiss onto her cheek and squeezed her arm.

"No more talking about who lives where for today, I promise. But Alice, by Easter time I will need to know. I have to make plans, especially now that I haven't got Ella to help."

Alice bit back her comment on the subject – that if he could only be a little less rigid in his thinking, Ella *would* be able to help right now, given that she was more than capable. No more arguments to ruin a sunny day, she reminded herself. Anyway, the hotel was his business.

"By Easter," she promised him, feeling her heart lurch.

And that was where they would leave this matter – for now, at least.

CHAPTER 24

It was such a relief to be in his own kitchen, using his own implements and having some time away from film crews and hotels. As he chopped dill and listened to the banter between Joby the pot washer and Tony, Symon felt his pulse begin to slow. In between filming more pieces for F&D he'd been busy talking to Perry, putting together a business plan with Ella and trying to think of ways to break the news of the change to his staff. Starting over was a risk, he knew that, but it was also a huge opportunity and every time he thought about it, Symon's heart cartwheeled with excitement.

Actually, that sensation might not just be down to his potential new business venture…

The truth was, Symon's thoughts had been whirling ever since he'd driven Ella to the manor house and confided in her about his plans. Instinct had told him she'd share his vision for the place, and she hadn't disappointed. Symon hadn't intended to tell her about his past but it had felt right and he'd known that if they were to work together she needed to know everything. A business partnership was like a marriage; secrets would only poison it. He'd also been certain that she would understand exactly why he'd felt the need to walk away from his life in Paris. Like him, Ella felt things very deeply and she too had been forced to find a way to cope. Whereas Symon had buried himself in work and cultivated a quiet persona, she had turned to her career and put her energies into becoming Evil Ella, the Polwenna Bay ice maiden and uber-bitch.

It puzzled Symon that nobody else could see that this was just an act. Ella reminded him of the stray cat he'd befriended in Paris. It had been the staff custom to grab a smoke in the narrow street that wiggled all the way down from Sacré-Coeur to Papillon Rouge. This was where the bins were stacked and, after dark, he could usually hear the scratching and scuffling of night-time scavengers. A small black cat often lurked in the shadows and Jean-Luc sometimes threw it scraps because he knew it would keep the rats away. Often, as Symon smoked there, blowing rings of heavy tobacco up into the starry sky, he would catch a glimpse of the creature. At first it had been wary, hissing and spitting when he'd stretched out his hand to caress it, but he'd seen the flicker of interest in the cat's eyes when it had caught the scent of the fish or meat he brought to tempt it. It had taken weeks of patience on Symon's part, and quite a few nasty scratches too, before the little cat had trusted him enough to come closer. It had been hurt and was wary, but after a while it would come when called, winding around his legs and raising its chin for a tickle. Earning the trust of this wild, fearful creature had been worth all the scratches and scars.

Metaphorically (and perhaps literally, for all he knew), Ella St Milton's claws could scratch too – and having witnessed how thoughtlessly her grandfather had treated her, Symon understood why. It would be hard to trust anyone if your own relatives could let you down so easily. He felt thankful for his own family who, although they might drive him to distraction at times, always had his back. Even Jimmy would do anything for his children. Like that wary little cat, Ella's trust would be hard won but worth more than gold.

She'd found her way beneath his guard, something that Symon hadn't expected. He'd not been looking to get involved with anyone – and even if he had been, Ella St Milton wouldn't have been top of his list, or even on his list in the first place. He'd known her all his life; Polwenna Bay was a small village, after all. She was slightly older than him, which when they were growing up had placed her as far out of his reach as the stars and the moon. It had also been a family joke that she'd had a thumping crush on Jake. Symon, as the younger and ginger brother, had always been in Jake's shadow. That hadn't stopped him admiring Ella from afar though, and when she'd mentioned Perry's sixteenth birthday party Symon had remembered straight away exactly what she'd been wearing that night. How could he have forgotten when he'd been unable to take his eyes off her? With her long blonde hair falling over her tanned bare shoulders, and with her slim figure swathed in a dress of shimmering green silk, she'd looked like a mermaid. She certainly couldn't have been more unobtainable if she'd dived to the bottom of the sea.

Symon wondered what the boy he'd been back then would say if he'd known that the man that he would become would end up a heartbeat away from making love to Ella in that very same parkland, amid a carpet of wild grasses and bluebells.

He probably wouldn't believe it. The adult version of Symon could hardly believe it.

He'd kissed Ella long and slowly, cupping her face in his hands and then running his fingers through her silky hair. He'd traced her mouth with his tongue, nipping at her lower lip with his teeth and hearing her gasp. It was a kiss that had begun as one thing, a moment of celebration, but that had caught fire to become something else entirely. He had never felt quite so out of control. Between kissing her, holding her and feeling her soft skin against his, Symon had felt as though he was losing his grasp on everything that had seemed so important only moments before. As soon as she'd melted in his arms, from the second her tongue touched his, Symon had known that he could have kissed her forever. Never in his life had he felt like this before; never had he seen anyone so beautiful or wanted them so much. Where this passion had sprung from Symon had no idea, but as Ella had kissed him back with an intensity that made him groan, he'd realised that he had to pull back before things got out of hand. His mind was reeling. He didn't want to let her go but if he didn't he was in danger of losing himself completely – and Ella deserved so much more. When Symon had finally forced himself to lift his mouth from hers, he'd felt as though something heavy had tumbled away.

Was it the past? The noise and heat of the kitchen receded as his thoughts drifted back again to that perfect afternoon…

"I already thought it was a great idea. You didn't have to kiss me," Ella had said shakily as she'd threaded her fingers through his hair and then traced the line of his jaw. "Unless you seal all your deals that way?"

Symon had laughed at this. "I can promise you I won't be kissing Perry Tregarrick like that! Or at all, in fact!"

"So this is a one-off? A celebration?"

She'd glanced up at him from under her eyelashes and his heart had melted when he'd glimpsed the uncertainty there.

"How can it be a one-off when it's the second time? Although I suppose officially it's the first time *I've* kissed you? Last time I seem to remember that you made all the running! There was I, innocently drinking my coffee, and wallop! It was like being attacked by a sink plunger!"

"A sink plunger! The cheek of it!" Ella had sat up and made a swipe at him. Symon had ducked and, catching her wrists, pinned her beneath him and kissed her until neither of them had any breath left.

"Who's the sink plunger now?" Ella had teased. Her make-up was gone, her cheeks were flushed and the usually poker-straight hair was ruffled and dusted with bluebells and blades of grass. Symon didn't think he'd ever seen her look so beautiful or so utterly desirable. It had taken all his control not to reach for her again and take her right there and then.

"I think we're quits," he'd said. Then, scrambling up, he'd held out his hand to Ella and pulled her to her feet. She was so light that he'd almost sent her flying. Symon had found himself thinking that he really must cook for her. From the way she'd bitten into his sample menu with such relish, he could tell that Ella had been holding back in all her appetites. He could hardly wait to satisfy every one of them. A strange feeling knotted in his chest and it took a few seconds before he recognised it.

Excitement. For the first time in almost as long as he could remember, Symon Tremaine was feeling excitement.

"Come on," he'd said, tenderly brushing the foliage from her hair. "Let's get going before I totally lose control and ravish you right here."

"That sounds like a lot of fun," Ella had mused, her cheeks still pink and her grey eyes shining.

"It certainly does but it could also be just a little awkward if Perry comes trundling by on his quad," Symon had pointed out. "I know he's oblivious to most things but I think I'll err on the side of caution, if it's all the same with you?"

She'd laughed. "Normally I'd have said that you never do anything else, but after today I know differently."

He'd laid his finger against her lips.

"What happens at the manor stays at the manor. We daren't let anyone know that Evil Ella has a seriously sexy and very badly behaved alter ego. Her image would be wrecked."

She'd shuddered. "That is most definitely staying classified information, alongside a certain YouTube clip."

"Christ, yes. I wouldn't want Granny Alice seeing that. We're definitely quits."

Symon had scooped up his rucksack and slung it over one shoulder. Hand in hand they'd wandered back to the house (which had taken them ages because they'd kept stopping to kiss), before seeking out Perry and sharing their plan.

Perry had been thrilled and full of ideas for grants and capitalising on the history of the place. Between them they'd decided that Symon would grit his teeth and carry on filming for as long as F&D wanted him, so that he could earn as much money as possible, while Ella would write a detailed business plan and see if she could liberate some of her savings from her share portfolio. Symon wasn't keen on this idea – accepting financial help from anyone went against everything he believed in – but Ella was adamant that if she was to be an equal partner then she had to help fund the venture.

"Perry's got the premises, and you've got your savings and your name, but what can I bring to the party?" she'd argued, after they'd returned from visiting Perry.

"You *are* the party," Symon had protested. "Besides, you bring your wedding-planning business and your management skills. Perry and I need those."

"You certainly do. He's always off on a tangent and your mind's usually on the next culinary creation," Ella had agreed. "Without me there'll be yurts and amazing food but not much else!" Then her expression had grown serious. "But teasing aside, I want to invest because I want to be part of this and I want to show my commitment too. Either we're in this together or not at all."

He'd taken her hands in his and kissed each in turn.

"We're definitely in this together," he'd promised, before kissing her again. After that, they hadn't talked about business again for quite a while...

The last few days had passed in a blur, partly because Symon was so busy and partly because he was in a state of delicious anticipation. Nothing more than kissing had taken place between him and Ella, but he was in no doubt this would change in the not-so-distant future, and the thought of it was driving him to distraction. In the meantime, Ella had a move to organise – she was going to crash in Tom Elliot's spare room – and Symon had filming to complete and a restaurant to run. He needed to stop daydreaming like some love-struck teenager and focus on what he was doing.

Especially when he was chopping up herbs!

As the blade missed his fingertips by a hair's breadth, Symon forced himself to focus. There would be lots of time to think about Ella and their plans for the manor, but for now he needed to keep all his fingers in one piece and his mind on the job. If they were to stand a chance of making a success of the place then his reputation as a chef was paramount. Maybe he could even get that second Michelin star?

Symon resumed his chopping but his thoughts were like a boat that kept slipping its mooring, and no matter what he did they kept drifting back to Ella. The connection he had with her was intense and, unlike Claudette, she was his equal in every way. It was like nothing he'd known before. Ella had an uncanny knack of seeing his vision almost before he did and she shared Symon's drive and passion for work. He already knew that he wanted a future with this girl and that he was falling head over heels for her. It was sudden and unexpected and illogical – yet it felt so natural, which was why he trusted it. Unlike the fiery and ultimately destructive passion he'd experienced with Claudette, his feelings for Ella filled him with a fizz of delicious expectation. With hindsight, Symon realised that his relationship with Claudette had been about the thrill of the forbidden and the dark danger of addiction. The uneven balance of power had thrown him out of kilter too; although it had added to the illicit excitement, it had also left him vulnerable. With Claudette, there had always been a sense of stomach-churning anxiety as well as lust. In contrast, Ella was his perfect match. Symon hadn't believed in soulmates before, but already he was starting to wonder whether he'd found his.

His phone buzzed deep in his pocket and, hoping it was Ella texting with an idea or to suggest meeting up, Symon put the knife down and wiped his hands on his apron.

Claudette

He frowned. Almost as though she could sense him slipping away from her, Claudette Marsaud had sent several messages over the past twenty-four hours. Symon hadn't read any of them. Thankfully, almost all he could think of now was Ella: it was a relief to look at Claudette's name and feel little more than a prickle of unease. Afraid that even opening one of her messages would allow her to creep back into his heart, Symon had deleted each of them straight away. He did the same now and then sighed. It was a painful chapter of his life but it was over. There were wonderful things to look forward to, he was sure of it.

"You all right, Chef?" Tony asked.

"Fine, mate, just got a lot on my mind with the filming," said Symon, pocketing the phone and returning to his chopping.

"Yeah, it must be tough being a celebrity chef," grinned his sous-chef, deep in the very glamorous job of picking out crab.

"You have no idea," Symon told him with a grimace. "It's hell."

Tony slung a handful of dead man's fingers into the guts bucket and, with his nose wrinkled, returned to their conversation. "Yeah. It looked bloody awful for Charlie Barton. Lots of money. Flash car. Time off. Shagging the boss."

"What?" Symon was suddenly ice cold.

"Charlie shagging Evil Ella? Klaus said he was always bragging about it," confided Tony. Splat went the crab's innards into the bucket. Symon felt as though his own were being ripped out and tossed in the bucket with them. "Apparently they were at it like rabbits. She even gave him a Range Rover. Hey! You should stick with the filming, boss, if celebrity chefs are Ella's thing. You never know, even you might get lucky!"

Symon's hands were shaking as he stared at Tony in disbelief. Suddenly he understood everything. Christ. What an idiot he'd been.

There was a clatter as his knife slipped onto the floor. Blood pooled on the countertop but Symon didn't flinch. The deep gash to his hand was nothing in comparison to the pain his heart was experiencing now that he knew the truth about Ella.

CHAPTER 25

Big Roger Pollard's shed had never enjoyed so much attention. Neither, it had to be said, had Big Roger Pollard.

Everyone was gathered in the Pollards' garden, a hilly affair just along the lane from the church, where a distinctly average shed was draped with faded bunting left over from the Diamond Jubilee. Everybody was agog to see what he'd been doing all these months, although it might be the promise of free drinks and nibbles that had really drawn a crowd. Eddie Penhalligan and his fishermen sons were working their way through a pile of curling ham sandwiches, Caspar Owen was scooping up handfuls of peanuts and even Sheila Keverne and Ivy Lawrence had made it up the hill for one of Mrs Pollard's rock cakes. There was a fairground atmosphere, partly down to the music playing from an old ghetto blaster and partly down to the presence of Silver Starr, who with the aid of one of her crystals was predicting to all and sundry what she thought would be in the shed.

"It's a watercraft," she was saying, eyes closed and body swaying. "I sense it will only reach the ocean after great strife and terrible destruction!"

"Sounds very Biblical," observed Jules. "What's in there, I wonder? Noah's ark?"

"Anyone seen dumb beasts trotting up here in pairs?" asked Chris the Cod.

"Only Big and Little Rog," bellowed Eddie. He glanced at his watch. "Well, come on then, Roger! What are we waiting for? My missus will have tea ready soon and I'd like to get a pint in first."

It was almost six in the evening and, although the days were drawing out now, the light was starting to fade. The pub crowd were getting twitchy. Nick and Emerald were perched on the garden wall clutching plastic cups of warm white wine and waiting for the big reveal. Emerald had to admit she was a bit perplexed. Why would anyone build a boat in their backyard and so far from the water?

"Because this is Cornwall and we like to do things arse about face," said Nick when she asked him. "And besides, you've met the Pollards. Do they strike you as the kind of people who do things in a methodical and logical manner?"

Emerald watched Little Rog trying to extricate his hand from a Pringles tube.

"I guess not," she giggled. Emerald liked her friends and family here in Polwenna Bay but they were a bit odd. She still wasn't quite sure when they were serious or when they were joking, a case in point illustrated perfectly by Big Roger Pollard's welcoming address.

"First of all, I would thank you for making the effort to come on up this evening but I know you're a nosey bunch of buggers and would have been sticking your beaks in anyway!" Big Rog announced. "I also know you'll all do anything for free booze and a sandwich, you bunch of bleddy freeloaders!"

"I'm insulted," huffed Sheila, through a mouthful of cake.

"Get on with it!" boomed Eddie Penhalligan, waving a sandwich. "What are we waiting for? If you take as long with this speech as you do to paint a window frame we're all going to die of old age."

There was a ripple of laughter.

"I'll have you know it takes skill and time to paint a window properly, Eddie Penhalligan!" said Big Rog. "These things can't be rushed."

"We do know. We're your customers!" shot back Eddie, enjoying his newly discovered talent for heckling as there was more laughter. "Cleared any drains lately, or should I look forward to mooring my trawler outside my house?"

Big Rog's face was red. "Those floods were not my fault! You come up here and say that!"

It was at this point that Jules stepped in to calm things down.

"We all know none of that was your fault and Eddie was only teasing, weren't you?"

"Course I was, mate," said Eddie. "I was pulling your chain! Come on! I want to see this famous boat."

"Shall we press on?" Jules asked, doing her best to move things forward.

"Dad's written a speech," piped up Little Rog. "Haven't you, Dad? We need the speech."

His father waved a tatty piece of paper in the air. "That's right, my boy! But, do you know what? I think we should just get to the main event."

He strode over to the shed, ducking under the Union Jack bunting, and threw the door open with pride. "Here she is!"

There was a wave of excitement as everyone surged forward for a look. Emerald hopped down from the wall and eventually managed to get a peek inside the shed too, where she saw a pretty little clinker boat. The wood gleamed, the brass work glowed and the vessel was clearly a labour of love, but it was still just a boat. Speculation regarding Big Roger's creation had ranged from a distillery to a cinema to a pole-dancing studio for Mrs Rog, so to discover that he really had been building a boat was a bit of an anti-climax.

"It's not a bar then," said Nick sadly.

"Or a pole-dancing club," sighed Caspar. "It's just a boat."

"Of course it's a bleddy boat!" Big Rog looked put out at this distinct lack of enthusiasm. "I told you all I was building a boat. What's the problem?"

"We thought the boat was a cover for something," explained Adam Harper. "A bit like the beach café was."

Big Rog looked shocked. "You all thought I was growing drugs?"

"That would have been more exciting than a boat. What do you think I look at all day?" asked fisherman Eddie.

"But what a great boat she is," Chris the Cod said kindly as Big Rog's face fell. The others all nodded hastily and made approving noises.

"You're very clever, Roger. The church hall roof will be nothing to you after this. I'll pencil you in for Monday, shall I?" said Jules.

Mollified, yet sensing he'd just been outmanoeuvred, Big Roger nodded.

"Well done, she's a beauty," Jonny St Milton commented admiringly. "I used to have one of those when I was a boy. We went out on it, Alice? Do you remember?"

Alice's eyes were bright and her cheeks pink. "Of course I do."

At least the elderly couple were talking again. Emerald was relieved to see this because she still blamed herself for causing trouble.

"I bet Adam Harper a tenner you'd built a bar in there," sighed Nick. "I've flipping well lost. It really was a boat."

"It's a great boat, Roger," Jules said. "I'll do the whole launch thing if you like? With prayers and champagne? God bless her and all who sail in her?"

Roger Pollard beamed at her. "Proper job!"

"Silly to waste the champagne on a boat," said Caspar quickly. "Maybe we could have that as a toast instead? A glass each?"

"How will you get the boat to the ocean?" Emerald wondered. It was a long and steep road down to the harbour. They didn't do things like this in San Francisco.

"It's on a trailer," Nick explained. "We'll tow it down with a car."

"The tide's in, so let's do it now," suggested Little Rog excitedly and there was a cheer at this. He dived into the shed and moments later called, "Err, Dad, how do we get her out?"

"Through the door, my boy!" Big Rog rolled his eyes. "How do you bleddy think we'll get her out? By magic?"

There was a scuffling and a bumping for a few moments but no boat emerged.

"Err, Dad?" called Little Rog. "I think it's stuck."

"Stuck? What do you mean, stuck?"

"I can't get it out the door."

"For heaven's sake, if you want something done do it yourself," said Big Rog to the others. He ducked into the shed.

"No! Not like that, you harris!"

There was more thumping and scraping, followed by a few grunts while everyone outside waited patiently for the boat to appear. And waited. And then waited some more. Finally, Big

Rog emerged with a sweaty face and an embarrassed expression.

"The boat's stuck."

Everyone gaped at him.

"What do you mean, *the boat's stuck?*" asked Mrs Pollard. "How can it possibly be stuck?"

Big Rog pulled off his cap and twisted it nervously in his hands. "It's too big to get out of the shed, love."

His wife stared at him. "You did measure the door, didn't you?"

The silence told everyone all they needed to know. Big Rog had built a boat that was stuck in his shed. Emerald felt Nick start to shake with silent laughter. She elbowed him in the ribs.

"Stop being mean!"

"I can't help it!" Tears were running down Nick's cheeks. "Only the Pollards could build a boat inside a shed and not think about how to get it out!"

The Pollards were now squabbling amongst themselves while everyone else laughed until their sides hurt.

"We can still get her out, Pa! We just have to take the side off the shed," said Little Rog eventually.

"That's right, my boy!" Big Rog looked relieved. Honour was saved and he clapped his hands together. "Fetch a crowbar, son, and we'll have the boat out in a jiffy."

"You'll do no such thing," said his wife. "My jasmine's climbing on that shed – and the clematis."

"I know you have a few plants growing on it, love, but needs must!"

Mrs Pollard placed her hands on her hips and glowered at him. "You are not going to pull my climbing jasmine down."

"But my boat's in there!"

"I don't care if you've got the *QM2* in there, Roger Pollard! You are not disturbing my plants!"

"What did I say? Great strife and terrible destruction," Silver Starr crowed. "My spirit guides are never wrong!"

"It's a shame they couldn't help Roger Pollard measure up," Nick whispered in Emerald's ear.

While the senior Pollards argued about whether or not to rip down the shed, everybody else busied themselves finishing off the wine and nibbles. By the time night had fallen and the windows in the village glowed with lamplight, it was Mrs Pollard and her plants one, Big Rog and Shed Armageddon nil. Gradually the villagers drifted away.

"Looks like the party's over," said Nick, once Alice and Jonny had kissed him and Emerald goodbye and Big Eddie and his crowd had departed for the pub. "I'm going for a drink. Want to come?"

She shook her head. "No, thanks. I'm going to FaceTime my mom and record my vlog."

"I'll come with you, Nick. These two will be arguing all night and by the time they've finished it will all be my fault anyway," said Little Rog gloomily. "Everything usually is."

"Yep. National debt. Global warming. All your fault," Nick teased. "You need some serious cheering up, Roger. Hey, Em, have you come up with any of those single cheerleader friends yet? I bet they'd go crazy for our English accents and even Rog here would be in with a chance!"

Emerald laughed. "You need to stop watching *High School Musical*. I really don't have any cheerleader friends and, before you ask again, I don't have any who work in Hooters either or who are Playboy Bunnies."

"You," said Nick gravely, "are an utter disgrace as an American sister. Oh well, looks like the pub it is, Rog."

Emerald was still smiling to herself as they went their separate ways; Nick and Little Rog turned left at the church to walk downhill into the harbour, while she turned right and took the steep lane away from the village. The night was dark and quiet except for the trembling hoots of owls. Clouds had drifted over the sky and wiped out the stars and the moon too, so that the only light she had was her iPhone torch. Usually the dark didn't bother Emerald in the least but, all the same, when the battery died and the beam of light went out her heart started to patter. Nick had taken great delight in telling Emerald all kinds of terrifying Cornish ghost stories, from ones about mysterious prowling black cats to tales of a phantom smuggler who haunted the caverns beneath the village. In the daylight it had been easy to dismiss these, but when you were walking in the pitch blackness and with only the looming shadows of familiar landmarks to guide you? Then it seemed very different. In her dark jeans and hoody, she felt as though she was melting into the night. Emerald could sense unworldly eyes watching her and she shivered.

She rounded the curve in the lane, yanking her backpack up onto her shoulders and readying herself for the steep climb up to the yard. The last thing she'd expected to see were two headlamp-yellow eyes bearing down on her out of the night. For a moment she was frozen in horror, dazzled by the full beam as her ears filled with the roar of a powerful engine in full throttle. Before she'd registered what was happening, the car was almost upon her.

There was no sidewalk here. How was she to get out of the way?

The vehicle was travelling downhill at such a pace Emerald didn't stand a chance of dodging it in time. All she could do was press herself into the hedgerow and hope this would save her. Thorns and twigs sliced into Emerald's arms and legs but she hardly noticed in her panic. *Breath in!* she told herself desperately.

It wasn't enough. The vehicle clipped Emerald and flipped her sideways until she was trapped between unforgiving metal and hawthorn. Then she slammed into the tarmac and there was nothing but a darkness a thousand times thicker than the blackness of a cloudy Cornish night.

CHAPTER 26

"OMG! Emerald Tremaine's been knocked down!"

Tom Elliot was wide-eyed as he delivered this news to Ella, who was busy packing up her office. Straightening up from filling boxes with all her files, Ella stared at him aghast. This explained why Symon hadn't returned any of her calls or text messages.

"Is she OK?"

"I think so," said Tom, "but I only just heard it myself. Apparently she was found in the lane up by the stables by some holidaymakers walking back to a cottage last night. She's in the hospital."

"Do they know what happened? Who hit her?" Abandoning her packing, Ella perched on the corner of her desk and did her best to ignore the cold dread seeping through her every cell. As she waited for Tom's reply she realised she was holding her breath.

"No idea. Hit and run apparently, at least that's what Betty Jago says. I thought I'd let you know, since you and Sy seem so *friendly* these days."

Tom lolled in the doorway, clearly gagging for some gossip. Ella ignored him.

"Haven't you got some work to do?"

"Err, I hate to point this out but you're not my boss anymore?" said Tom. "See how the place is already going to pieces without you?"

But Ella wasn't in the mood to banter with Tom. She grabbed her jacket from the back of the chair and shrugged it on. The packing she would finish later. Right now she had several very urgent things to see to.

As she walked out of the hotel, looking out over the choppy sea and at the louring clouds that heralded a change in the weather, her brother was headed in the opposite direction and on foot for once rather than behind the wheel of his sports car.

"Teddy, I was hoping to catch you," she began, but her brother just held his hand up as though warding her off and continued on his way.

"I can't stop right now, sis. Far too much to do! Some of us have a hotel to run, you know!"

Ella clenched her fists and counted to ten. By the time she'd finished Teddy was leaping up the steps to reception as though he hadn't a care in the world. There was no point asking for a lift.

Irritated, Ella walked down the hill into the village. She eyed the sky and the churning water with concern. It looked like rain to her and the wind was already whipping up the waves in the bay. A squall was marching across the horizon, blurring the sky and sea together in a watery grey smudge, and if she didn't hurry Ella knew she'd get soaked.

Ella made it to The Plump Seagull just as the heavens opened. It was only early morning but already the place was buzzing with activity. Tara was folding napkins and Kelly was busy restocking the bar area, both women singing along to Pirate FM as they worked. It was a far cry from the usual quiet that Ella insisted upon for her guests, and she found herself thinking that maybe it didn't hurt for the staff to have some fun. When she and Symon were running the manor together this would be just the kind of work atmosphere she would aim for. A sense of being part of a valued team drew people together far more effectively than rigid rules ever could.

Careful! The ice maiden really was melting, thought Ella. She'd be taking them out for team bonding days next.

"Hello there," she said, spotting Symon seated at a table studying menus with a determined intensity. His left hand was swathed in a bandage and she wondered what he'd done. Cut it cooking? Burned it? She wished she'd been the one who'd dressed it and tended to him. Her heart constricted with tenderness.

He looked up. "Oh. It's you."

Rather than the warm tone and smiles Ella had grown used to, Symon was cool. Was it because he was in his place of work or that she had interrupted? Wrong-footed momentarily, Ella said, "Sorry if I'm disturbing you. You weren't answering your phone."

"No. I wasn't."

This wasn't much better.

"I was worried about Emerald," Ella said. "And you. What's happened to your hand?"

Symon glanced down at it as though he'd barely noticed. "Just a cut. It's nothing important. Emerald's in a worse way. She's concussed and she's broken her arm. Jules and Granny are at the hospital now."

Ella's hand flew to her mouth. "That's awful."

"Yes."

More stony monosyllables. Why was he so off with her?

"Kelly, give me a hand in the kitchen, please?" said Tara, nudging the younger girl. Switching off the radio, they tactfully left Ella and Symon alone together.

Symon didn't speak for a moment and Ella was gripped by unease. What had happened? What had changed? Her hands tingled with fear. This aloofness was frightening her and not being close to him was unbearable.

"Why didn't you tell me?" he said finally.

"Why didn't I tell you what?"

"That you were screwing Charlie Barton? Did you really think I wouldn't find out? Come on, Ella! Kitchen staff love to gossip. Your thing for chefs is common knowledge, apparently. After me, who next? Tony? Klaus? Rick bloody Stein?

Cold horror swamped her. Oh God. She should have known that Charlie bloody Barton would come back to haunt her.

"Please, Symon, let me explain—"

"You don't need to explain!" snapped Symon, cutting her off. "It's all totally self-explanatory, thanks Ella. There was I feeling sorry for you and thinking how badly Charlie had behaved when all the time you'd been sleeping with him."

"It didn't mean anything!"

"Of course it didn't! It never does to women like you," he snarled. "Out with the old and in with the new, eh? Isn't that how it goes with you lot?"

"No! It isn't like that!"

"It's exactly like that," said Symon bitterly. "Come on, Ella. You can drop the wide-eyed and innocent act now. You use people to get what you want. You wanted a celebrity chef so you slept with Charlie and got him. You needed somebody to bail you out and here I was. It's how you've always operated but I was actually stupid enough to think I was falling in love with you and that maybe you felt the same. What an idiot. You must have laughed so hard when you checked back in with lover boy."

Ella's heart was hammering in her throat. Only minutes ago she would have been turning cartwheels at the mention of love.

Now these were the most painful words she'd ever heard. She had to make him see that Charlie had meant nothing. She'd never let Charlie into her heart the way she'd let Symon Tremaine in.

"That's utter nonsense! Like I said, Charlie meant nothing! It was just a stupid fling and it was over almost as soon as it started. I'm not proud of being involved with him and I swear to God we're not in touch now."

He laughed harshly. "I should have known what was really going on when you said he had your car."

"He took it in payment! He was practically blackmailing me!" Ella cried. "Just listen, will you? I need you to know nothing serious went on between me and Charlie."

Symon gave her a cold look. "For once, Ella, this isn't about what you need."

"Charlie meant nothing. It was just fun. Yes, I was stupid to get involved with him, but it was never serious. He didn't mean anything to me, whereas you... You're everything."

She'd never been so honest with anyone in her life and Ella's throat tightened because suddenly she realised exactly what Symon Tremaine had come to mean to her. Against all the odds and without her even noticing, he'd edged closer and closer, slipping into her hopes and dreams and even her future. She had trusted him in a way that she'd never trusted anyone before. She'd let him see her, the real her. If he pushed her away now it would be a rejection in every respect.

"That's very touching, Ella." There was a sharp edge to Symon's voice that she'd never heard before. "The trouble is, we both know it's utter nonsense. No doubt you said the same to Charlie and, who knows, maybe even Jake? I'll have to ask him."

Ella gasped. These words were so cruel she actually felt as though she'd been slapped. She couldn't believe Symon was so angry just because she'd not told him about Charlie.

"How many times can I tell you that Charlie meant nothing?" she said. "I didn't mention him because it didn't even occur to me that I needed to! That's how little he actually featured in my life! It's not because he's some major love affair I'm guarding. It's because he was a stupid, meaningless fling. I've regretted it every day since!"

"Just like the one that we nearly had, I suppose? Lucky we stopped when we did. I'd hate to be the latest notch on your bedpost. And if you're trying to bed all the TV chefs in the land, then I guess Gordon and Jamie had better watch out."

The sarcasm in his voice was betrayed by the briefest flicker of pain in those blue eyes, and instantly Ella understood that none of this was really about her.

This was about Symon. Or maybe more accurately it was about Claudette.

Hadn't the other woman told Symon he was just a fling? Made him feel that what they'd shared was nothing to her when it had meant the world to him? Like Ella, Symon felt things deeply and, like her, he would revert to whatever defence mechanism had worked before. By his own admission he'd shut Claudette out of his life and walked away, and now he was going to do the same to Ella.

She couldn't let him. They were at the start of something special and they couldn't lose it. Not over a stupid misunderstanding.

"What we have isn't meaningless and you know it," said Ella quietly. "That's why you're terrified."

His mouth curled scornfully. "Hardly."

"Yes, you are." Ella felt as though she had nothing to lose now. There was no point holding back. "You're terrified of real relationships where a woman is actually flesh and blood and not some idealised vision up on a pedestal. Like your mother was and like Claudette was too."

"Spare me the cod psychology," he spat.

But Ella had the bit between her teeth now.

"I'm sorry if you had a bad time in the past and I'm sorry if Claudette let you down and hurt you but *I'm not her*! Women are human, Symon. We make mistakes. We do things we regret. We sleep with the wrong people. We make bad choices. We have pasts. That's real life. I've never pretended to be perfect and I've never lied to you either. If I misled you about Charlie then I'm sorry but you've misled me too!"

"I have not!" Symon grated. "I've been nothing but open and honest with you."

Ella shook her head.

"You might have told me about your past but you also let me believe that it was safe to be myself and that it was all right to tell you everything – but that was a lie, wasn't it? I haven't lived up to some unobtainable goal you placed there for me to reach. And do you know what? Maybe it's just as well you're disappointed in me now because with a conditional love like yours nobody could ever be good enough! So I'm sorry if you feel like I've let you down, Symon, but you've let me down too!"

Then she flew from the restaurant and out into the street. It was raining hard now but that didn't matter to Ella. She could hardly tell where the raindrops ended and her tears started. She felt as though her heart was splintering into a million sharp pieces, each one stabbing her repeatedly as his words echoed through her mind. The pain was unbearable.

How had something so wonderful been snatched away so quickly?

Once again she was alone; unloved and unlovable. And this time as she stood sobbing in the rain, her hair plastered to her cheeks and her clothes drenched, she didn't even have Evil Ella to call upon. No matter how hard she tried it seemed that her ice-maiden alter ego was long gone and no amount of wishing would summon her back. This new, hurting and vulnerable version of Ella St Milton looked frighteningly as though she was here to stay. The thought made her cry even harder.

Symon watched Ella go and then slumped at the table with his head in his hands. He'd been so angry about Charlie that when she'd walked into the restaurant he'd been unable to contain himself. White-hot jealousy had coursed through him; the idea of Ella being with Charlie turned his stomach. He wasn't a fool and he knew Ella had been with other guys, but Charlie Barton? That smirking, preening, swaggering idiot? Symon had almost thrown up at the thought and when Ella had admitted it, he'd thought he would explode.

Why did he feel so angry? Why did it matter so much that she hadn't mentioned Charlie to him? Why was he feeling this way?

Symon stomped up and down the restaurant, trying to calm himself down, but the words Ella had fired at him replayed over and over again in his head. It was all nonsense. Of course he hadn't let her down. She'd let him down by not being truthful with him. How could he trust her? He should have learned his lesson the last time.

"You might have told me about your past but you also let me believe that it was safe to be myself and that it was all right to tell you everything – but that was a lie, wasn't it?"

It was all utter nonsense, of course. He wasn't that
unrealistic but there had to be honesty in relationships.
Otherwise what was the point? He'd been on the edge of
trusting Ella in every way – in business and in love – and to
find that she'd been keeping secrets had been a huge shock to
him. It reminded him of Claudette (who'd been a consummate
keeper of secrets, and of secret lovers), and he'd sworn to
never go down that route again.

"Symon, are you OK?"

Tara popped her head around the service door just as Symon
completed another lap of the restaurant.

"I'm fine."

"*You* might be, but the soles of your shoes won't last long if
you keep this up!" She smiled at him but her eyes were
worried. "Look, Symon, I overheard some of what just went
on."

Symon groaned. That meant that they'd all heard. Great. Just
great. The kitchen staff would have a field day.

"Did you know that Ella was seeing Charlie?"

Tara slipped into the room and closed the door behind her. "I
think that was common knowledge, Symon, but even if it
wasn't you shouldn't hold that against her."

"Why not? Ella uses people. Charlie first and then me. Christ.
I can't believe I didn't listen to Mo or Jake. They know what
she's really like."

Tara poured him a brandy from the bar. "Have this and calm down. Besides, you know Mo's a law unto herself and can hold a grudge like no one else. And Jake won't say anything against Ella even though things ended badly between them."

Symon necked the drink. The burning warmth in his throat did little to comfort him, Instead, it reminded him of his past: in his mind's eye, he saw a bare-chested young man downing cognac and showing off to a dark-eyed woman whose mouth curved in wry amusement.

"I've been so stupid," he said bleakly. "I trusted her."

Who was he talking about? Ella or Claudette? The two were starting to blur and Symon closed his eyes in defeat. He needed to stay away from love; his judgement was not to be relied on.

"I don't think trusting Ella was wrong," said Tara slowly. "I think your instincts are spot on with her. You can tell me it's none of my business, but I think she's in love with you too. She's changed since she's been working with you; everyone says so. She's warmer and more human."

Symon laughed bitterly. "You've been reading too many of Caspar's novels."

"I have not," said Tara, looking offended. "I just know that being with Richard has made me a better person and that sometimes finding the right person is all it takes. Ella trusts you and from what I've seen of her she doesn't give that trust lightly, Symon. Don't blow it."

Once Tara returned to her work, Symon mulled these words over. Nevertheless, he was sure there was nothing anyone could say now that would change his feelings. A lie was a lie even if it was by omission. Ella hadn't told him the truth, so how could he ever put his faith in her again? He didn't think he could even bear to work with her at the manor now, let alone trust her with his heart. She'd let him down and he couldn't see a way forward.

He had no choice but to stay well away from Ella St Milton, no matter how much that was going to hurt.

CHAPTER 27

Emerald's head hurt. Really hurt and even opening her eyes felt like an effort.

"How are you doing, love?" Her grandmother's voice was filled with worry.

Not wanting to give the elderly woman any more stress, Emerald forced herself to look animated. "I'm feeling much better," she fibbed. There was no way she could tell Alice it felt as though a line-dancing festival was taking place inside her skull. When she'd been hit by the car she must have walloped it with quite some force. The doctors in the emergency room had all agreed that she'd got off rather lightly with mild concussion and a broken arm. The unspoken sentiment was that she was lucky not to have been killed.

Emerald was very shaken. One minute she'd been trying to dive out of the way of the speeding vehicle and the next she was waking up in an ambulance. She'd panicked at first but the paramedic had soothed her and promised to call her family, which had made Emerald cry harder because her mom was thousands of miles away in California. She might be eighteen and in the middle of her adventure of a lifetime, but there was nobody Emerald wanted more at that moment than Leaf. Her mom might be flaky at times but she was still her mom and Emerald missed her dreadfully. As she'd lain on the trolley, with an oxygen mask pressed over her face and tears trickling out of the corners of her eyes, she'd realised that she hadn't needed to travel all the way to England to find her family: she already had one.

Leaf was her family.

"How are you doing?" Jimmy asked solicitously. "Is the arm settling down?"

Emerald nodded. Her arm was hurting but some heavy-duty painkillers were taking care of that. It had been pinned in two places and would take some time to heal. All the simple things she took for granted, like getting dressed or making a drink, were going to be very awkward indeed. And what about looking after Mo's horses? How would she manage?

"I haven't done the horse for Mo!" Emerald cried, struggling to sit up. The sudden movement yanked her drip and an alarm began to bleep.

"The horses are just fine. Jake and Summer are helping Mo," Jules said, placing a hand on Emerald's shoulder and easing her back onto the pillows.

"And Ashley has quite enough money to pay for help," added Jimmy, who was sitting at the bedside and working his way through the box of candy Alice had produced. "There's nothing for you to worry about except for getting better."

Her father's grey hair, usually in a ponytail, was looking dishevelled where he'd been running his hands through it in agitation for most of the night. Jimmy must be exhausted, Emerald thought, because he'd arrived at the hospital only ten minutes after the ambulance and had stayed at her side ever since. When they'd set her arm and she'd sobbed with pain, Jimmy had held her other hand and told her stories about the time Zak broke his collarbone falling out of the tree house.

"He was lucky to get away with that," Jimmy had recalled. "Zak had borrowed a trawl from Big Eddie to make a scramble net, and if Ed had got his hands on your brother a broken collarbone would have been the least of his injuries!"

He'd gone on to recount her siblings' other childhood injuries and illnesses, from chickenpox to concussion, and as she'd listened Emerald had remembered all the times that Leaf had sat by her bedside cooling her forehead when she had a fever or singing to her to soothe her to sleep after a bad dream. Jimmy was a good father in his own way – his love for his children rang true in his every word, and there were years and years of care and affection woven through the stories that he'd told her – but these weren't her stories, were they? These were the childhood memories of her siblings and the echoes of the past they shared with their father. She had her own memories and stories but they were shared with her mom and their life in America. That was home.

As she lay in her hospital bed, Emerald was struck by the irony that she'd come all the way to England to find her roots, only to discover they were to be found exactly where she'd started.

"I want to go home," she said quietly.

"That shouldn't be long now," smiled the nurse who'd come to turn off the alarm. She picked up Emerald's chart from the foot of the bed and squinted at it. "You're doing really well, love. I expect you'll be discharged tomorrow."

"Oh! Isn't that wonderful!" Alice squeezed Emerald's hand and beamed at her. "You can come home tomorrow! We'll make your bedroom ready for you at Seaspray and I'll cook your favourite dinner to welcome you back."

"Cool," said Emerald listlessly.

The elderly woman's face furrowed. "Oh love, I've just realised I haven't a clue what your favourite food is."

But Emerald hadn't been thinking about Seaspray. When she'd thought of going home it was the tiny rental apartment in Sausalito that she'd been picturing, with its peeling mint paint on the woodwork, dusty backyard, vibrant splashes of bougainvillea and ticking ceiling fan in the den. Home was the cloudless blue skies and bright colours of California, the traffic-choked freeway – and her mom, who would have known to welcome Emerald back with refried beans and tacos. Homesickness clawed at her heart and tears spilled over her cheeks. Emerald wanted to be there so much it hurt.

"Can I call my mom?" she whispered.

"Oh, love, of course you can," said Alice. She passed Emerald a tissue. "You must miss her very much. But it's still the middle of the night in the States. Shall we call her a little later?"

Emerald couldn't reply. Shaken from the accident and missing home so badly, she started to sob.

"Oh, love!" said Alice helplessly.

"I'm sorry, Granny," wept Emerald, "but I miss my mom so much."

"Of course you do," said Jules. "There's no one like your mum when you're poorly. I even miss mine, and she used to dose me up with cod-liver oil."

Emerald smiled through her tears. "That sounds gross."

Jules grimaced. "It certainly was. In fact, the thought of it makes my stomach churn even all these years on."

"I've already spoken to your mum, love," said Jimmy, once Emerald had blown her nose and Alice had mopped up her tears. "I called her last night while you were having your arm set. She's on her way."

Emerald stared at him. She couldn't quite believe what she was hearing. Leaf was coming here?

"For real?"

He smiled. "For real. I promise! Not that I could have stopped her if I tried. As soon as she heard what had happened she was ready to swim the Atlantic if she had to."

"That's mothers for you," said Alice.

But Emerald was worried. "She hasn't got any money! How will she afford it?" The tears, never far from the surface today, started to fall again. "I've caused so much trouble for you all."

"No, you haven't!" said Jimmy fiercely. "None of this is your fault, Emerald. And as for the ticket here? It's all taken care of. I've already booked and paid for the flight and Leaf will be here tomorrow. It's the very least I can do for you, Emerald. I'm sorry I've handled everything so badly and I'm sorry if I've been a disappointment to you as a father."

Emerald raised herself up on her good elbow and smiled at him.

"Never," she said quietly. "You could never be a disappointment. Thank you, so much! Thank you, *Dad*."

And this time it was Jimmy's turn to well up.

"Have the police got any idea what happened?" Jules asked Alice once visiting time was over and they were driving home. The countryside blurred past them in smudges of greens and browns and splatters of daffodils in the hedgerows, but for once the glory of a Cornish spring was completely passing Jules by; still shocked by the state they'd found Emerald in, she could only see the deep cuts to the girl's head and the angry purple and red bruises blooming against her tanned skin. The pinned arm was plastered, but even the cheerful pink cast couldn't detract from the fact that it was covering a nasty injury. Who could have hit her and left her for dead?

Alice shook her head. "The police have nothing to go on and Emerald says it happened so fast that she didn't see anything that can help them."

"So it's a hit and run?"

"Not necessarily. It was very dark, Emerald's torch wasn't working and she was wearing black," Alice pointed out. "Whoever hit her might have thought they clipped a deer or a badger."

Jules found this hard to believe. "How could you possibly mistake a person for a badger?"

"If you were driving fast you might?" Alice didn't sound convinced. "There are lots of badgers and deer up at the top. They live in Fernside woods, where there's lots of cover, and they quite often run out into the lane. Jake hit a badger in the truck once and it did a huge amount of damage."

The car had reached the top of Polwenna Bay and, as always, the view took Jules's breath away. The bad weather had drifted out into the English Channel and now the water was a kaleidoscope of shifting blues and turquoises below the houses and narrow streets. The thought that somebody down there, one of their friends or neighbours, could have knocked Emerald down and knowingly left her alone and injured in the dark was unbearable. Jules simply couldn't believe it. She *wouldn't* believe it.

"It can't have been deliberate," she agreed. "All the same though, I'm going to keep an eye out for any cars with dents. It might even be worth popping over to the local garage and asking if they've had any requests for bodywork?"

"I'm sure the police will have already thought of that, love," said Alice, pouring cold water on Jules's attempts to solve crime. "I would just wait and see. In my experience these things have a habit of coming to light."

Jules nodded. Alice was right. But how long this would take was anyone's guess. She just hoped that something happened soon before somebody else was hurt. Or worse.

As she packed up her belongings over at the Polwenna Bay Hotel, Ella St Milton was all cried out. Since she and Symon had exchanged words she'd had far too much time on her hands to mull events over. Usually she was flat out with work, so it felt strange to have free time. Not wanting to think, Ella had kept busy by emptying her apartment and driving her belongings down to Tom's small cottage. With Charlie having taken her car, Ella had been using the hotel's microvan instead. Narrow and nippy, it was perfect for wiggling through the village's tiny streets and she was irritated to discover that it was being used just when she was set to move the last of her things. Jonny's Jag was parked outside the hotel, but given that Ella and her grandfather still weren't talking, she didn't feel right about borrowing it. Besides, it was a headache trying to squeeze the Jag through streets originally designed for one horse power.

Ella checked her watch. It was early afternoon and, since the Easter holidays had yet to begin, the village would be fairly quiet. She had only two boxes and a wheelie bag left, so she could easily cram these into Teddy's little Audi and run in and out of Tom's place in minutes. Then she could scoot over to the manor and see if Perry was about. Ella might not be Symon's favourite person anymore, but she was still a businesswoman and the potential the house had as a future wedding venue was not to be discounted. If only she could summon Evil Ella. Her alter ego's cool approach and cutting comments were the shield she needed to face Symon again.

But Evil Ella wouldn't come when called, which made the new, emotional Ella weep even harder. Somehow falling for Symon Tremaine had taken away her armour – and, without it, Ella wasn't sure how she'd survive.

Well, not by sobbing and feeling sorry for herself, she thought now as she sealed the final box and glanced around the flat that had been hers for so long. The flat was up on the top floor and had big windows that let in vast pools of light, which spilled onto the waxed oak boards and made the white paint gleam. Ella had chosen the fittings and furniture herself. Spending rare days off in small interior design shops had been a guilty pleasure, and she'd loved picking out things like the perfect driftwood piece or a glass sculpture to complement it. She would miss this little sanctuary and her life here at the hotel more than she could ever say.

But terrifyingly, this wasn't nearly as much as she would miss the friendship she'd had with Symon and the beautiful dreams she had dared to weave for what might lie ahead.

Ella lugged the next lot of her belongings down the stairs and through the warren of corridors leading to the back of the hotel. She would never be able to take this route now without remembering how Symon had taken her hand that day and quietly guided her to safety. Her hand in his had felt so right and Ella had felt a sense of peace she hadn't experienced since... well, actually since she must have been very small. For as long as she could recall Ella's relationships had been about arguing and point-scoring. From her parents' rows and the tug-of-love access visits (which in reality had been more about each party annoying the other as much as possible than a desire to see the children), through to squabbling with Ted, standing up to her grandfather and playing mind games with boyfriends, every single relationship had been about protecting herself and making sure she didn't get hurt.

How ironic that it was this fledging relationship with Symon Tremaine, which had never proceeded beyond bone-melting kisses and which had never asked anything of her except that she was completely herself, that had hurt Ella the most...

She mustn't brood on it. Symon had made his feelings clear. He loathed her.

The family's vehicles were kept in the old coach house at the back of the hotel, once filled with prancing thoroughbreds and carriage horses but now home to far greater horse power. Jonny's pride and joy of a classic Bentley slumbered under a dust sheet and until recently Ella's Audi and Range Rover had resided there too. The little hotel van was often tucked just inside the entrance. Ella was seeking Teddy's sleek Audi A8, which was always kept here ready for a quick getaway.

There it was, under a cover for once. This kind of care was unlike her brother, who couldn't usually be bothered to look after things. Whipping the cover off, Ella was about to open the Audi's door and slide onto the driver's seat when she spotted something that made her stomach turn to water.

The left-hand wing mirror was dangling from the door, and wires were spilling from the side of the car like exposed veins and arteries. The paint was scratched, the mirror was shattered and there was no doubt about it: this car had been in a collision with something.

Or someone.

Ella threw up. It felt as though the world was spinning around and around, and for a moment she thought she would pass out. Teddy must have hit Emerald Tremaine and left her for dead. There was no other explanation.

As though in a dream she retraced her steps back to the hotel, where she slipped into the ladies' room to sluice her mouth and wash her face and hands. Once she was restored to something resembling normal, Ella walked to the hotel office. There she found Teddy sitting at her desk with his feet up scrolling through Facebook.

"I don't know what you made such a song and dance about, sis," he said when he saw her. "This job's a piece of cake."

Ella was not in the mood. She strode up to the desk, swiped his feet off the polished surface and, leaning forward until her eyeballs almost touched his, hissed, "What the hell's happened to your car?"

"Whoa! Chillax! I never knew you liked it so much," said her brother, shrinking back.

It took all Ella's control not to grab him by the tie and throttle the truth out of him.

"I am not messing about, Ted! What happened to the car? The wing mirror's hanging off!"

"Keep your hair on. It's under warranty! Jesus, Ella, what the hell is wrong with you? Is it time of the month or something?"

"Just tell me what happened! What did you hit?"

Ella was shouting now and probably the whole of the hotel could hear her, but she was beyond caring. If her brother was capable of leaving a young girl injured in a dark lane then Ella had to know. She felt responsible by association and she had to put things right.

"Christ. Keep your wig on." Teddy looked about six as his bottom lip jutted out. "I was driving back from Fowey yesterday evening on the back roads—"

"Had you been drinking?" Ella demanded but she already knew the answer. The locals always used the back roads if they thought they'd had a few too many.

Teddy shrugged. "I had a couple of drinks but I wasn't pissed and I didn't crash, if that's what you're thinking, sis. I clipped a deer as I came down Stable Hill. It was in the hedge and I didn't even see it. It was bloody lucky it wasn't anything bigger; I could have really damaged the car."

Ella's knees buckled and she sagged against the desk. If Teddy had been driving anything larger Emerald would be dead.

"What?" said Teddy. "You've gone a really funny colour."

"That wasn't a deer, Ted. It was a person."

Her brother stared at her in disbelief. "What? No it wasn't. It couldn't have been. I didn't see anyone."

"You wouldn't have done, if she was on the passenger side." Ella's mouth filled with metallic-tasting saliva and she swallowed it frantically. She couldn't be sick again. "Ted, last night Emerald Tremaine was knocked down on that hill. She's in hospital."

"That wasn't me. It couldn't have been. I never saw anyone," Teddy's face was white. "No way. I never hit her and don't you *dare* start saying that I did."

"Ted, you did. It was an accident and I know you didn't mean to but you hit Emerald."

"You don't have any proof." He was on his feet now and pacing the office, one hand loosening his tie while the other raked through his blond hair. "You can't prove that."

Ella's stomach turned again with disgust. "You haven't even asked if she's all right."

Teddy stopped dead. "Oh Christ, Ella. She isn't…"

"No. A broken arm and some bruises, luckily, but the police are treating it as a hit and run."

"Thank God." Teddy passed a shaking hand over his face. "So she's OK and there's nothing to link it to me, is there? She didn't see anything? I certainly didn't see her."

Ella couldn't believe what she was hearing. "That's hardly the point, Ted! You hit her!"

"What if I did? What the fuck was the silly cow doing, walking along in the dark like that? She was practically asking to be run over!"

"She was walking home!" Ella yelled. "And you were driving too fast and probably half pissed as usual!"

"You take that back! There's no proof it was anything to do with me!"

"Except the broken wing mirror!" Ella screamed. "You have *got* to go to the police. You have to tell them what happened."

"Are you mental? What on earth would I do that for? I can get the bloody car fixed, no questions, and nobody will ever know. If I tell the police I could lose my licence."

"You could," she agreed. "You might face prison too. But, Ted, they will find out in the end."

"How will they?" His eyes narrowed. "Would you drop me in it? My own sister? What is this? Revenge for the old man preferring me? Jealous because I've got your job and you can't bear it?"

Ella was stunned. "Do you really think I would use a girl's injuries to further my own career or score petty points? Is that the kind of person you honestly think I am?"

He shrugged. "Evil Ella, right?"

"No! Wrong! Nothing is worth that. No hotel or career!" Ella insisted. "I'm asking you to do it because it's the right thing to do and because no matter what you've become recently, deep down inside I *know* you're not the sort of person who injures a young girl, even by accident, and doesn't take responsibility. You have to own up, Ted! You can't hide something this serious!"

"I totally agree, Ella. He absolutely can't and I won't let him."

Jonny St Milton stood in the doorway. He was leaning heavily on his walking stick and looked every one of his eighty or so years. Behind him was Tom Elliot, eyes wide and mouth open, clutching a sheaf of papers that slid suddenly from his grasp and drifted to the floor. In the heat of their discussion, both arrivals had gone unnoticed by Ella and Teddy.

"So much for family loyalty," Teddy spat.

Jonny glanced at Ella. He couldn't quite look her in the eye. "Unfortunately, I think that's been misplaced for quite a while. Now, Edward St Milton, are you going to call the police? Or am I?"

CHAPTER 28

Symon was upstairs in his apartment, sprawled on the sofa and flicking through the digital channels. The prepping for the evening's service was completed, there was a break in his filming schedule, thank goodness, and he had some time to kill before he and Nick left to visit Emerald. He'd turned his phone off, his staff had left until The Plump Seagull opened for the evening's service and he had a rare window of opportunity where there was nothing for him to do but relax.

The problem was, Symon seemed to have forgotten how this was done. He was having trouble switching off his brain. No matter how many times he flipped through property shows, quizzes, old movies and Jeremy Kyle repeats, Symon found it impossible to focus on anything. All he could think about was Ella and Charlie Barton and how close he'd come to falling for another woman who was only interested in a trophy chef. Claudette had been excited by his status as a rising star, but only if he came with a guarantee, and Ella had only cared about the kudos that Symon could bring to the hotel.

His heart ached because she'd done a good job of persuading him otherwise. He'd almost fallen for it too. What an idiot he'd been and how Ella must have laughed. If he wasn't supposed to be driving to the hospital later, Symon would have been tempted to hit the whiskey and drink himself into oblivion.

He was contemplating his next move when the doorbell shrilled. Symon ignored it. There was no one due to visit and nobody he wanted to see. Or rather, and more accurately, the person he longed to see wouldn't be knocking on his door again. Not after the things he'd said to her earlier on.

The bell shrilled a second time and then a third. Whoever they were, they were certainly persistent. Curiosity got the better of him and Symon padded down the stairs and opened the restaurant door, his mouth falling open when he saw the identity of his visitor.

Had he been drinking and not noticed?

"*Bonjour, chéri,*" said Claudette Marsaud, stretching up onto tiptoes and kissing his cheeks. "*Ça va?*"

Ça va? Symon was rendered utterly speechless. It was as though two totally separate worlds had just collided, because here on his doorstep – standing in the narrow cobbled lane with the soundtrack of seagulls and the chortling River Wenn playing in the background – was the very woman who had haunted his dreams for so long. Clad in a stylish wrap dress, with a Louis Vuitton bag on her shoulder and not a hair out of place, she was looking every bit as chic as though she'd just strolled off the Champs-Élysées. As Symon caught a hint of her familiar perfume his senses reeled and he clung onto the doorframe as though this grip was all that could keep him from falling back through time and becoming the man he'd once been.

The man who had loved her and adored her and who would have done anything for her. The man she'd rejected.

"Aren't you going to invite me in?" Claudette Marsaud asked, tilting her head at him as those slanting dark eyes glittered with promises. "When I have travelled so far?"

Somehow Symon managed to find his voice. "Claudette. What are you doing here?"

"I have come to see you, of course! Why else would I be here? It is not for the English weather or the cuisine!" she laughed.

The sound of her laughter was every bit as musical and enchanting as Symon remembered, but something about it set his teeth on edge. Maybe it was because the weather was beautiful today, a little breezy but a gorgeous spring day nevertheless, or that he was tired of English cooking being the butt of jokes? Symon wasn't sure, but he was riled.

"So, this is the famous Fat Bird?" she was saying, sliding past Symon and into the building. Her breast brushed his arm (deliberately, he knew, because it was one of her old tricks), and his treacherous body reacted as it always had.

"Plump Seagull," he corrected automatically, shutting the door and leaning against it with his arms crossed. "Look, Claudette, I know this isn't a social visit. Why are you here?"

But Claudette wasn't listening. She was too busy stalking around the restaurant, picking up menus and running a manicured nail over the bar. She had an intense look on her face that told him she was busy appraising what she saw and calculating how it could be improved. Jean-Luc had once commented that she was the brains of the operation and, as the saying went, had an eye for business and a body for sin. A cold sweat of shame broke out between Symon's shoulder blades as he recalled this conversation. Had the older man suspected that his protégé was in love with his wife? Probably. Most men who met Claudette were captivated. As he watched her sashay past tables and chairs, the dress belted tightly to accentuate the hand-span waist and her buttocks swaying seductively, Symon knew that she was very conscious of the effect she had on the opposite sex. There had been a time when he couldn't have stood and watched like this without being consumed with the urge to touch her and draw her close, sinking his face into the silky fall of dark hair and pulling her hard against him, and he knew she was more than aware of this. His passion for her had been primeval and all-consuming but it had also been toxic, poisoning everything he had held dear.

She spun on her heel, clapping her hands in delight. "Oh, Symon! *C'est très enchanteur! Tu es si intelligent!*"

In the past her praise had had the power to light up cities, and he would have gone to the ends of the earth to hear it.

Now, he felt the dull ache of cynicism. How often had she given him a flash of hope that he might mean something to her? That she truly admired him? The truth was that whenever she'd felt Symon start to slip away from her, Claudette had tossed him a compliment and a dark-eyed promise.

"Thank you," he said, shortly. Christ, he needed a drink. As Claudette nosed about, Symon headed to the bar and poured himself a whiskey. He downed it straight away, then poured another. Sod it. Nick would have to drive to the hospital.

"I think that the menu could be a little more adventurous," she continued critically, "and also the décor in here is a little, how you say, unoriginal? But it is charming. And a Michelin star too, *non*? You always did have such… potential."

They both knew she wasn't alluding to his skills in the kitchen. Symon had been in relationships before he met Claudette – it was impossible not to meet girls when you lived in a seasonal seaside town brimming with holidaymakers clad in shorts and tiny tops and all desperate for a summer romance – but it was Claudette who'd taught him how to please a woman, the places to kiss and caress and the words to make her melt…

In spite of everything, Symon's pulse quickened at the memories of those snatched hours with her in his room, the blinds drawn against the harsh noon sun and the feel of her sweat-slicked skin against his. He pushed this image away and replaced it with another, one that sliced through him like jagged glass through a wrist.

"I need a man, Symon, not a boy. This has been fun, but leave Jean-Luc for you? Maybe when you have your own restaurant, with a Michelin star. Perhaps then."

When he'd fled his Parisian life and returned to Polwenna Bay, a huge part of him had been determined to prove to Claudette that he was the man she needed. He could run his own critically acclaimed restaurant, he could have the write-ups in the press and he could win the coveted Michelin stars too. Then she would see. Then she would want him.

But somewhere along the way this had stopped being about her.

"I owe a lot to you and to Jean-Luc," he said evenly.

"Of course. We both knew you were talented," Claudette agreed. She wiggled her way back to him until she was standing so close that he could see the pulse fluttering in her neck. The flawlessly made-up face looked up at him and he felt hypnotised as her dark eyes held his.

"You always had extra talents, Symon. I have missed them. I missed you."

He'd missed her too, but his lonely hours spent yearning for Claudette had shortened and thoughts of her had grown fewer as The Plump Seagull had taken on a life of its own. Polwenna Bay had filled the void. She was from another life.

She was so close now that he could have held her in his arms, crushed her mouth with his and taken her right there and then against the wall if he'd wanted to. The glitter in her eyes and the arch of her brows seemed to be daring him to do it.

Then, abruptly, she undid her dress and let it fall to the floor. She was naked except for the skimpiest thong and sheer black stockings.

What the hell!

Unfortunately for his visitor, this reveal had the opposite effect to the one she'd intended. Symon leapt backwards, knocking the whiskey tumbler flying and showering them both with amber droplets.

"Jesus, Claudette! Cover yourself up!" he gasped, glancing around in panic in case Granny Alice or, God forbid, Sheila Keverne should trundle by. "What the hell are you thinking?"

But Claudette didn't seem at all perturbed to be standing topless in his restaurant and in broad daylight.

"So English now! You didn't always used to be such a prude!"

She reached to grab his shirt to pull him closer, but her fingers grasped only air as Symon backed even further away, feeling like one of Mo's horses cornered by the vet. Claudette might be stunning and have a figure that women half her age would kill for, but as she stood before him, wearing only wisps of black lace and Chanel Number Five, Symon thought the situation couldn't be less sexy. She'd come to see him just so that she could flash her underwear without any warning? Seriously?

It was a terrible, contrived cliché and suddenly it struck Symon as being funny. She might just as well have turned up in a trench coat like some dodgy strippergram. Symon couldn't help himself; he started to laugh and once he started he simply couldn't stop.

"*Qu'est-ce qu'il y a de si drôle?*" snapped Claudette, snatching up her dress and wrapping it around herself. Her dark eyes flashed with fury. "Why are you laughing at me?"

"Not at you! At this situation!" Symon gasped, wiping his eyes on his sleeve. "Oh, come on Claudette! You must see how ridiculous it is. We haven't seen each other for years and suddenly you're down to your underwear. This is Cornwall in April! You're lucky not to catch your death of cold!"

Claudette stared at him for a minute and then she too started to laugh. Symon had always loved her laughter. It was low and rasping, husky from years of smoking and drinking, and it brought back memories of red wine, Gauloises and talking until the sun rose.

"I'll make us a coffee," said Symon tactfully. "Then we can catch up."

Once they were sitting at a table, Claudette in her dress again and looking awkward, Symon poured them both a strong black coffee. Now they were merely two old acquaintances catching up.

He hoped.

"Is Jean-Luc well?"

She shrugged. "I think so. We have, how you say? We have smashed up."

"Broken up?" Symon's brain was whirling. Not so long ago he would have been thrilled to think she was free; now he just felt weary. "That's a shame, Claudette. In spite of everything I always thought you were a great couple."

"*Oui.*" She stared into the coffee and when she looked up her expression was mournful. "It's very sad but now I think is a good time for you and I to begin a new life, don't you agree? We were always good together."

But Symon shook his head. "We weren't. It was an affair that should never have happened. We betrayed Jean-Luc."

"Pah! Jean-Luc doesn't care what I do! Do you not think he has other women? Do you think he has been a saint?"

"So why not leave him before? Why not come with me when I asked you to?"

Claudette looked at Symon as though he was being an idiot. "Because you had nothing to offer me. No future. Papillon Rouge was my life."

He nodded. At the time he hadn't understood – but now that he had The Plump Seagull, Symon had more insight into how passionately she must have felt about her restaurant business. Look how hard he was fighting for his. He'd even sold his soul to the Food and Drink Channel.

Hold on…

Was this the key to her return?

"Did you see me on the television?" Symon demanded as suspicion took hold. Of course. It made perfect sense. When he'd been destitute and heartbroken, Claudette hadn't been interested in him, the real him, but now that he had a Michelin star and it looked as though a successful television career beckoned she was declaring her love and leaving her husband?

"Of course," said Claudette, as though this was obvious. "I read the papers too. I have been watching your career for a long time, waiting for the perfect moment when we can be together. This is it. So I have come."

The woman sitting opposite was still beautiful and sexy and, if she'd paid this visit a few months ago, Symon suspected he'd have been jumping for joy and planning a triumphant return to Paris. He certainly wouldn't be wasting time drinking coffee when Claudette was wearing stockings and heels. Part of him, the hurt and angry part still smarting from Ella's betrayal, was sorely tempted to take Claudette upstairs anyway, but he knew this would be a mistake. Claudette might have held his heart for a long time but she was calculating and opportunistic and had no loyalty to anyone except herself; he could see this so clearly now and knew beyond all doubt that whatever hold she'd once had over him was well and truly broken now.

The truth was that Symon Tremaine had stopped yearning for Claudette a long time ago – and from the moment Ella St Milton had first kissed him, it was Ella who had haunted his dreams instead.

"You need to go back home and talk to Jean-Luc," he said gently.

She frowned. "Why? We are both free and you have your career now. Come back to Paris with me. We can start a Fat Bird there. It will be magnificent!"

He laughed. "There aren't any fat birds in Paris! Or plump seagulls, rather. Besides, my life is here. I don't want to go to Paris." He took a deep breath. This was hard but he had to be honest. "It's over, Claudette. I don't want to be with you. I don't love you."

She stared at him. Incomprehension was written across her beautiful face.

"You are telling me it's finished?"

"It's been finished since the day I left," he said, and he knew this was true. He didn't love this woman. He didn't want to start a new restaurant with *her*, or stay up all night making plans for their future. He didn't want to hold Claudette or kiss her or make love to her or talk to her until the sun faded. It was over.

"You're in love with someone else, aren't you?" hissed Claudette. "Don't deny it. You would never have said 'no' to me otherwise."

"What?"

"You are in love with another woman." Claudette stood up, tugging at the belt of her dress and smoothing her hair. "I can see it in your eyes, *chéri*; you don't need to pretend. There is someone else."

Symon laughed in astonishment. "What on earth makes you say that?"

"A woman can tell these things, Symon. I can see it is too late for me. I have my pride. I will not beg."

"I wouldn't want you to," he said.

Claudette leaned across the table and dropped a kiss onto his cheek.

"She's a very lucky girl, whoever she is. You must love her a great deal. Be happy."

Symon remained seated at the table staring into space long after the door had clicked shut behind Claudette and the tapping of her heels on the cobbles had faded away. His hands were shaking, but not from the shock of his ex-lover's unexpected visit. No. That was nothing but the ending of a long story, the last sentence of a book he had once loved to read.

Symon was trembling because he knew Claudette was right. He was in love with Ella. Charlie Barton and all the other misunderstandings didn't matter one bit in comparison to how he felt about this spiky, determined and utterly incredible woman.

He loved her and he had done since that first fleeting kiss.

Symon loved Ella St Milton and he had absolutely no idea what to do about this – but he did know someone who might. He reached for his phone. It was time to give Tom Elliot a call.

CHAPTER 29

"Vicar! Vicar!"

Sheila Keverne scuttled across the street to catch Jules, her wicker trolley bumping behind her over the cobbles and her breath coming in sharp gasps. Jules knew this look well: Sheila had a juicy morsel of top-quality gossip and she was dying to share it. Now she had Jules in her sight there would be no escape. Greyhounds were more likely to ignore rabbits.

Jules sighed inwardly. She'd been hoping to catch Danny at the marina for a quiet few moments. They hadn't seen each other for a couple of days and tonight he was going to visit Emerald with Symon and Nick, so their usual Wednesday evening together was on hold. Tomorrow was Maundy Thursday, the start of the Easter celebrations, and Jules would be flat out with services and special events. There would be hardly a minute to spend together. When would they ever get a moment to talk about his job and their future? Even Danny seemed to be avoiding the issue.

As Sheila bore down on her Jules contemplated ducking into a doorway or diving down one of the narrow side streets – but would Jesus have done this? If He'd hidden from his followers rather than caring for them, Christianity wouldn't have had quite the same impact on the world. Still, Jules suspected that even Jesus would have had to call on all his reserves of love and patience to deal with Sheila Keverne on a mission. Sending up a quick prayer for even more patience today, Jules girded her loins and waved back.

"Hello, Sheila! How can I help you? Is it about the Easter Egg Hunt?"

Jules really hoped not. The Polwenna Bay Easter Egg Hunt was fast becoming the bane of her life. For bickering among her flock, it was right up there with the infamous Polwenna Bay naked calendar. Danny, who had kindly agreed to take charge of the event, was close to strangling Sheila. So far she'd taken exception to chocolate as prizes ("It's bad for the kiddies' teeth, Vicar!"), decided that cardboard eggs filled with a mini prize were too expensive and done her best to change the date too ("Our Lord rose on a Sunday, Vicar, as you well know!"). Jules was sorely tempted to cancel the whole deal. She had enough to contend with on Easter Sunday without twenty children turning St Wenn's upside down! Having the hunt on the Saturday made much better sense. In any case, Sheila was too late. In a desperate bid to avoid any more squabbles, Jules had collected the eggs from Seaspray and already given them to the Pollards with strict instructions to hide them in the churchyard. Danny had quite enough on his plate with Emerald's injury and looking after Alice, so Jules had decided to take some of the burden. He'd already done the hard work of organising the banners and the eggs, so now it was her turn to help him. Sometimes a girl had to take the bull by the horns, or in this case the Easter bunny by the tail!

"Oh no, no," panted Sheila, hand on her heart as she recovered from her sprint down the street. "It's much more important than that!" She paused for emphasis. "Vicar, you'll never believe this but it was Teddy St Milton who knocked down that poor girl!"

"What?" Jules wasn't sure she'd heard correctly.

"That hooligan Teddy St Milton! He was the one who ran young Emerald over and left her for dead. I'm not at all surprised. He drives way too fast, doesn't he? I said so only the other day to Betty Jago! That boy will kill us all, I said!"

"Sheila, you can't go about saying things like that without any proof," admonished Jules. Sometimes she really did feel as though all her hard-written sermons on the evils of gossip were in vain. Would it make any difference if rather than slaving over them she just watched *EastEnders* instead and downloaded a ready-made homily? She was beginning to wonder.

But Sheila was shaking her head. "It's true, Vicar. Meg Trewiddy told me. Her daughter is a chambermaid at the hotel and she heard it from Tom Elliot. All the staff have been told. Teddy St Milton's gone to the police station to make a statement."

Jules couldn't believe it. Teddy was reckless and drove like a moron; all the same, she'd never have dreamed he was the kind who could leave a girl for dead. He was an idiot but she'd never thought he was bad.

"Why didn't he stop and help her?" she wondered. It broke her heart to think of poor Emerald hurt and alone in the dark.

"According to Meg he thought he'd hit a deer. His sister saw the damage to the car and she guessed what had happened," Sheila continued, loving every dramatic minute of telling this story. "She confronted him and that was when Teddy realised what he'd done. Apparently their grandfather's devastated."

Jules could only imagine. Poor Jonny. Teddy was the light of his life.

"It was very brave of Ella to do that," she said. Ella St Milton was a tricky customer but Jules had long suspected there was more to her than met the eye. She also had a feeling that Symon thought so too…

"Anyway, I just thought I'd let you know. Better be on my way. I can't stand here talking to you all day," Sheila said, her eyes lighting up when she spotted Kursa Penwarren stepping out of her front door. "Yoo hoo! Kursa! Wait a moment!"

And she was off again, the wicker trolley bounding behind her and her raincoat billowing like Superman's cape. Gossip Woman, thought Jules fondly. Sheila meant well but speaking to her did feel a bit like being in the middle of a force-nine gale.

Goodness, this was a lot to take in. Did Alice know, or any of the others? Jules imagined that Jonny would have called her; her heart went out to him because that wouldn't be an easy conversation. He and Alice had been bickering about their marriage for weeks now. Would this be the final straw for their relationship?

Jules hoped not. They adored each other and deserved this late chance of happiness. With a heavy heart she headed to the marina to find Danny. He would know best what to do and how to help heal his family. All she could do was be there, for the Tremaines and for the St Miltons.

If Ella had stopped to think about it she would never have confronted Teddy while there was a chance that their grandfather might overhear. The shock was far too much for him and as he sat slumped at the desk, with his head in his hands and his face a ghastly shade of grey, she was truly frightened for him. After Teddy had stormed out of the room, presumably to drive into the next town and report the accident to the local police, Jonny had called Alice Tremaine and broken the news. Ella had tactfully removed herself to the window, where she'd watched the seagulls attacking today's rubbish and had contemplated how much everything had changed since she'd last watched their squabbles.

"I'm so sorry, Ella."

Her grandfather's voice, as dry as rustling autumn leaves, broke into her musings.

"You've got nothing to be sorry for," she told him.

Jonny removed his glasses and rubbed his eyes wearily. When he replaced his spectacles, Ella was shocked to see that his eyes were red. Her grandfather never cried.

"I have everything to be sorry for," he said. "I didn't listen to you when you warned me that Teddy was spending too much money and behaving wildly. I turned a blind eye and I indulged him. I have to take my share of the blame."

Ella didn't know what to say. It was true.

"You love him," she said helplessly.

"Yes, yes," Jonny waved his hand. He hated talking about emotion. "I love you both, damn it, but Alice is right. I'm a silly old fool. I let old-fashioned values and the idea of a family name blind me to all Teddy's faults and I overlooked you, Ella. I know that now."

Ella was a little embarrassed by his admission. "I always understood why. You only wanted to do the right thing."

Jonny leaned forward. "That's as maybe but I made a mistake, Ella. I don't know if you can forgive me for the things I said to you and the way I behaved?"

For a moment Ella was tempted to tell him that she wasn't sure. He'd hurt her. Let her down. Betrayed her. She could berate him now and say her piece. She could let him know just how much it had hurt to see the business she loved so much snatched away from her, to be made to feel that she was worthless and forced to move out of her flat. These words were poised on her tongue like divers on the edge of a springboard and all she had to do was let them leap.

But how could she? Jonny was old and tired and he had made a mistake. What good would it do now for her to make him feel even worse? Would it change the past? Make her feel any better? Mend Emerald's injuries? Jonny wasn't a fool. He knew that his judgement had been in error. With this thought, all the bitterness and anger she'd been nursing vanished. Besides, by snatching the hotel away from her Jonny had actually done something rather marvellous, Ella now realised. He had forced her to rethink her game plan, evaluate her skills and look about her for opportunities that could be grasped with both hands and made to work. Without the loss of the business would she have ever thought of Polwenna Manor as a venue or seen the potential of working with Perry and Symon?

Would she have kissed Symon in the long grass and bluebells and finally known what it felt like to fall in love?

Ella knew the answer. Jonny's choice had given her the gift of independence and, even more precious, a beautiful memory that – as much as it now broke her heart – she knew she would treasure until she was as old as he was.

"There's nothing to forgive," she said, and she meant it too.

"So will you come back to the hotel? Run it again for me? Move back into your flat?" her grandfather asked hopefully. "We can put all of this behind us, can't we?"

This was the moment Ella had dreamed about but now it had arrived she knew what her decision was.

"It's already behind us, Grandpa. We need to be there to help Ted," she told him, giving the old man a hug. "If he's prosecuted he's going to need all the support we can give him. I promise I'll be there but we can't be responsible for his actions. Teddy has to face up to those and you have to let him. It's the only thing that will save him from himself."

"When did you get so wise?" sighed Jonny and Ella laughed at this.

"I'm not wise, Grandpa. I've made some huge mistakes. Charlie Barton for one."

"Ah yes." He looked thoughtful. "I liked his replacement though. Symon Tremaine is a good man. A steady hand on the tiller. I think he makes you happy too?"

Ella didn't trust herself to reply. Symon had made her heart soar and losing him before they'd even had a chance to discover where their feelings might take them was intensely painful.

"And I know the hotel makes you happy," Jonny pressed. "Will you have your job back? Please? I promise I'll stay out of all the decisions and if Ally will have me I'll take myself to Seaspray and never bother you again."

"You don't need to do that, Grandpa. I'm not going to come back to the hotel. Give Tom Elliot the chance to run it instead. He's a fantastic manager and more than ready for the opportunity."

"Is this because you're angry with me?" Jonny asked sadly.

Ella shook her head. "Not at all. Grandpa, I don't want to punish you or make a point or anything like that, but I would like the chance to do something myself, if that makes sense? I want to see what *I* can achieve without the St Milton name and the silver spoons. I'd like to make it on my own so that I can look at my business when I'm your age and know I built it myself through my own hard work, not just because I was born into the right family."

As she said this it felt like a huge weight slid from her shoulders and Ella knew without a shadow of a doubt that she had made the right decision.

"I'm very proud of you," Jonny told her and his eyes glistened.

These quiet words were the balm that Ella had needed for so long. Her grandfather was proud of her. She hadn't let him down. That meant the world.

"I'm proud of you too," she said, blinking back tears. "Now, if I promise to move back into my flat for a bit and help Tom take over, would you please go and tell Alice you love her and will move into Seaspray as soon as she'll have you?"

Jonny's answer was to be on his feet in an instant. Laughing, Ella passed him his walking stick and his coat. As he left, she crossed her fingers that at least one St Milton would get their happy ending.

CHAPTER 30

The village was filling up with holidaymakers as though the warm spring sunshine was a beacon guiding them through the main street and past the gift shops, with their dusty piles of last season's buckets and spades, to the beach. As Ella steered Jonny's big Jag through the crowds she prayed that she didn't catch a wing on one of the postcard stands or scrape the paintwork when creeping through the narrowest stretch between the pasty shop and the hairdressers. As she passed these pinch points, the visitors flattened themselves against the walls or ducked into doorways and Ella waved her thanks. They would never have any idea just how close they had come to having their toes squashed!

The tide was out and the sandy beach was sprinkled with windbreaks and towels while the determined British public made the most of the rare sunny afternoon. Knowing that the harbour would be empty for at least the next few hours, Ella reversed the Jag carefully onto the slipway and pulled the handbrake on as hard as she could. It was a cheeky parking place but now that it was officially the holiday season the local traffic warden would be on the lookout for rogue vehicles. The ownership of the slip and the seabed was a contentious issue, but so far the council hadn't managed to claim it. Ella knew that the car would be safe here while she retrieved her boxes from Tom's place.

Abandoning the car, Ella made her way through the bustling streets towards the village green, where Tom rented a cottage. Was it her imagination or were people looking at her askance? Granted, Ivy Lawrence looked at most people as though she hated them and Kursa Penwarren always said hello, but as Ella fought her way against the tide of visitors she was sure the locals were talking about her. They must already know about Teddy.

The village gossip machine was alive and kicking then. Ella and Tom had spoken to all the staff and told them what was happening. No doubt they'd all been on Facebook or texting the minute she'd left the room. The St Miltons were probably already trending on Twitter.

Ella bit her lip. She was terribly worried for her brother but, in his favour, he really hadn't known he'd hit Emerald and by all accounts she was going to be just fine. Maybe this was the start of things getting better for them all? Perhaps she would even be able to find Symon and make him understand that Charlie Barton had just been a stupid and meaningless mistake?

Hope flooded her. Everything felt possible when the sun shone and the village teemed with life.

Filled with determination, Ella took a sharp left into the twisty back lane that ran beside the River Wenn and past The Plump Seagull. It was late afternoon and Symon was bound to be there, since he had no filming scheduled at the hotel. They could have an hour at least to talk. She'd paused to fish out her phone to call Tom and let him know she'd be a while, when the clip-clop of heels on cobbles caused her to look up.

A striking woman with a chic black bob, immaculate make-up and a gorgeous wrap dress was walking towards the restaurant. With the latest Louis Vuitton bag looped over her arm and her feet encased in high-heeled shoes, it was obvious that she wasn't headed for the beach. Ella recognised her straight away.

It was the woman from Symon's YouTube clip.

It was Claudette Marsaud.

As though frozen, Ella remained in the street pretending to be engrossed in her phone but watching Claudette out of the corner of her eye. She saw the French woman ring the doorbell and drum her nails impatiently before ringing it a couple more times. Eventually the door opened and Symon stepped out. He was wearing an unbuttoned shirt and soft frayed jeans and his feet were bare. With his hair loose and tousled, he looked as though he'd only just tumbled out of bed.

Claudette kissed him on both cheeks, spoke to him for a moment and then vanished inside.

Ella was no fool. She knew what this meant.

She turned sharply on her heel, hurrying away from the restaurant as fast as she could without trampling any holidaymakers. Somehow she made it through the warren of lanes, over the bridge and past the village green without bursting into tears or being accosted by Sheila Keverne or Ivy Lawrence. Ramming the key into the lock, Ella fell into Tom's cottage, slamming the door behind her and panting raggedly. There was a sharp pain below her breastbone; she pressed the heels of her hands against it, but no matter how hard she tried to rub it away the agony refused to shift.

Ella slid down the door and into a heap on the floor. All of the boxes and cases she'd moved out of the hotel were stacked beside her there. She knew she needed to fetch them and carry them through the village and back to the car, but at this moment she didn't even have the strength to make it to the first case, let alone lift and carry all the bags. She didn't have the strength to do anything at all.

Ella was utterly defeated. The events of the past few weeks felt overwhelming. Charlie Barton quitting. The wedding. Symon stepping in. The filming. Her grandfather's choice. Her unexpected feelings for Symon. Their amazing kiss at the manor. All the plans for the future. Teddy's accident. Seeing Claudette…

It was as though she'd been balancing on a high wire while spinning plates: so long as she hadn't tried to think about it, all had been well, but the moment she'd acknowledged what she was trying to cope with, the whole lot had come crashing down around her.

The world hadn't ended, Ella knew that, but at this moment it felt like it. Alone and unseen, she clasped her knees against her chest and wept. She knew there was no hope and that crying wouldn't help, but everything hurt so much that once the tears started to fall she didn't think they would ever stop. She cried for the fledging love that would never take flight, for the dreams of the manor, for Teddy, for her hopeless parents and most of all because she couldn't bear the thought of Symon being with Claudette. That idea totally slew her.

Eventually, Ella cried herself out. Time had passed, an hour at least, and the sun's rays were lower as they sloped in through a small sash window. Ella supposed she had better rescue the car before the tide came in and floated it away to France. Jonny's day had been bad enough already without that happening.

Hauling herself up from the floor, Ella crossed the room to the sink and splashed some cold water onto her face. She probably looked like a goblin and her make-up was long gone. Still, what did any of that matter now? She mopped her face with a Polwenna Bay tea towel and pulled her damp hair up into a messy top knot. There. Hopefully she wouldn't frighten the holidaymakers too much. She'd leave her things here and sort them out another time. Maybe she should visit her mother for a few weeks? Some Floridian sunshine might help.

Yeah. Right. Ella shook her head in despair. No amount of sunshine could make her feel better. Still, a few thousand miles of distance might help.

She picked up her keys and was heading to the door when the sharp rap of knuckles made her jump. Then the letter box rattled.

"Ella? Are you in there?" a voice called.

She jumped. It was Symon.

There was another rattle.

"Ella?" he called again. "If you're in there, please open the door!"

Astonished, Ella did as requested. She couldn't resist the chance to see him and her heart raced as she gulped in the sight of Symon standing on the doorstep. The low sun behind him turned his hair to flame and glanced off the pure angles of his beautiful bone structure. When his eyes locked with hers it took all Ella's strength not to hurl herself into his arms.

"What are you doing here?" she said, and her voice sounded croaky and strange.

"Looking for you, of course," he answered, as though this was obvious.

"So you've found me." Ella turned away, not wanting Symon to see her blotchy face. "Look, I'm sorry about Teddy knocking Emerald over. I had no idea and as soon as I found out I—"

"Tom told me what you did, and it's incredible and brave and so like you, but I'm not here about that," Symon said quietly. "I'm here to talk to you, Ella. I *have* to talk to you."

But Ella didn't want to talk. She couldn't even bear to look at him knowing that only an hour before he'd been kissing Claudette on the restaurant step.

"I was just sorting out some bits and pieces and I'm really busy," she said coolly. "I really don't have time or the inclination to tell you yet again that nothing serious happened with Charlie Barton or that I wasn't on some secret mission to steal your skills for the hotel or add you to my celebrity chef collection."

Symon didn't say a word. Oh, sod it. She might as well carry on. If he'd made this much effort to find her and continue the fight he was never going to forgive her – and anyway, he was back with Claudette. There was nothing to lose.

"Charlie was totally meaningless and I wish to God it had never happened but it did and I never loved him! Not like I love—"

Oh God. What was happening to her lately? Ella felt a wave of humiliation break over her. She hoped he hadn't noticed her slip. She was shocked at it herself, shocked and frightened at the intensity of her feelings, and she couldn't bear to see him sneer at her admission.

But Symon wasn't gloating.

"I know," he said softly. "It's the same for me."

She looked at him in confusion. "What's that supposed to mean? What's the same? What do you know?"

"I understand. Ella, I know things get heated in restaurants and it's so easy to get swept away and make mistakes under pressure. Passions run wild. I've been there, remember? It's easy to fall in love, but not so easy to act on it or handle it properly. Or even recognise the real thing when you see it."

Oh. He was talking about Claudette. Of course he was. Disappointment swamped her and she took a steadying breath as she fought to keep her emotions in check. Evil Ella might be gone but Calm and Collected Ella might still make an appearance, along with Don't Make a Total Fool of Yourself Ella if she tried hard enough.

"I'm glad you and Claudette have worked things through," she said stiffly. "Congratulations."

Symon frowned. "What?"

"You and Claudette Marsaud. I saw her, Symon," Ella said wearily. "She's here at the restaurant, isn't she? It's fine. I'm pleased for you. I know how you feel about her and—"

"No, you don't." Cutting her off, he stepped forward and took her hands, holding them tightly and pulling her hard against him. Ella could feel his heart racing through the thin cotton of his shirt. "Claudette was here, Ella, but she's gone away now and for good."

"But you love her," Ella whispered. She didn't understand.

"I don't," said Symon. "I thought I loved her once but it wasn't real. It was an infatuation. It wasn't love; I know that now."

"How do you know that now? What changed?" It didn't make sense. Claudette was beautiful and she had come all this way to find him. What was wrong?

Symon released her hands and cupped her face in his fingers, staring down at Ella as though he never wanted to stop looking.

"How do I know? That's simple. The reason I know is because I never once felt with her the way I feel when I'm with you."

"And how is that?" she whispered.

"That the world is filled with possibilities and sunshine. The sky stretches for ever when we talk about our plans and share our ideas. It's exciting, intoxicating, addictive and also the easiest thing in the world. We see things the same way, Ella. We share a vision."

"We do," she agreed.

"And it sounds crazy but we're the same, you and I. We feel things deeply but we've been hurt and that's taught us to hide away. We bury ourselves in work and present a front to everyone else. But you saw through mine, Ella, and I know I've seen through yours. You're not cold and you're not the bitch you like to pretend you are. You're warm and loving and you have so much to give. I see you and you see me."

Ella nodded. "I thought so too but what about Claudette? Charlie was a silly fling but you loved her for years."

There was conviction in his expression. "I promise you that all the time I thought I cared for Claudette I never once felt like my world had ended the way I did when I found out about Charlie. I'm falling in love with you, Ella. I know it's fast and probably way too soon to tell you but I can't keep this feeling secret. I'm crazy about you. I can't think about anything else. Not even cooking!"

She couldn't speak.

"I know I overreacted, but to think that what meant the world to me could mean so little to you was unbearable," he continued. "The only way I can describe it? It felt like my heart had been thrown into a Kenwood Chef on high speed."

"That," said Ella sternly, "has to be the most unromantic thing I have ever heard."

Symon grinned and she loved the way his eyes lit up. "Is it? It's true though. You crept under my guard, Ella St Milton, and slipped into my heart. I have no idea how but you're there."

"And you did the same to me," she said. "How did you do it, Symon Tremaine? How did this happen?"

His fingers caressed her face. "How does any chef make the perfect dish? I followed a recipe of course! Take one restaurant, add a sprinkle of write-ups, mix in a Michelin star and a handful of celebrity chefs and let the villagers stir!"

Ella began to laugh at this but his finger slipped to her lips, quietening her.

"I haven't finished yet. You know how particular we chefs can be and this recipe's still incomplete. I still need the one magic ingredient."

She tilted her head back and looked up at him questioningly. "And what's that?"

"You," Symon said simply. Then he dipped his head and kissed her, and Ella melted like butter icing on a warm day. They had shared kisses before but none had been this tender or had felt so right. As they held each other until the sun sank below the village rooftops and shadows slipped into the room, kissing and laughing with the sheer wonder of it, Ella knew beyond all doubt that Symon was absolutely right.

Together, she knew that they had found the perfect recipe for love.

THE END

Epilogue

The weather couldn't have been more perfect for Easter. The sunshine had decided to spend its holidays in Cornwall and, apart from a few wisps of lazily drifting cloud, the sky was a perfect powder blue. Jules stood in the churchyard and gazed out across the bay, watching the little tripping boats and listening to the excited shrieks and squeals from the beach as brave bathers dared to dip their toes into the sea. From this vantage point the sea might look as clear and blue as the Caribbean but Jules knew it would be bitterly cold. You wouldn't find any of the locals venturing near it without a wetsuit.

Jules loved Easter the most of all the holidays, in both an ecclesiastical and a secular sense. Of course, the crucifixion and resurrection were key to her faith and their message of hope meant everything to her, but she also loved seeing the world come back to life after the long winter. Not only was the village full of visitors once more, and not only were all the gift shops open again with souvenirs displayed in the windows, but Nature was yawning and stretching too as she woke up in a burst of green shoots, primroses and jaunty daffodils. The churchyard couldn't have been more colourful if Tess's pupils, now assembling excitedly by the gate, had come in armed with their brushes to paint it for today's Easter Egg Hunt.

In spite of Sheila Keverne's best efforts, everything was ready to go. The Pollards had done a sterling job of hiding the eggs and Big Rog, who was still being teased about his boat, had even managed to mow the grass beforehand. Now the air was meadow scented – and if Jules closed her eyes, the smell of freshly cut grass and the warm sunshine on her face transported her straight to the summertime. Bliss.

"We're all ready, Vicar, and we've found some ingenious hiding places if I do say so myself," said Big Rog, trundling over to her and looking very pleased with himself.

"Not *too* ingenious, I hope?" Jules asked. Earlier on she'd been pottering about in St Wenn's and had discovered one egg on the lectern and another in the font. She'd held her breath when checking the communion chalice but luckily that had escaped the Pollards' attentions. "We did agree outside only, remember?"

Big Rog nodded. "I've told my boy. He's very disappointed, mind. He had some cracking hiding places."

Jules reckoned Little Rog would get over it. She hoped Danny wouldn't mind Big Rog taking over. She wasn't sure where he'd got to though.

She glanced across the churchyard, hoping to see Danny, but there was still no sign of him. Nick was here, chatting away to

Emerald and her mum and looking very excited. Emerald, pale and bruised but thankfully in one piece and discharged from hospital, was rolling her eyes while her mother, a very pretty woman with long blonde plaits and who didn't look much older than Emerald, laughed. If vicars were allowed to place bets, then Jules's money was on Nick doing his best to find out whether Leaf had ever been a Playboy Bunny. He truly was the limit.

"Churchyard only," she said firmly. "Besides, the whole point is that the children are supposed to find the eggs. You did put them in accessible places, didn't you?"

"Ah," said Big Rog. He scratched his head. "Well, the thing is, Vicar—"

"Jules, can we get started? The children are getting overexcited and we're already ten minutes late." Tess Hamilton had joined them, looking fraught as she did her best to keep control of the children, who were literally bouncing with agitation.

Jules checked her watch. She'd been waiting for Danny to bring the banners and the flags but he was running very late now. There was no sign of Morgan either, who was the official photographer. She hoped everything was all right at Seaspray. Jules had been flat out with Easter services but the last time she'd been at the house everything had seemed good. Leaf had been sleeping off jet lag, Emerald had been resting and being fussed over by Jimmy and, incredibly, Jonny St Milton appeared to have moved in.

"Separate bedrooms, of course, until we're married," Alice had said to Jules, flushing like a sixteen-year-old. "Not that there'll be any chance of hanky-panky with his dicky heart and my bad hip!"

Jules had laughed. "It's all right, Alice! You don't need to justify anything to me. Just let me know when you want the banns read and I'll be on it!"

"I think I may have to get in the queue. Symon and Ella seem very close all of a sudden," Alice had replied.

Sure enough, something had shifted between those two and Jules was so glad. She had a soft spot for Symon, the quiet sounding board of the family, and she'd long suspected that he nursed a secret sadness. Admittedly Ella had always been hard to warm to, but Jules knew people built their defences in different ways and for different reasons. Underneath the icy exterior there had been a frightened little girl and Jules knew that learning to trust again was the bravest thing a person could do. Even Mo, whose teeth were set on edge at the sight of her old nemesis with Symon, had been forced to admit that she had nothing but admiration for how Ella had handled Teddy's behaviour and for Ella's support for her grandfather following the fallout. Poor Jonny was devastated. Although everyone understood that Teddy genuinely hadn't realised what he'd done, his fast driving and wild behaviour had raised eyebrows in Polwenna Bay for some time. Whatever happened next, and whatever the police decided to do, there wasn't a great deal of sympathy for him.

While Tess told off her charges and Roger Pollard sidled off muttering something ominous about ladders, Jules cast her eyes over the barbecue, where Symon was busy preparing some rather exotic burgers and Ella was mixing up a marinade. They were chatting away easily and Jules realised she'd never seen Ella smile so much.

Or at all, actually. *My goodness,* thought Jules. *What a change.*

Every few minutes Symon stopped what he was doing to pull Ella close and kiss her gently or to simply touch her cheek. He couldn't tear himself away from her for a second and it was obvious that Ella felt the same way. Jules was moved because it was true what they said: there really was a perfect person for everyone. Still, maybe they should focus on preparing the lunch? At this rate it would be a miracle if the burgers even made it onto the grill!

"Shall I let them begin?" Tess asked. "I don't think we can keep the kids waiting much longer."

The crowd of children was growing bigger by the second and the air of excitement was palpable. Jules hadn't a clue where Danny was but she couldn't hold the Easter Egg Hunt up any longer. She would have a riot on her hands.

She nodded at Tess. "Let's do this."

Tess herded the children forward with a skill that Jules was very envious of. Rounding up her church council was like trying to herd fog. Maybe Tess would be interested in joining if or when Danny took the job in London? Not that Jules wanted to think about this today when the sun was shining. In fact, she was working hard *not* to think about what was going to happen in the months ahead and she had a feeling that Danny was avoiding the subject too.

Come on, Jules told herself sharply, *focus on what you're doing! Worry about Danny later.* She forced a cheerful expression onto her face and clapped her hands.

"Hello everyone! Welcome to our Easter Egg Hunt! I hope you all have a lovely time. Just remember though, no leaving the churchyard to look for eggs. There's no need, because they're all here."

"And no pushing or shoving," added Tess, in a stern teacher voice. "I'm watching you all!"

"Ready! Set! Go!" said Jules, and instantly a pool of small people spilled across the grass shouting and squealing as they raced to discover the hiding places. The Pollards had done a good job though, because they were certainly taking their time to find any.

"Jules! Jules!"

It was Danny, charging across the churchyard and looking agitated. "Haven't you picked up my messages? I've been trying to call you for over half an hour!"

Jules felt her jeans pocket. "I must have left my phone in the house."

"I can't find the bloody eggs anywhere!" Danny said frantically. "I was going to hide them this morning, I know it's last minute but I've been flat out, and I left them in the kitchen and now they've gone."

"Oh, Dan, I'm so sorry!" Jules felt dreadful for worrying him. "Didn't Big Rog tell you? I picked the eggs up from Seaspray to save you a job. He's hidden them already, so don't worry, the Easter Egg Hunt is going ahead."

"What?" said Danny.

"The Easter Egg Hunt has started already. Look!" Jules swept her hand across the scene, where small people were scrabbling under rocks, searching through tufts of grass and lifting up flowerpots. There was a fair bit of elbowing and pushing going on too; it was rather like a chocolatey version of the Next sale.

Danny stared at Jules. The expression on his face looked a bit like horror.

"You've hidden the eggs? Already? All of them?"

"It's an Easter Egg Hunt, so yes!"

"Where, Jules? Where are they hidden?" Danny's voice rose and several heads turned. "I need to know!"

This was weird. "Dan, I haven't a clue where they are. It's a *hunt.* Besides I didn't hide them, the Pollards did."

Jules had hardly finished her sentence before Danny was sprinting through the children in the direction of Big Rog. Alarmed, she followed him. She hadn't seen Danny this worked up or, quite frankly, this peculiar since the days when he was drinking heavily.

"Roger! I need to know where you've put the eggs!" he was saying, bearing down on the surprised builder. "There was a blue stripy cardboard one. Where did you put it?"

"I dunno, Danny. There were hundreds of blooming eggs. It could be anywhere."

"You need to find it," Danny ordered. "Now."

Her boyfriend might no longer be on active service commanding a squadron, but Big Rog jumped to attention straight away and with no questions asked. Minutes later he was dragging his son through the crowd and back to Danny.

"Blue with stripes. Cardboard. Have you seen it, son?"

"Why are you so teasy?" grumbled Little Rog. "It's just a bleddy egg."

"Just answer the question!" Danny bellowed and Little Rog jumped, almost saluting.

"I did see it! It was quite big. I thought it must be a special prize so I hid it in a special place."

The children were discovering their treasure now and cries of excitement rang through the air. Jules laid a hand on Danny's arm.

"One of them will find it soon, Dan, don't worry."

"I don't want one of them to find it!" Danny cried. "That's the last thing I want." He turned to Little Rog. "Where was that special place? Think!"

In answer, Little Rog trotted off and moments later returned with a stepladder. Jules had known the Pollards for some time now and she'd thought that nothing else they ever did now could surprise her, but a ladder? In disbelief she watched Little Rog prop it against the church porch, scoot up the rungs and rummage in the gutter.

"What on earth?" she spluttered. "This is a kiddies' Easter egg hunt. How on earth are they supposed to find eggs up there?"

"Find good hiding places, you said," muttered Little Rog.

"Don't make it too easy, you said," added his father, looking sulky.

Jules was speechless. Maybe next time they could chuck the eggs in the harbour and get the children to dive for them? Or how about the moon? That should do it.

Little Rog scooped out a handful of sludge and leaf mould. "Here he is!"

In his hand was a very sad Easter egg, the once shiny cardboard now pulpy and speckled with dirt. This didn't seem to bother Danny though, who practically wrestled Little Rog from the ladder to take possession of this sorry prize.

"Shall I get the rest while I'm up here?" asked Little Rog.

The rest?

"Unless you want to do a risk assessment and then tell Miss Hamilton that her children have to climb ladders, yes!" Jules said, exasperated. Her Boss really was testing her patience in this parish. She must try harder.

As Little Rog scurried back up the ladder, Danny examined the ruined Easter egg.

"This isn't quite what I had in mind," he said to Jules with a rueful smile.

"Danny," Jules said slowly, "I may be being thick here, but what exactly did you have in mind? Why are you hiding eggs in the gutter with the Pollards?"

Danny started to laugh. His blue eye crinkled and soon he was doubled over, gasping and wheezing with mirth.

"The Pollards were not in on this, I promise!" he said as he sank awkwardly onto his knees.

"Dan! What are you doing?" Jules gasped. "It's muddy!"

But Danny wasn't worried about the state of the grass.

"This is for you," he said, reaching out and placing the sodden cardboard egg in her hand. "It's your Easter egg, Jules. I must admit that my hiding place wasn't nearly as ingenious as Little Rog's though – I was going to put it in a bunch of daffodils!"

"Why are you giving me this? Why are you kneeling on the grass?" Jules's heart was starting to do some very strange things. It was skipping about all over the place as she suddenly allowed herself to imagine… to hope…

"Open it," Danny said, so Jules did and she was hardly able to believe what she saw. Inside the pulpy cardboard was a box.

A ring box.

"I know it's not chocolate," Danny added when she didn't say anything. "But I hope it's the next best thing?"

Jules's hands were shaking so much she could hardly open the sprung lid, but when she did she knew this was better than anything Cadbury produced. Inside the box, nestled on a bed of midnight-black velvet, was a beautiful diamond solitaire.

She looked at Danny in shock. "Is this what I think it is?"

Nodding, Danny reached for her hand. "This isn't quite the way I pictured this moment but yes, it's a ring – and in a way maybe it's right that I've given it to you in the very spot where you first tore a strip off me all that time ago? After all, it was your words that made me realise I had a choice. I could either carry on spiralling downwards or I could choose to look at what I did have. You changed my world that day and now you are my world. So, Jules Mathieson, I know I'm a bit wonky and sometimes a big bit grumpy, but I truly do love you with all my heart. Will you marry me?"

"Yes!" Jules cried and then Danny was on his feet and she was hugging and kissing him. "Yes! Of course I'll marry you!"

She wiped the tears from her eyes as all around them their friends and neighbours clapped and cheered. Danny slipped the ring onto her finger and held her close.

"I'm the luckiest man in the world," he whispered.

"Lucky that the Pollards are in charge today, you mean," laughed Jules, holding up her left hand and admiring the way the ring sparkled in the April sunshine. "Anyone normal would have hidden that egg under a bush. Then there'd have been a very surprised six-year-old wearing this!"

"You know me, I never do things the easy way," Danny said. Then they were surrounded by everyone wanting to congratulate them. Jules held Danny's hand tightly and knew that she had never been as happy. There was only one cloud lurking on her horizon...

"You are going to be my stepmother. Fact," said Morgan, tugging on her tee shirt. He looked concerned. "Will Dad live with you at the vicarage or will you live in Seaspray?"

Jules turned to Danny. "Well?" she asked him quietly. "Where do you think we should live?"

Danny kissed her softly and, taking her hand, led Jules away from the crowd until they were at the edge of the churchyard and looking out over the bay.

"I've been meaning to talk to you about that, Jules," he said slowly. "How do you feel about moving to London?"

To be continued in Polwenna Bay 6

Sign up for Ruth's Newsletter to find out about future books as soon as they're released!

I really hope you have enjoyed reading this book. If you did I would really appreciate a review on Amazon. It makes all the difference for a writer.

Amazon UK

Amazon.com

ABOUT THE AUTHOR

Ruth Saberton is the bestselling author of *Katy Carter Wants a Hero* and *Escape for the Summer*. She also writes upmarket commercial fiction under the pen names Jessica Fox, Georgie Carter and Holly Cavendish.

Born in London, Ruth now lives in beautiful Cornwall. She has travelled to many places and recently returned from living in the Caribbean but nothing compares to the rugged beauty of the Cornish coast. Ruth loves to chat with readers so please do feel free to look her up on Facebook and follow her on Twitter.

Twitter: @ruthsaberton
Facebook: Ruth Saberton
www.ruthsaberton.com

Printed in Great Britain
by Amazon

81814771R00253